AN UN**OF**FICIAL MINECRAFTERS GRAPHIC NOVEL FOR FANS OF THE AQUATIC UPDATE

JOURNEY TO THE OCEAN'S END

THE S.Q.U.I.D. SQUAD #5

MEGAN MILLER

SKY PONY PRESS
NEW YORK

This book is not authorized or sponsored by Microsoft Corp., Mojang AB, Notch Development AB or Scholastic Inc., or any other person or entity owning or controlling rights in the Minecraft name, trademark, or copyrights.

This book is not authorized or sponsored by Microsoft Corp., Mojang AB, Notch Development AB or Scholastic Inc., or any other person or entity owning or controlling rights in the Minecraft name, trademark, or copyrights.

Sky Pony Press books may be purchased in bulk at special discounts for sales promotion, corporate gifts, fund-raising, or educational purposes. Special editions can also be created to specifications. For details, contact the Special Sales Department, Sky Pony Press, 307 West 36th Street, 11th Floor, New York, NY 10018 or info@skyhorsepublishing.com.

Minecraft® is a registered trademark of Notch Development AB.
The Minecraft game is copyright © Mojang AB.

Visit our website at www.skyponypress.com.

10 9 8 7 6 5 4 3 2 1

Library of Congress Cataloging-in-Publication Data is available on file.

Cover design by Kai Texel
Cover and interior art by Megan Miller

Print ISBN: 978-1-5107-6500-9
Ebook ISBN: 978-1-5107-6575-7

Printed in China

Introduction

It is a dire time in the world. The Evil Pillagers are conquering villages and destroying the villagers' culture and libraries.

But far out at sea live the Book Guardians, a secret group of miners and villagers helping to save the libraries' precious books. Before the books can be destroyed by Pillagers, the Book Guardians carry them secretly by boat to their hidden underwater ravine headquarters. Here a small group of three families collects the books and stores them for better times—for when the Pillagers are defeated.

While the grown-ups (a.k.a. GUs) are checking deliveries, securing books, making plans, and double-checking those plans, the children—Inky, Luke, and Max—are meeting new friends and solving mysteries.

And that's not all. After helping the dolphins, they were gifted with the GOLDEN DUST MAGIC OF SPEAKING TO CREATURES. So, yes, they can talk to their underwater neighbors: the creatures, fish, and squid with whom they share their new home.

The Pillagers, however, have mounted a new offensive and fort near the Book Guardians' hidden ravine home. The Book Guardians know they must escape soon to avoid capture. They've been given directions to a faraway safe location, the Ocean's End, by a mysterious stranger, Tara. But will their escape plan be enough to save the books, and themselves?

Meet the S.Q.U.I.D. Squad

INKY

Clever. Enjoys organizing stuff. Pulled one too many squid tentacles. Knows what words like acronym mean. Mostly likes to play by the rules.

LUKE

Also clever, a little rebellious, and enjoys delivering a good speech. He sees himself as the leader, but Inky and Max have other ideas.

MAX

Brave. Leaves Inky and Luke in the dust when it comes to crafting stuff really, really fast. Their secret club name was his idea—the Super Qualified Underwater Investigation Detective . . . er . . . Squad. Just say "Squid Squad," it's easier.

And also, meet . . .

EMI

Lives in a cottage on the other side of the coral reef. Has a lot of informative books about the life aquatic that Inky, Luke, and Max need to read, like, STAT.

SOFI

Inky's mom. She's good at redstone and can spot a secret redstone door a mile off. So she has ALREADY figured out that Inky, Luke, and Max have made their OWN secret underwater cave headquarters INSIDE OF the Book Guardians' own secret underwater ravine headquarters. She hasn't even told anyone else about it.

ABS

Sofi's brother. He's really nice and can haul chests of books like you wouldn't believe.

ZANE

Max's dad. He goes on a lot of secret boat missions to find new villagers who want to save their books.

NEHA

Zane's sister. She's pretty nice, too.

PER AND JUN

Luke's mom and dad. Per is also fond of speeches and Jun tries to let him know when they go on too long. They go out with Zane on his missions sometimes.

MABEL

Gruff on the outside, sweet on the inside.

Chapter 1
Escape Route

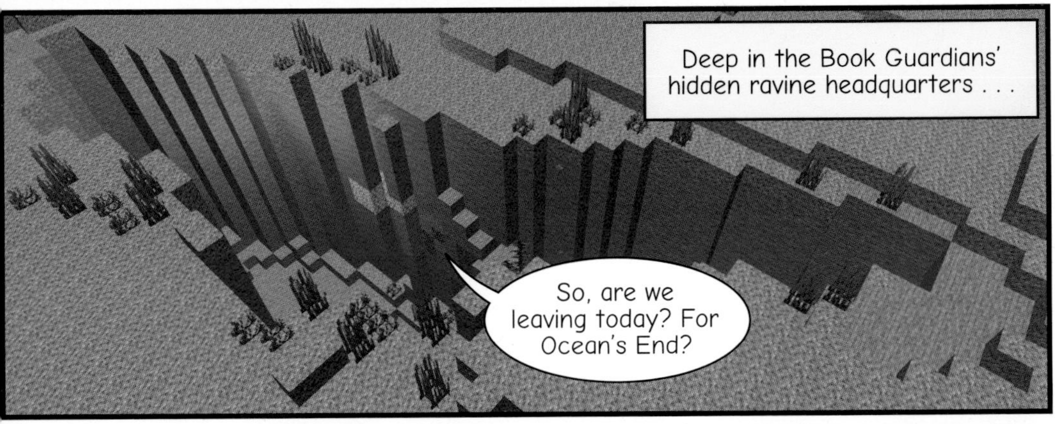
Deep in the Book Guardians' hidden ravine headquarters . . .
So, are we leaving today? For Ocean's End?

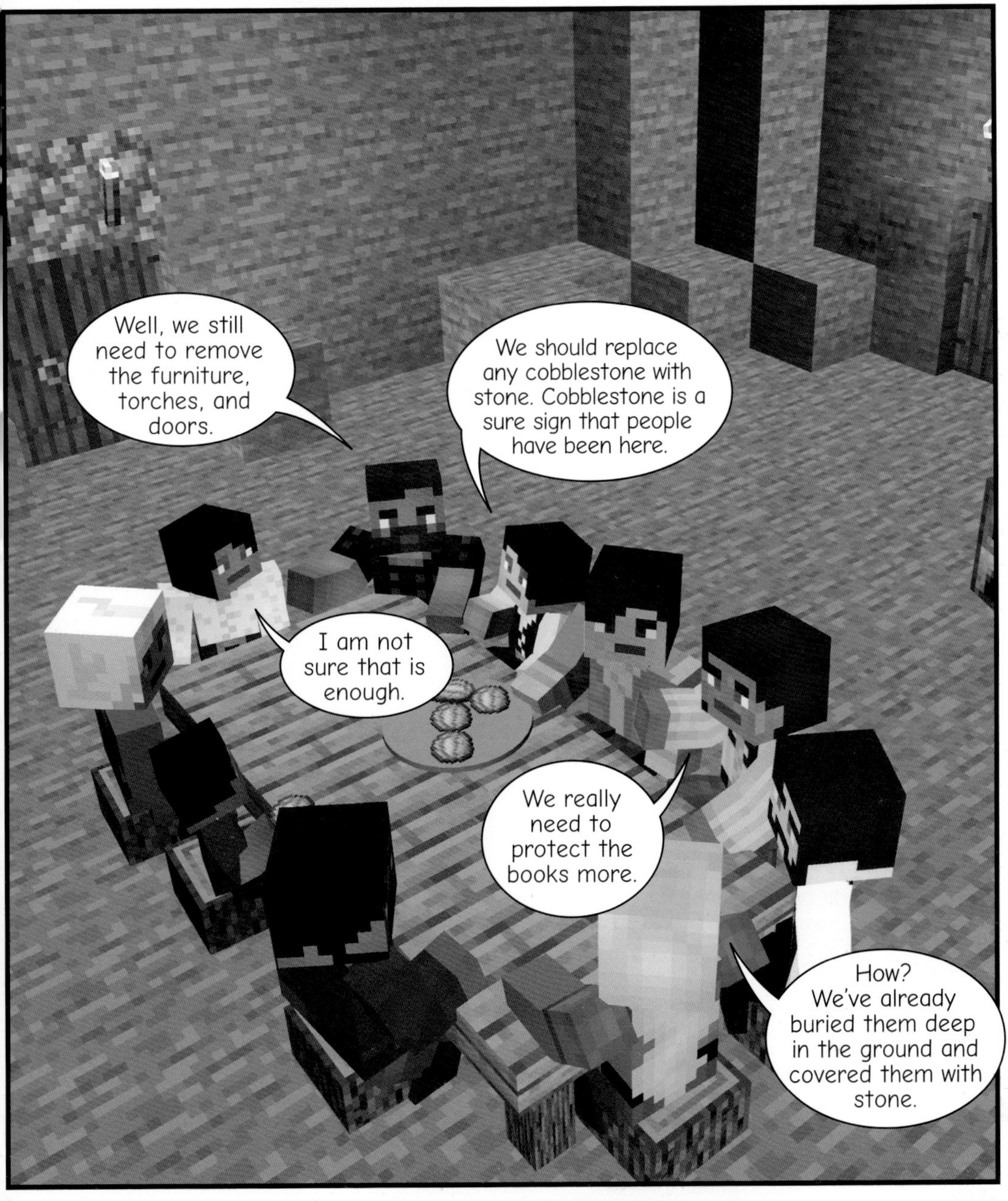
Well, we still need to remove the furniture, torches, and doors.
We should replace any cobblestone with stone. Cobblestone is a sure sign that people have been here.
I am not sure that is enough.
We really need to protect the books more.
How? We've already buried them deep in the ground and covered them with stone.

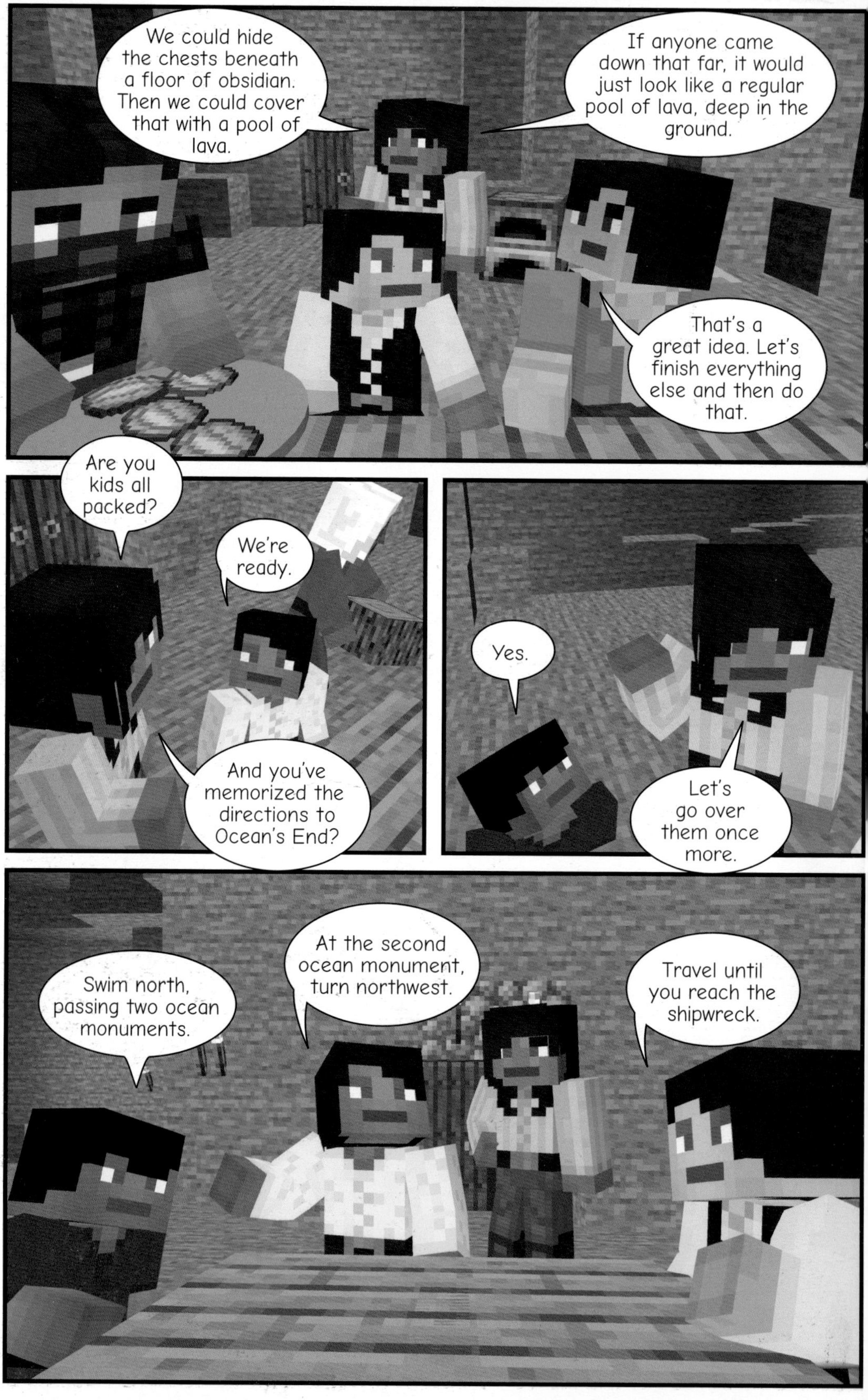
We could hide the chests beneath a floor of obsidian. Then we could cover that with a pool of lava.
If anyone came down that far, it would just look like a regular pool of lava, deep in the ground.
That's a great idea. Let's finish everything else and then do that.
Are you kids all packed?
We're ready.
And you've memorized the directions to Ocean's End?
Yes.
Let's go over them once more.
Swim north, passing two ocean monuments.
At the second ocean monument, turn northwest.
Travel until you reach the shipwreck.

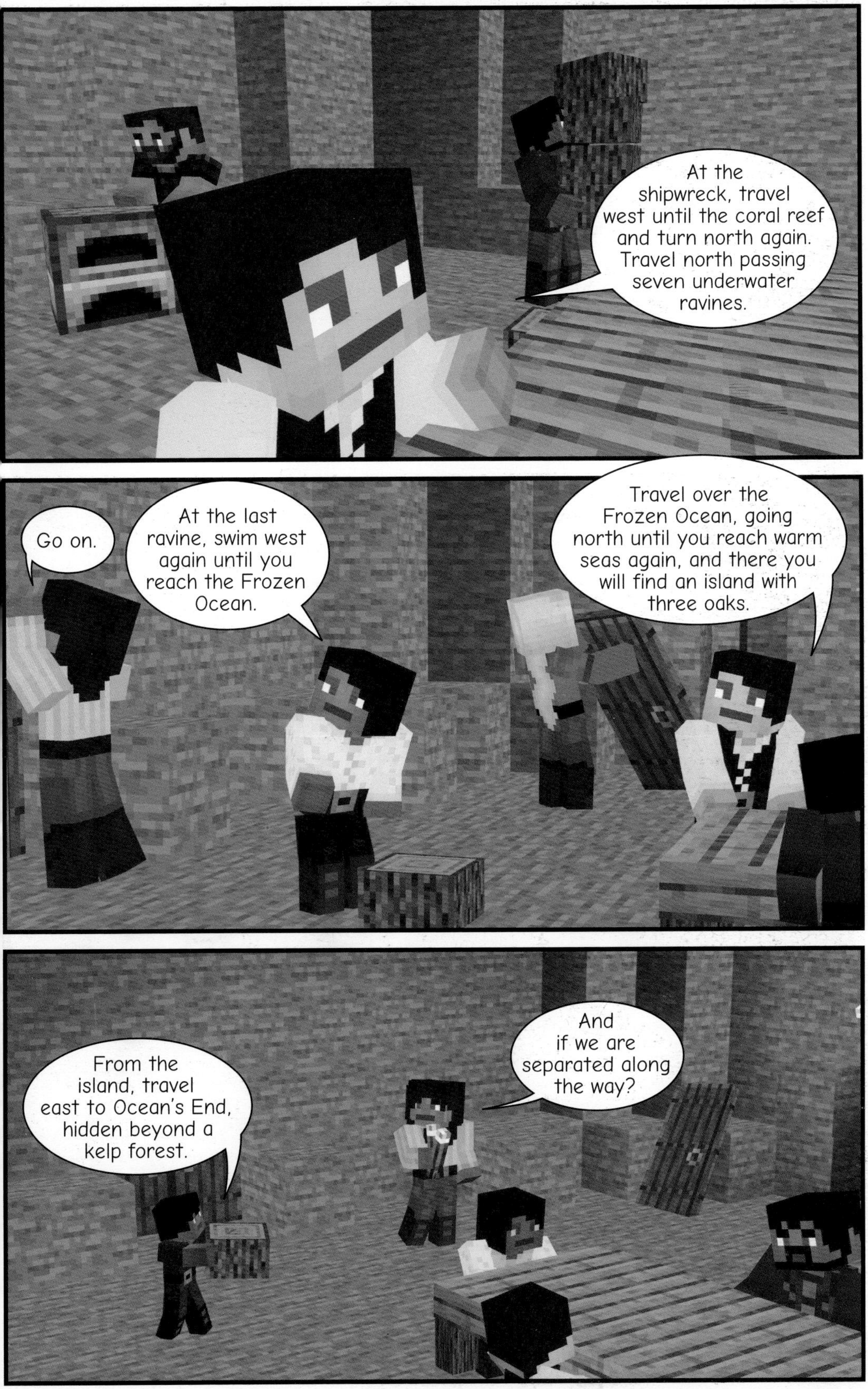
At the shipwreck, travel west until the coral reef and turn north again. Travel north passing seven underwater ravines.
Go on.
At the last ravine, swim west again until you reach the Frozen Ocean.
Travel over the Frozen Ocean, going north until you reach warm seas again, and there you will find an island with three oaks.
From the island, travel east to Ocean's End, hidden beyond a kelp forest.
And if we are separated along the way?

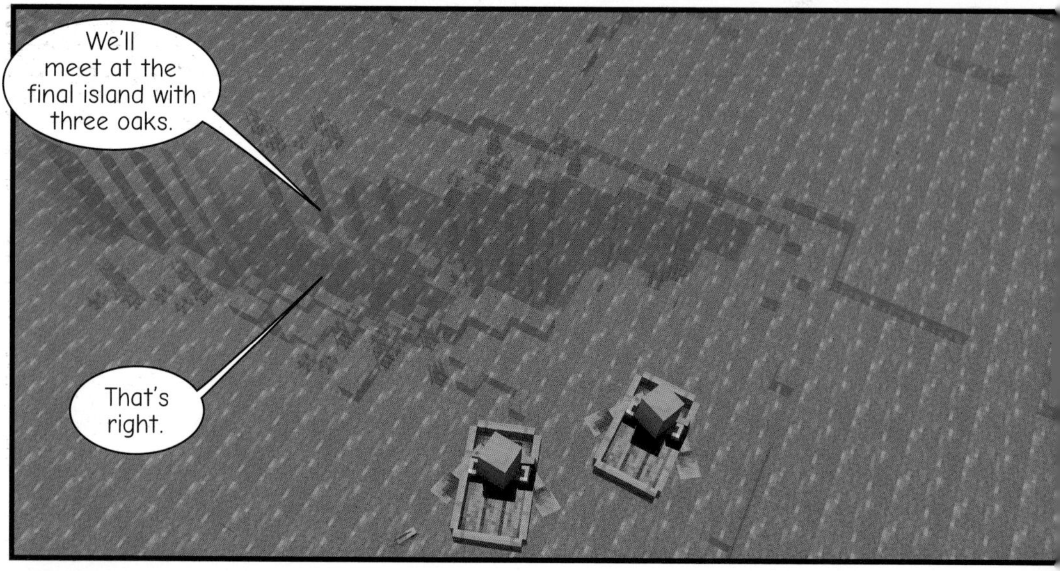
We'll meet at the final island with three oaks.
That's right.

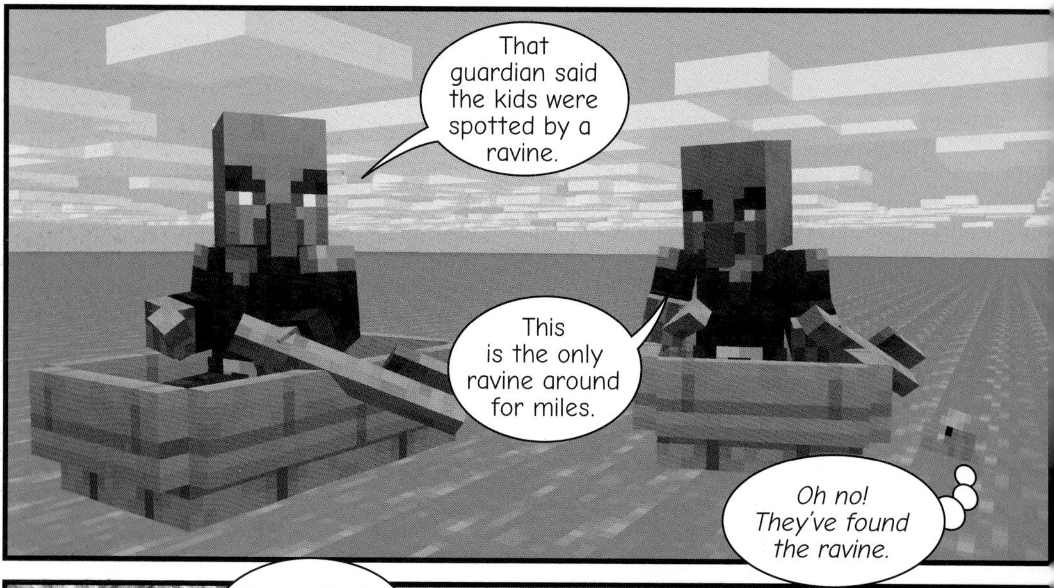
That guardian said the kids were spotted by a ravine.
This is the only ravine around for miles.
Oh no! They've found the ravine.

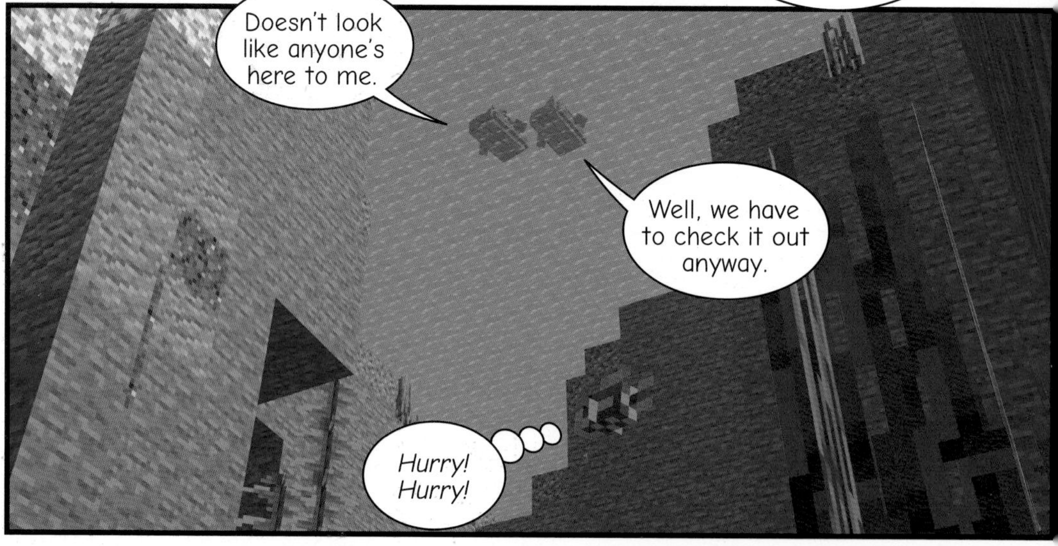
Doesn't look like anyone's here to me.
Well, we have to check it out anyway.
Hurry! Hurry!

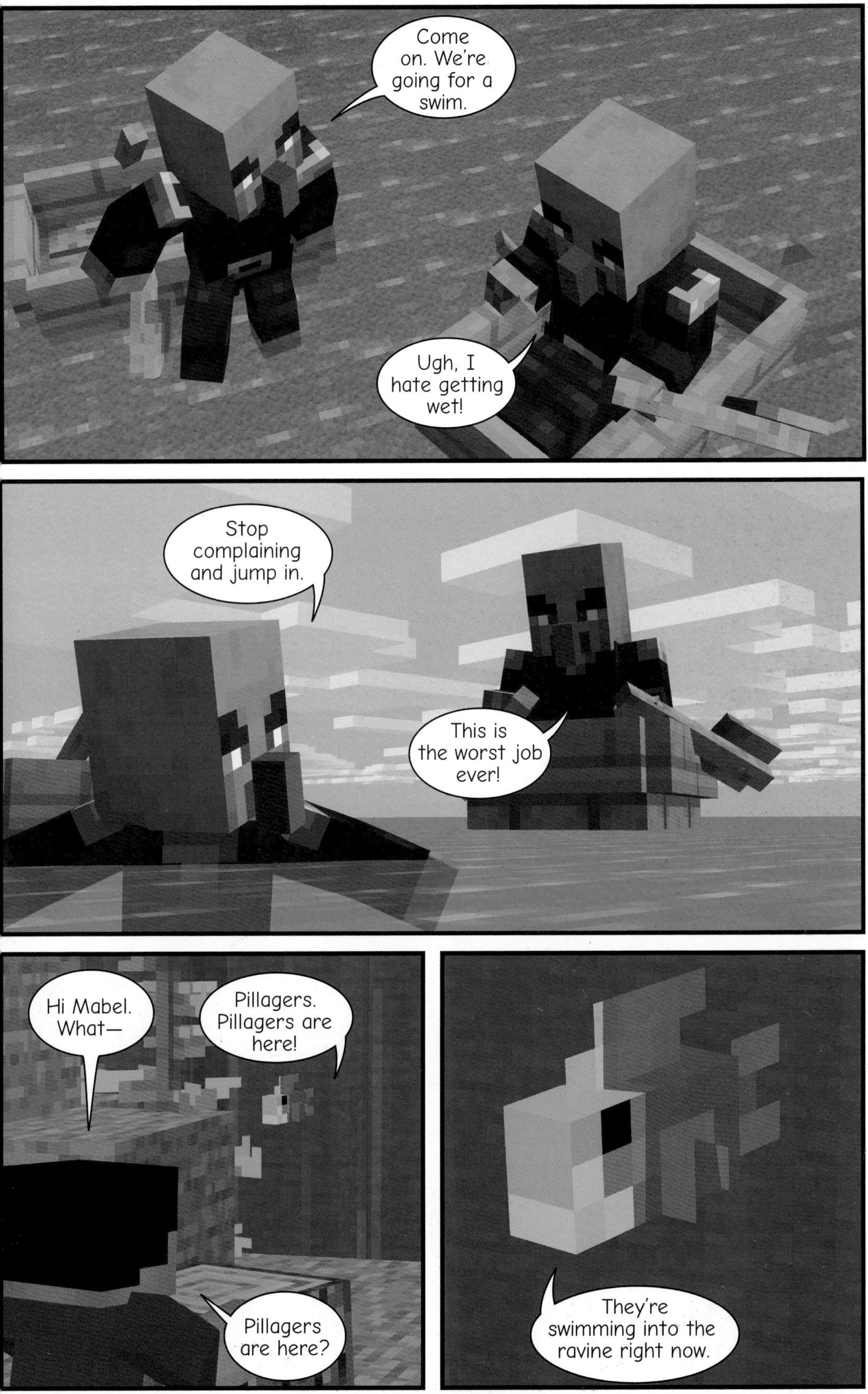
Come on. We're going for a swim.
Ugh, I hate getting wet!
Stop complaining and jump in.
This is the worst job ever!
Hi Mabel. What—
Pillagers. Pillagers are here!
Pillagers are here?
They're swimming into the ravine right now.

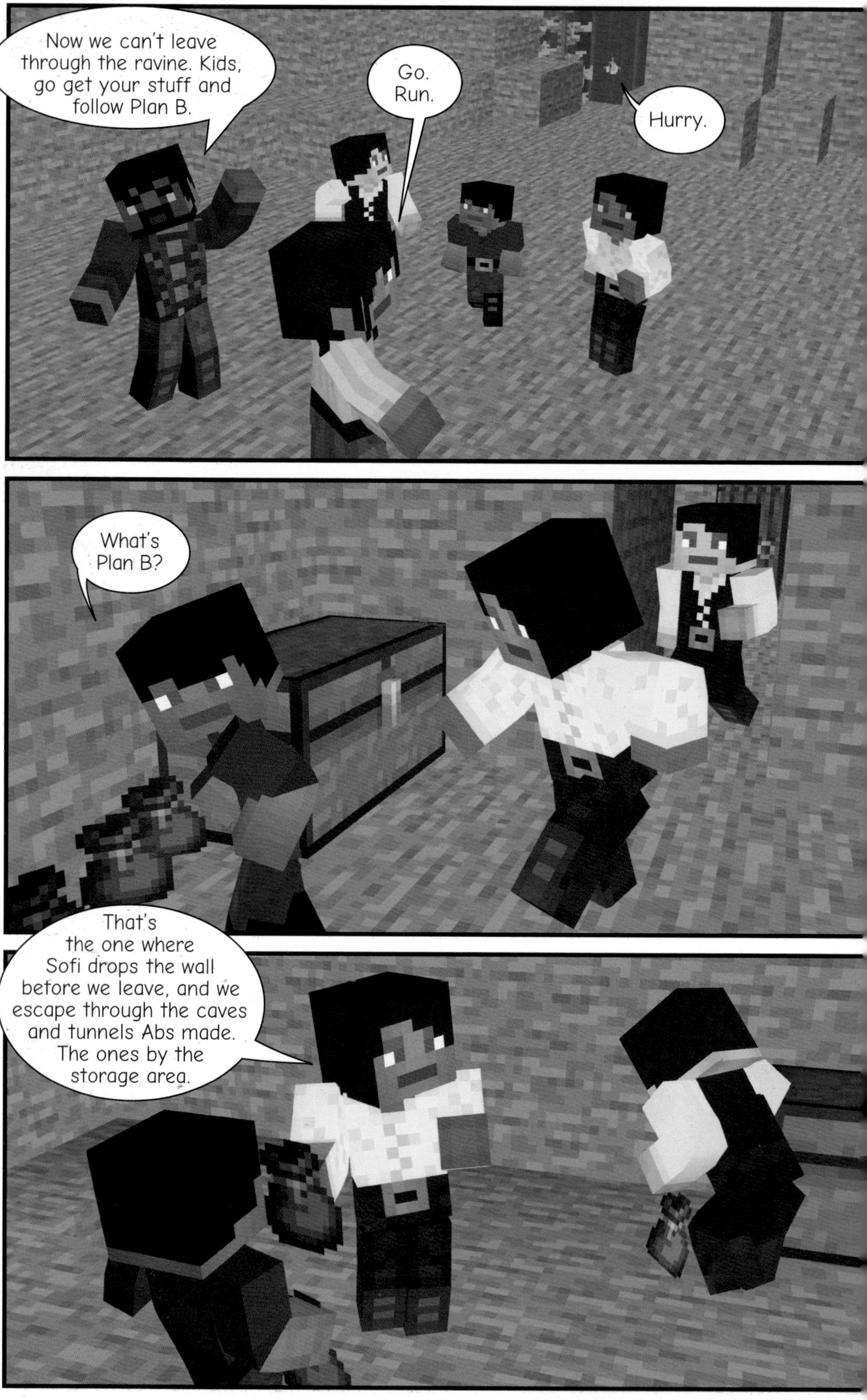
Now we can't leave through the ravine. Kids, go get your stuff and follow Plan B.
Go. Run.
Hurry.
What's Plan B?
That's the one where Sofi drops the wall before we leave, and we escape through the caves and tunnels Abs made. The ones by the storage area.

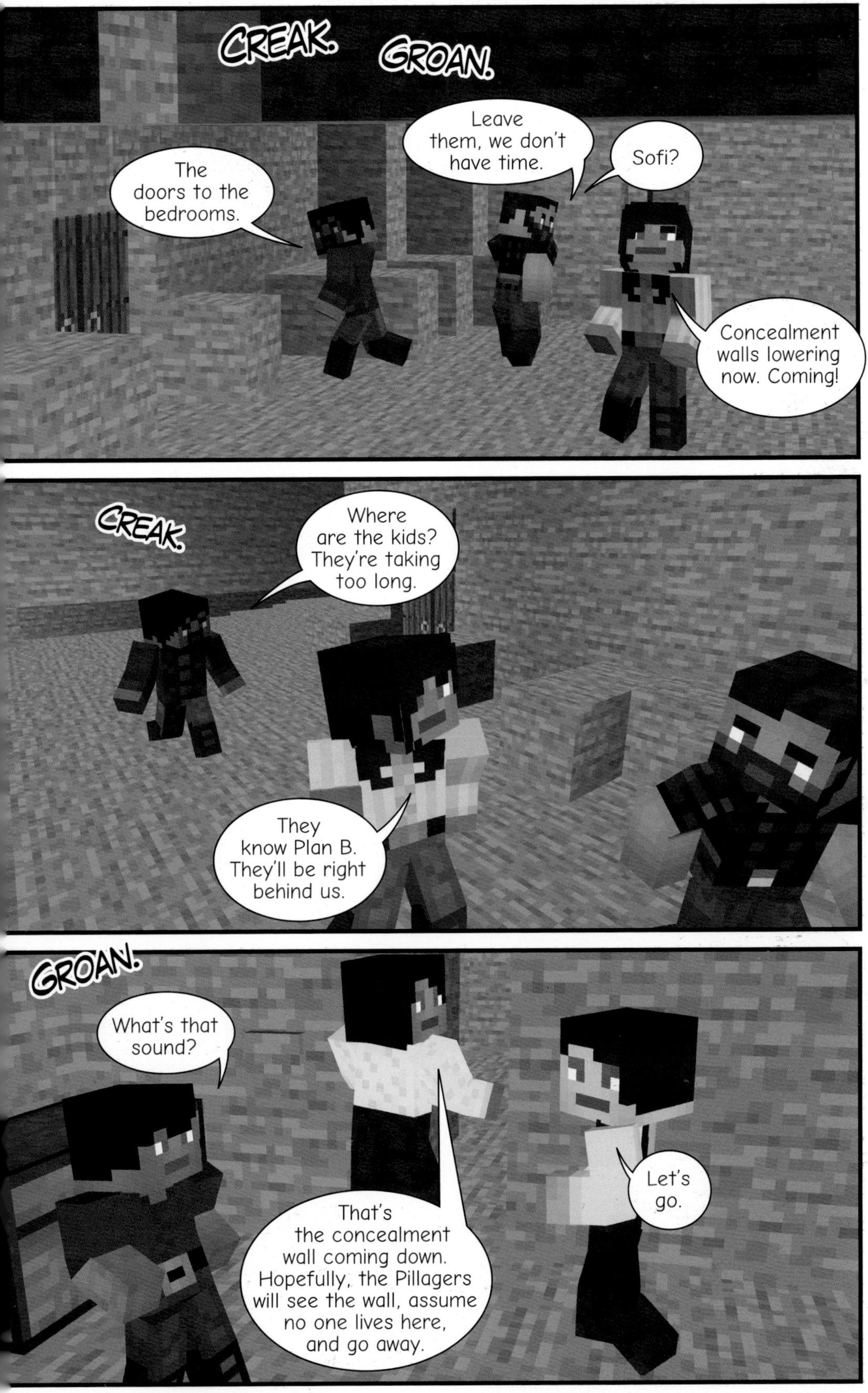
CREAK.
GROAN.
The doors to the bedrooms.
Leave them, we don't have time.
Sofi?
Concealment walls lowering now. Coming!
CREAK.
Where are the kids? They're taking too long.
They know Plan B. They'll be right behind us.
GROAN.
What's that sound?
That's the concealment wall coming down. Hopefully, the Pillagers will see the wall, assume no one lives here, and go away.
Let's go.

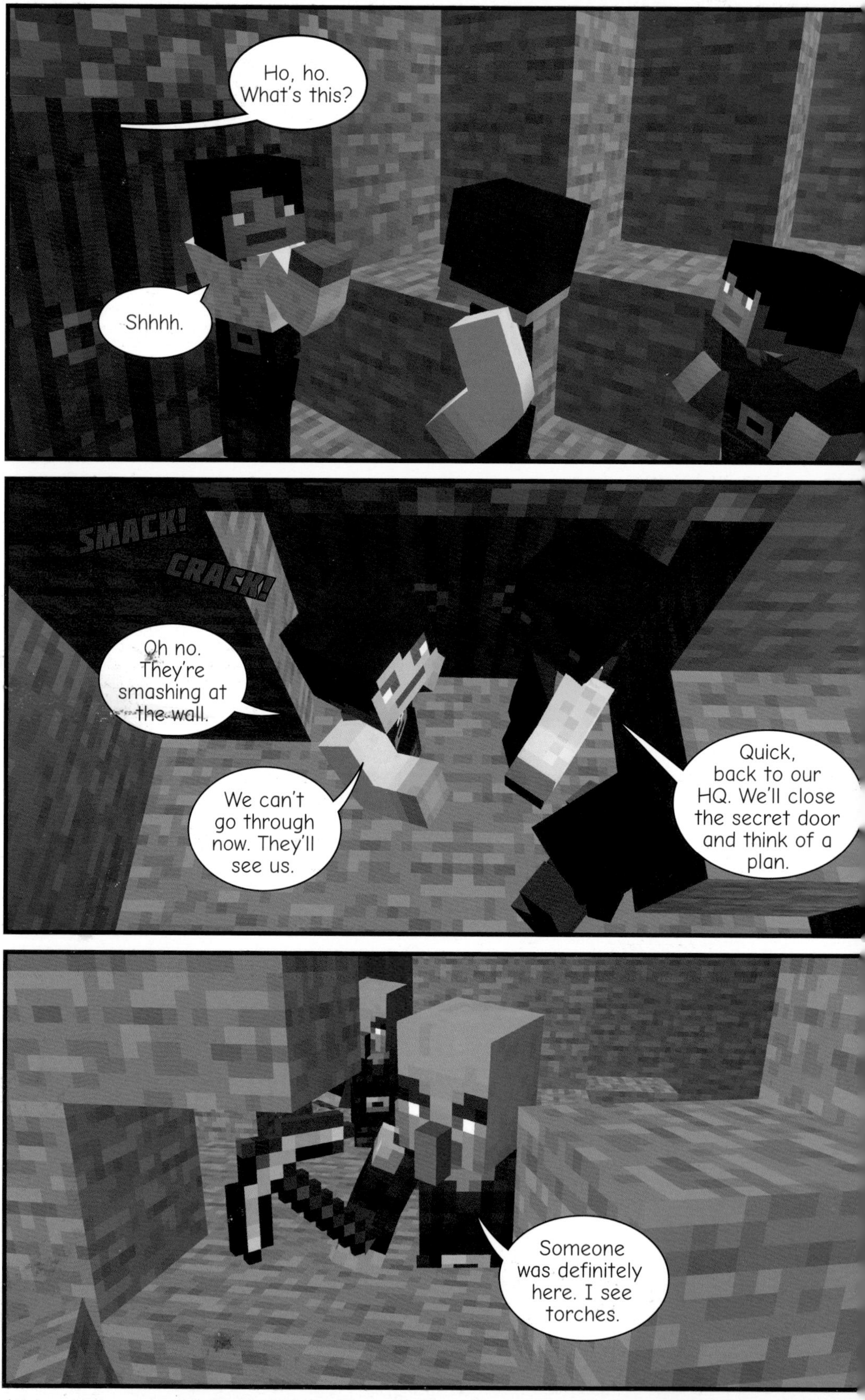
Ho, ho. What's this?
Shhhh.
SMACK!
CRACK!
Oh no. They're smashing at the wall.
We can't go through now. They'll see us.
Quick, back to our HQ. We'll close the secret door and think of a plan.
Someone was definitely here. I see torches.

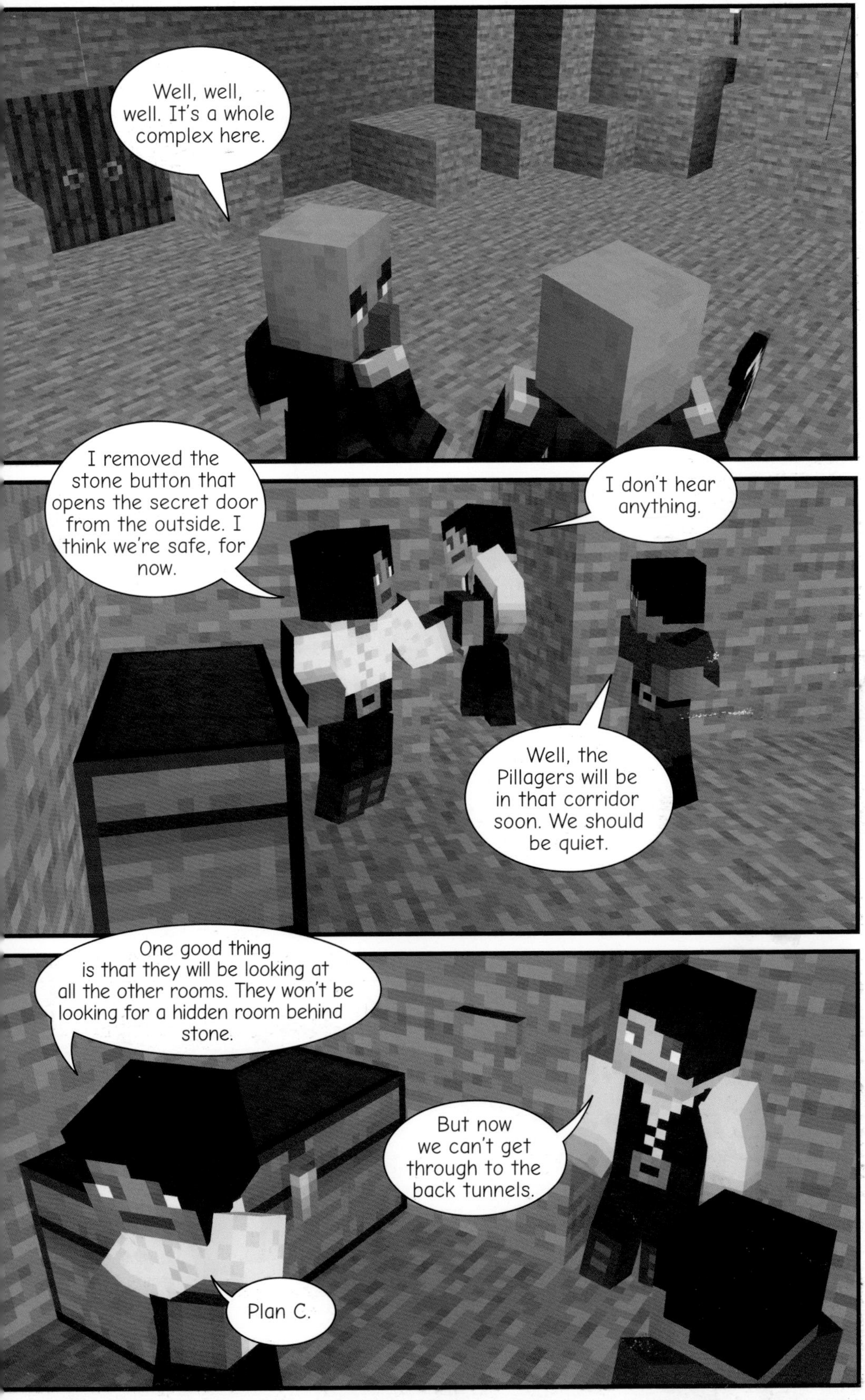
Well, well, well. It's a whole complex here.
I removed the stone button that opens the secret door from the outside. I think we're safe, for now.
I don't hear anything.
Well, the Pillagers will be in that corridor soon. We should be quiet.
One good thing is that they will be looking at all the other rooms. They won't be looking for a hidden room behind stone.
But now we can't get through to the back tunnels.
Plan C.

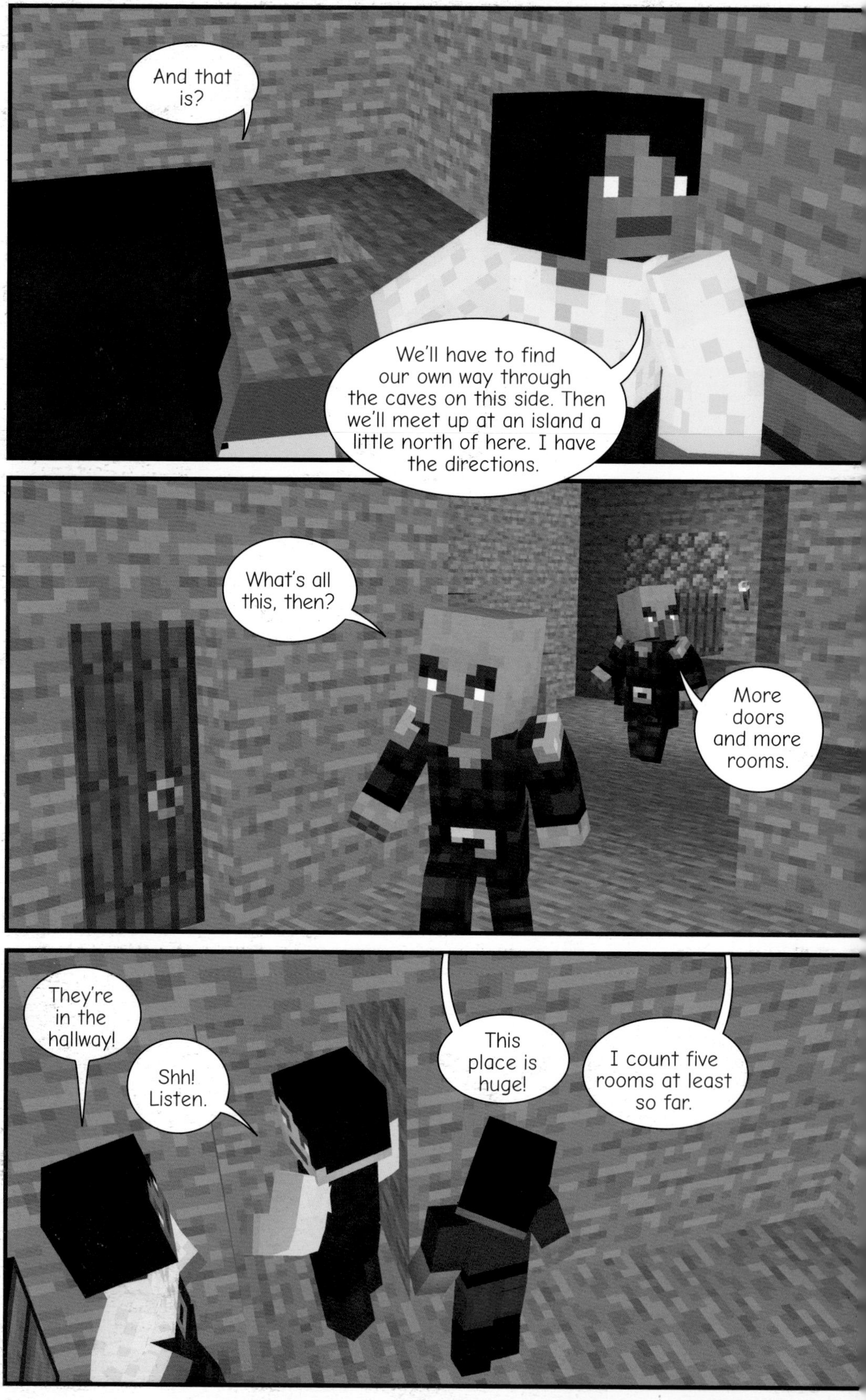
And that is?
We'll have to find our own way through the caves on this side. Then we'll meet up at an island a little north of here. I have the directions.
What's all this, then?
More doors and more rooms.
They're in the hallway!
Shh! Listen.
This place is huge!
I count five rooms at least so far.

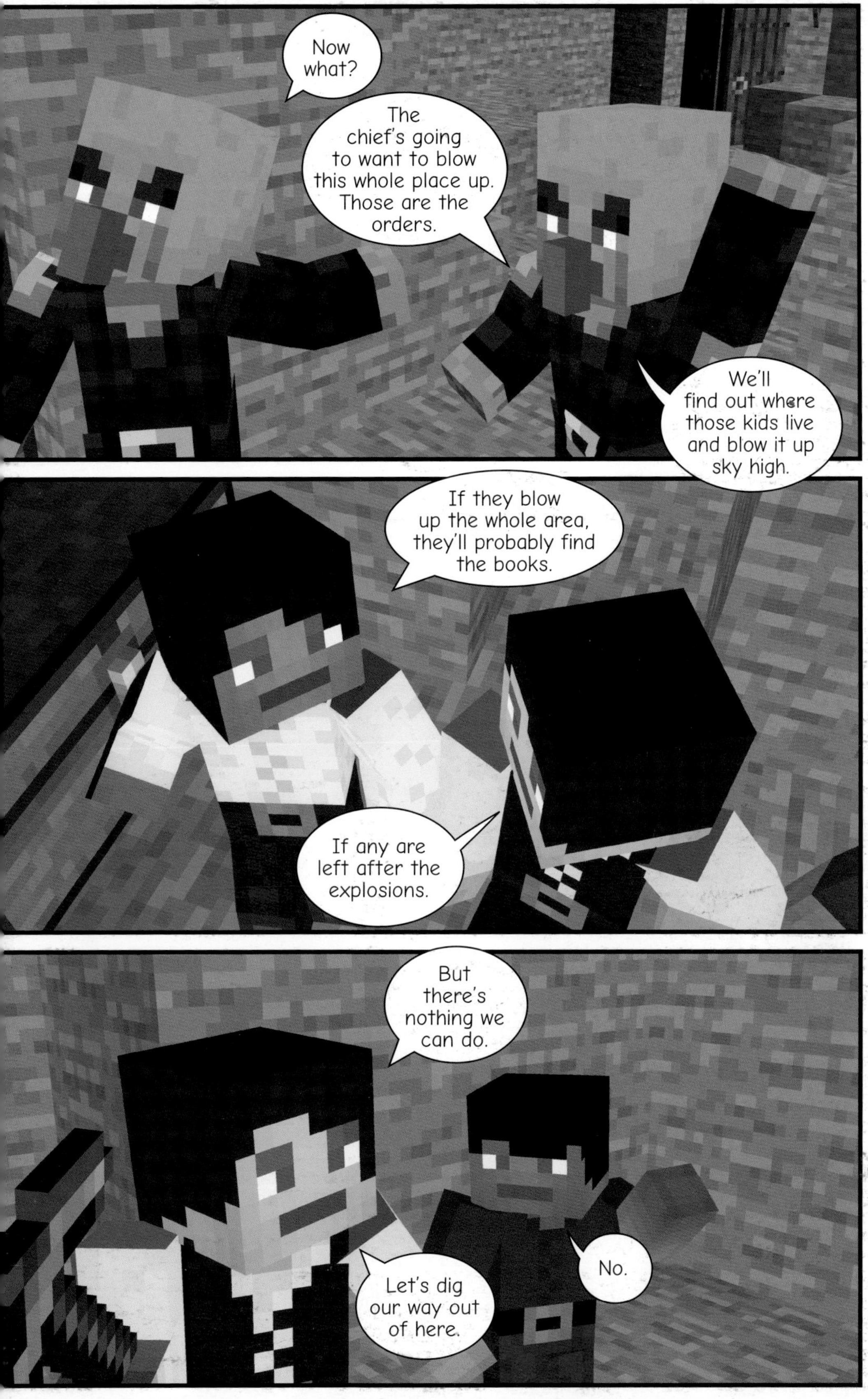

Now what?
The chief's going to want to blow this whole place up. Those are the orders.
We'll find out where those kids live and blow it up sky high.
If they blow up the whole area, they'll probably find the books.
If any are left after the explosions.
But there's nothing we can do.
Let's dig our way out of here.
No.

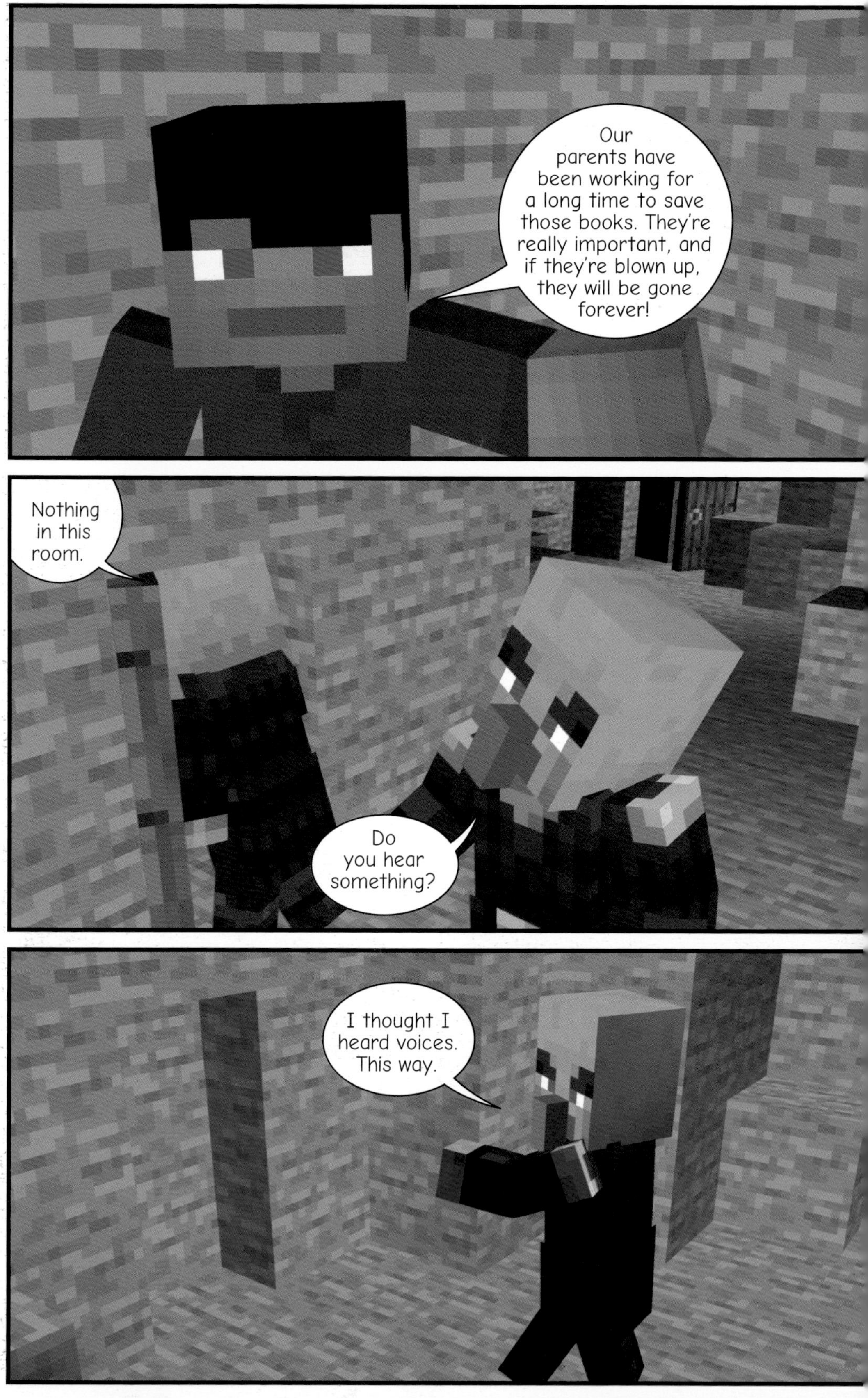
Our parents have been working for a long time to save those books. They're really important, and if they're blown up, they will be gone forever!
Nothing in this room.
Do you hear something?
I thought I heard voices. This way.

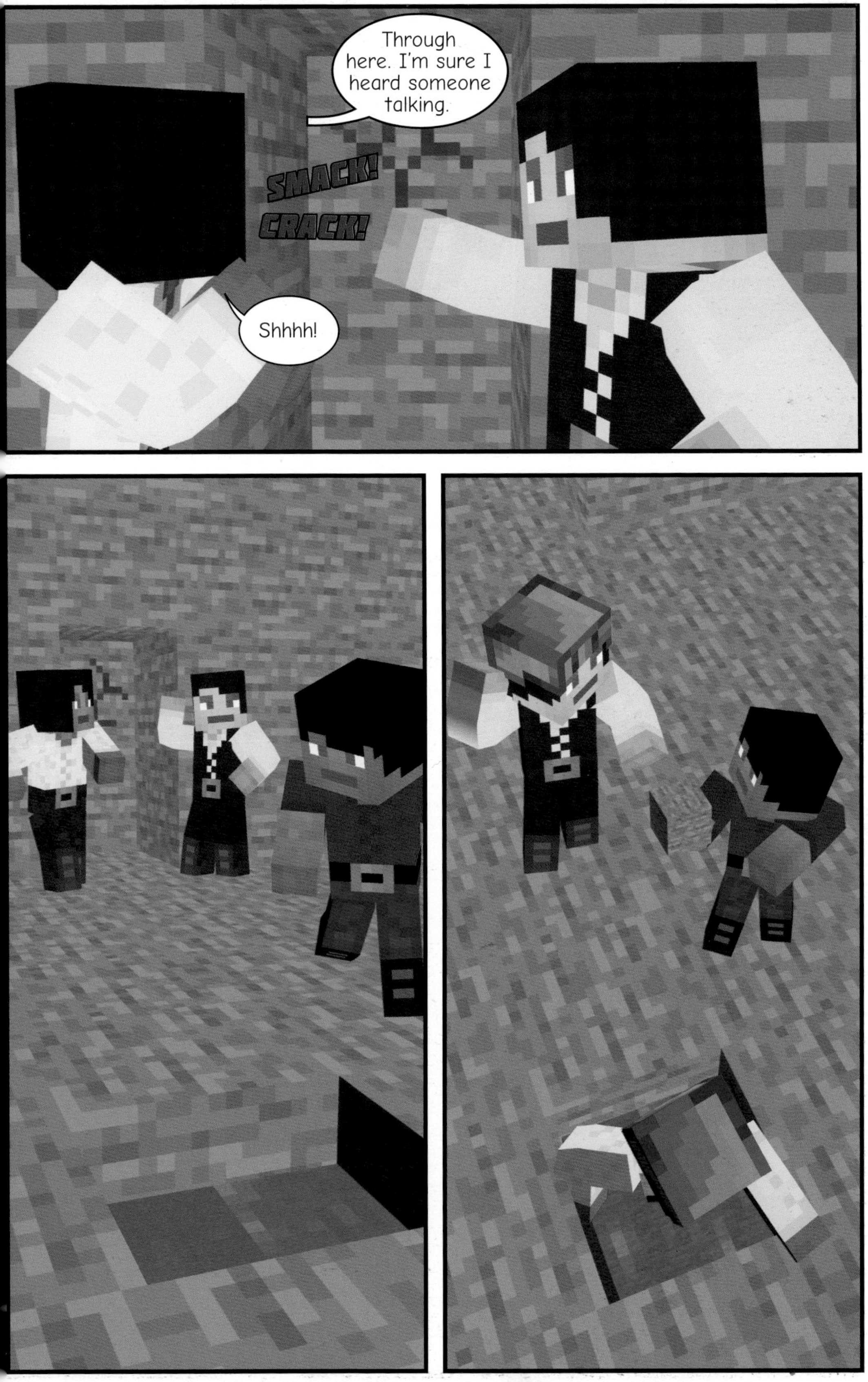
Through here. I'm sure I heard someone talking.
SMACK!
CRACK!
Shhhh!

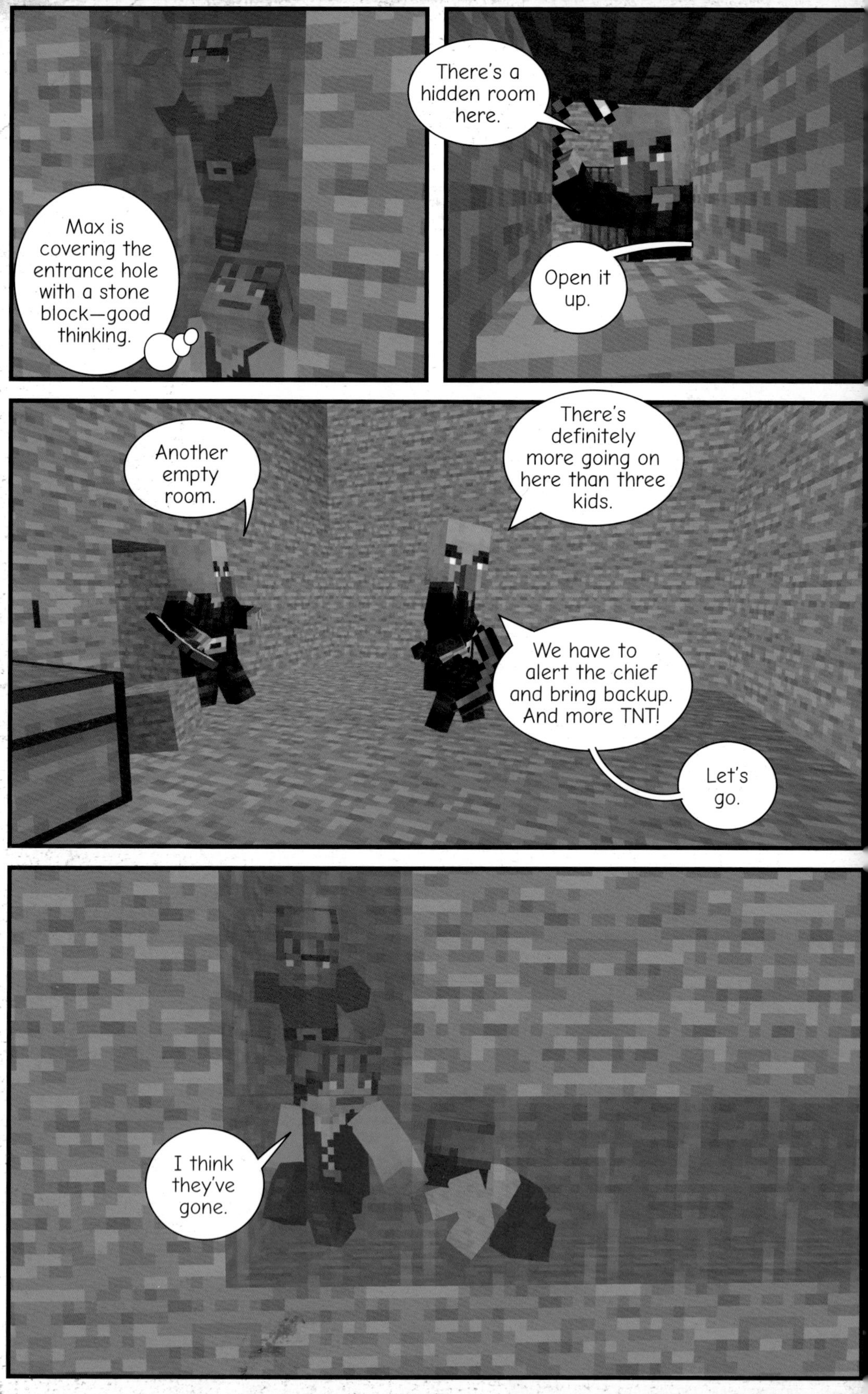
Max is covering the entrance hole with a stone block—good thinking.
There's a hidden room here.
Open it up.
Another empty room.
There's definitely more going on here than three kids.
We have to alert the chief and bring backup. And more TNT!
Let's go.
I think they've gone.

Chapter 2
Well, Goodbye Home

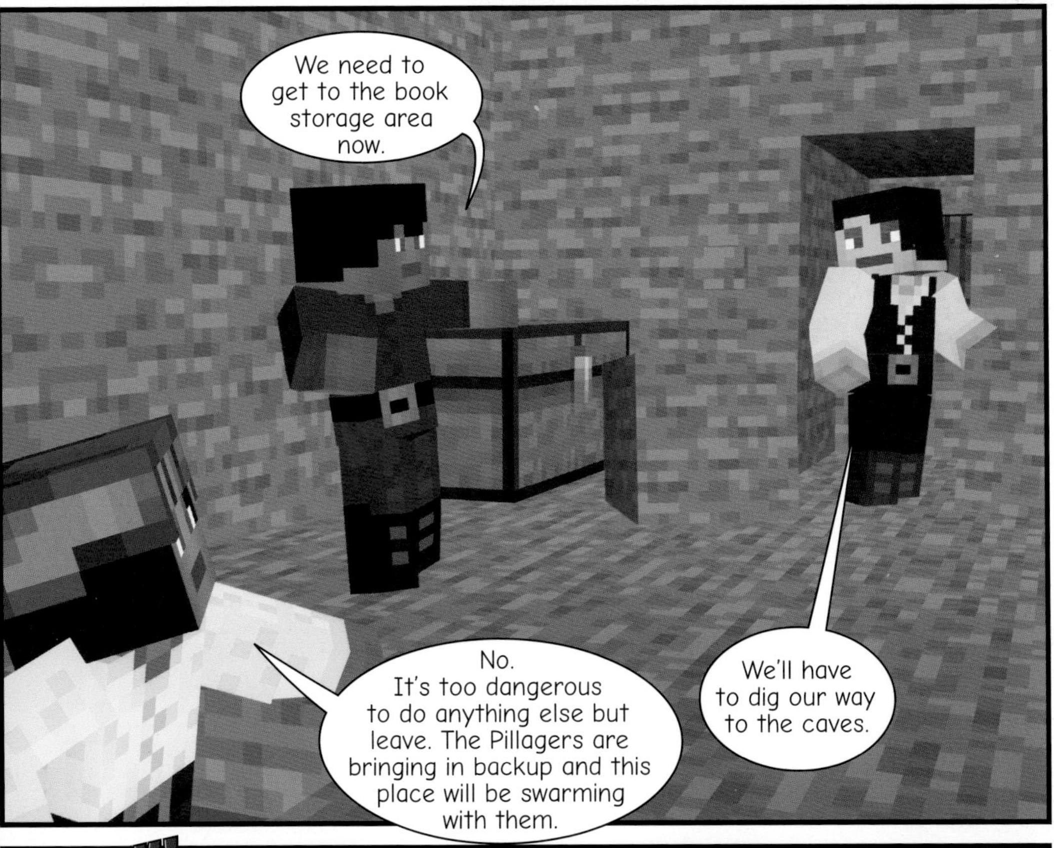
We need to get to the book storage area now.
We'll have to dig our way to the caves.
No.
It's too dangerous to do anything else but leave. The Pillagers are bringing in backup and this place will be swarming with them.

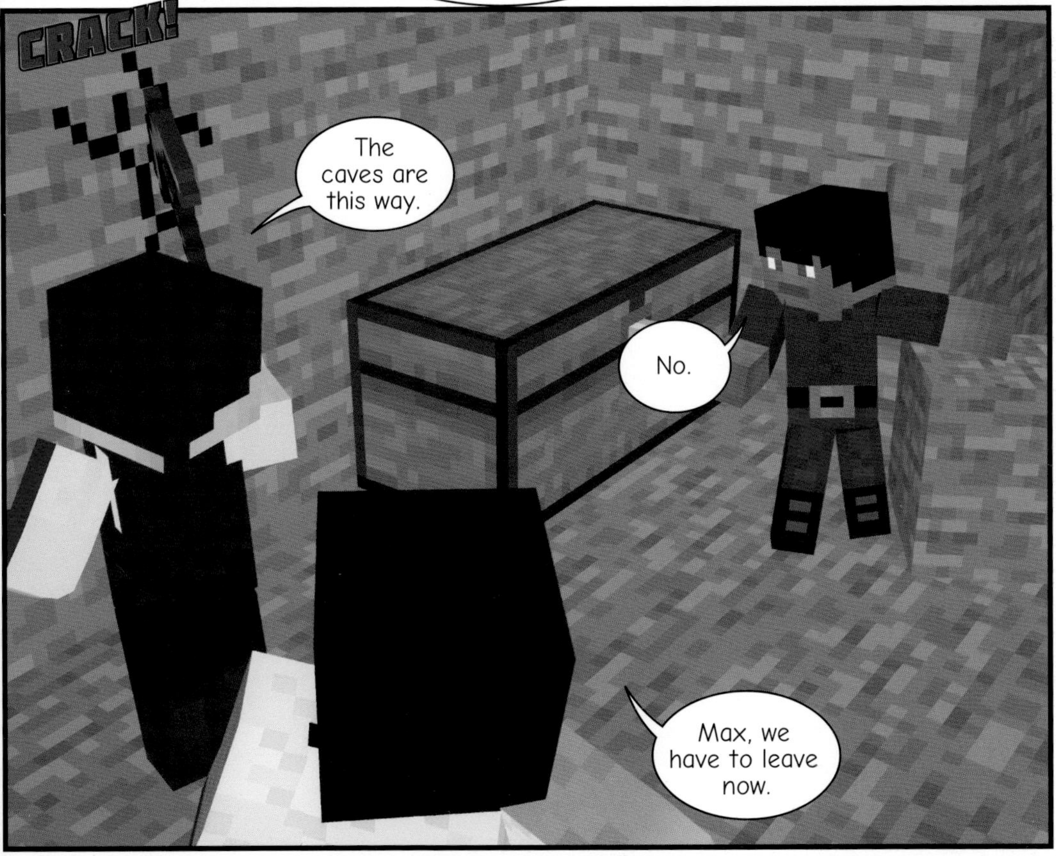
CRACK!
The caves are this way.
No.
Max, we have to leave now.

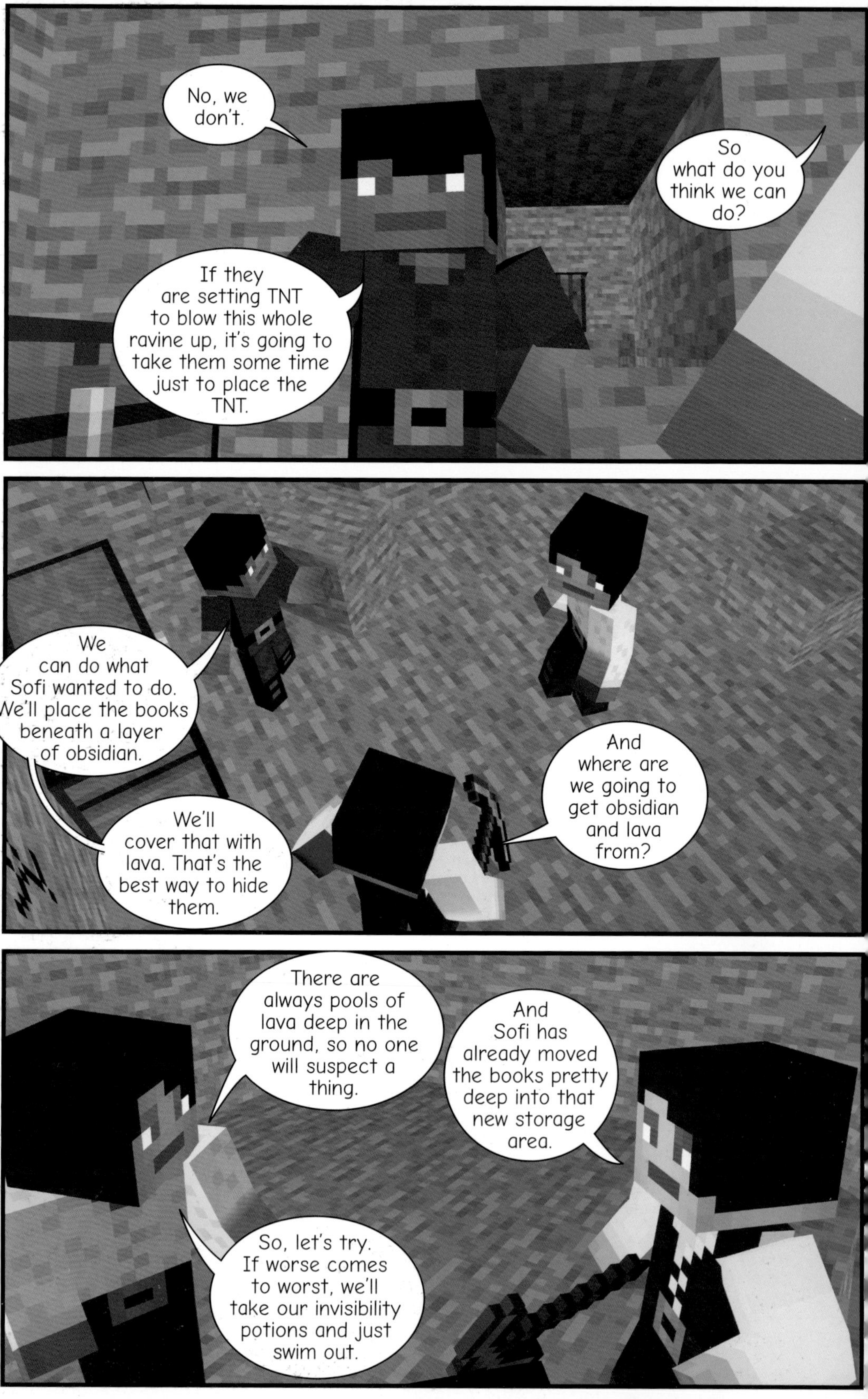
No, we don't.
So what do you think we can do?
If they are setting TNT to blow this whole ravine up, it's going to take them some time just to place the TNT.
We can do what Sofi wanted to do. We'll place the books beneath a layer of obsidian.
We'll cover that with lava. That's the best way to hide them.
And where are we going to get obsidian and lava from?
There are always pools of lava deep in the ground, so no one will suspect a thing.
And Sofi has already moved the books pretty deep into that new storage area.
So, let's try. If worse comes to worst, we'll take our invisibility potions and just swim out.

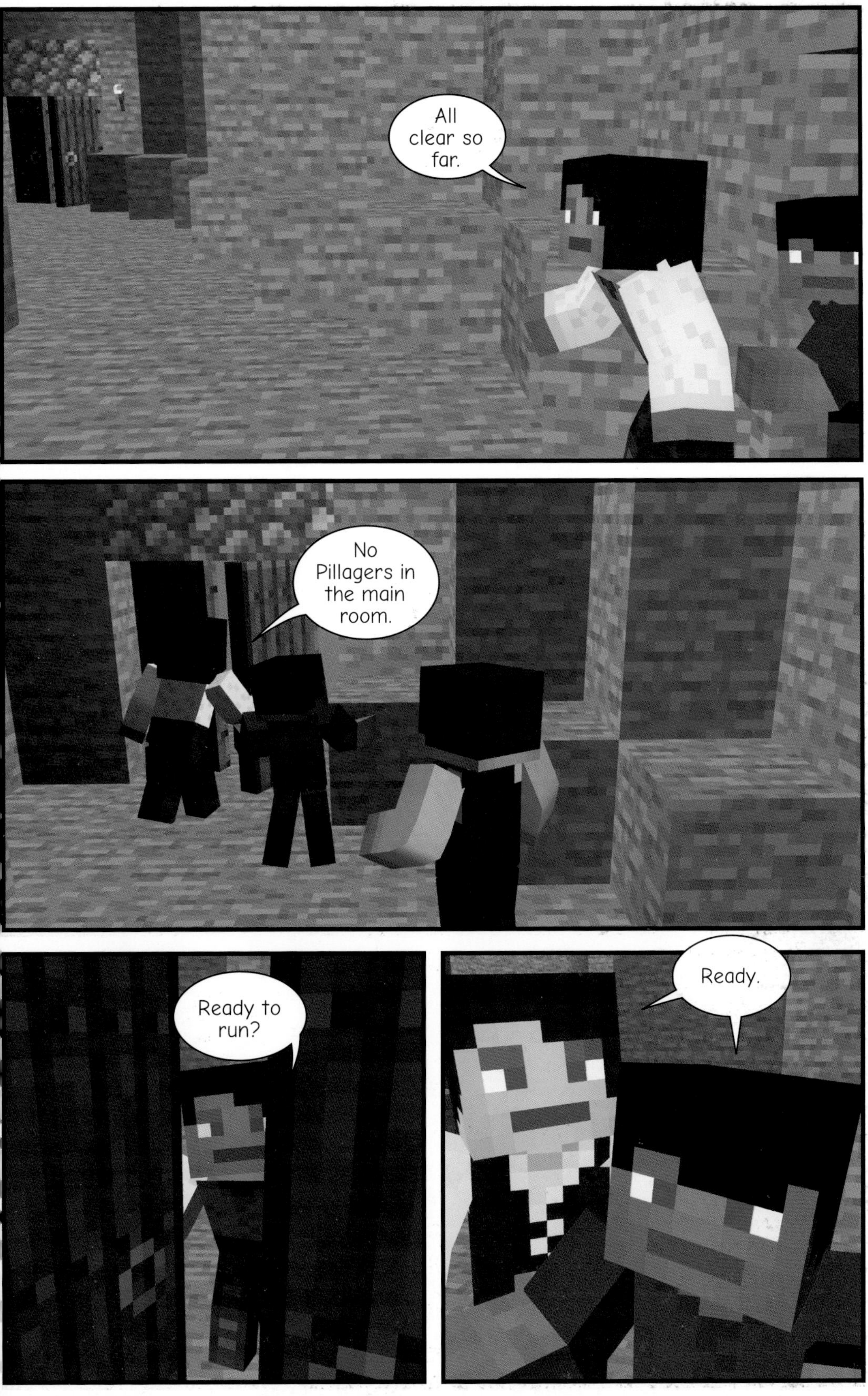
All clear so far.
No Pillagers in the main room.
Ready to run?
Ready.

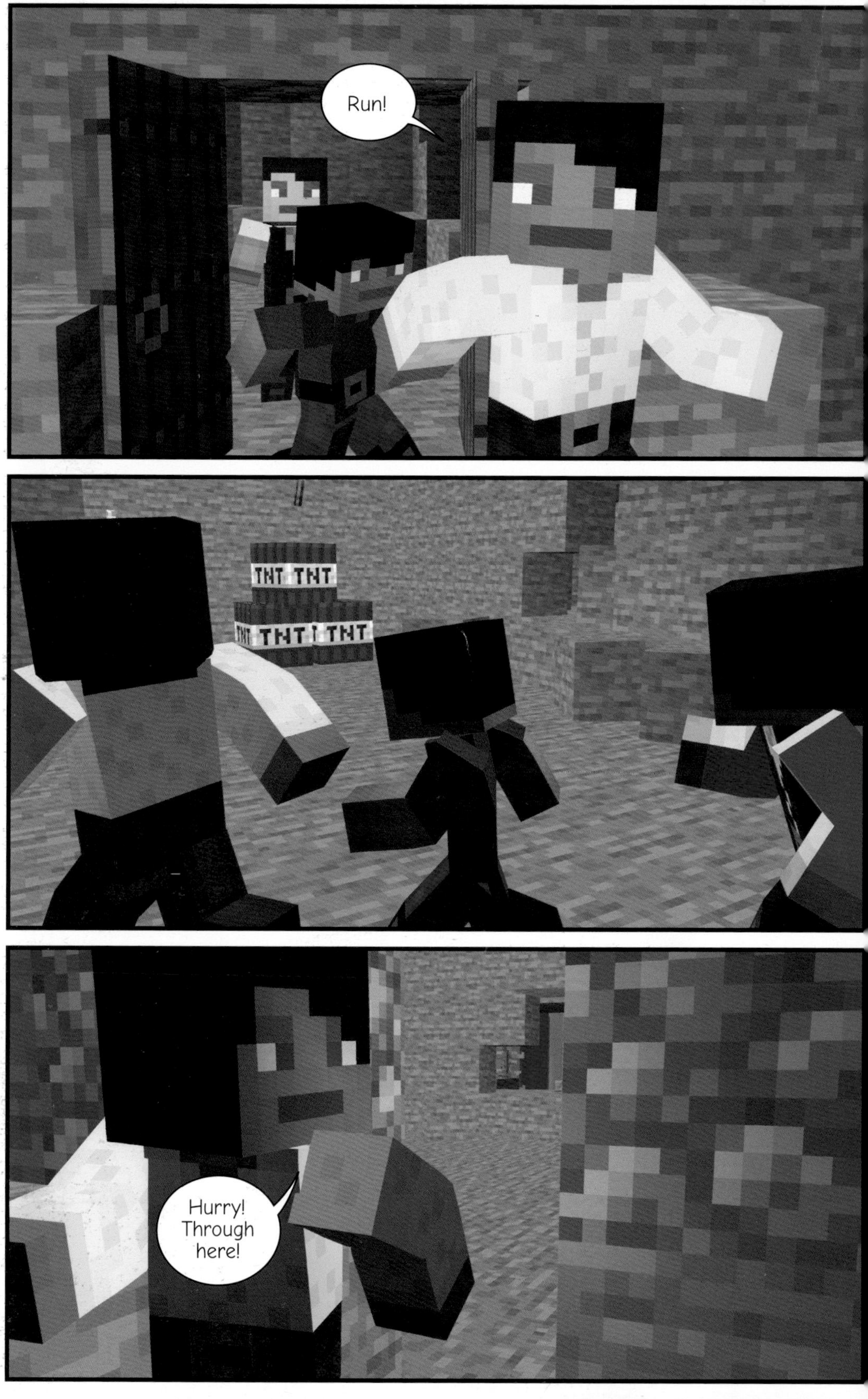
Run!
TNT TNT
TNT TNT
Hurry! Through here!

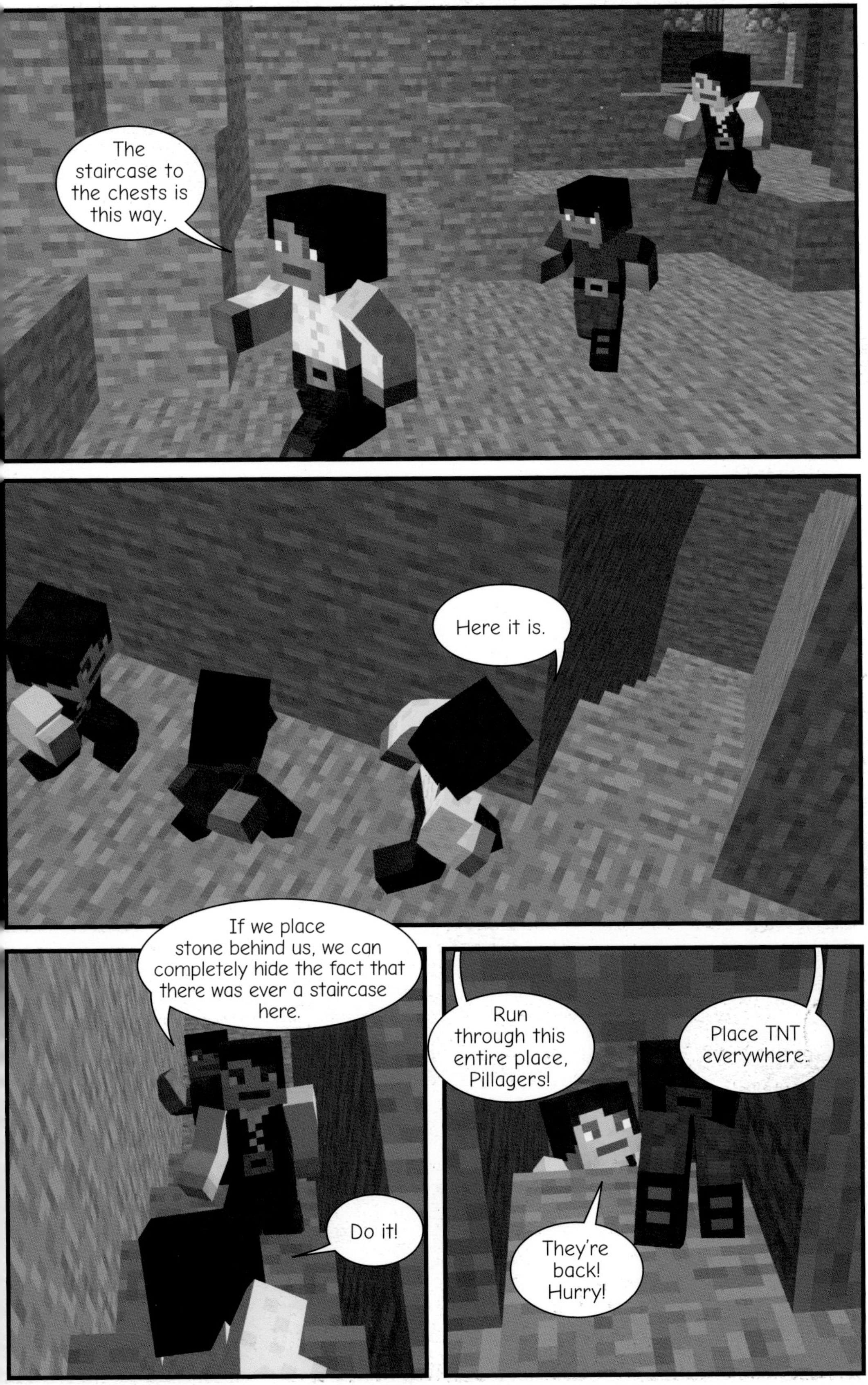
The staircase to the chests is this way.
Here it is.
If we place stone behind us, we can completely hide the fact that there was ever a staircase here.
Do it!
Run through this entire place, Pillagers!
Place TNT everywhere.
They're back! Hurry!

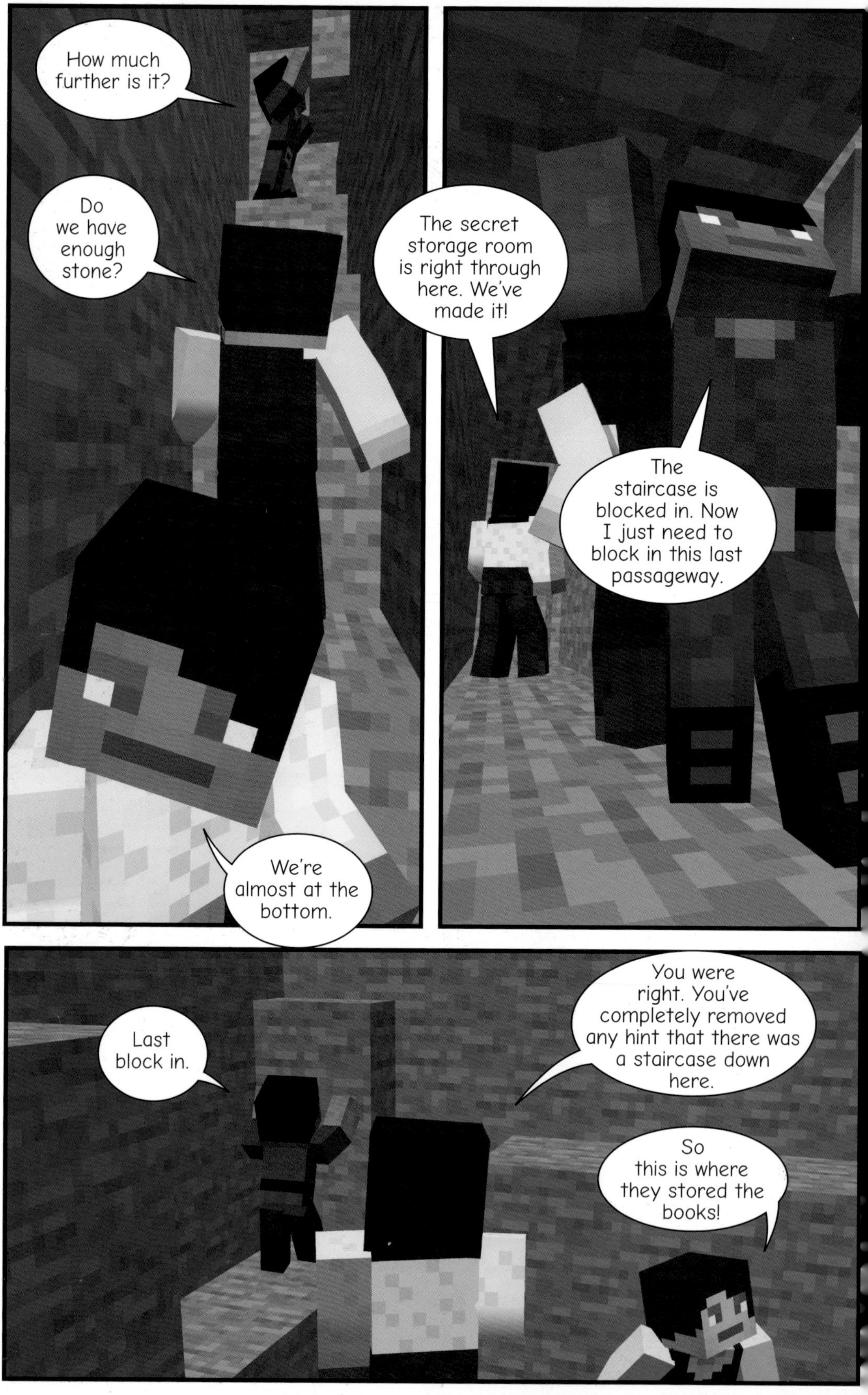
How much further is it?
Do we have enough stone?
We're almost at the bottom.
The secret storage room is right through here. We've made it!
The staircase is blocked in. Now I just need to block in this last passageway.
Last block in.
You were right. You've completely removed any hint that there was a staircase down here.
So this is where they stored the books!

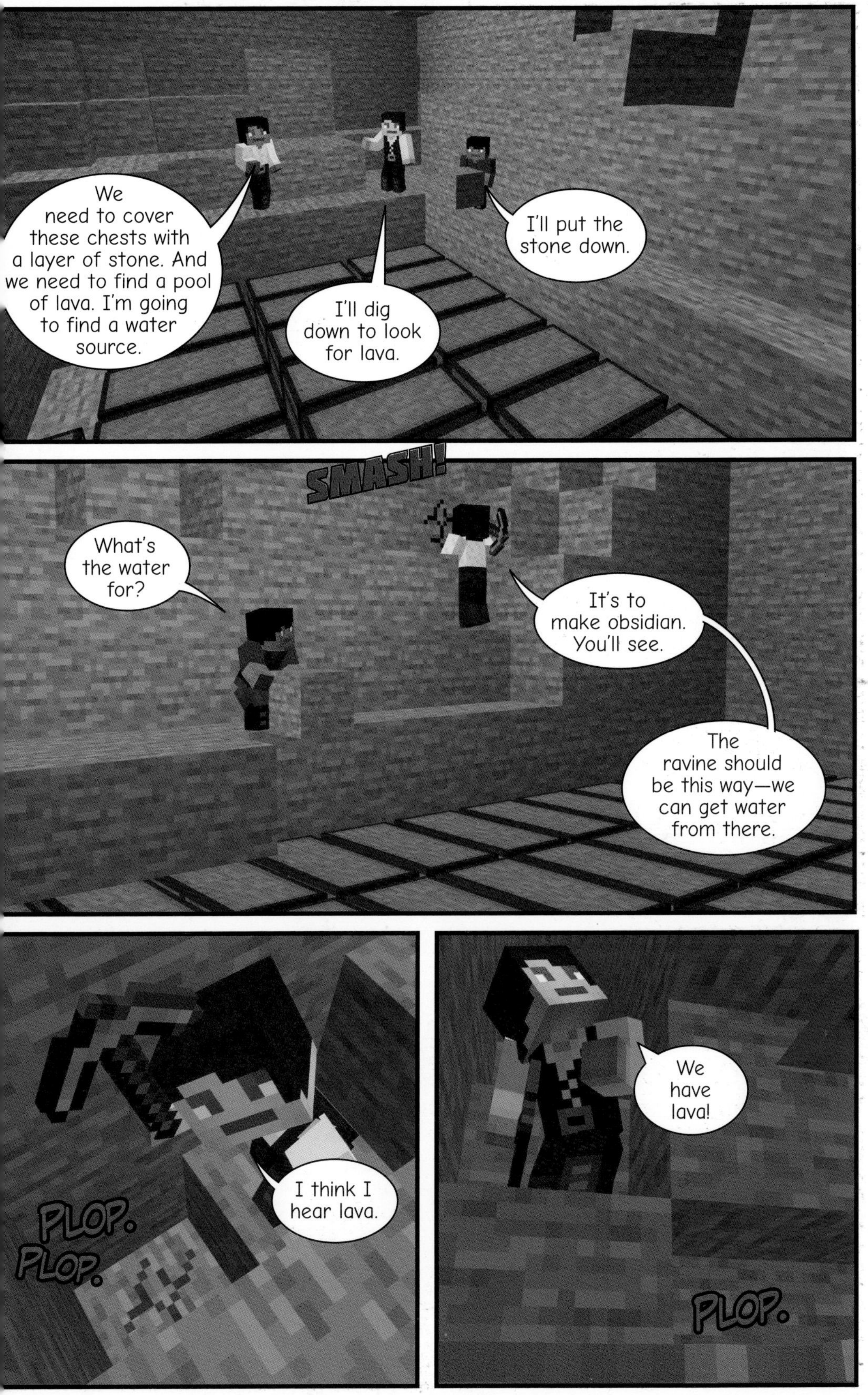
We need to cover these chests with a layer of stone. And we need to find a pool of lava. I'm going to find a water source.
I'll dig down to look for lava.
I'll put the stone down.
SMASH!
What's the water for?
It's to make obsidian. You'll see.
The ravine should be this way—we can get water from there.
PLOP. PLOP.
I think I hear lava.
We have lava!
PLOP.

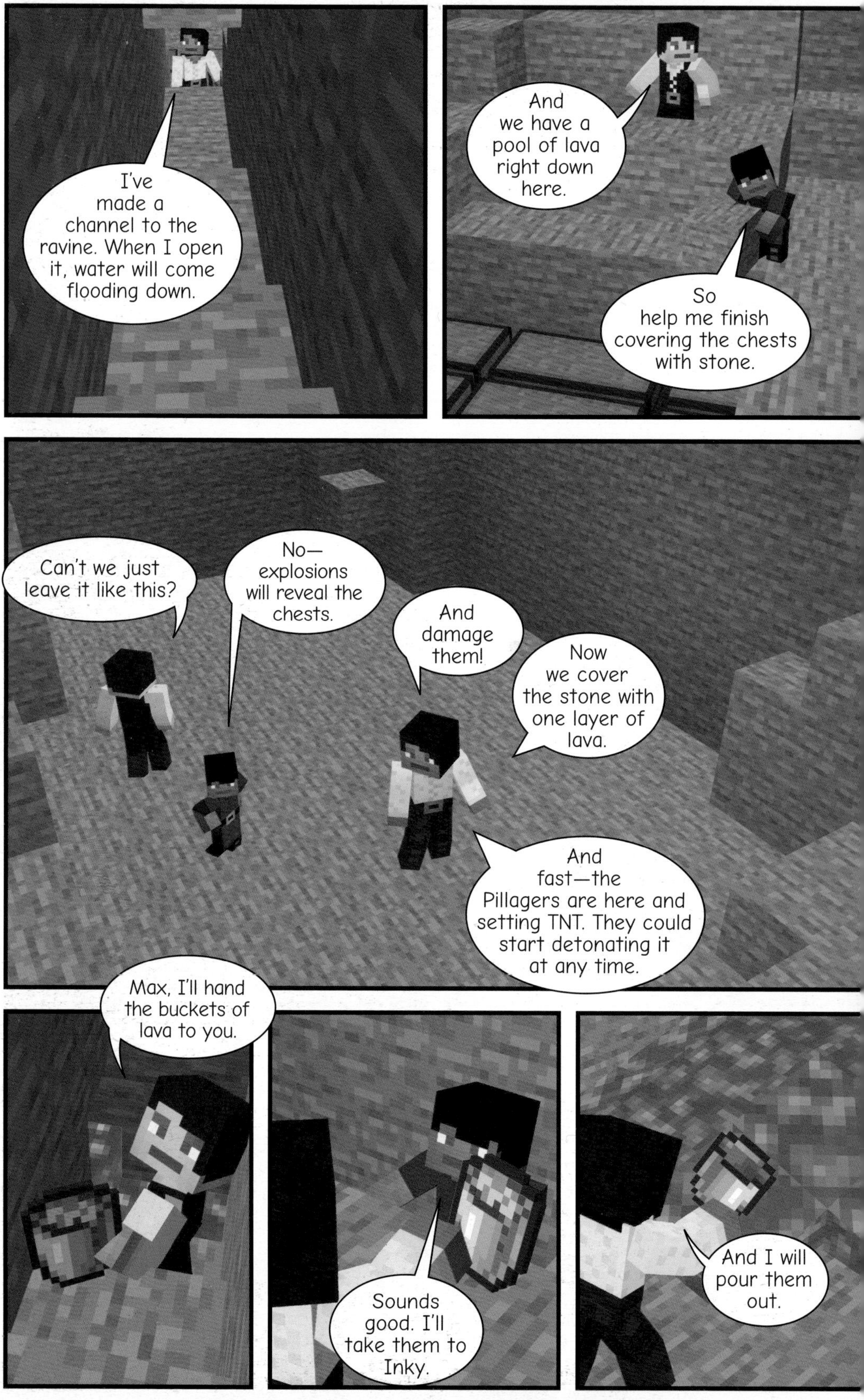
I've made a channel to the ravine. When I open it, water will come flooding down.
And we have a pool of lava right down here.
So help me finish covering the chests with stone.
Can't we just leave it like this?
No—explosions will reveal the chests.
And damage them!
Now we cover the stone with one layer of lava.
And fast—the Pillagers are here and setting TNT. They could start detonating it at any time.
Max, I'll hand the buckets of lava to you.
Sounds good. I'll take them to Inky.
And I will pour them out.

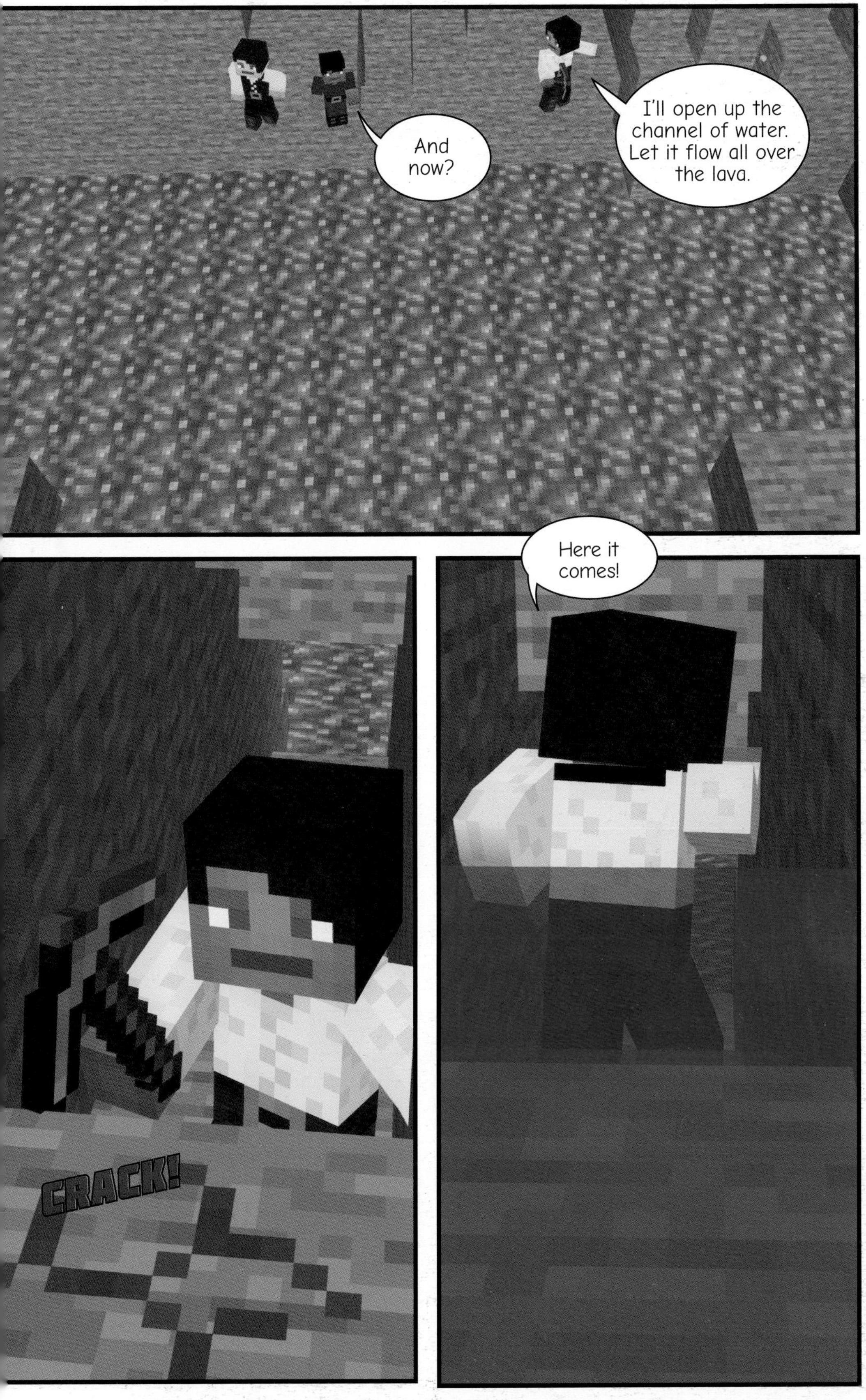
And now?
I'll open up the channel of water. Let it flow all over the lava.
CRACK!
Here it comes!

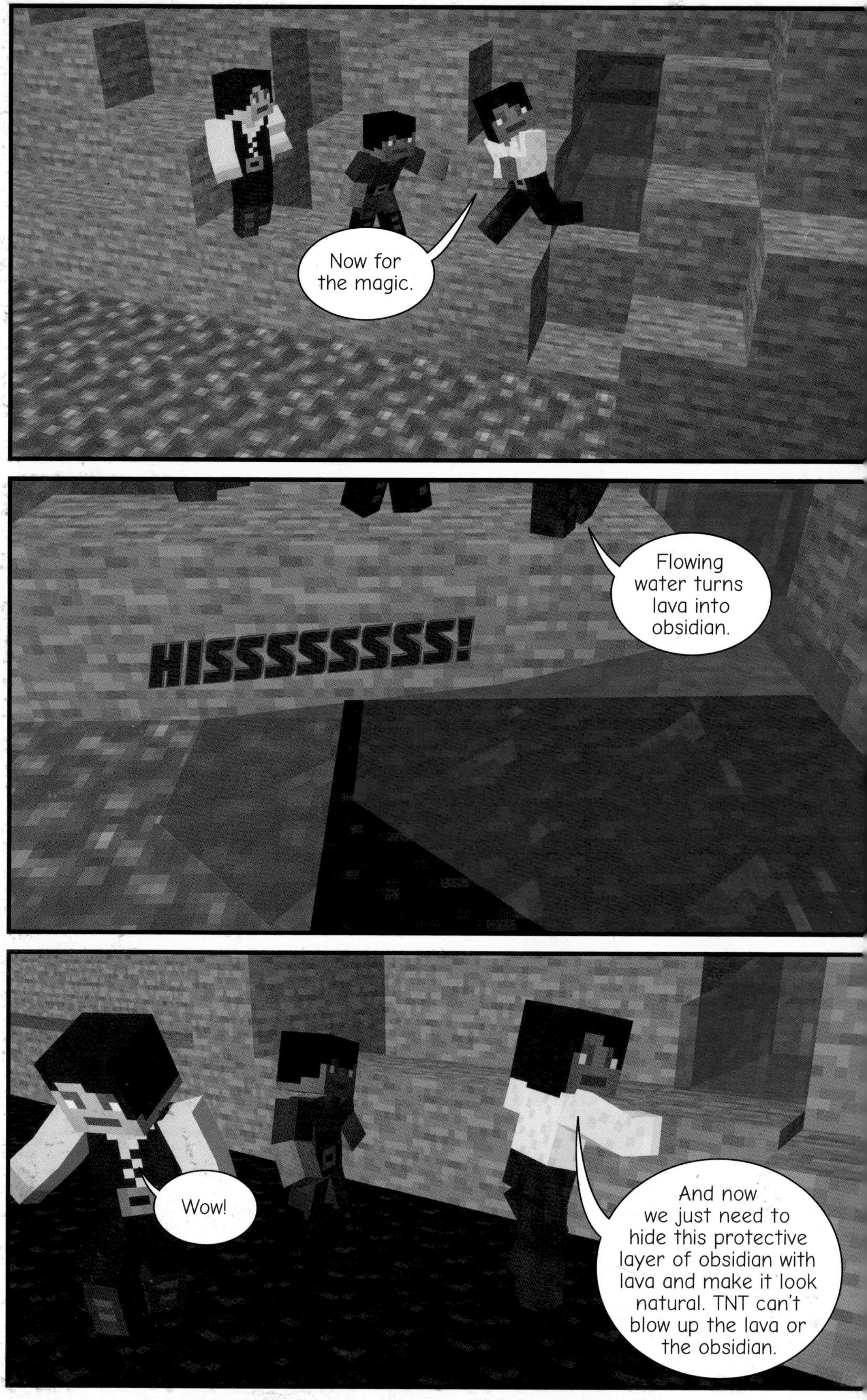
Now for the magic.
HISSSSSSS!
Flowing water turns lava into obsidian.
Wow!
And now we just need to hide this protective layer of obsidian with lava and make it look natural. TNT can't blow up the lava or the obsidian.

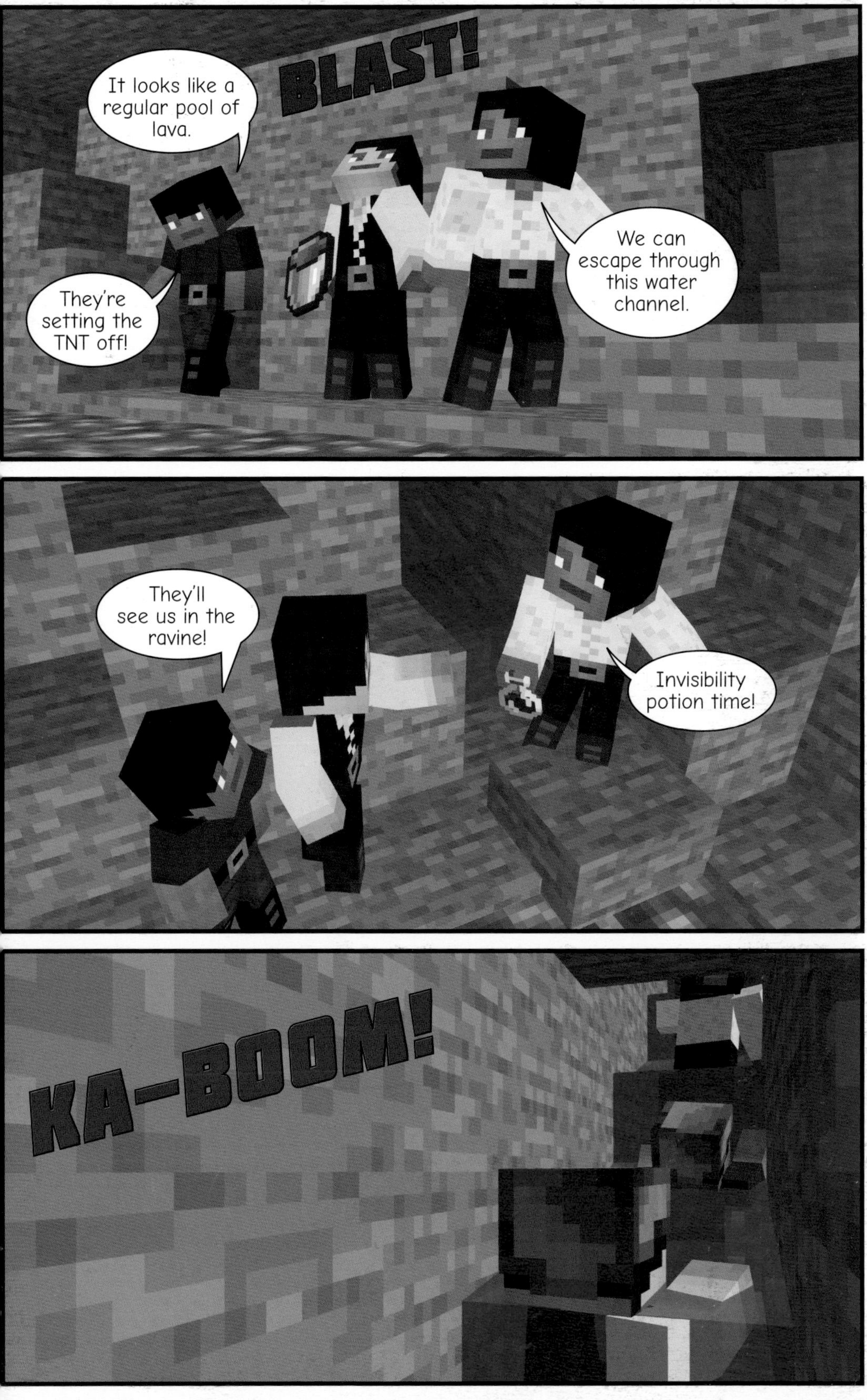
It looks like a regular pool of lava.
BLAST!
They're setting the TNT off!
We can escape through this water channel.
They'll see us in the ravine!
Invisibility potion time!
KA-BOOM!

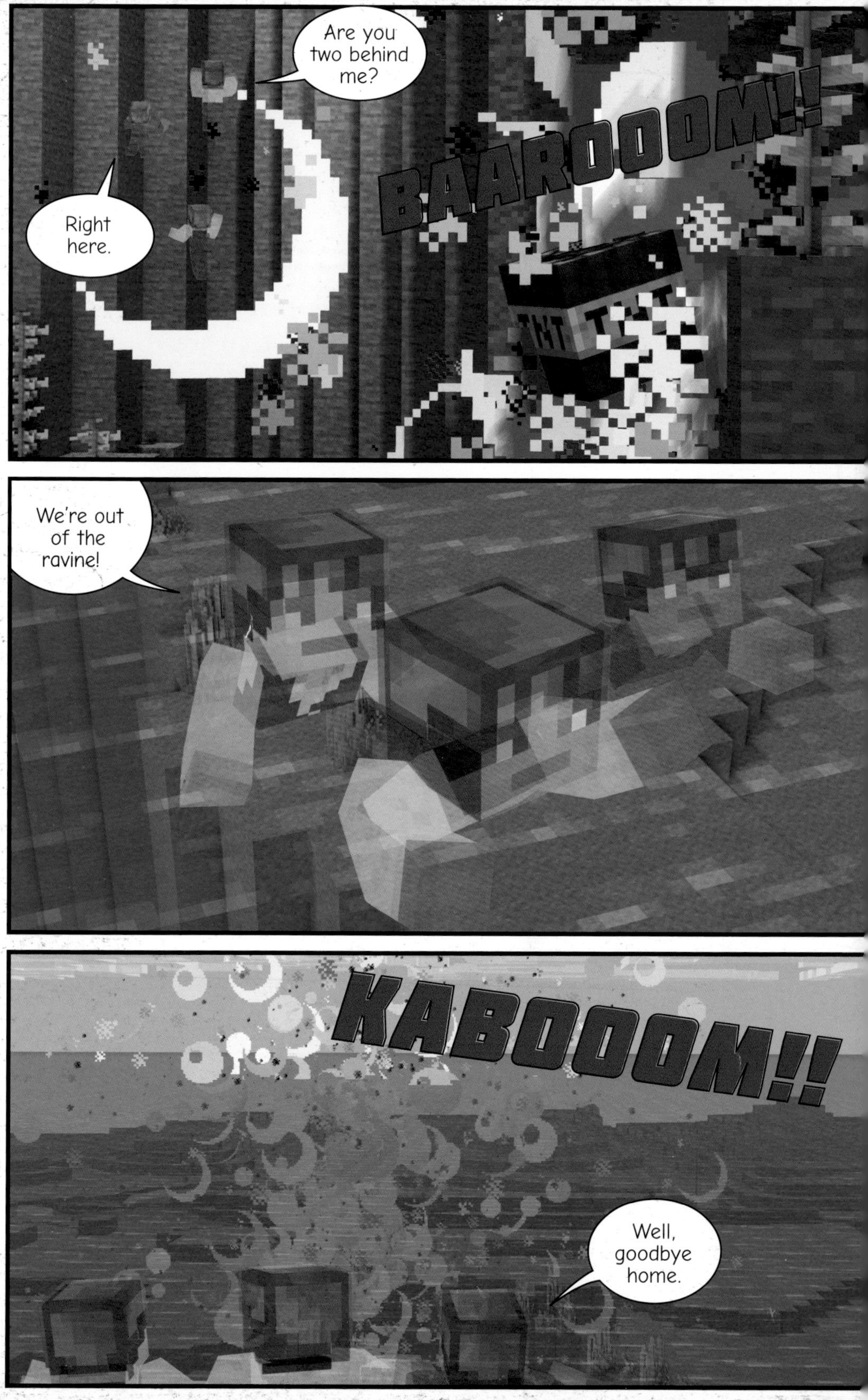
Are you two behind me?
Right here.
BAAROOOM!!
We're out of the ravine!
KABOOOOM!!
Well, goodbye home.

Chapter 3
A New Plan

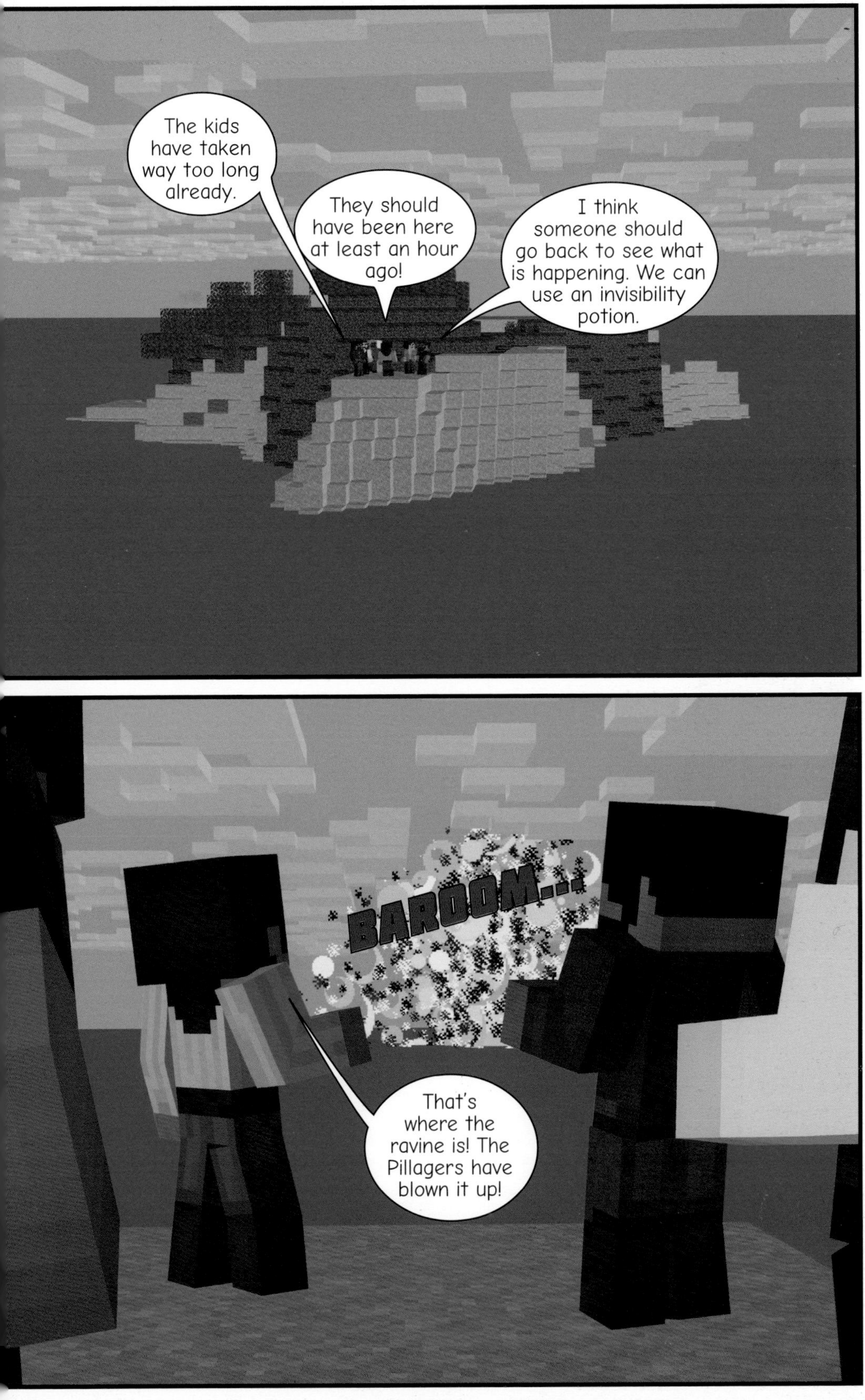
The kids have taken way too long already.
They should have been here at least an hour ago!
I think someone should go back to see what is happening. We can use an invisibility potion.
BAROOM...!
That's where the ravine is! The Pillagers have blown it up!

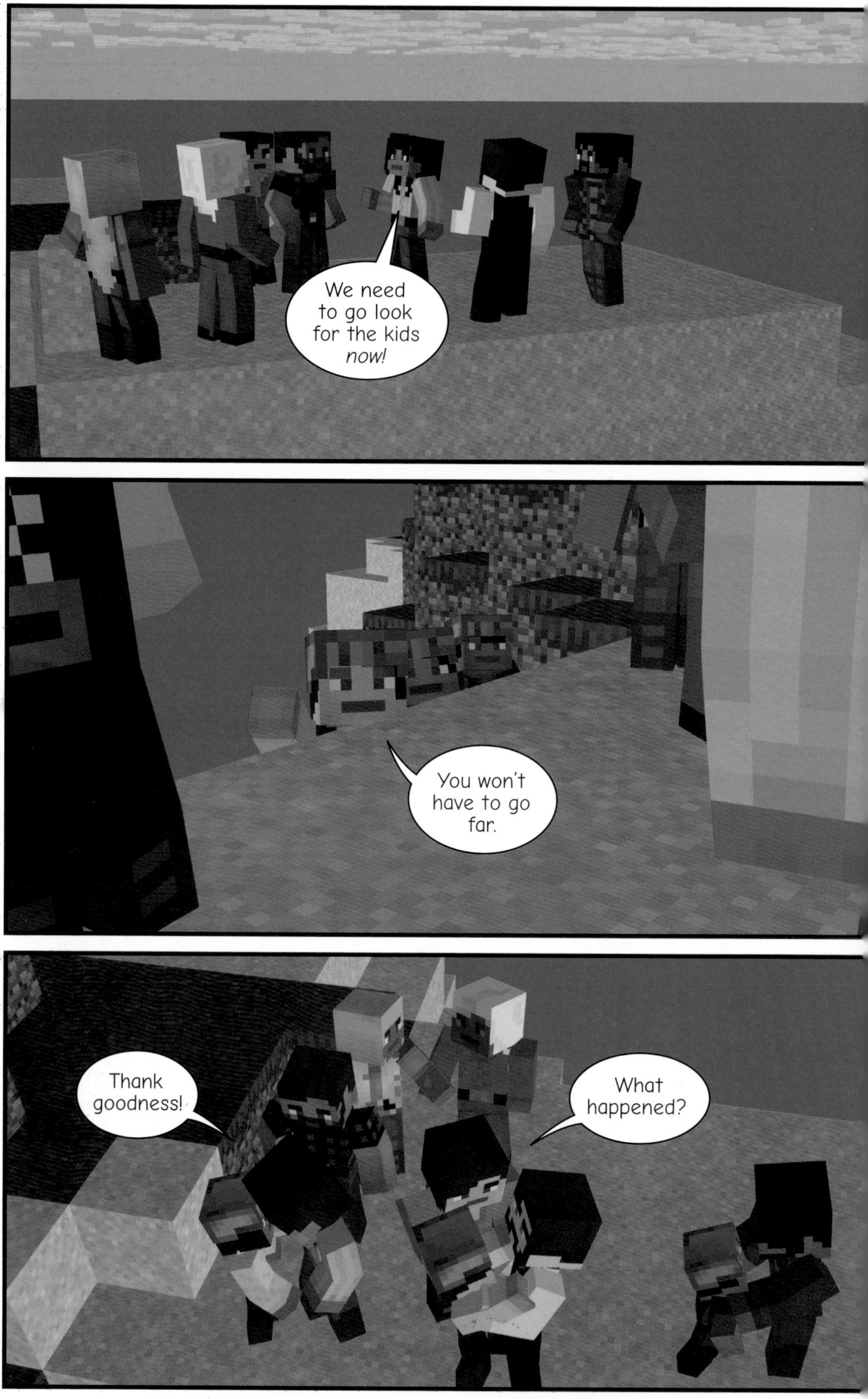
We need to go look for the kids *now!*
You won't have to go far.
Thank goodness!
What happened?

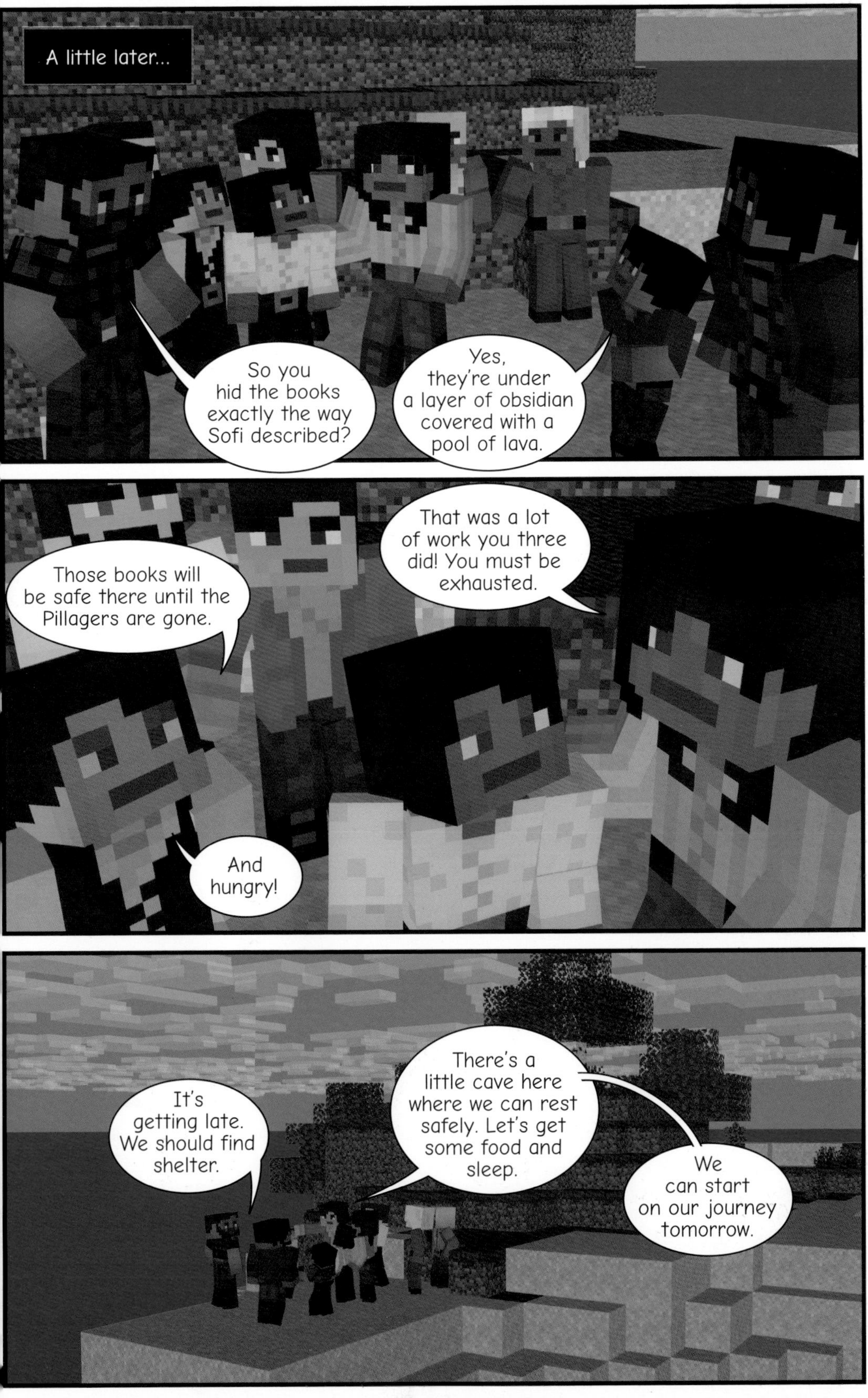
A little later...
So you hid the books exactly the way Sofi described?
Yes, they're under a layer of obsidian covered with a pool of lava.
Those books will be safe there until the Pillagers are gone.
That was a lot of work you three did! You must be exhausted.
And hungry!
It's getting late. We should find shelter.
There's a little cave here where we can rest safely. Let's get some food and sleep.
We can start on our journey tomorrow.

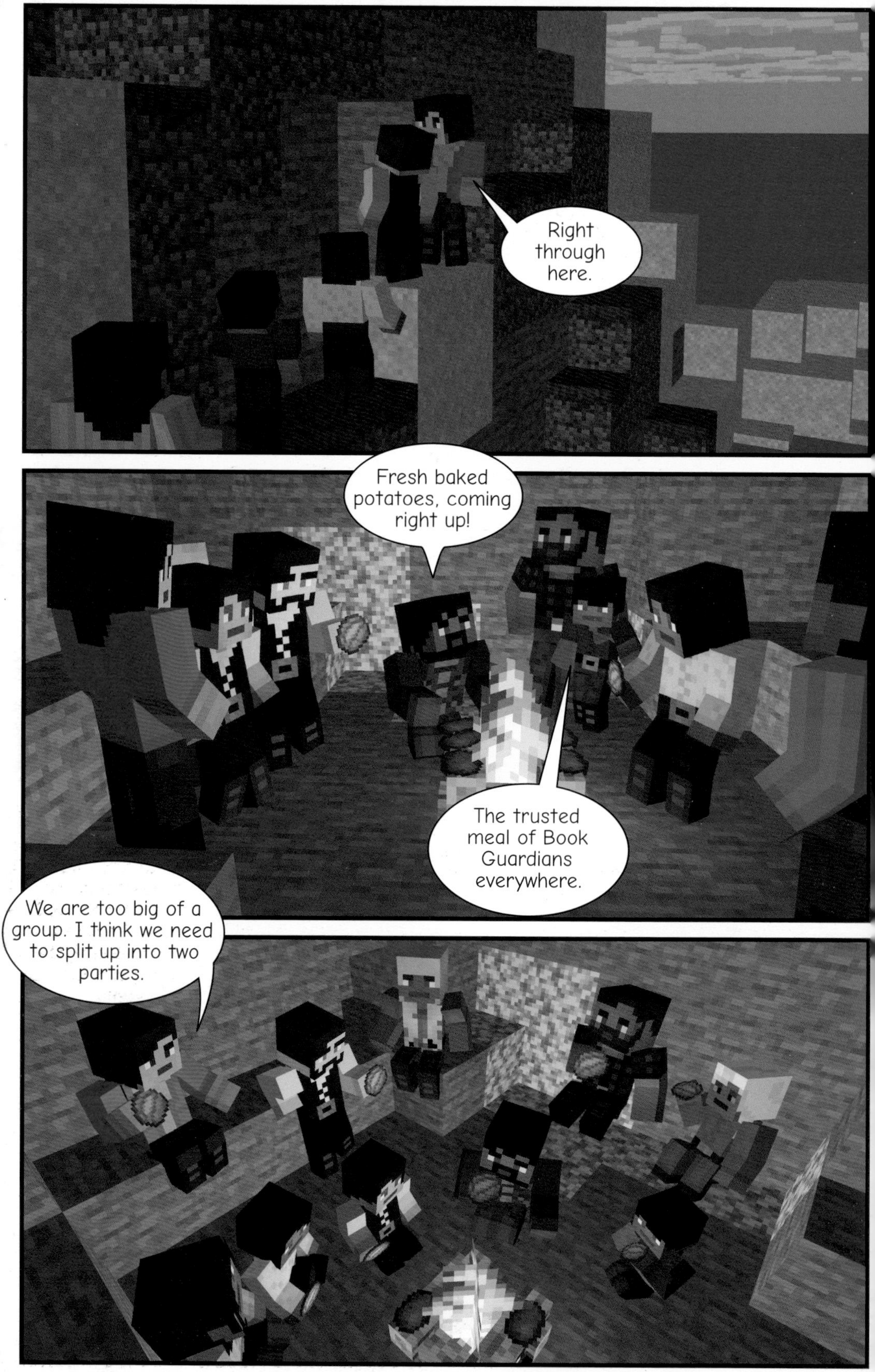
Right through here.
Fresh baked potatoes, coming right up!
The trusted meal of Book Guardians everywhere.
We are too big of a group. I think we need to split up into two parties.

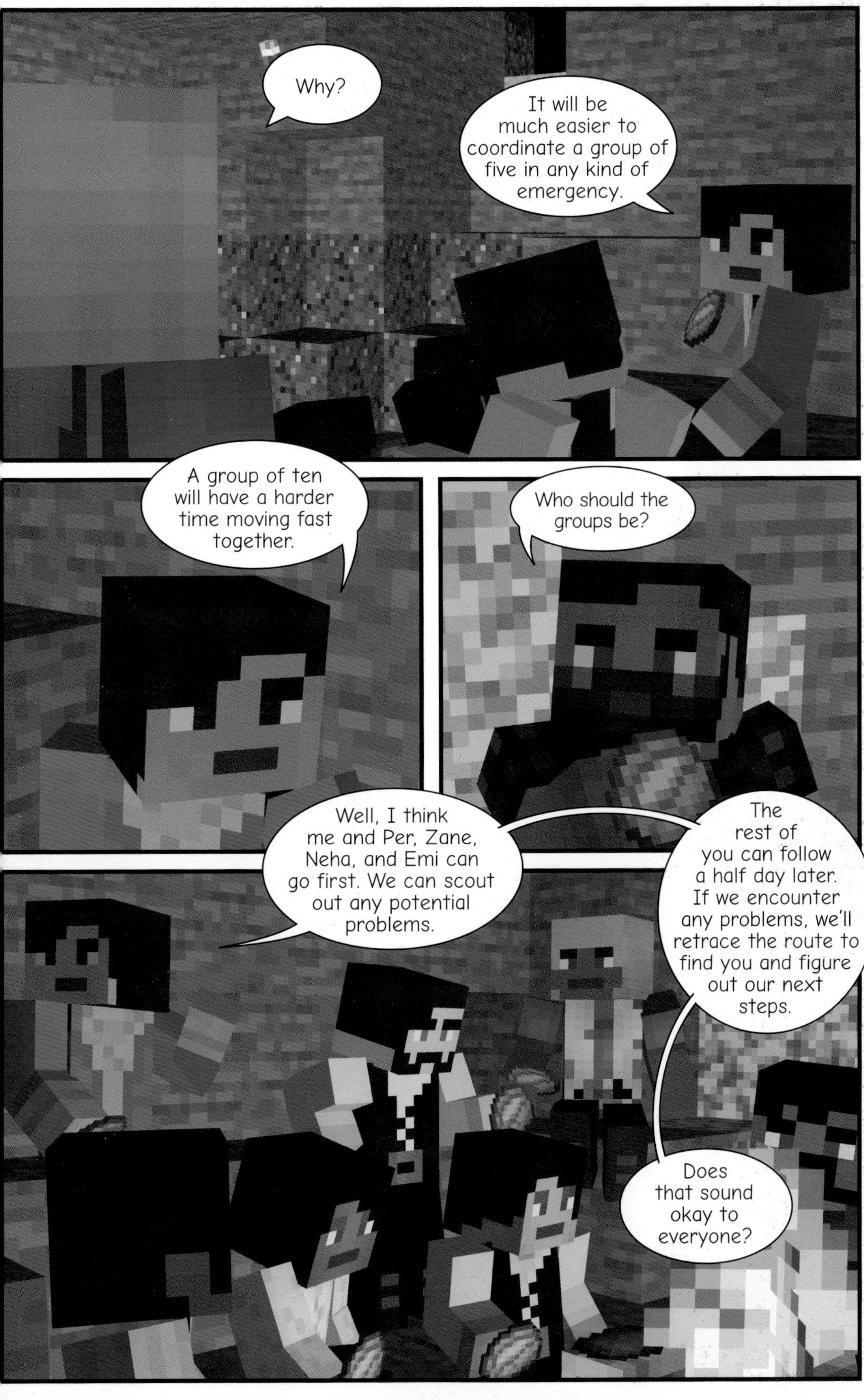
Why?
It will be much easier to coordinate a group of five in any kind of emergency.
A group of ten will have a harder time moving fast together.
Who should the groups be?
Well, I think me and Per, Zane, Neha, and Emi can go first. We can scout out any potential problems.
The rest of you can follow a half day later. If we encounter any problems, we'll retrace the route to find you and figure out our next steps.
Does that sound okay to everyone?

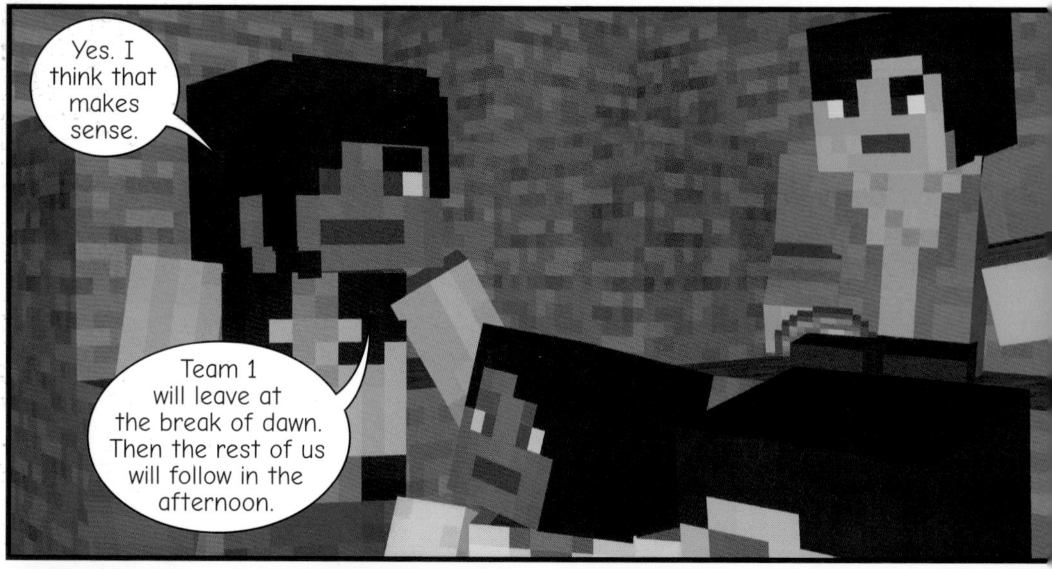
Yes. I think that makes sense.
Team 1 will leave at the break of dawn. Then the rest of us will follow in the afternoon.

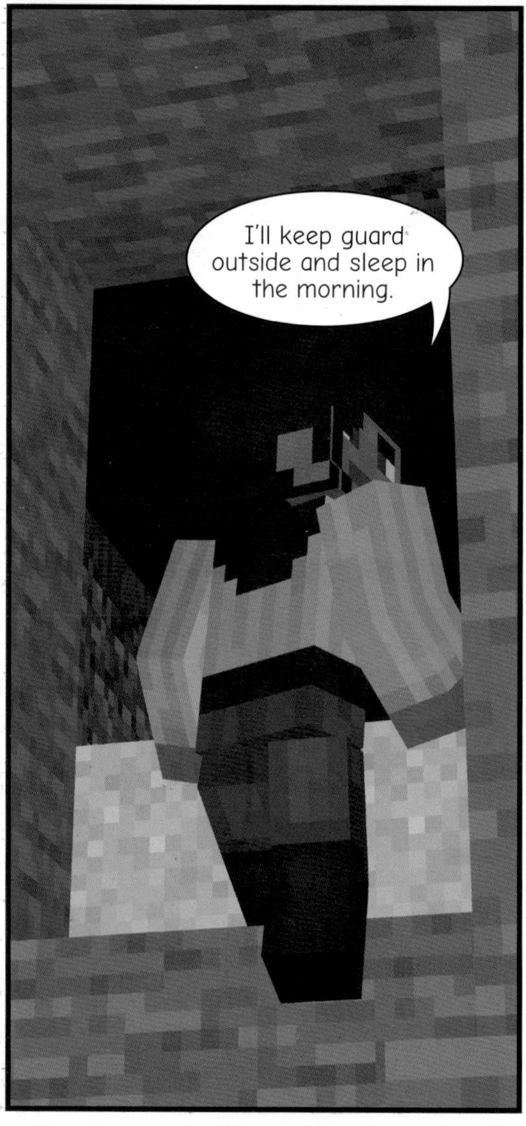
I'll keep guard outside and sleep in the morning.

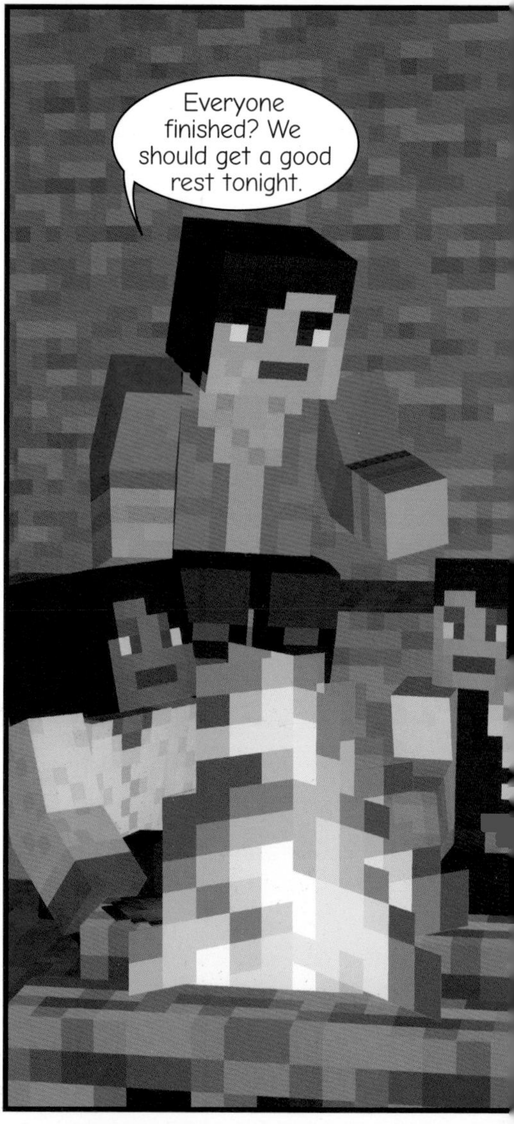
Everyone finished? We should get a good rest tonight.

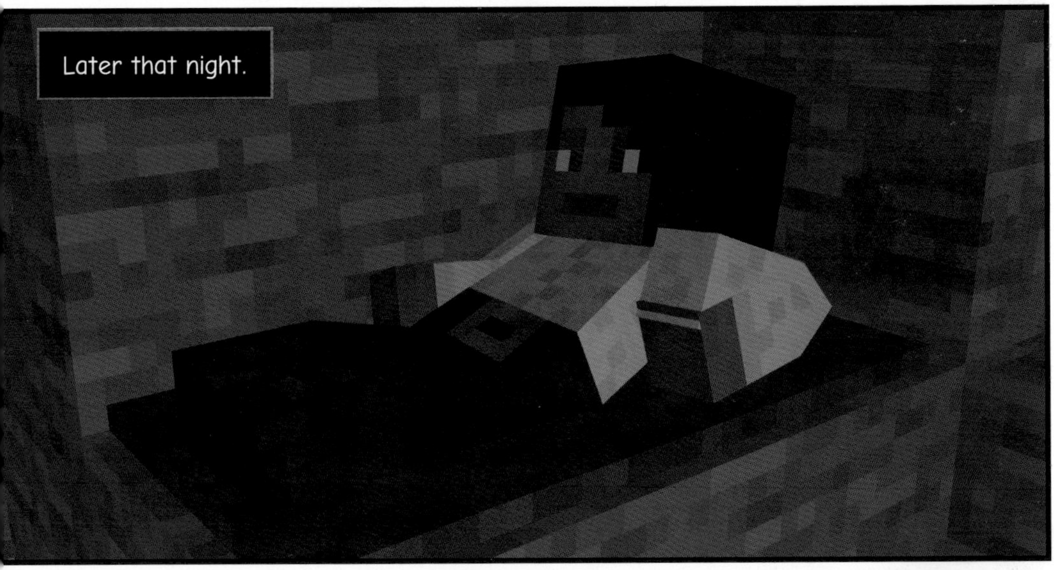
Later that night.
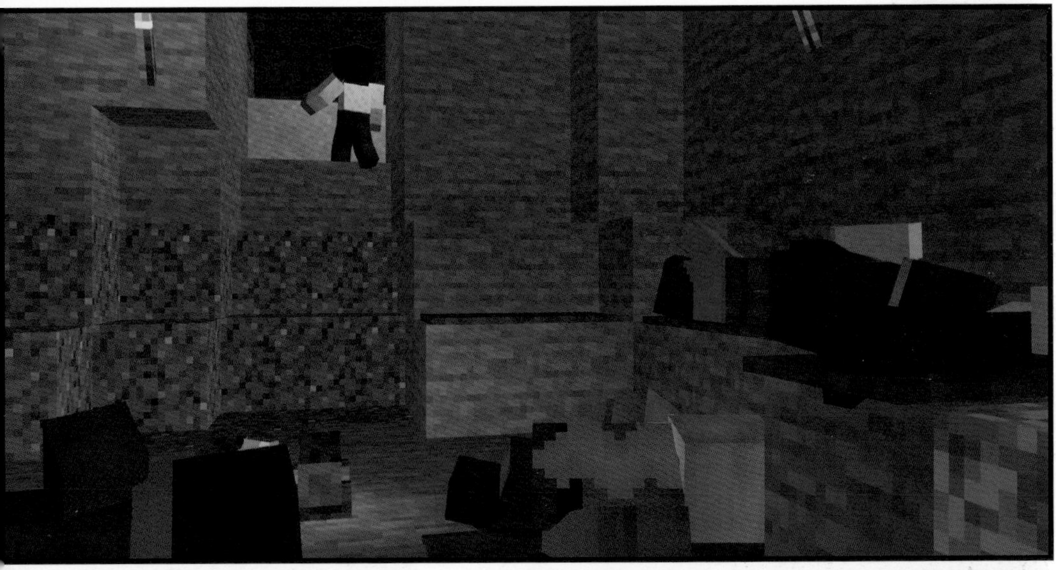
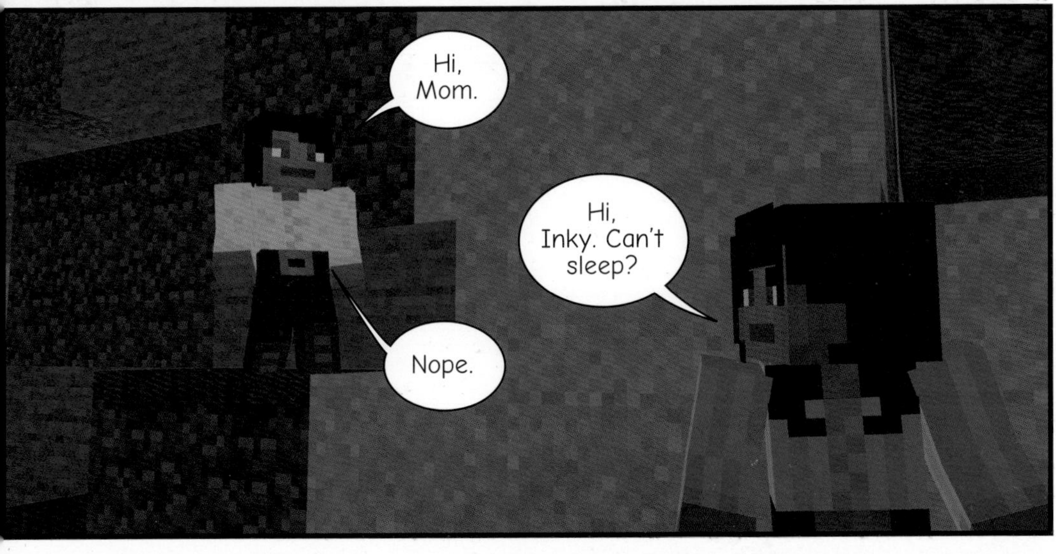
Hi,
Mom.
Hi,
Inky. Can't
sleep?
Nope.

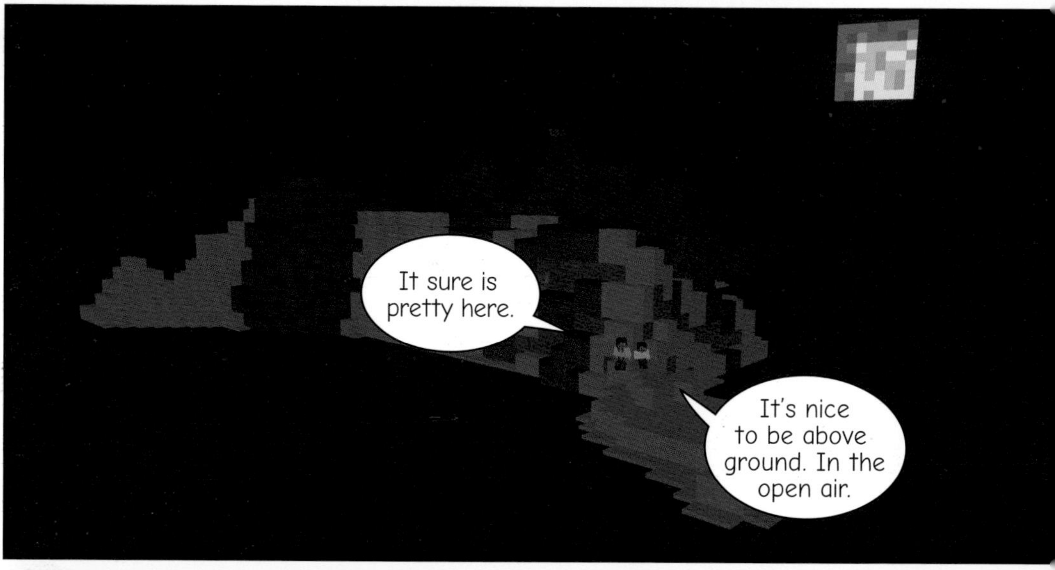
It sure is pretty here.
It's nice to be above ground. In the open air.

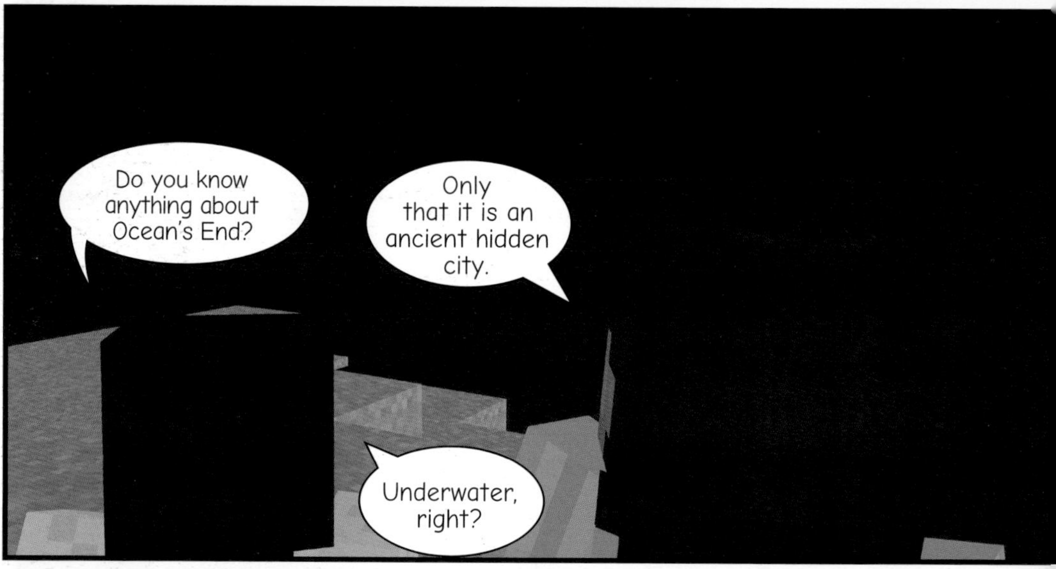
Do you know anything about Ocean's End?
Only that it is an ancient hidden city.
Underwater, right?

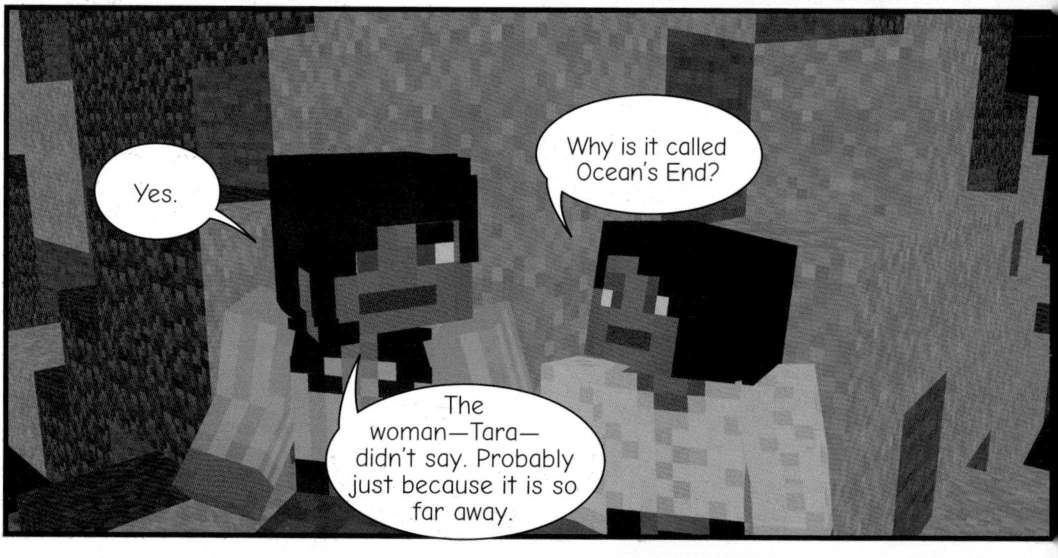
Yes.
Why is it called Ocean's End?
The woman—Tara—didn't say. Probably just because it is so far away.

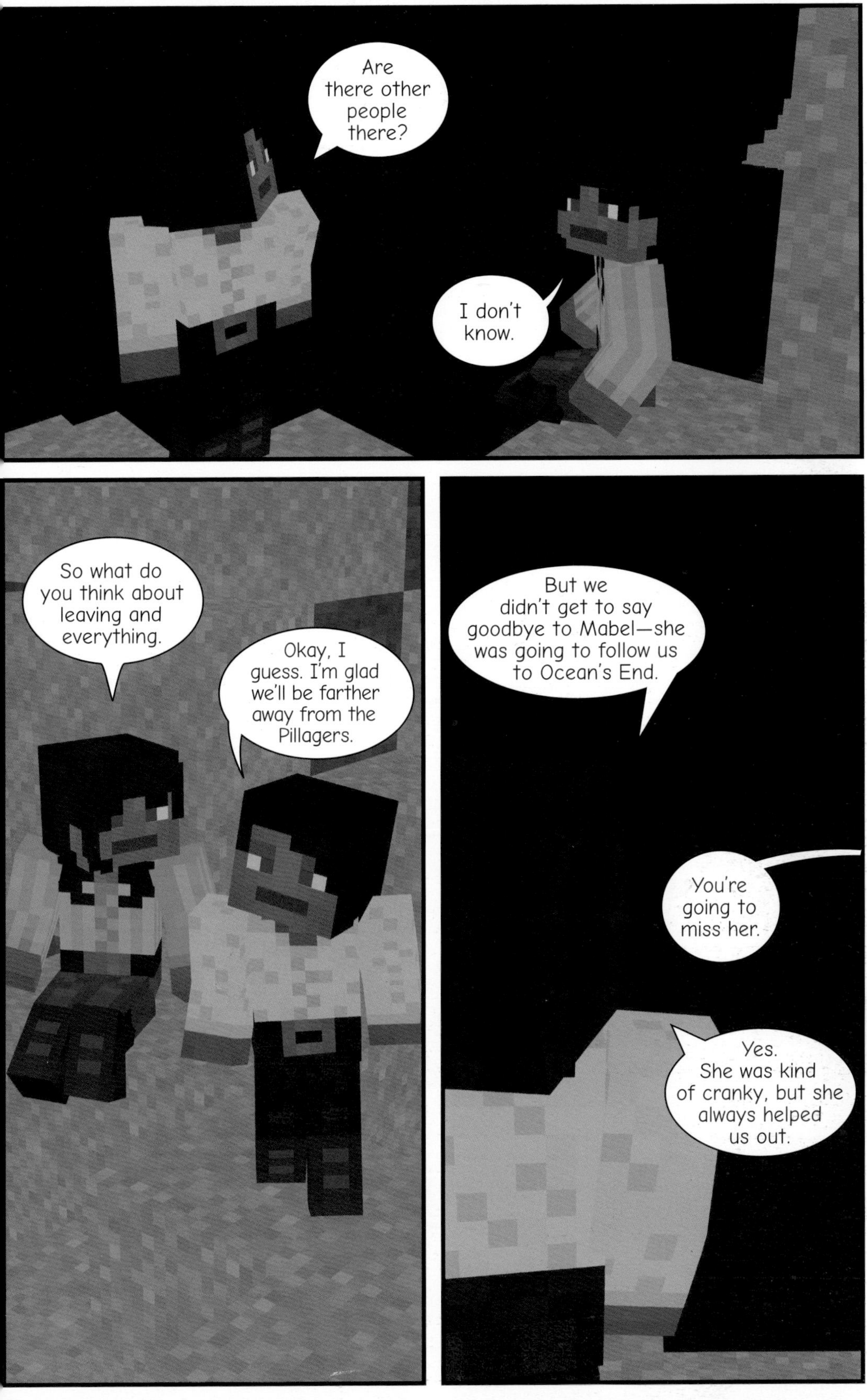
Are there other people there?
I don't know.
So what do you think about leaving and everything.
Okay, I guess. I'm glad we'll be farther away from the Pillagers.
But we didn't get to say goodbye to Mabel—she was going to follow us to Ocean's End.
You're going to miss her.
Yes. She was kind of cranky, but she always helped us out.

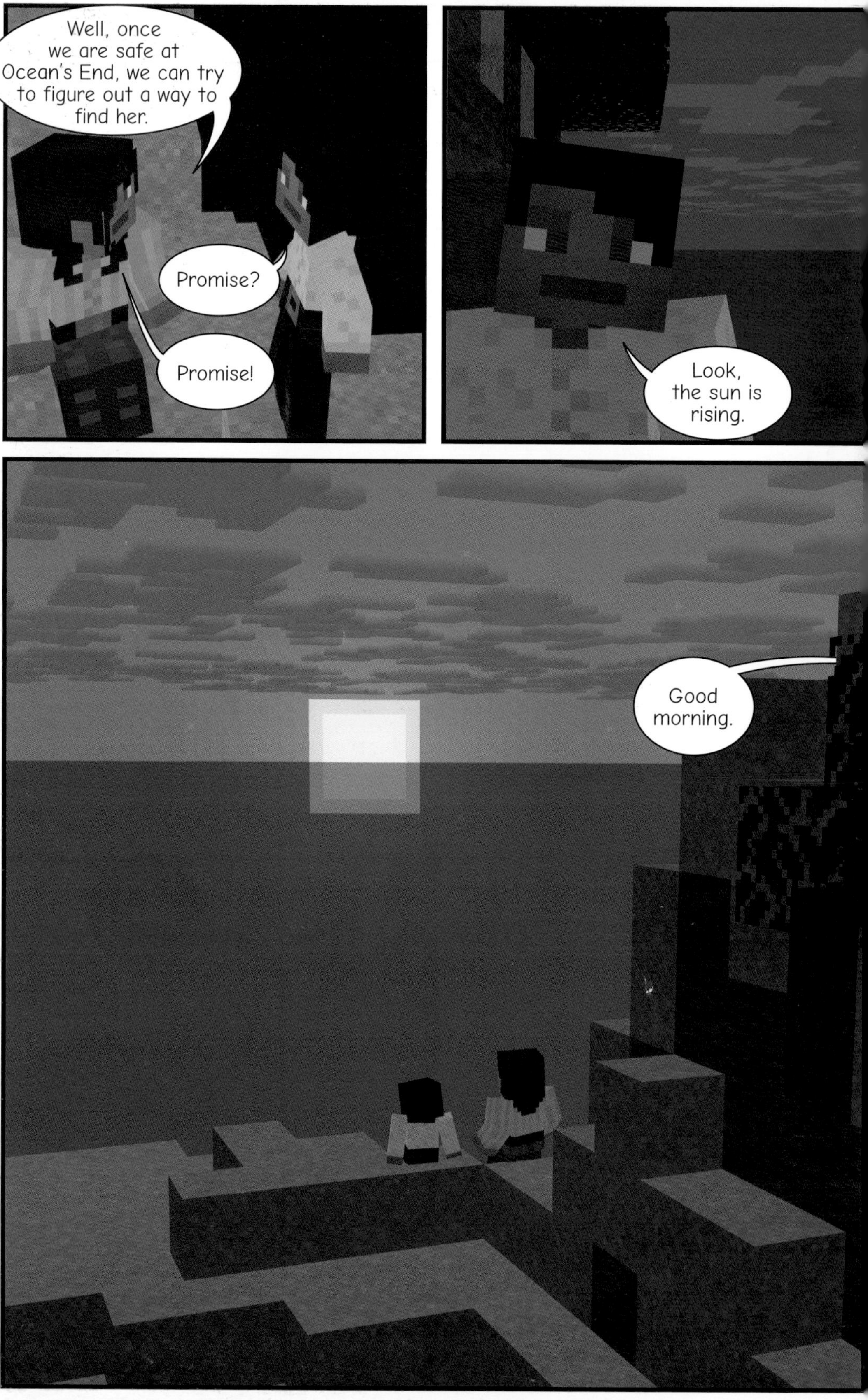
Well, once we are safe at Ocean's End, we can try to figure out a way to find her.
Promise?
Promise!
Look, the sun is rising.
Good morning.

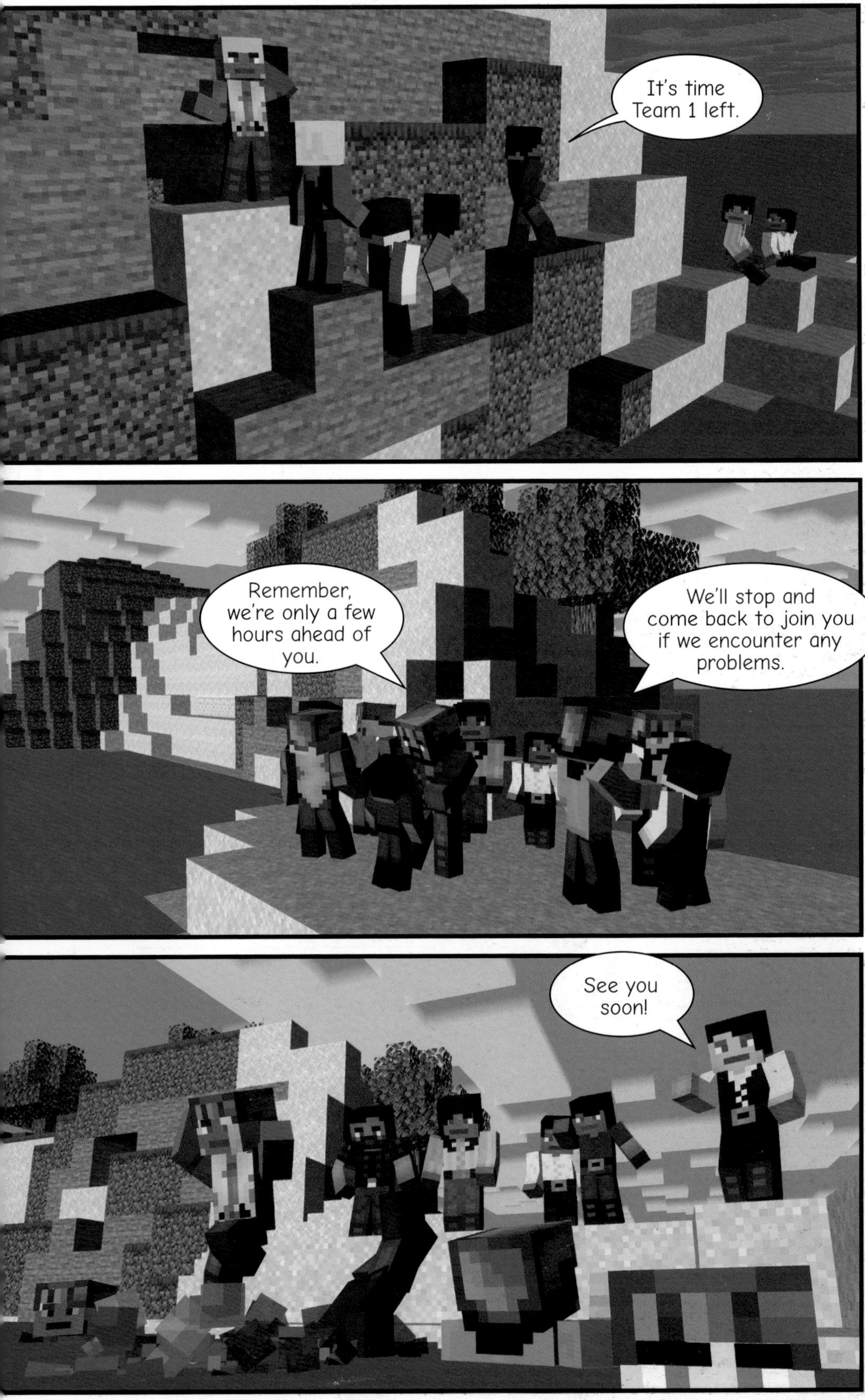

It's time Team 1 left.
Remember, we're only a few hours ahead of you.
We'll stop and come back to join you if we encounter any problems.
See you soon!

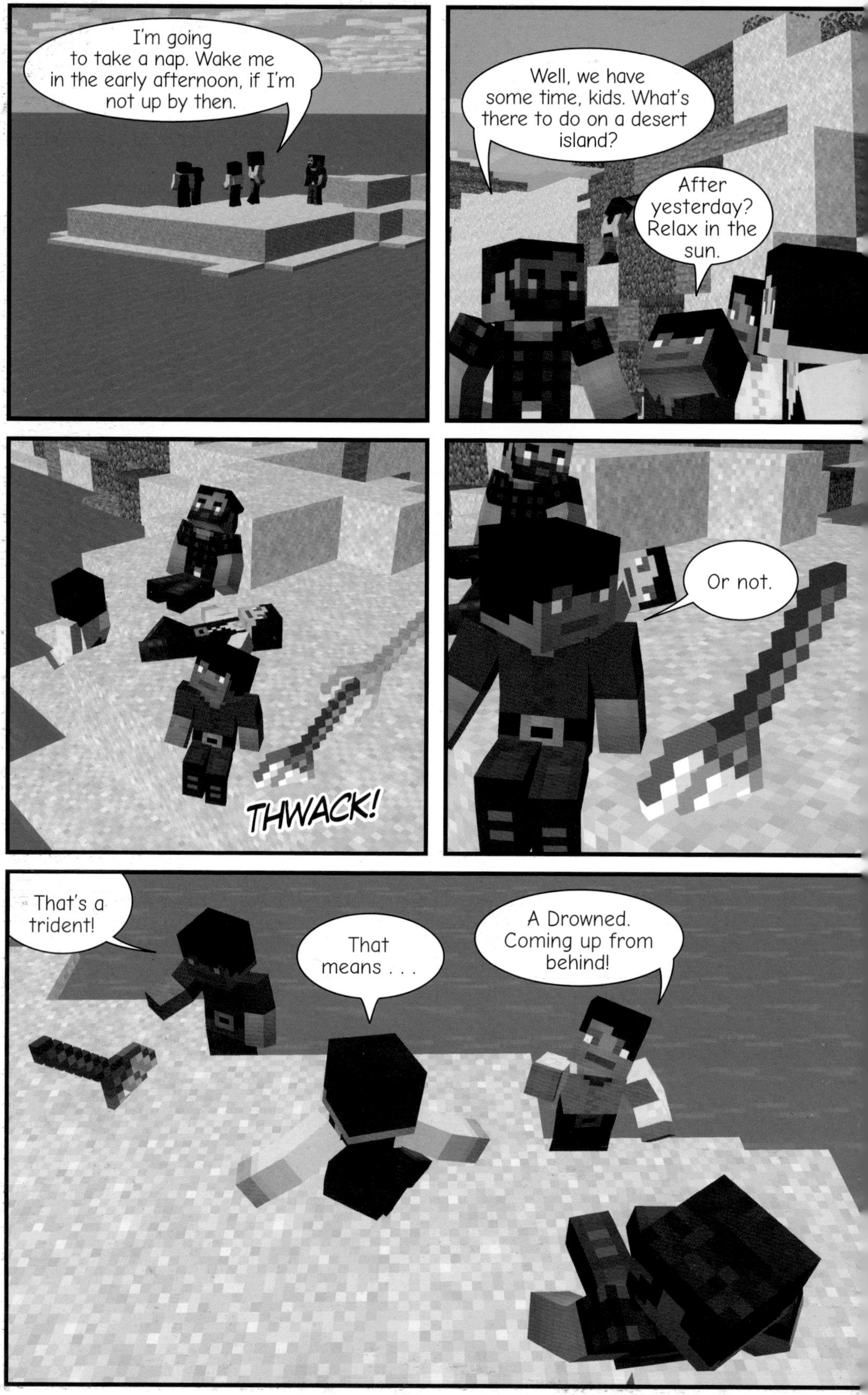
I'm going to take a nap. Wake me in the early afternoon, if I'm not up by then.
Well, we have some time, kids. What's there to do on a desert island?
After yesterday? Relax in the sun.
THWACK!
Or not.
That's a trident!
That means . . .
A Drowned. Coming up from behind!

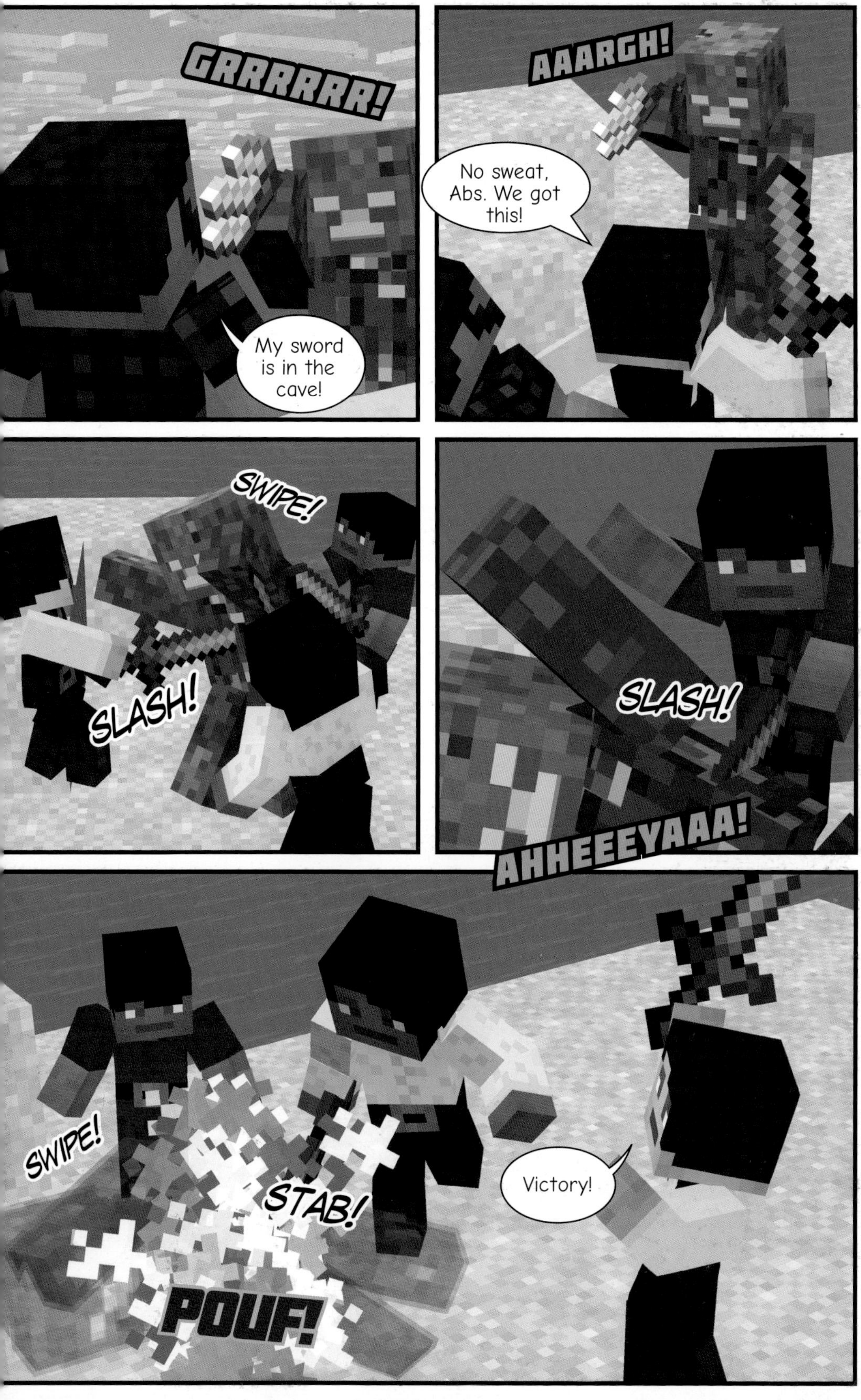
GRRRRRRR!
My sword is in the cave!
AAARGH!
No sweat, Abs. We got this!
SWIPE!
SLASH!
SLASH!
AHHEEEYAAA!
SWIPE!
STAB!
POUF!
Victory!

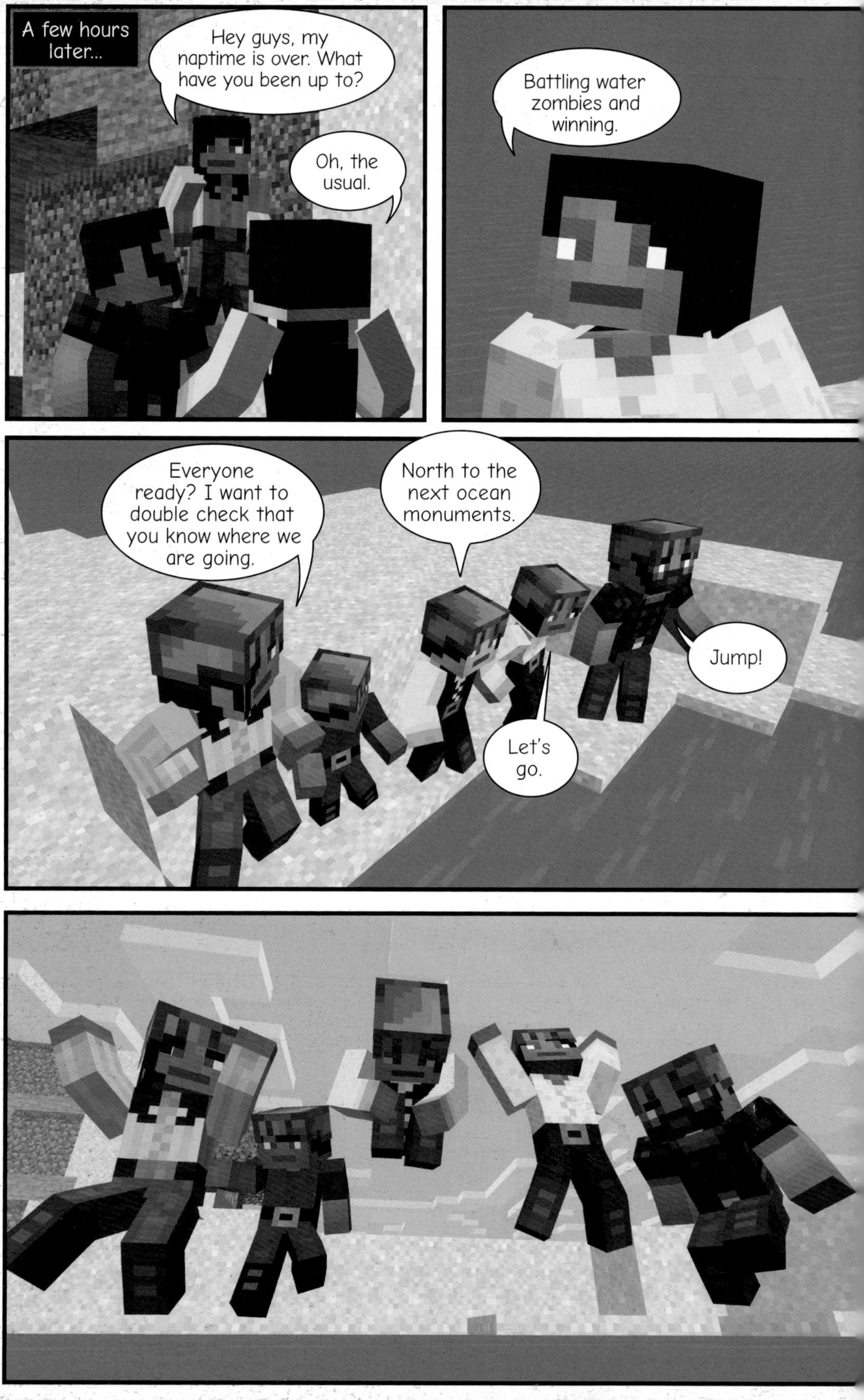

A few hours later...
Hey guys, my naptime is over. What have you been up to?
Oh, the usual.
Battling water zombies and winning.
Everyone ready? I want to double check that you know where we are going.
North to the next ocean monuments.
Jump!
Let's go.

Chapter 4
Guardians
vs. Pillagers

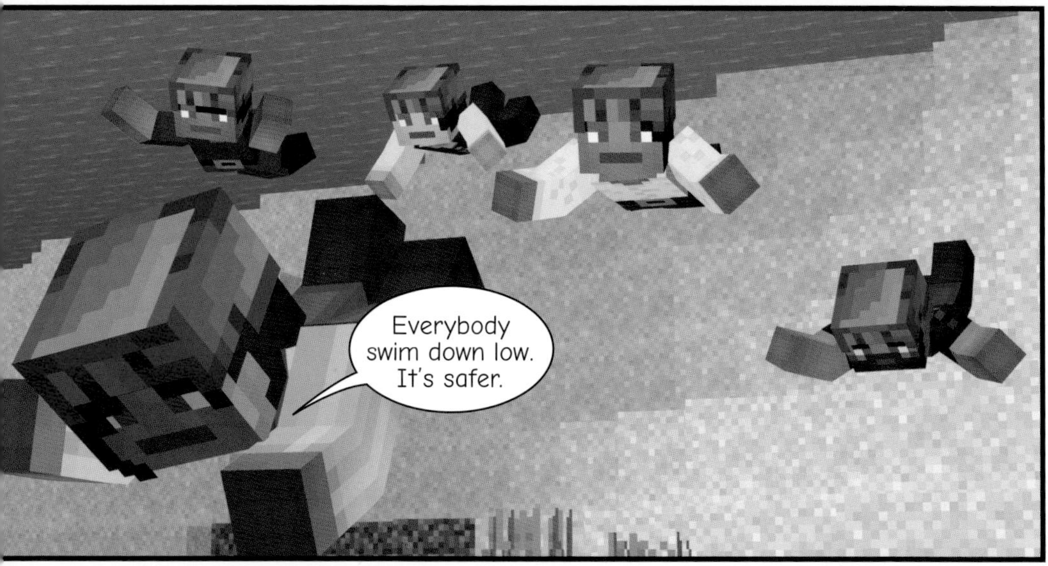
Everybody swim down low. It's safer.

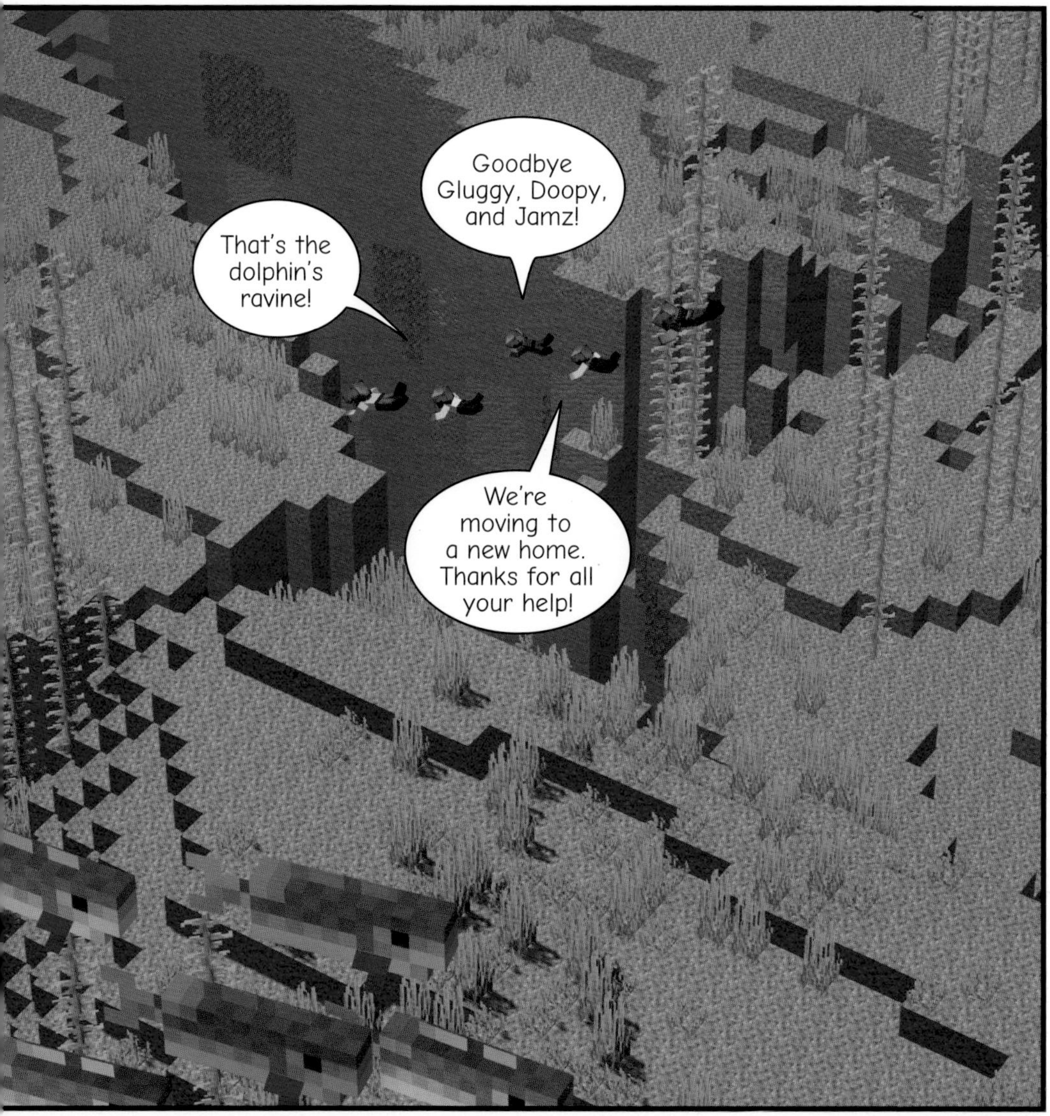
Goodbye Gluggy, Doopy, and Jamz!
That's the dolphin's ravine!
We're moving to a new home. Thanks for all your help!

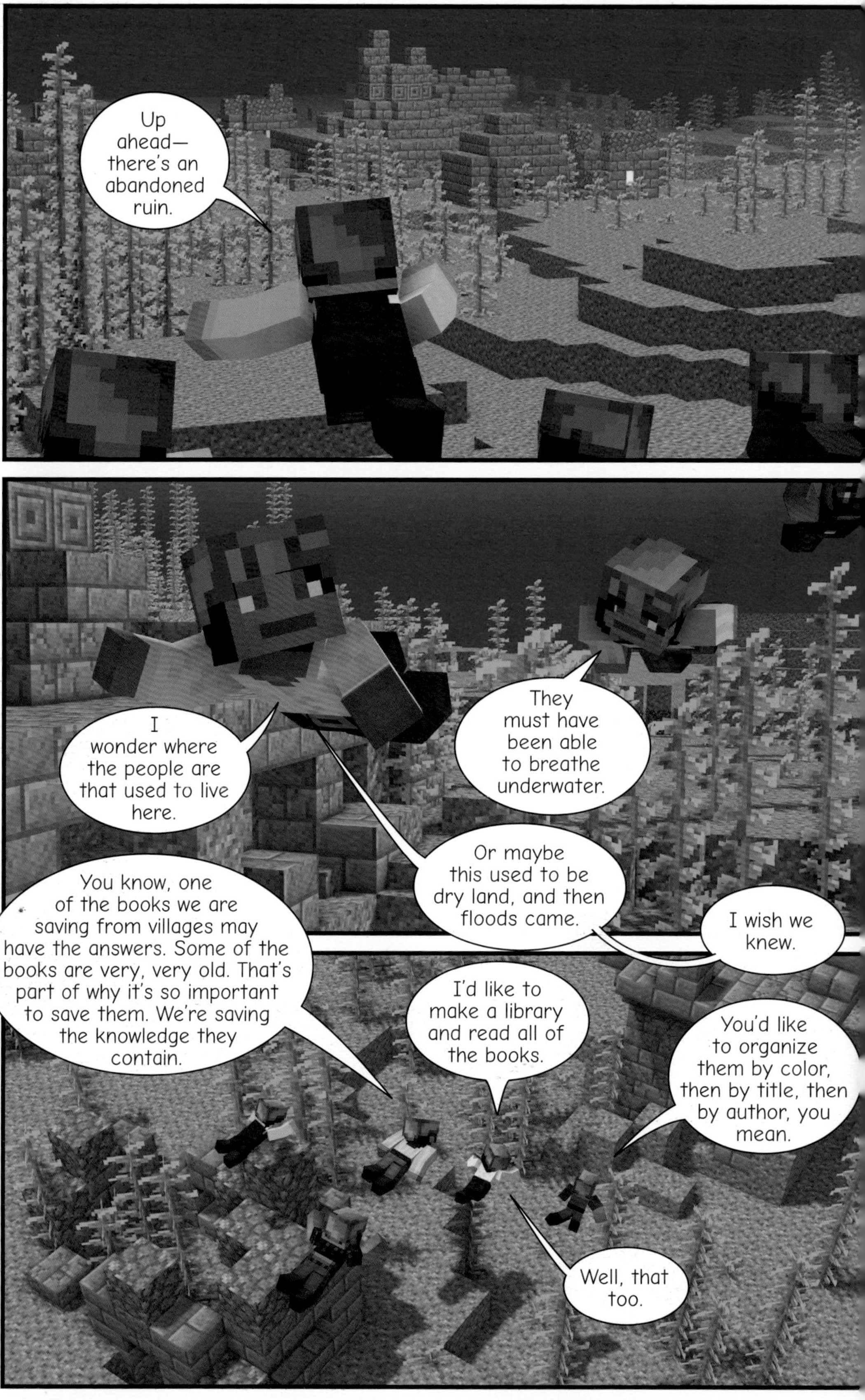

Up ahead— there's an abandoned ruin.
I wonder where the people are that used to live here.
They must have been able to breathe underwater.
Or maybe this used to be dry land, and then floods came.
I wish we knew.
You know, one of the books we are saving from villages may have the answers. Some of the books are very, very old. That's part of why it's so important to save them. We're saving the knowledge they contain.
I'd like to make a library and read all of the books.
You'd like to organize them by color, then by title, then by author, you mean.
Well, that too.

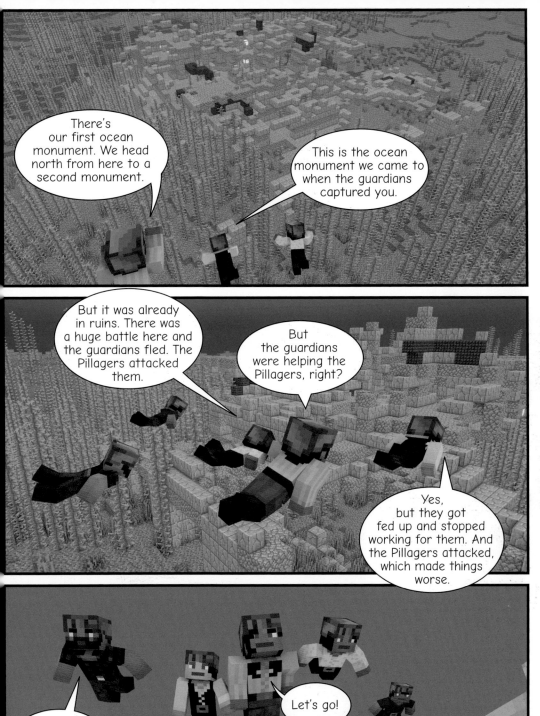

There's our first ocean monument. We head north from here to a second monument.

This is the ocean monument we came to when the guardians captured you.

But it was already in ruins. There was a huge battle here and the guardians fled. The Pillagers attacked them.

But the guardians were helping the Pillagers, right?

Yes, but they got fed up and stopped working for them. And the Pillagers attacked, which made things worse.

Well, at least this one is free from guardians.

Let's go!

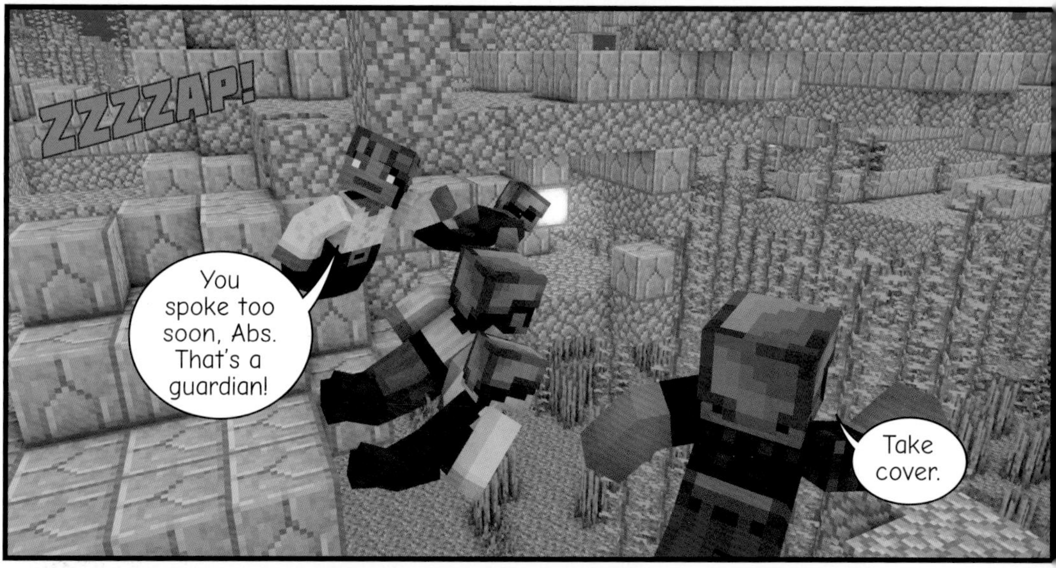
ZZZZAP!
You spoke too soon, Abs. That's a guardian!
Take cover.

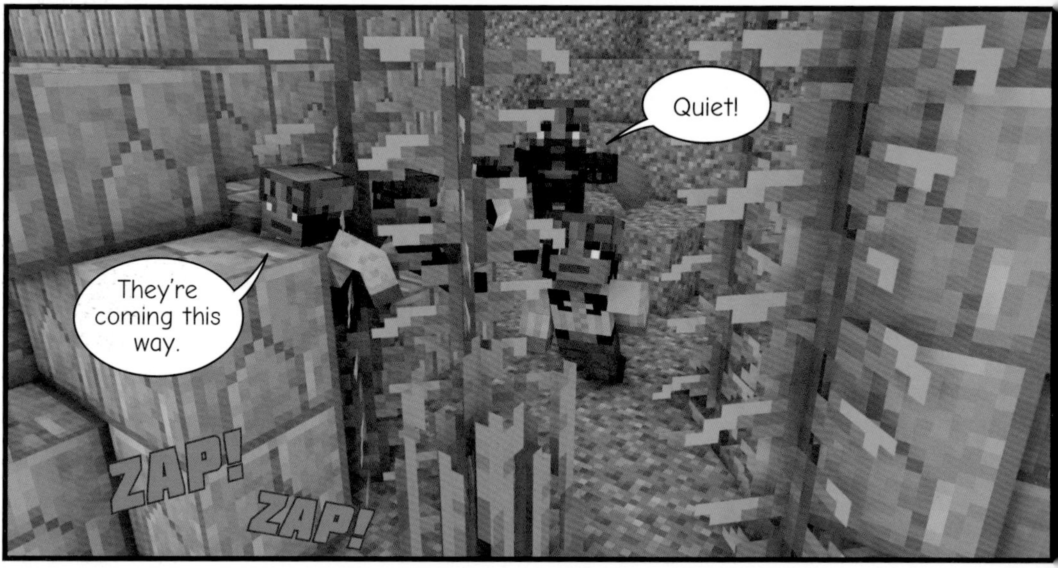
They're coming this way.
Quiet!
ZAP!
ZAP!

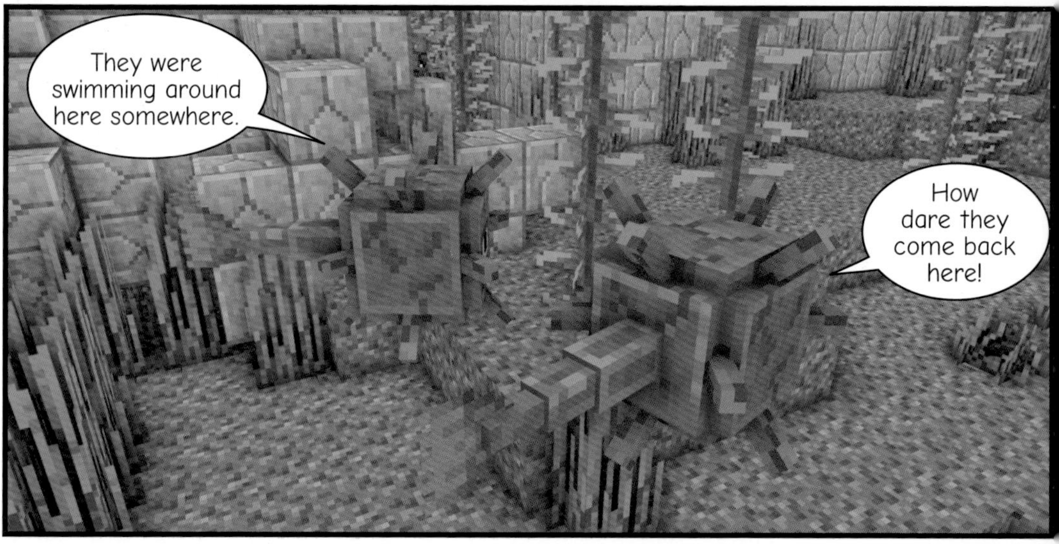
They were swimming around here somewhere.
How dare they come back here!

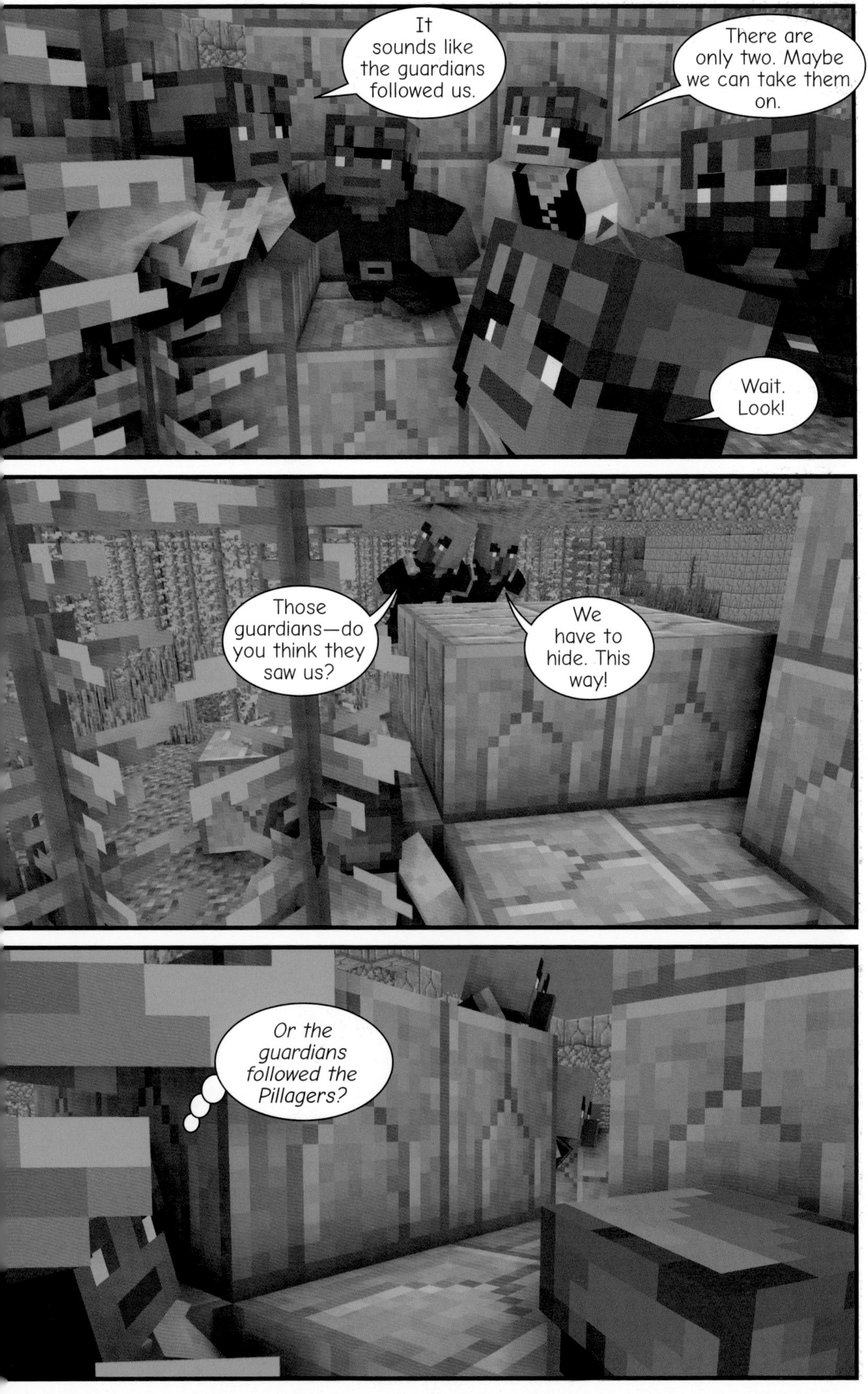
It sounds like the guardians followed us.
There are only two. Maybe we can take them on.
Wait. Look!
Those guardians—do you think they saw us?
We have to hide. This way!
Or the guardians followed the Pillagers?

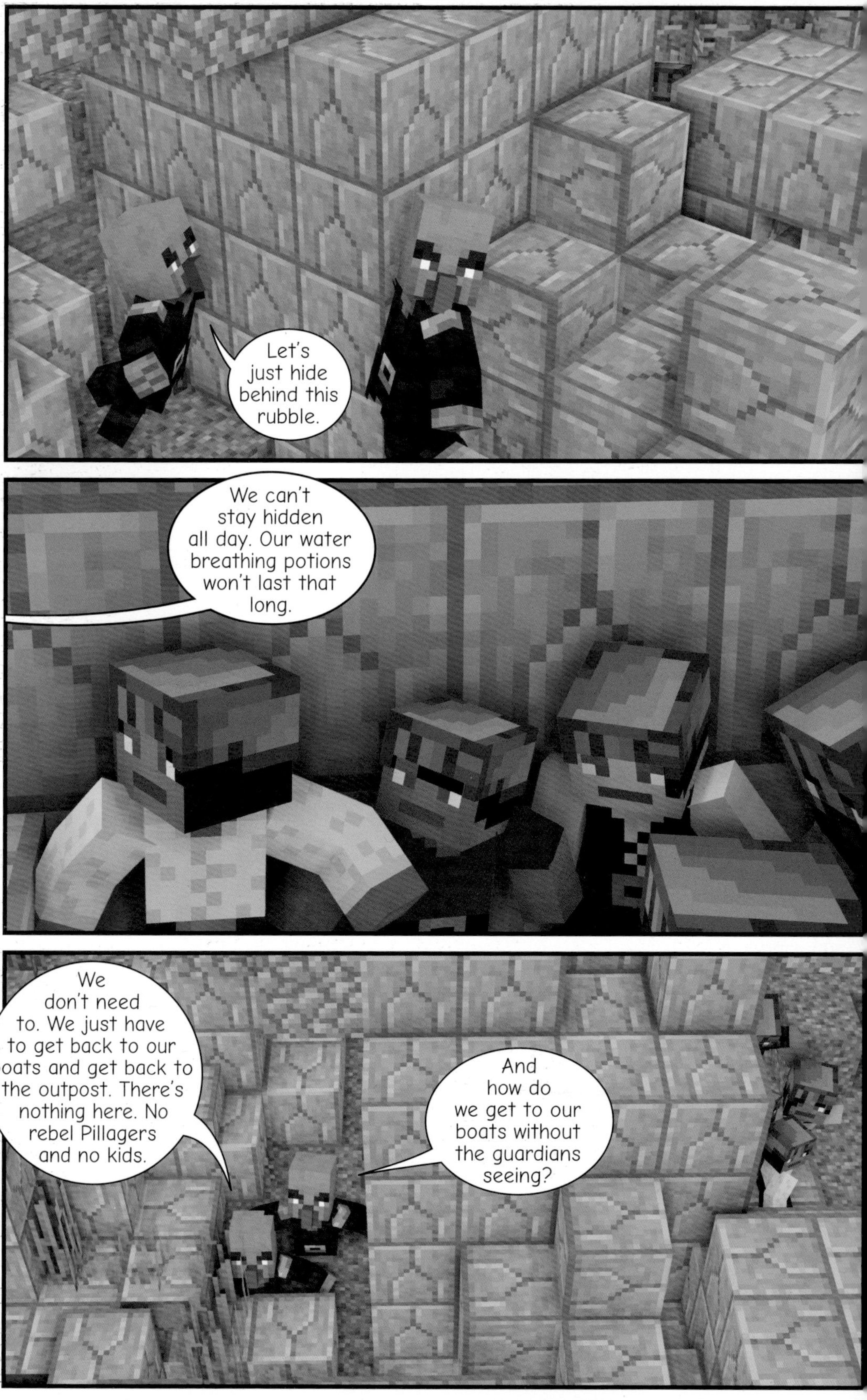
Let's just hide behind this rubble.
We can't stay hidden all day. Our water breathing potions won't last that long.
We don't need to. We just have to get back to our boats and get back to the outpost. There's nothing here. No rebel Pillagers and no kids.
And how do we get to our boats without the guardians seeing?

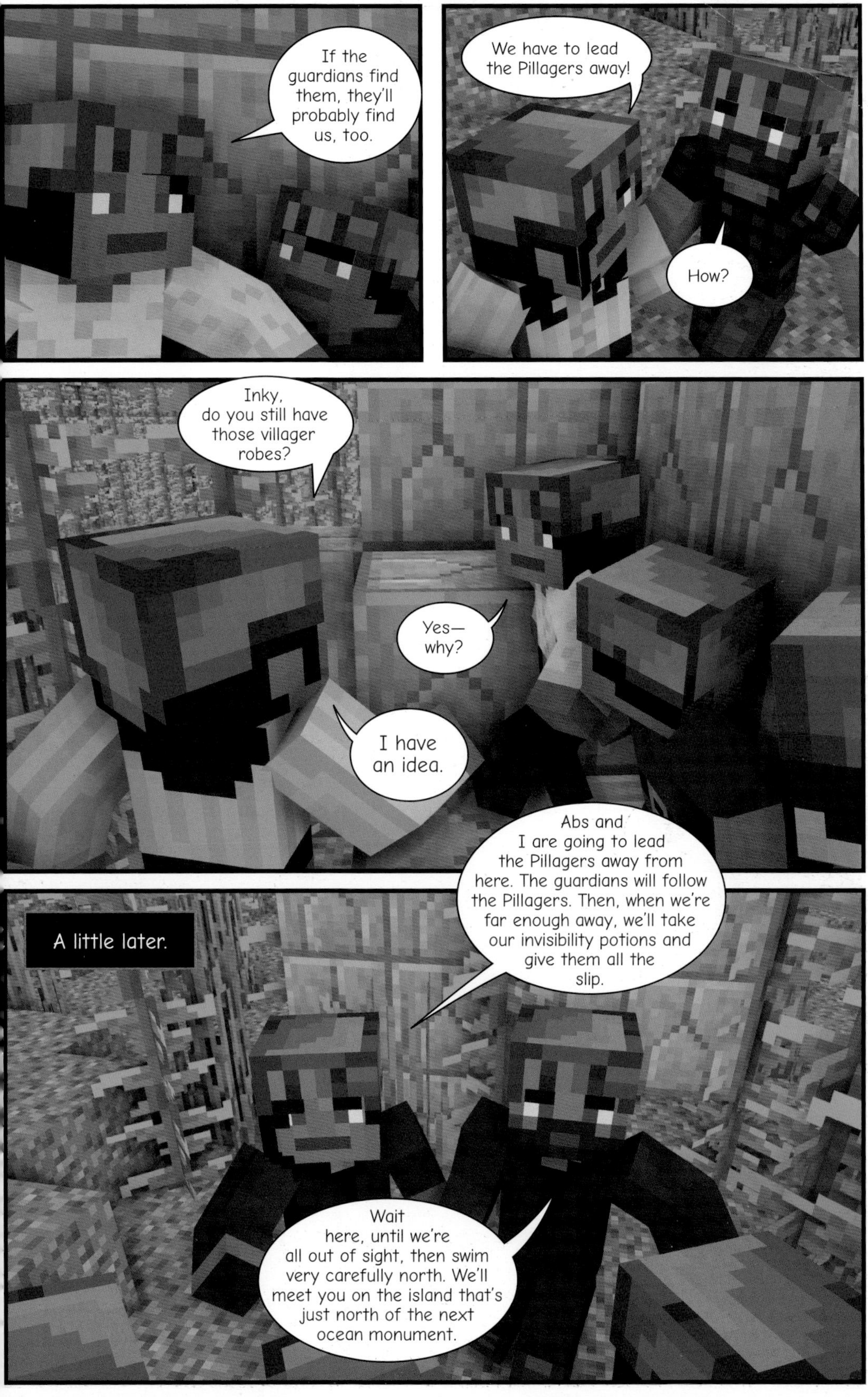
If the guardians find them, they'll probably find us, too.
We have to lead the Pillagers away!
How?
Inky, do you still have those villager robes?
Yes— why?
I have an idea.
Abs and I are going to lead the Pillagers away from here. The guardians will follow the Pillagers. Then, when we're far enough away, we'll take our invisibility potions and give them all the slip.
A little later.
Wait here, until we're all out of sight, then swim very carefully north. We'll meet you on the island that's just north of the next ocean monument.

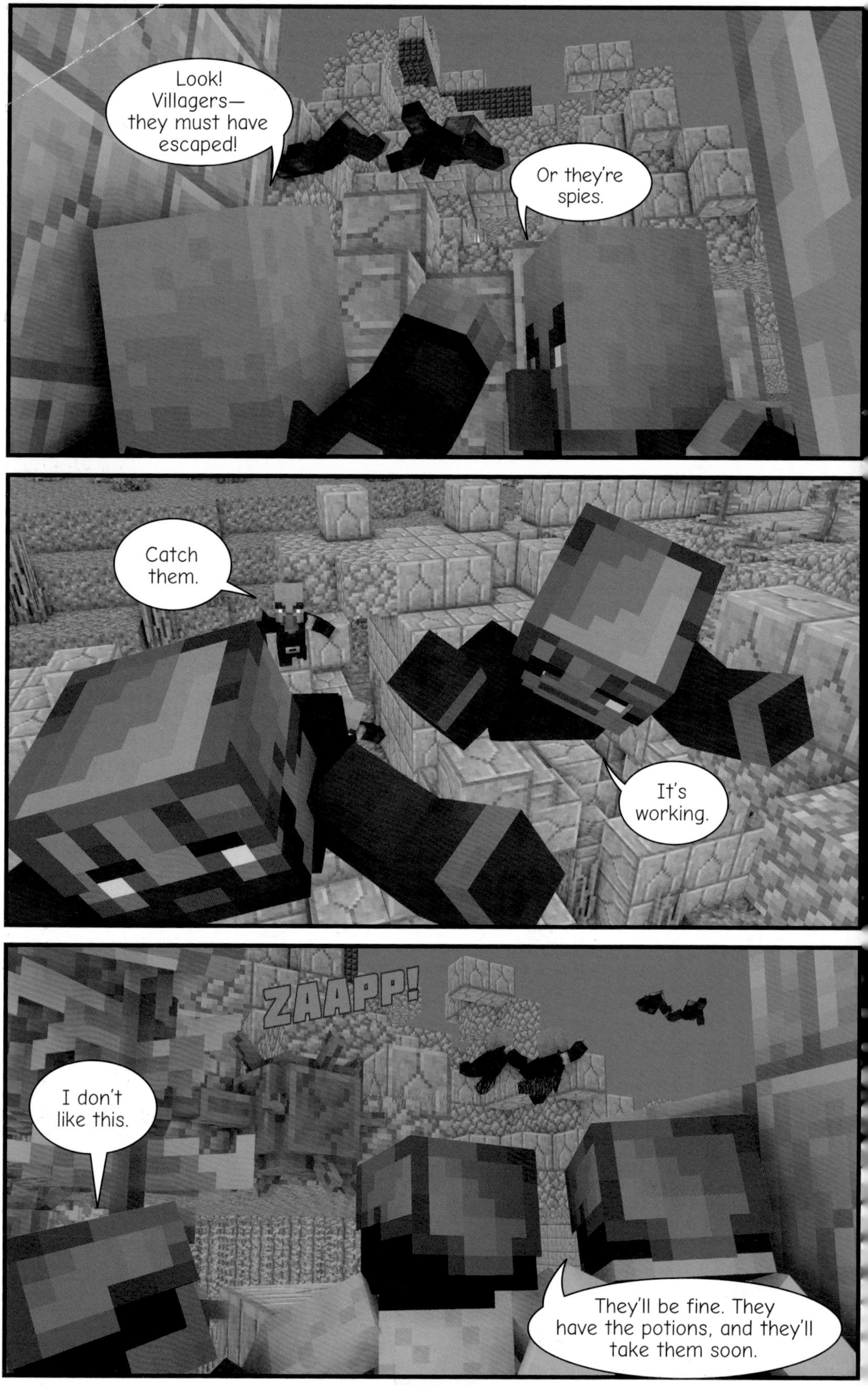
Look! Villagers—they must have escaped!
Or they're spies.
Catch them.
It's working.
ZAAPP!
I don't like this.
They'll be fine. They have the potions, and they'll take them soon.

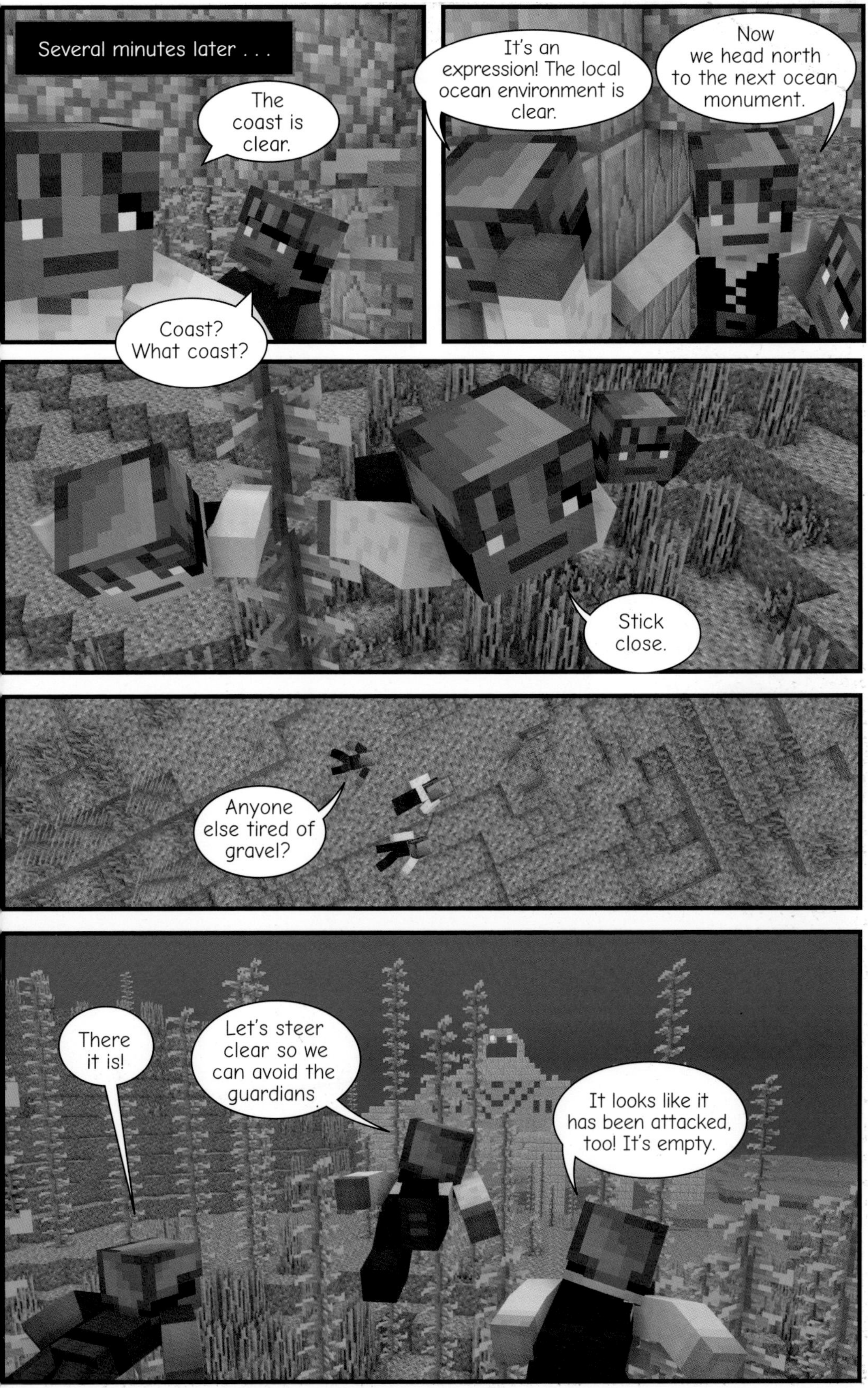

Several minutes later . . .
The coast is clear.
Coast? What coast?
It's an expression! The local ocean environment is clear.
Now we head north to the next ocean monument.
Stick close.
Anyone else tired of gravel?
There it is!
Let's steer clear so we can avoid the guardians
It looks like it has been attacked, too! It's empty.

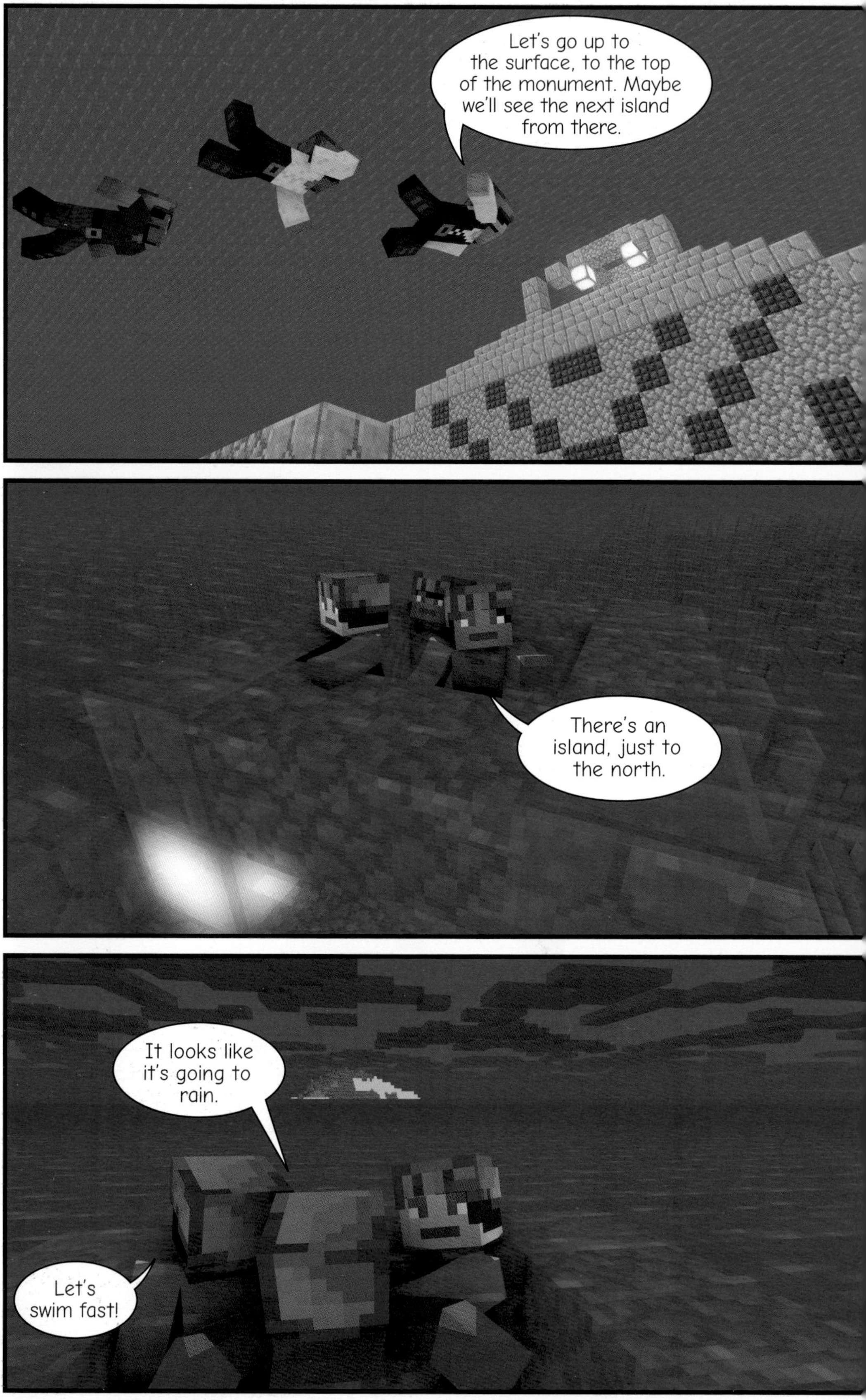
Let's go up to the surface, to the top of the monument. Maybe we'll see the next island from there.
There's an island, just to the north.
It looks like it's going to rain.
Let's swim fast!

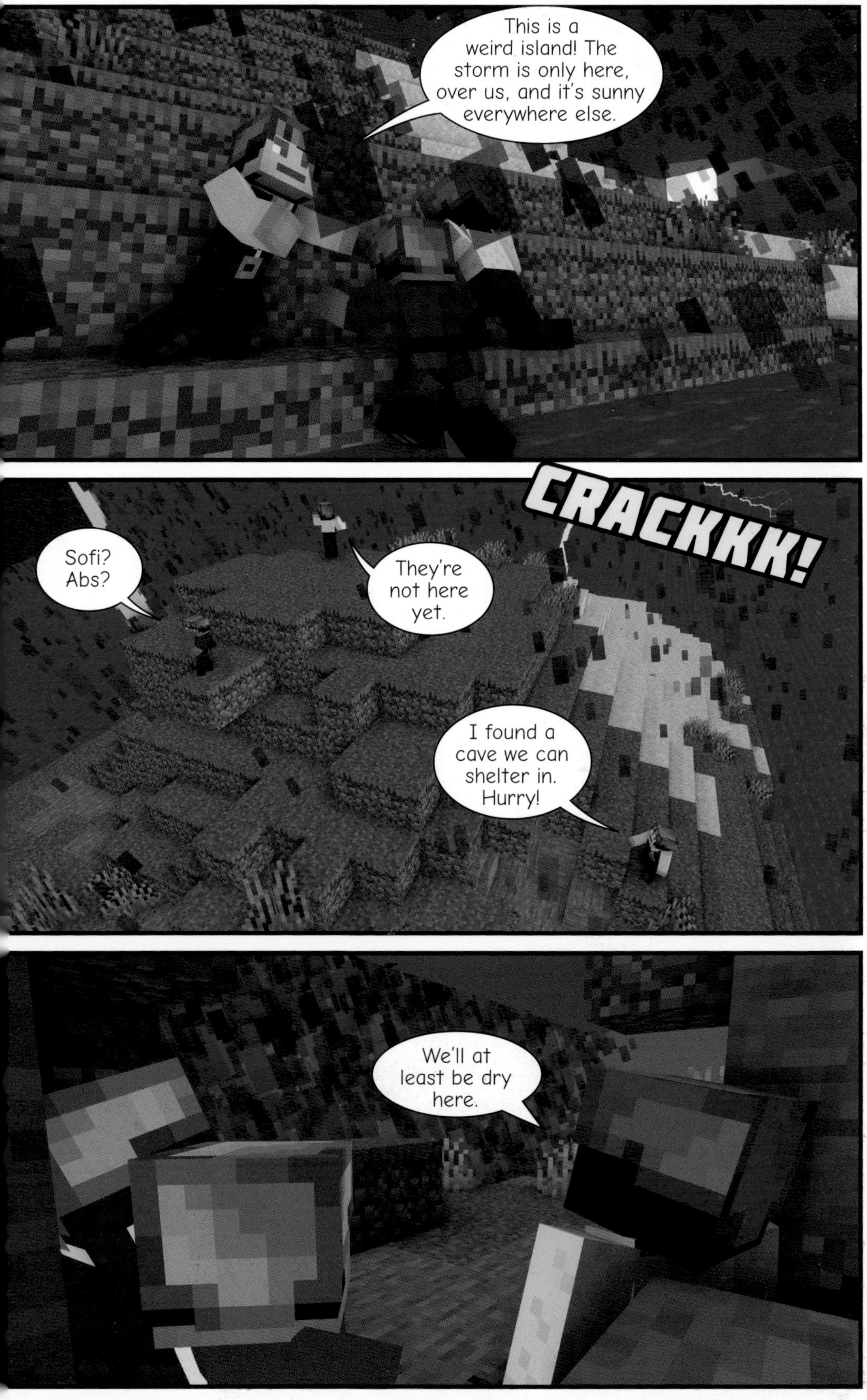
This is a weird island! The storm is only here, over us, and it's sunny everywhere else.
CRACKKK!
Sofi? Abs?
They're not here yet.
I found a cave we can shelter in. Hurry!
We'll at least be dry here.

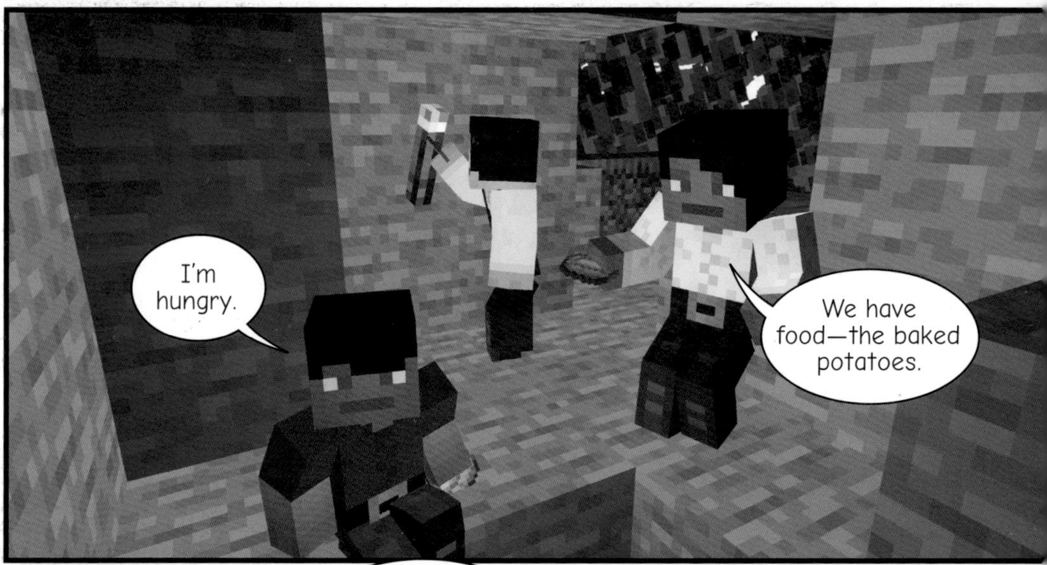
I'm hungry.
We have food—the baked potatoes.

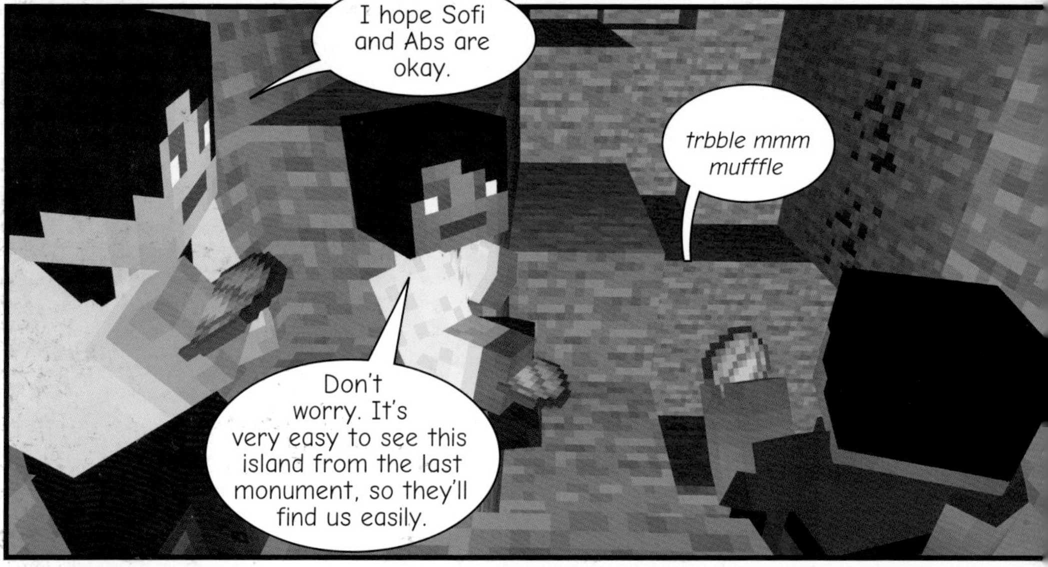
I hope Sofi and Abs are okay.
trbble mmm mufffle
Don't worry. It's very easy to see this island from the last monument, so they'll find us easily.

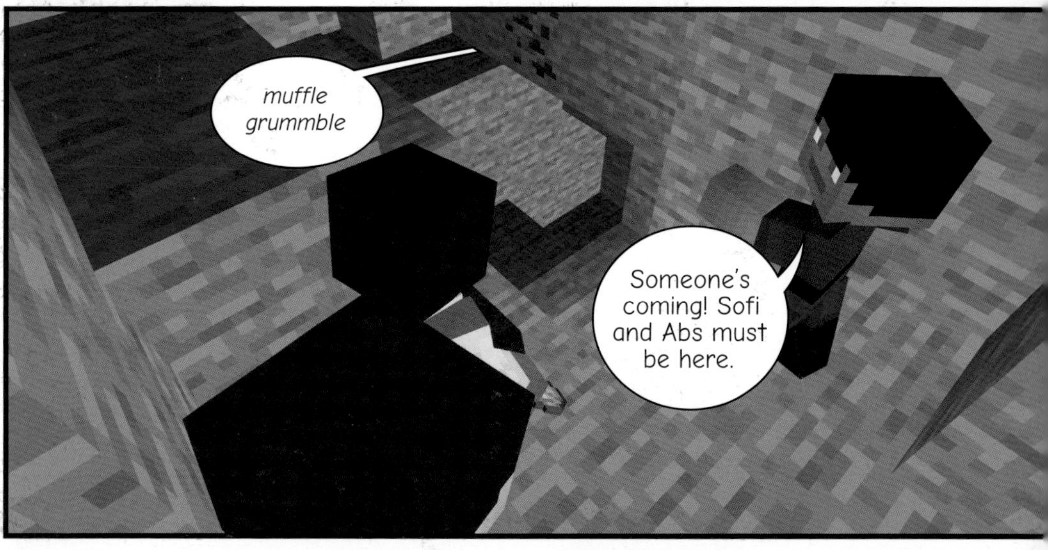
muffle grummble
Someone's coming! Sofi and Abs must be here.

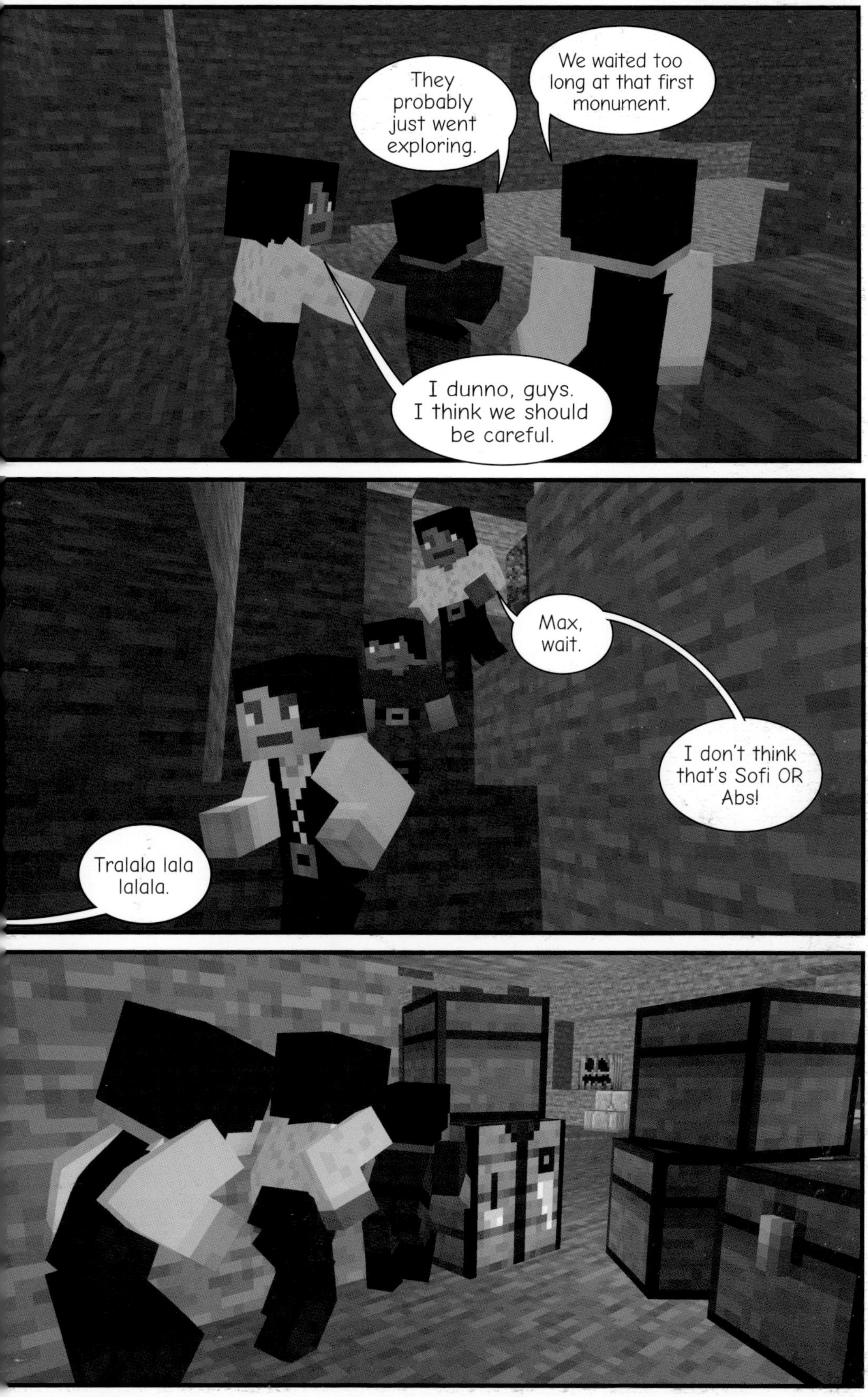
They probably just went exploring.
We waited too long at that first monument.
I dunno, guys. I think we should be careful.
Max, wait.
I don't think that's Sofi OR Abs!
Tralala lala lalala.

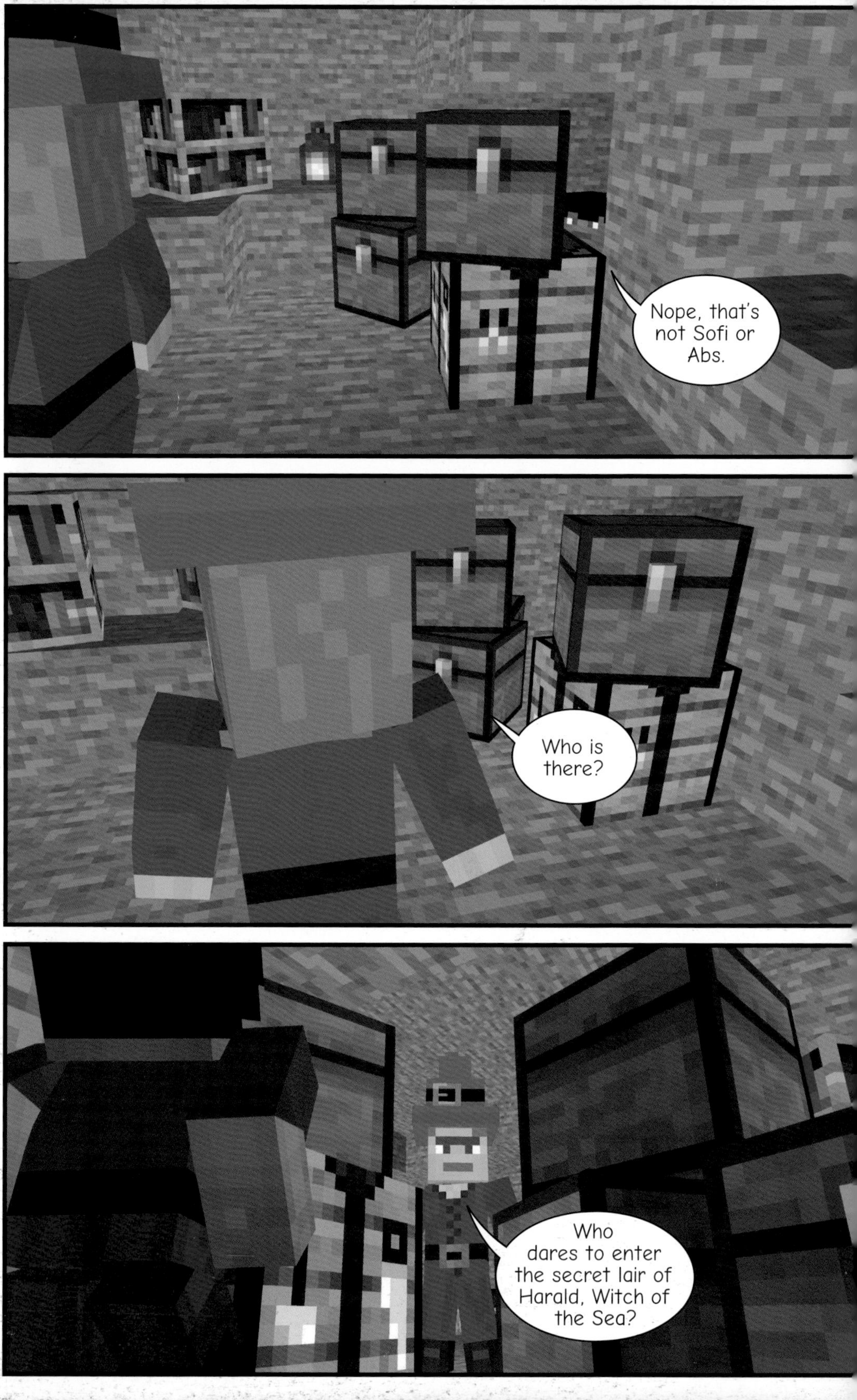
Nope, that's not Sofi or Abs.
Who is there?
Who dares to enter the secret lair of Harald, Witch of the Sea?

Chapter 5
The End

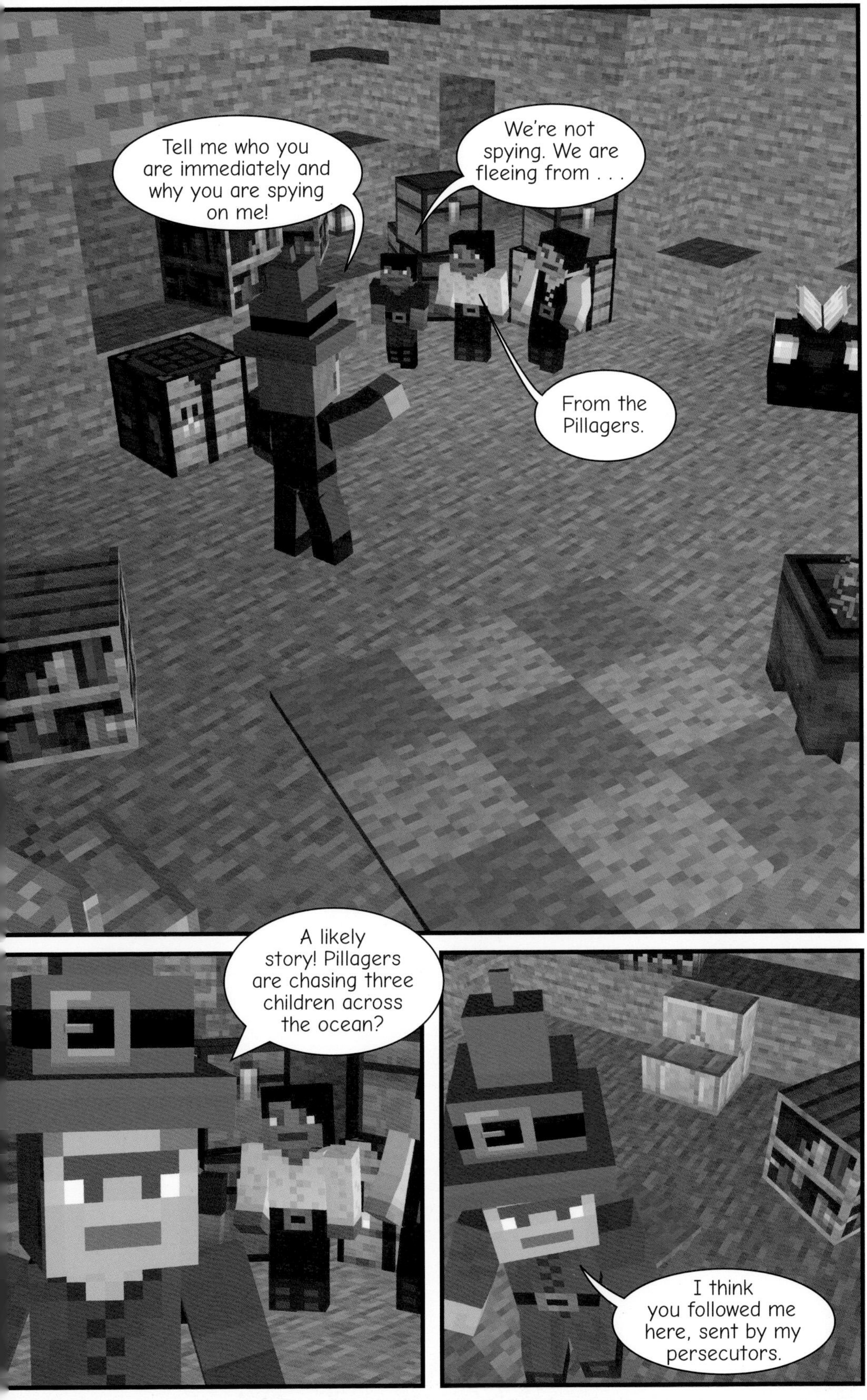
Tell me who you are immediately and why you are spying on me!
We're not spying. We are fleeing from . . .
From the Pillagers.
A likely story! Pillagers are chasing three children across the ocean?
I think you followed me here, sent by my persecutors.

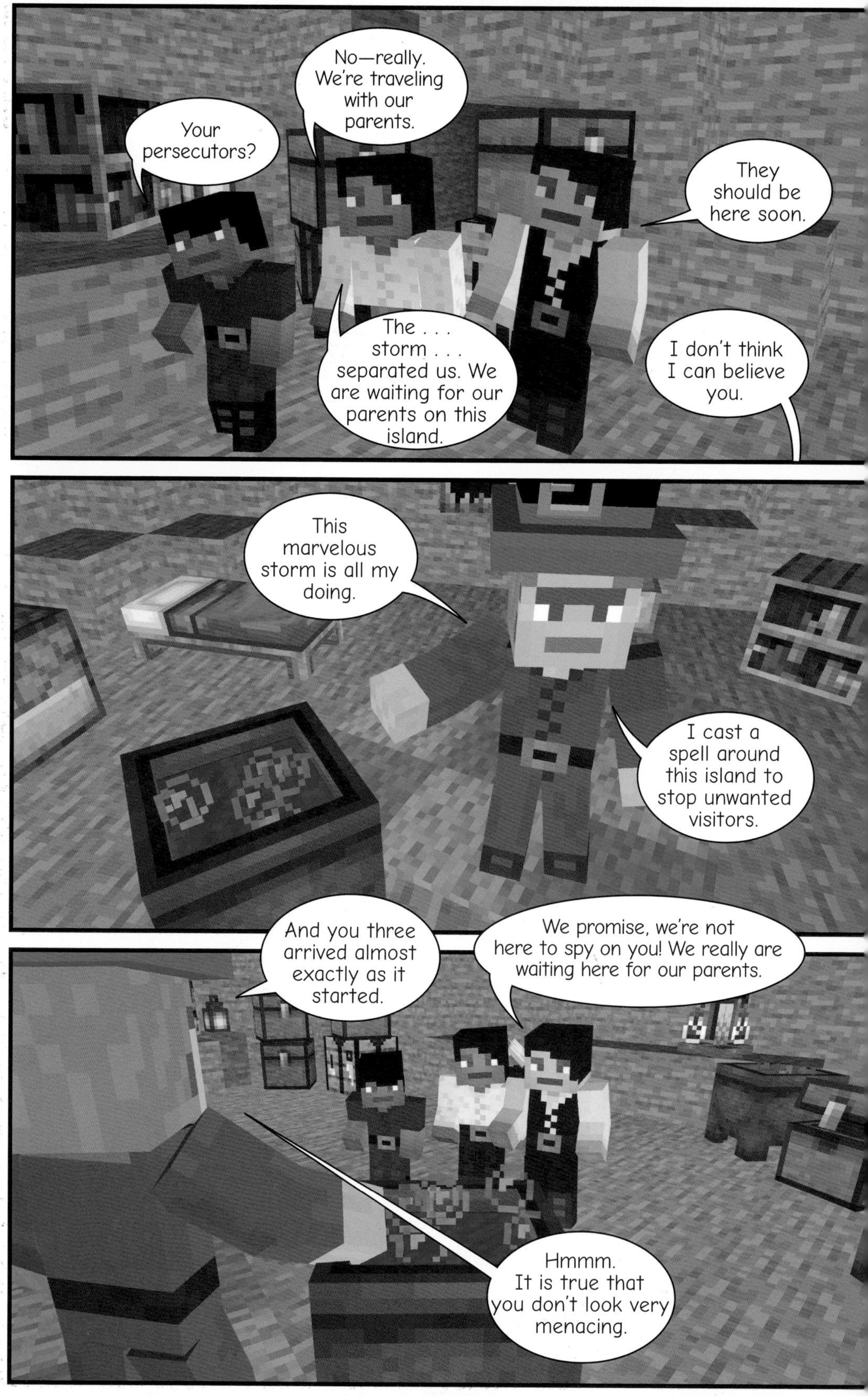
Your persecutors?
No—really. We're traveling with our parents.
They should be here soon.
The . . . storm . . . separated us. We are waiting for our parents on this island.
I don't think I can believe you.
This marvelous storm is all my doing.
I cast a spell around this island to stop unwanted visitors.
And you three arrived almost exactly as it started.
We promise, we're not here to spy on you! We really are waiting here for our parents.
Hmmm. It is true that you don't look very menacing.

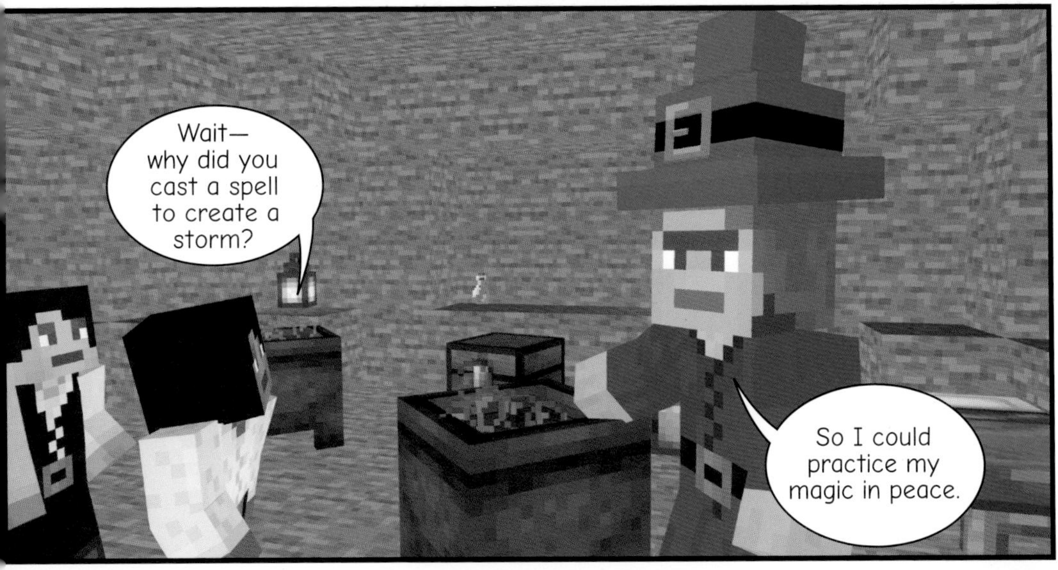
Wait—
why did you
cast a spell
to create a
storm?
So I could
practice my
magic in peace.

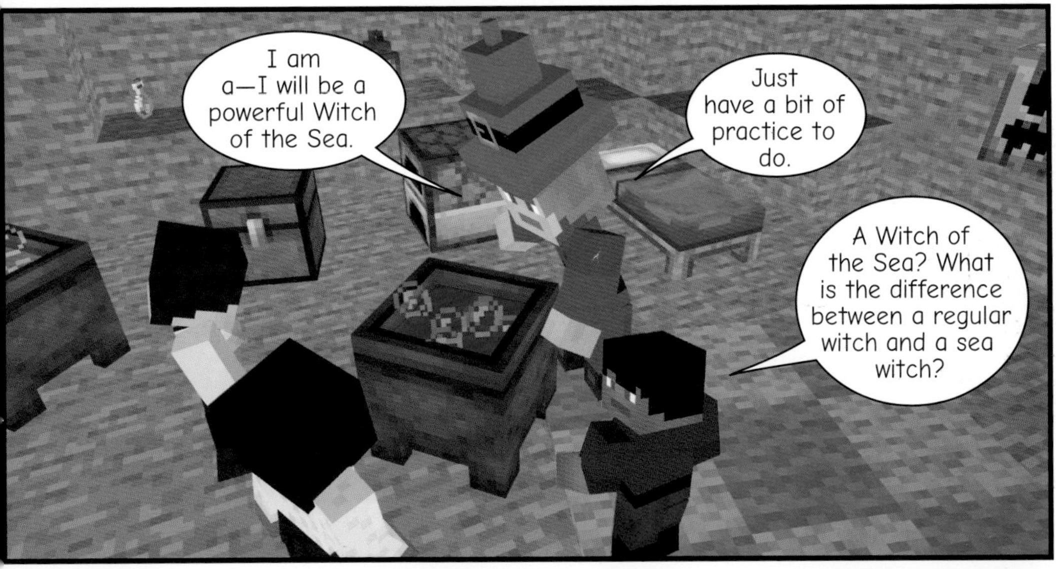
I am
a—I will be a
powerful Witch
of the Sea.
Just
have a bit of
practice to
do.
A Witch of
the Sea? What
is the difference
between a regular
witch and a sea
witch?

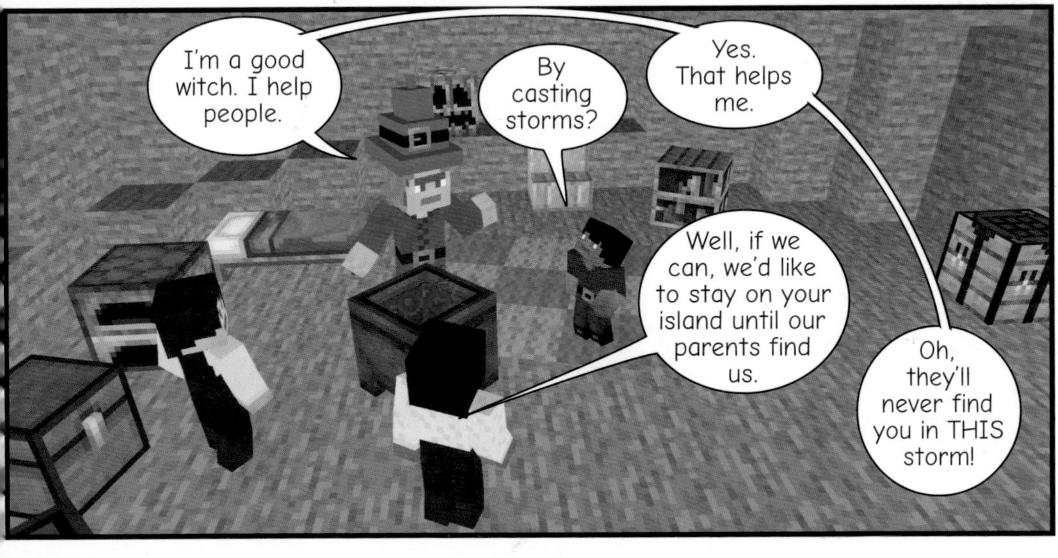
I'm a good
witch. I help
people.
By
casting
storms?
Yes.
That helps
me.
Well, if we
can, we'd like
to stay on your
island until our
parents find
us.
Oh,
they'll
never find
you in THIS
storm!

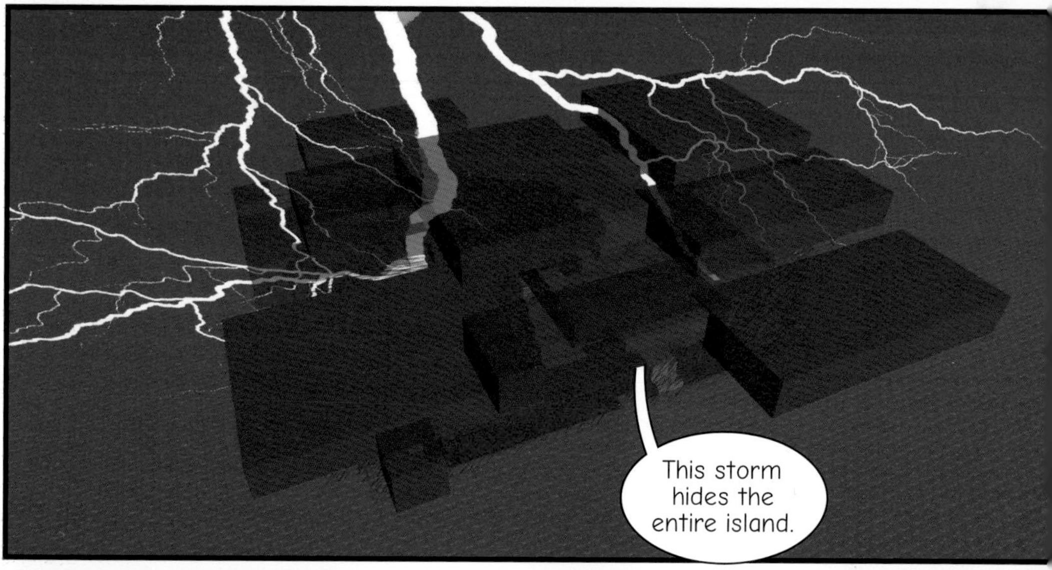
This storm hides the entire island.

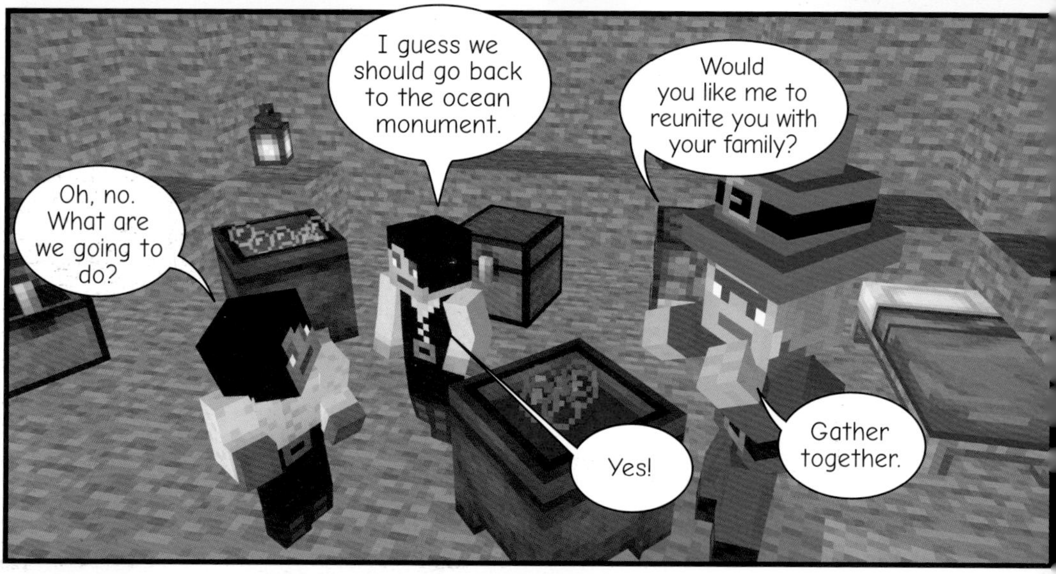
Oh, no. What are we going to do?
I guess we should go back to the ocean monument.
Would you like me to reunite you with your family?
Yes!
Gather together.

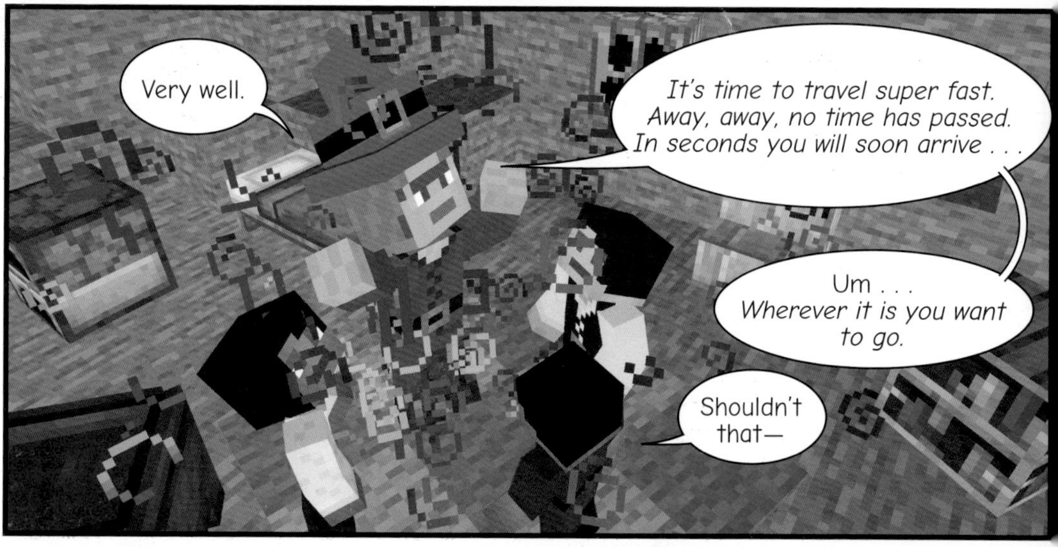
Very well.
It's time to travel super fast. Away, away, no time has passed. In seconds you will soon arrive . . .
Um . . . *Wherever it is you want to go.*
Shouldn't that—

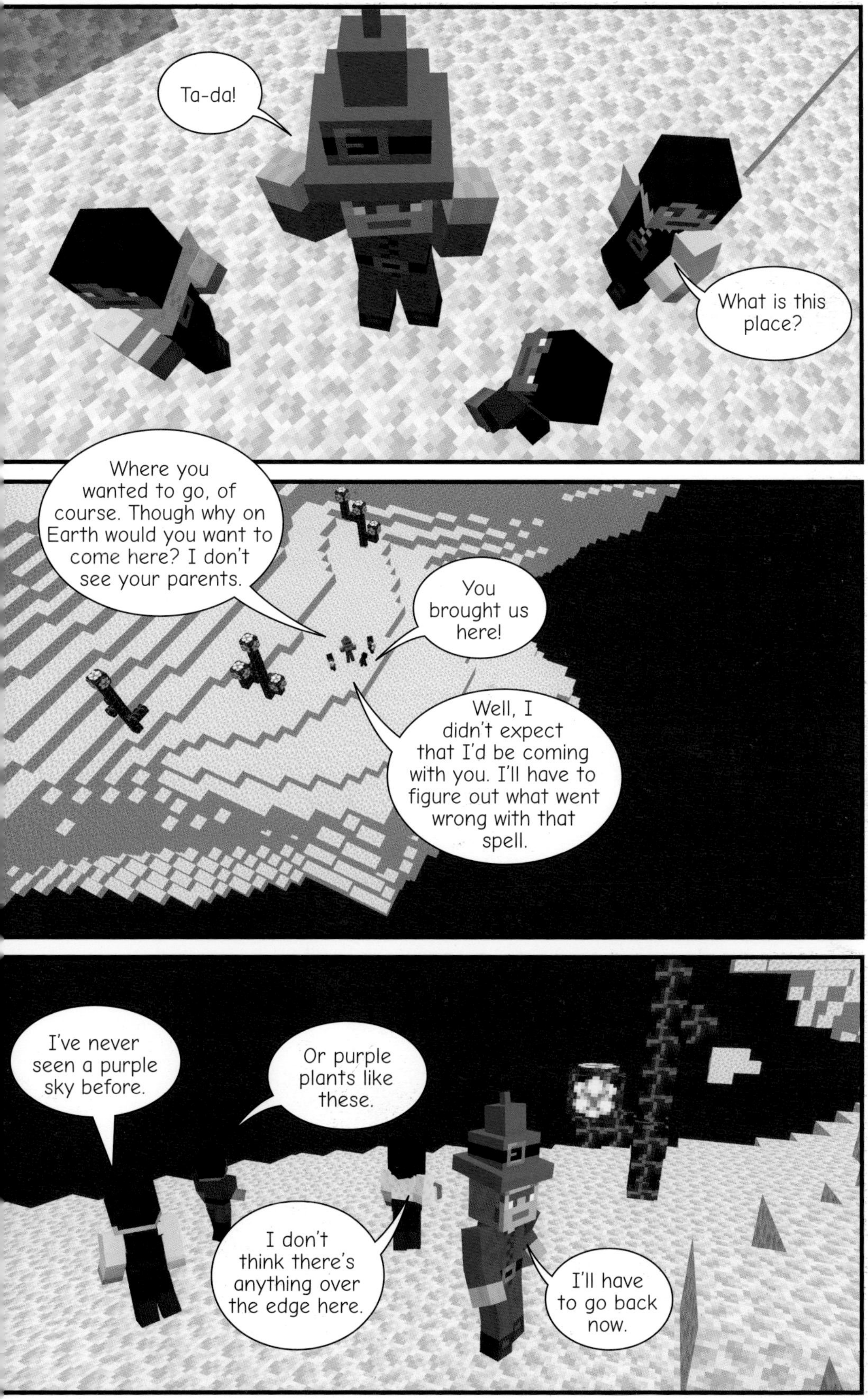
Ta-da!
What is this place?
Where you wanted to go, of course. Though why on Earth would you want to come here? I don't see your parents.
You brought us here!
Well, I didn't expect that I'd be coming with you. I'll have to figure out what went wrong with that spell.
I've never seen a purple sky before.
Or purple plants like these.
I don't think there's anything over the edge here.
I'll have to go back now.

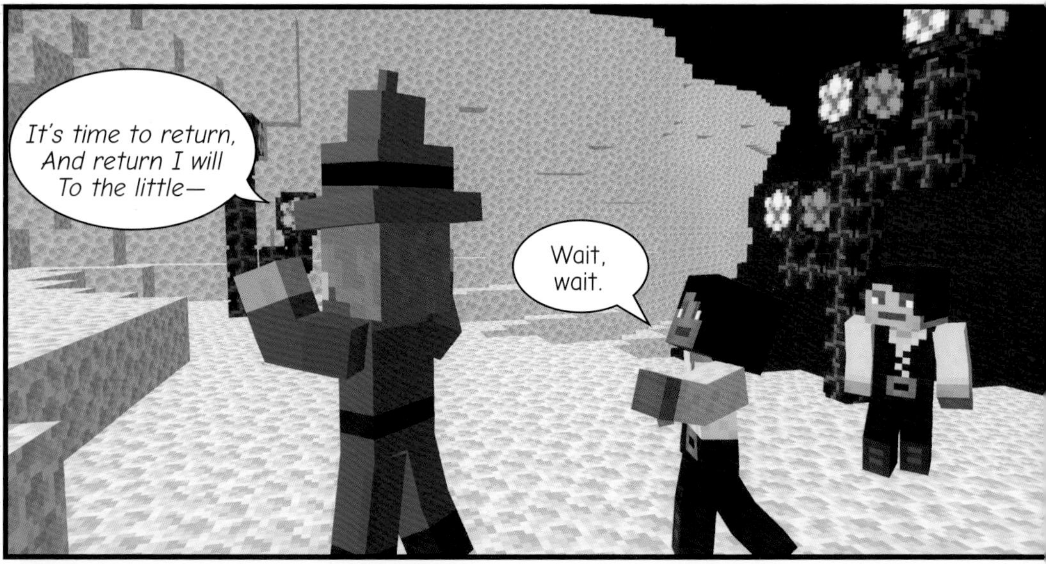
It's time to return, And return I will To the little—
Wait, wait.

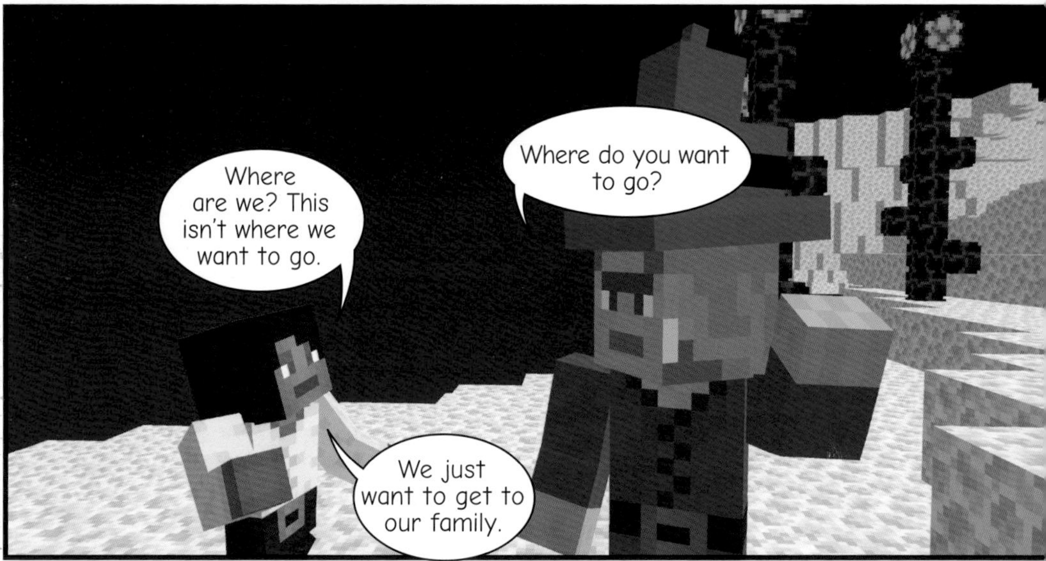
Where are we? This isn't where we want to go.
Where do you want to go?
We just want to get to our family.

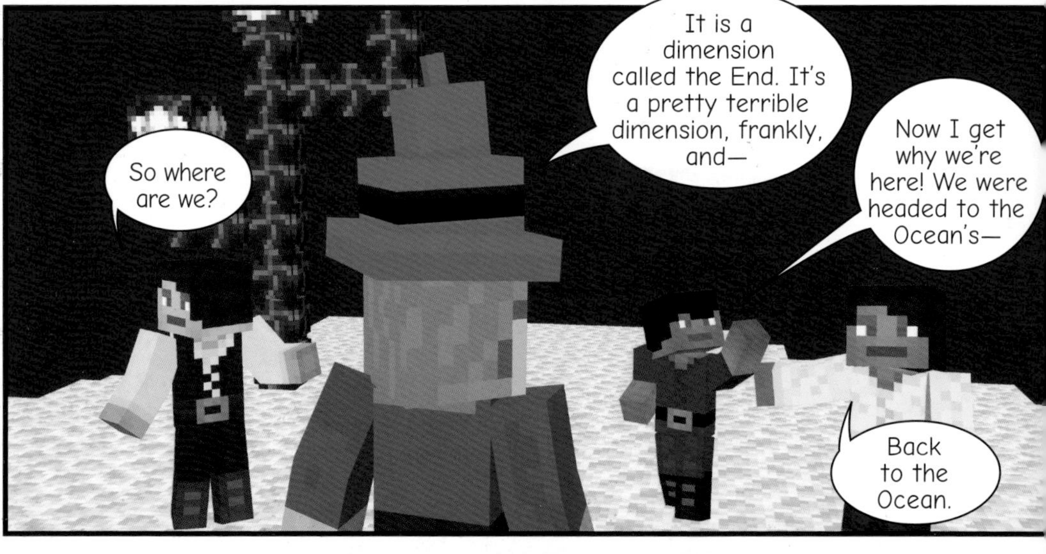
So where are we?
It is a dimension called the End. It's a pretty terrible dimension, frankly, and—
Now I get why we're here! We were headed to the Ocean's—
Back to the Ocean.

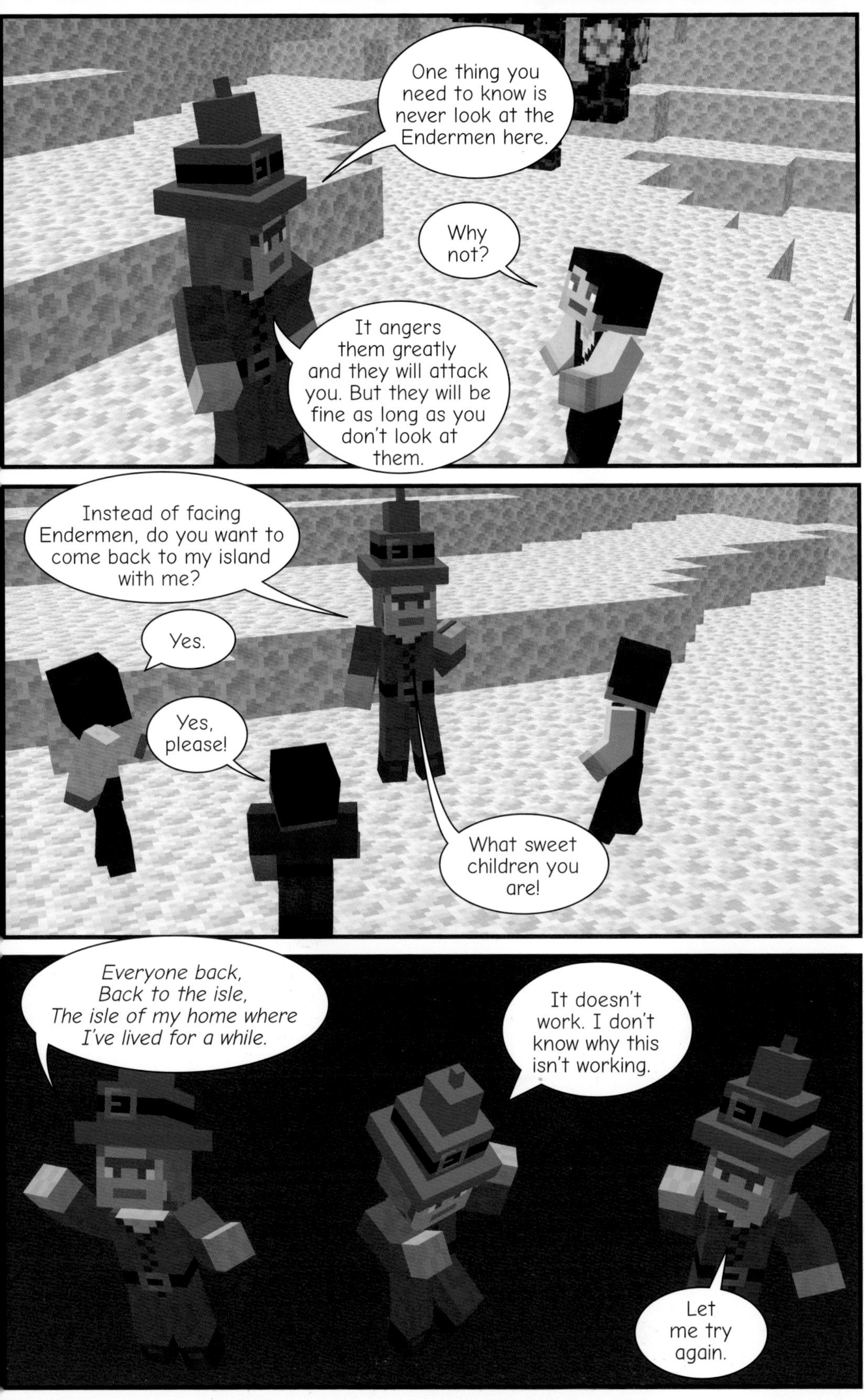
One thing you need to know is never look at the Endermen here.
Why not?
It angers them greatly and they will attack you. But they will be fine as long as you don't look at them.
Instead of facing Endermen, do you want to come back to my island with me?
Yes.
Yes, please!
What sweet children you are!
Everyone back, Back to the isle, The isle of my home where I've lived for a while.
It doesn't work. I don't know why this isn't working.
Let me try again.

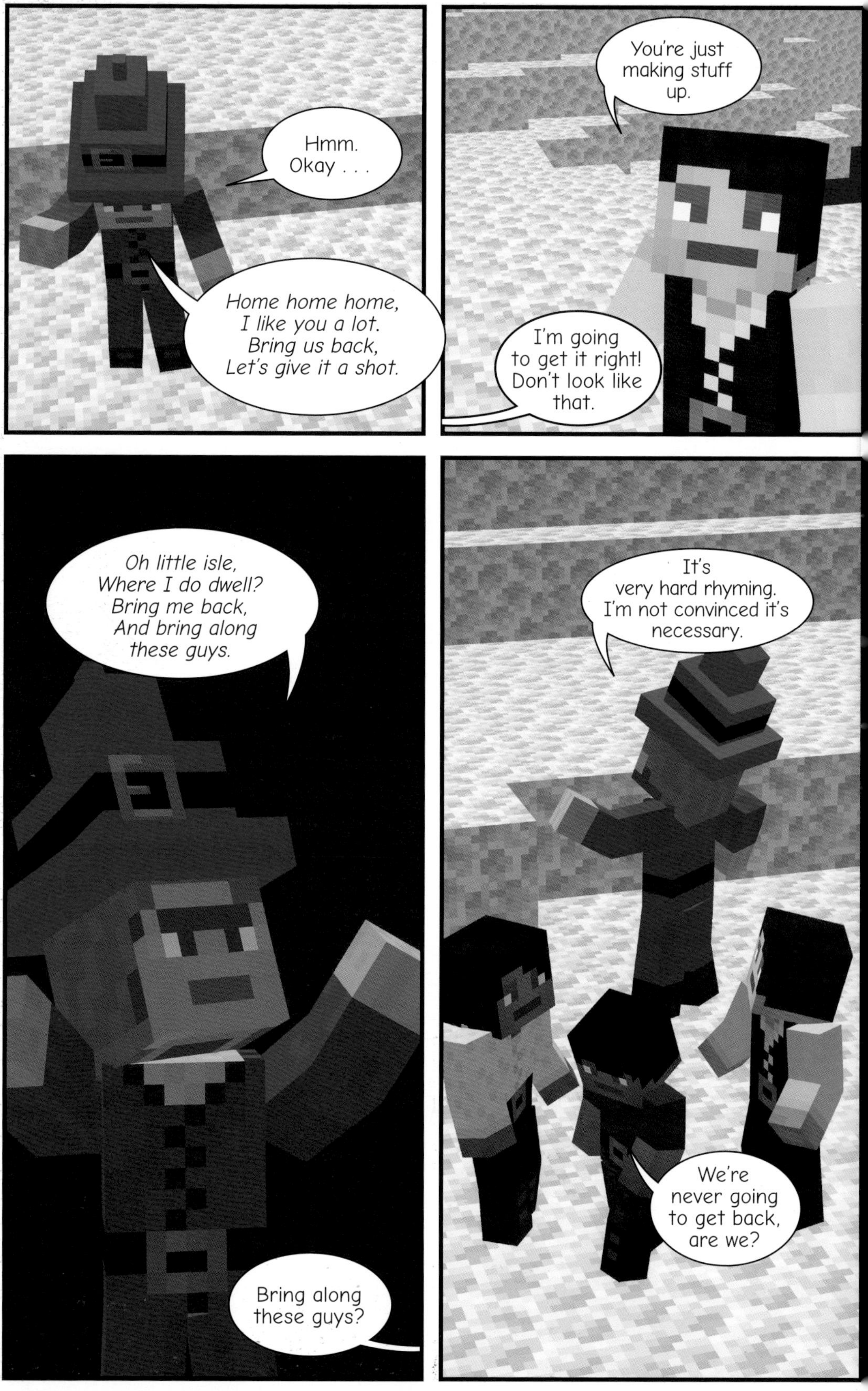
Hmm. Okay . . .
Home home home, I like you a lot. Bring us back, Let's give it a shot.
You're just making stuff up.
I'm going to get it right! Don't look like that.
Oh little isle, Where I do dwell? Bring me back, And bring along these guys.
Bring along these guys?
It's very hard rhyming. I'm not convinced it's necessary.
We're never going to get back, are we?

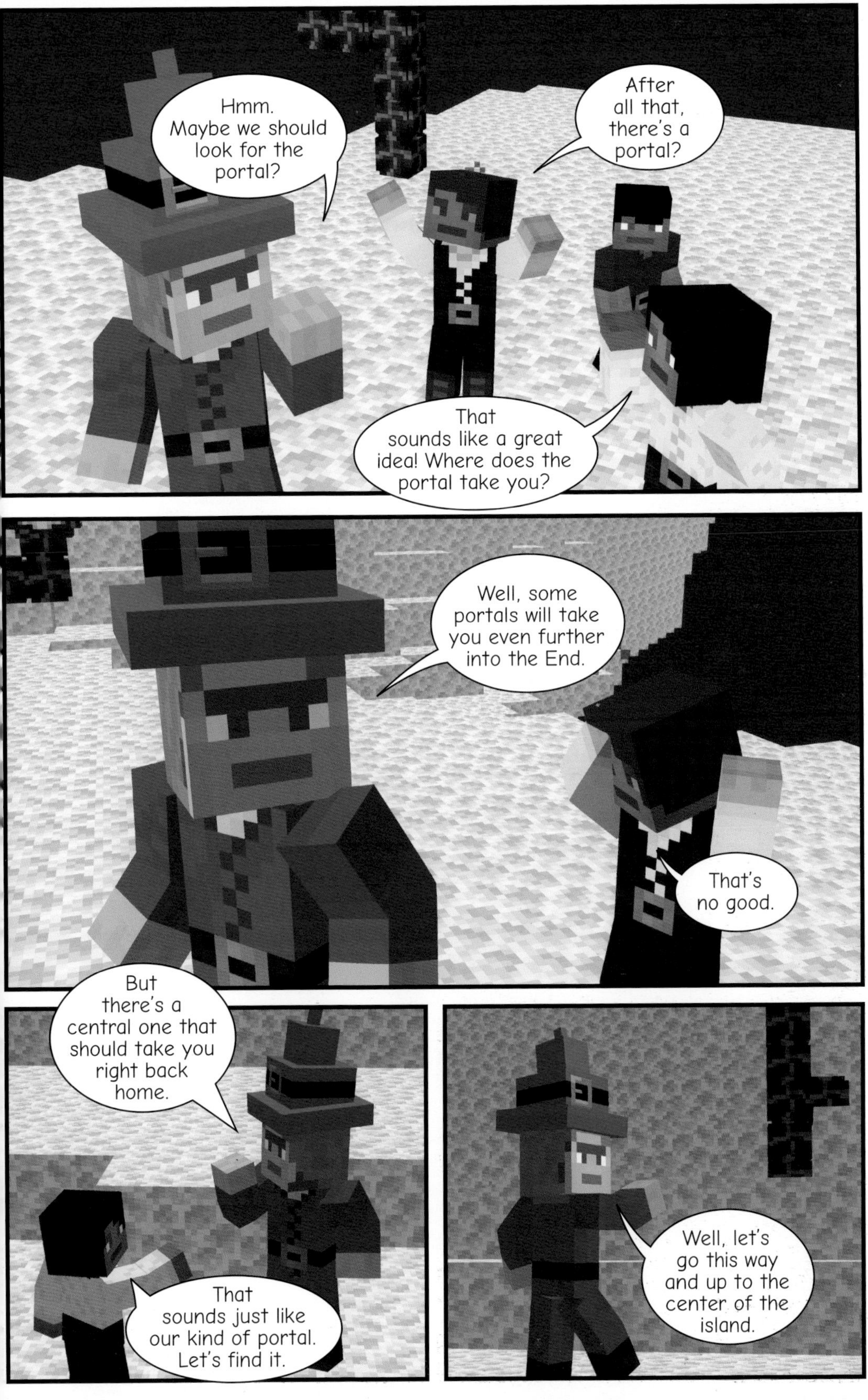
Hmm. Maybe we should look for the portal?
After all that, there's a portal?
That sounds like a great idea! Where does the portal take you?
Well, some portals will take you even further into the End.
That's no good.
But there's a central one that should take you right back home.
That sounds just like our kind of portal. Let's find it.
Well, let's go this way and up to the center of the island.

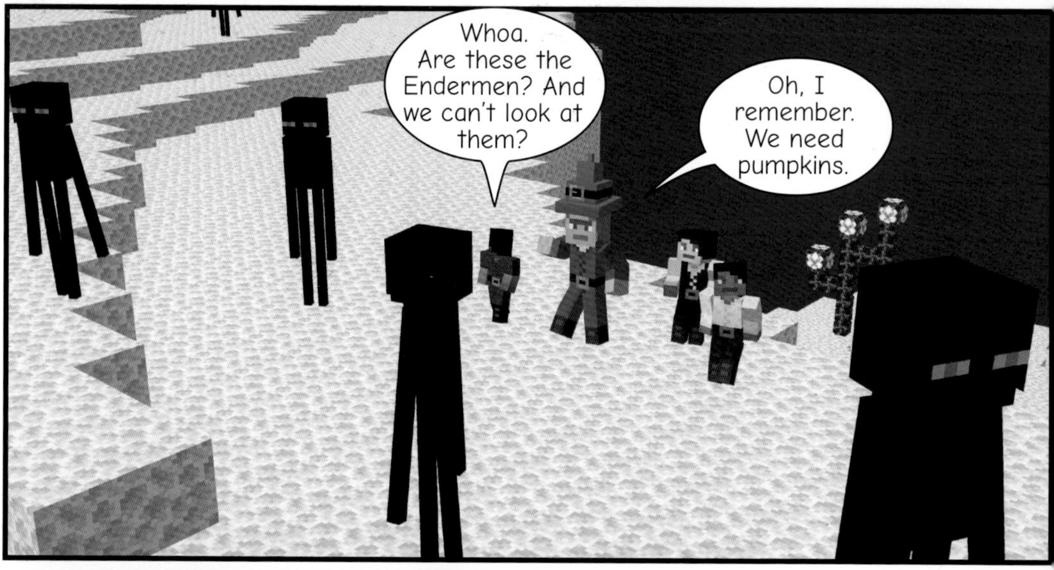
Whoa. Are these the Endermen? And we can't look at them?
Oh, I remember. We need pumpkins.

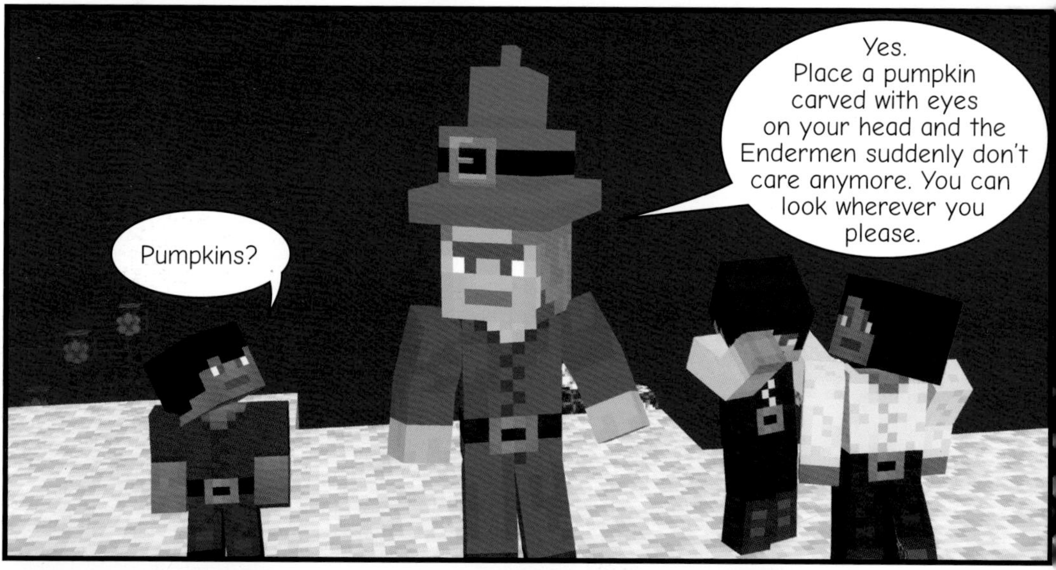
Yes. Place a pumpkin carved with eyes on your head and the Endermen suddenly don't care anymore. You can look wherever you please.
Pumpkins?

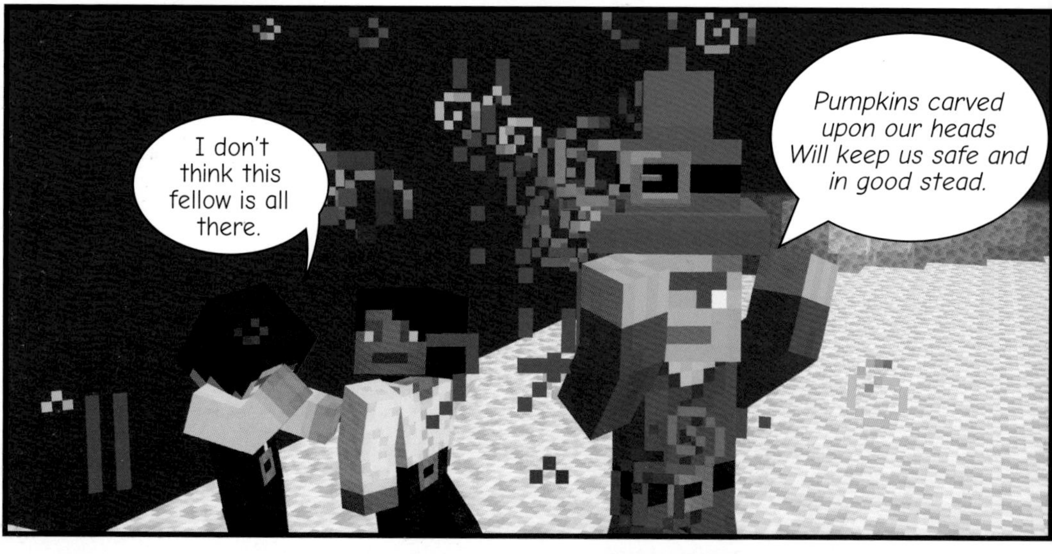
I don't think this fellow is all there.
Pumpkins carved upon our heads Will keep us safe and in good stead.

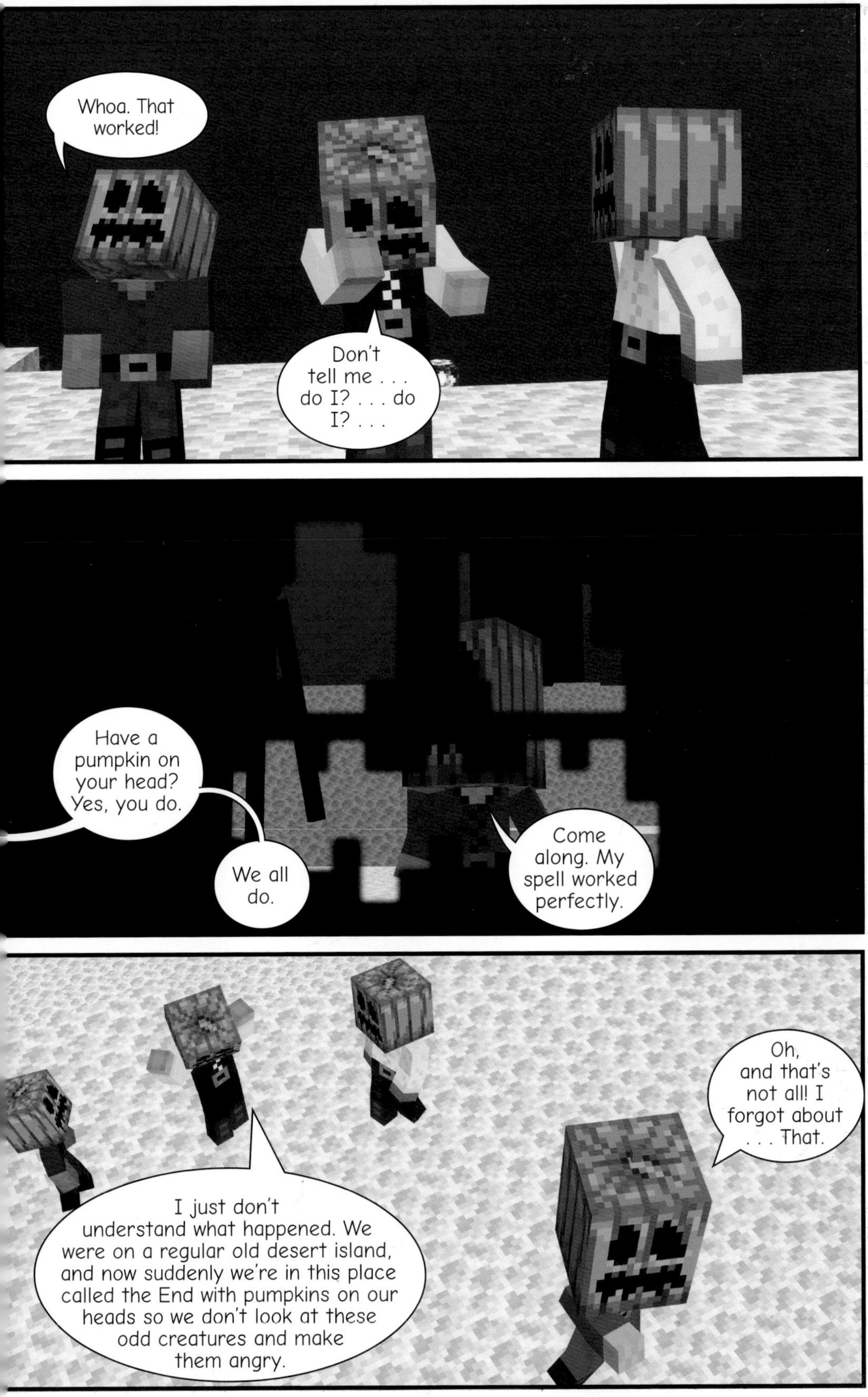
Whoa. That worked!
Don't tell me . . . do I? . . . do I? . . .
Have a pumpkin on your head? Yes, you do.
We all do.
Come along. My spell worked perfectly.
I just don't understand what happened. We were on a regular old desert island, and now suddenly we're in this place called the End with pumpkins on our heads so we don't look at these odd creatures and make them angry.
Oh, and that's not all! I forgot about . . . That.

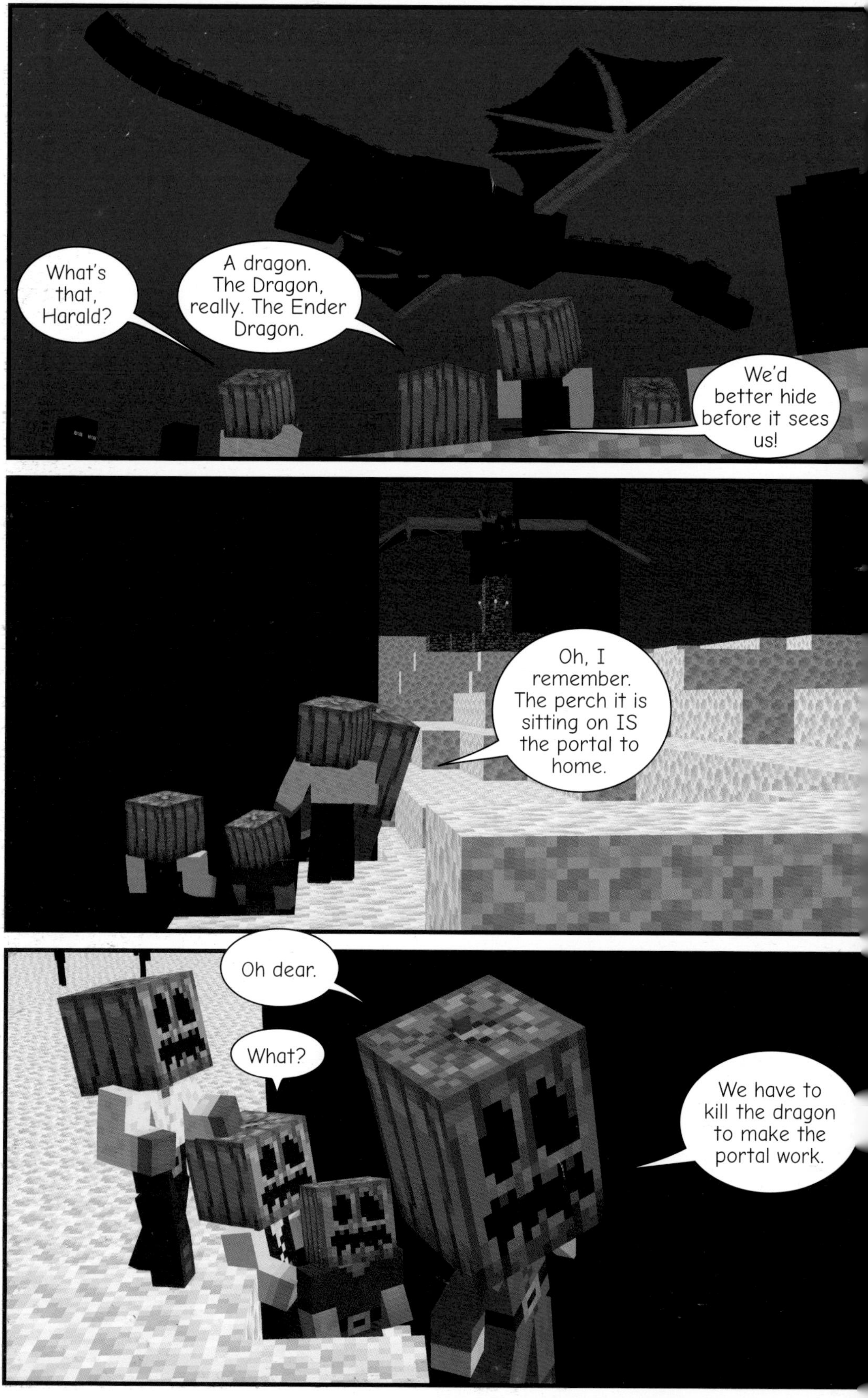
What's that, Harald?
A dragon. The Dragon, really. The Ender Dragon.
We'd better hide before it sees us!
Oh, I remember. The perch it is sitting on IS the portal to home.
Oh dear.
What?
We have to kill the dragon to make the portal work.

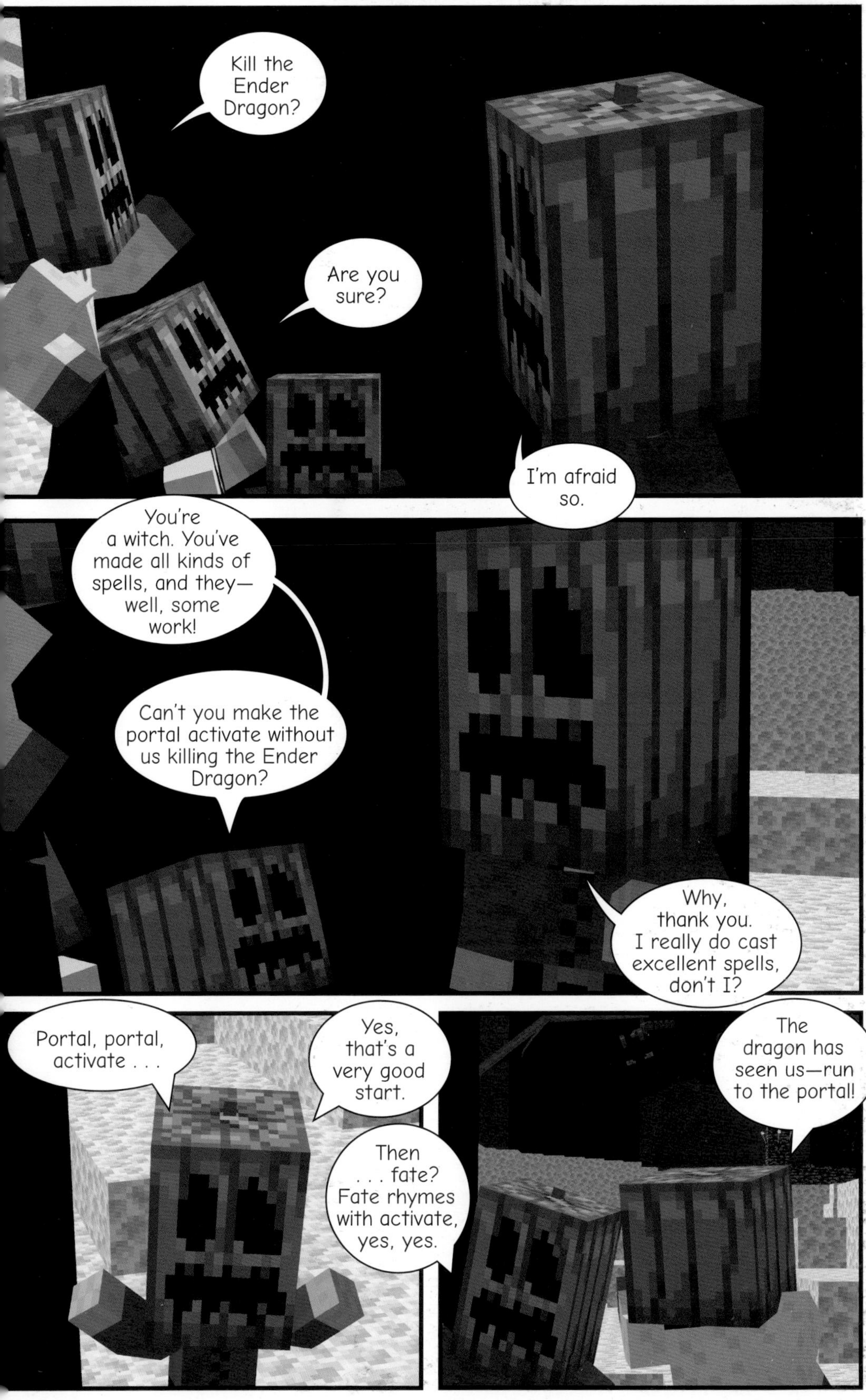
Kill the Ender Dragon?
Are you sure?
I'm afraid so.
You're a witch. You've made all kinds of spells, and they—well, some work!
Can't you make the portal activate without us killing the Ender Dragon?
Why, thank you. I really do cast excellent spells, don't I?
Portal, portal, activate . . .
Yes, that's a very good start.
Then . . . fate? Fate rhymes with activate, yes, yes.
The dragon has seen us—run to the portal!

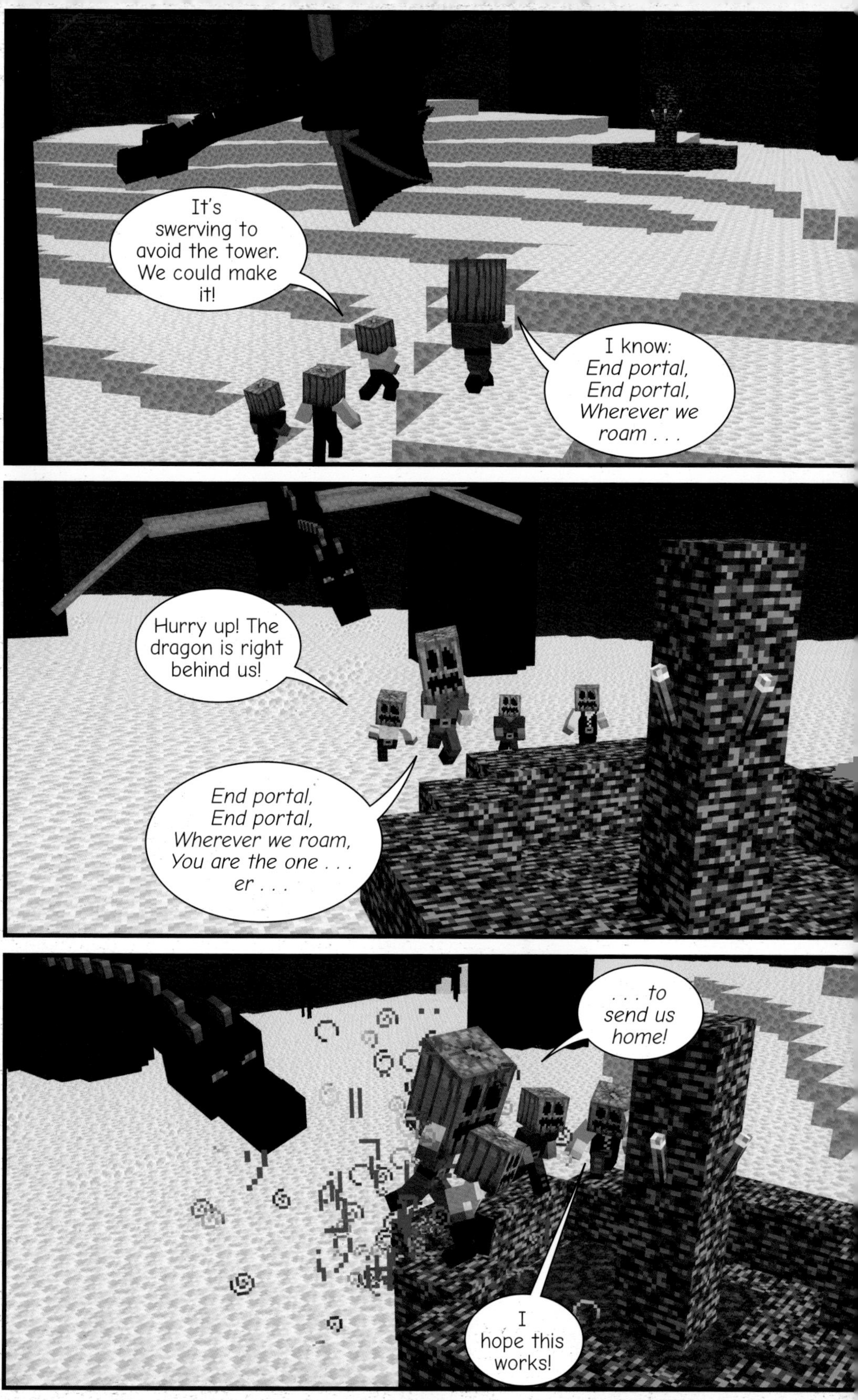
It's swerving to avoid the tower. We could make it!
I know: *End portal, End portal, Wherever we roam . . .*
Hurry up! The dragon is right behind us!
End portal, End portal, Wherever we roam, You are the one . . . er . . .
. . . to send us home!
I hope this works!

Chapter 6
Bad Witch

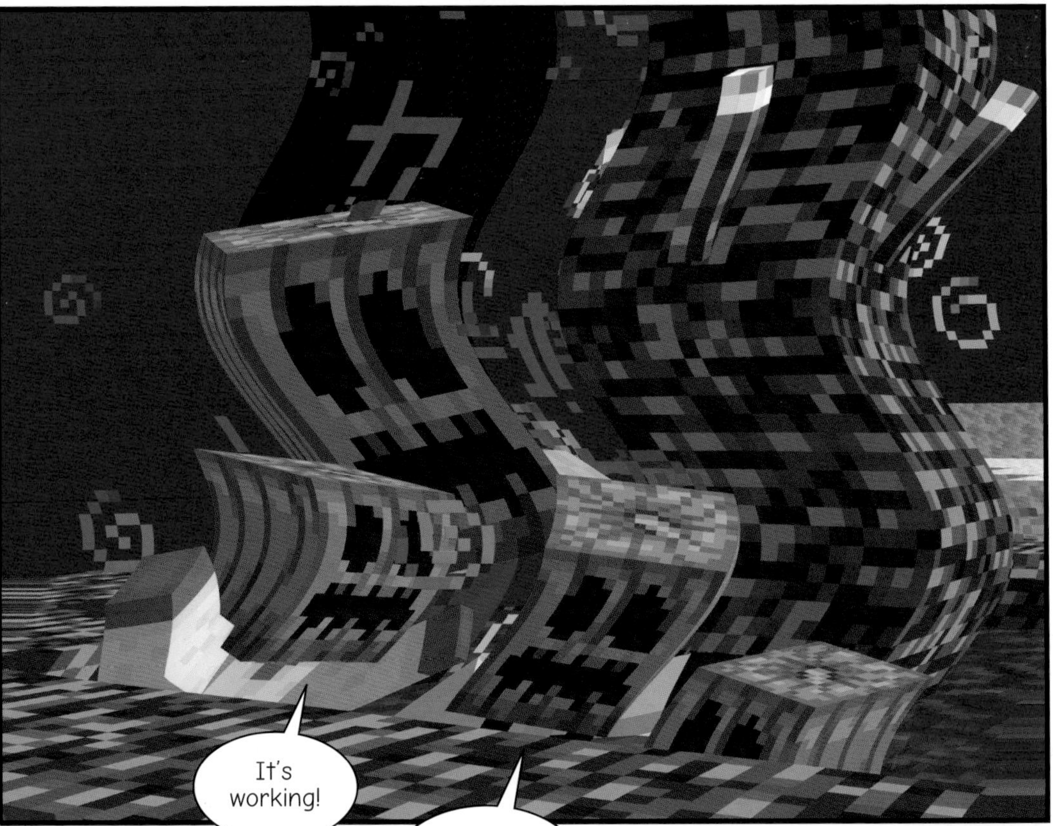
It's working!
Well, it's taking us somewhere.

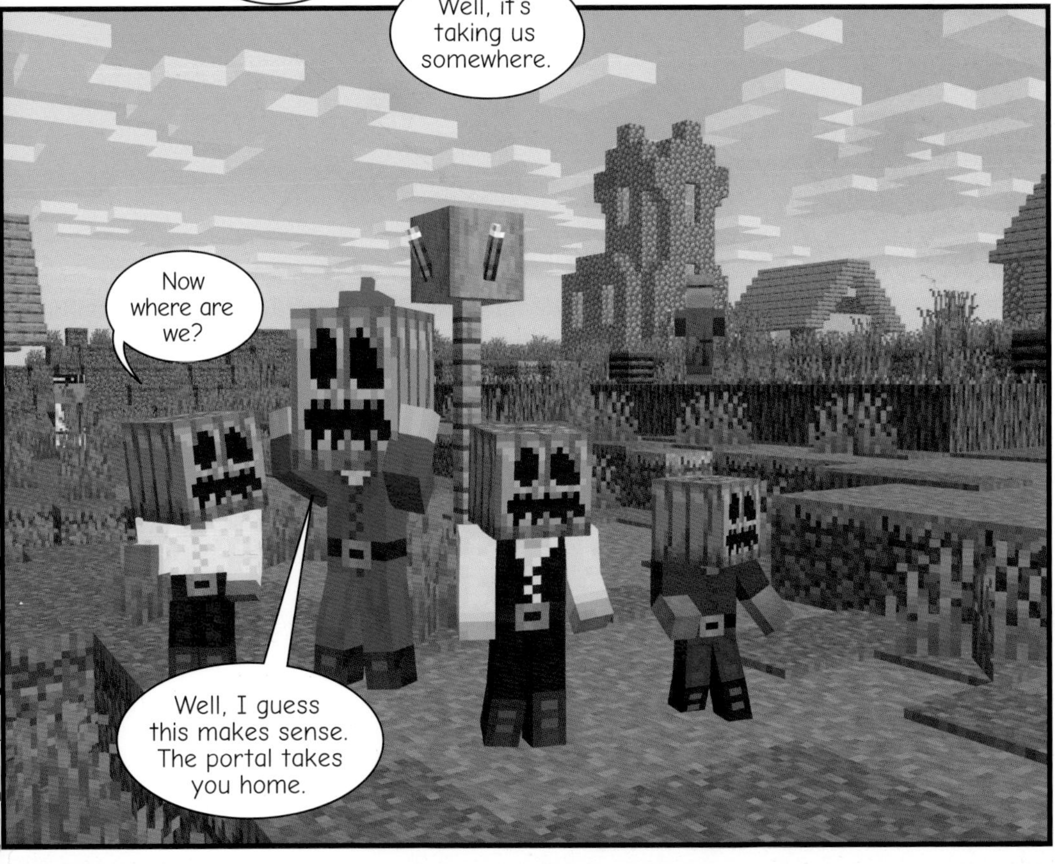
Now where are we?
Well, I guess this makes sense. The portal takes you home.

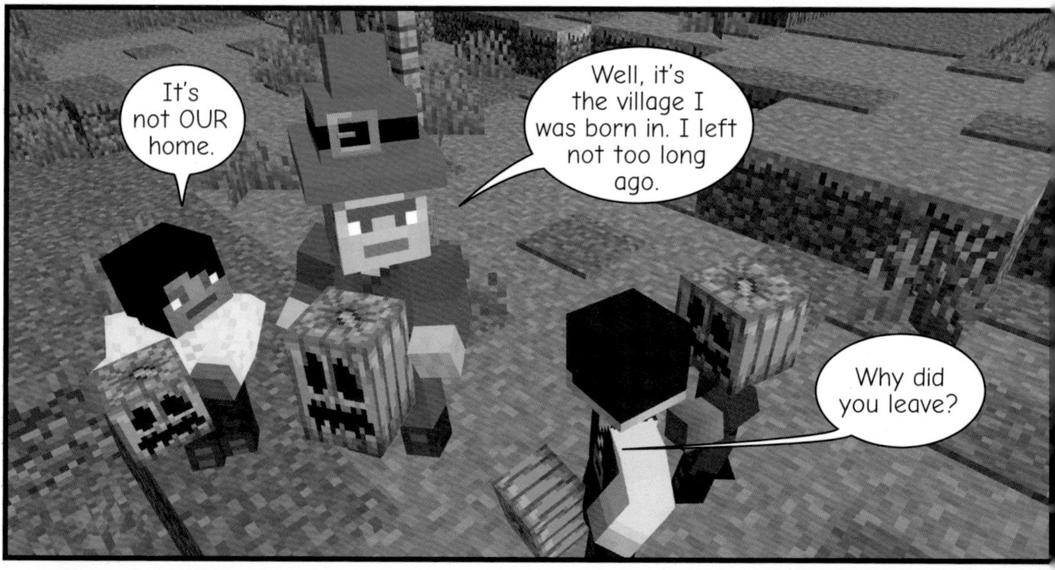
It's not OUR home.
Well, it's the village I was born in. I left not too long ago.
Why did you leave?

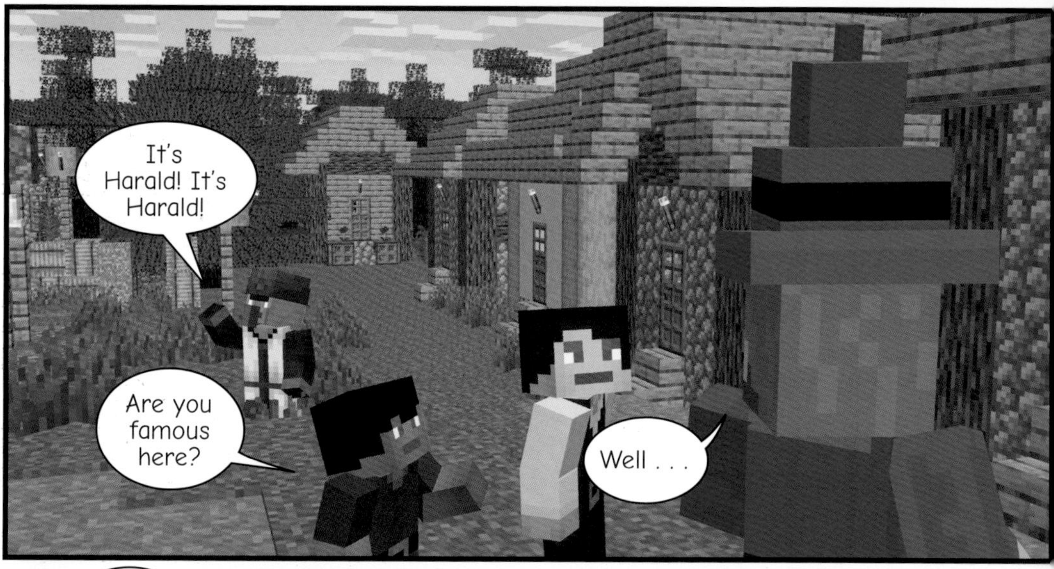
It's Harald! It's Harald!
Are you famous here?
Well . . .

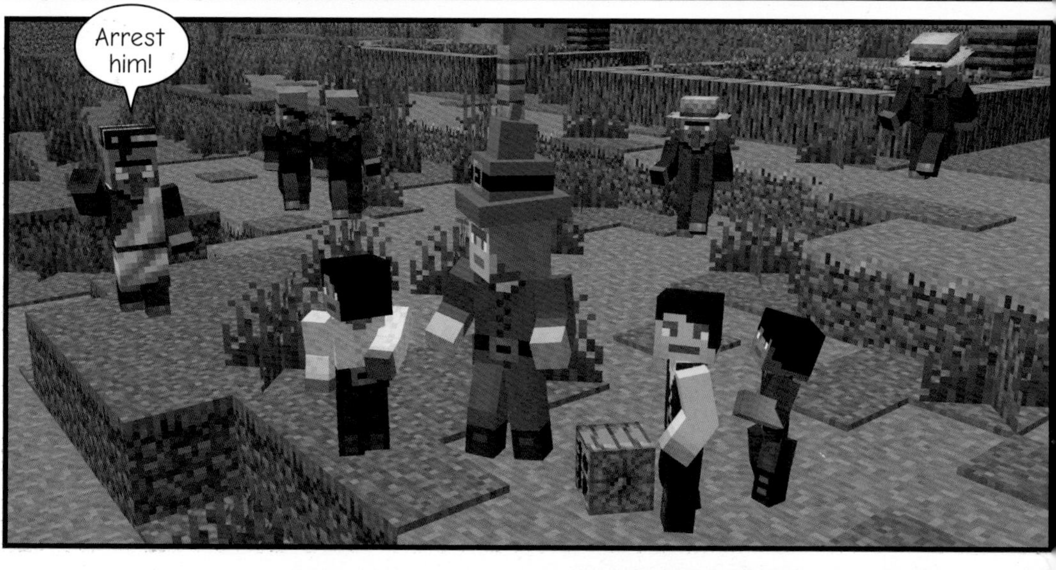
Arrest him!

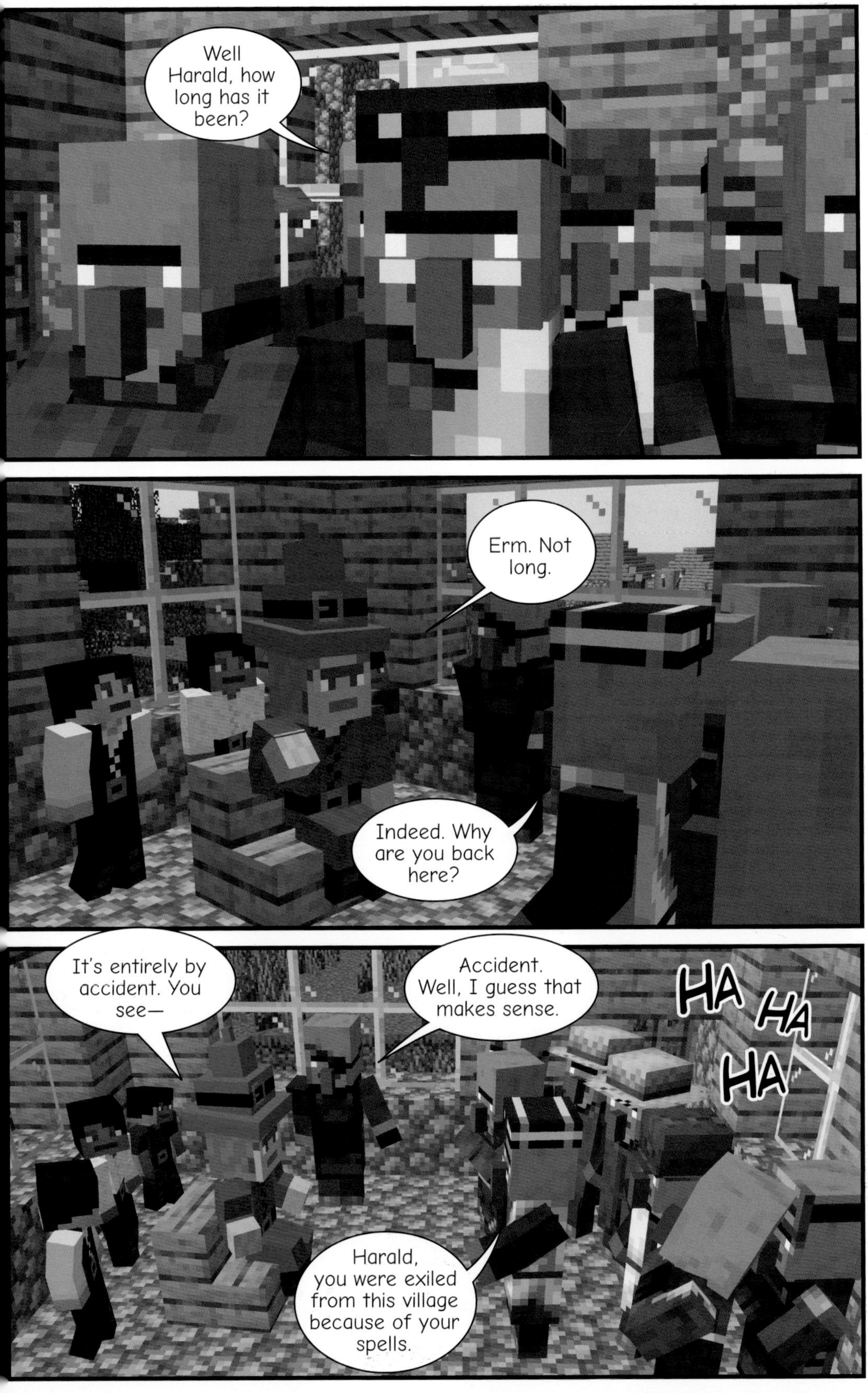
Well Harald, how long has it been?
Erm. Not long.
Indeed. Why are you back here?
It's entirely by accident. You see—
Accident. Well, I guess that makes sense.
HA HA HA
Harald, you were exiled from this village because of your spells.

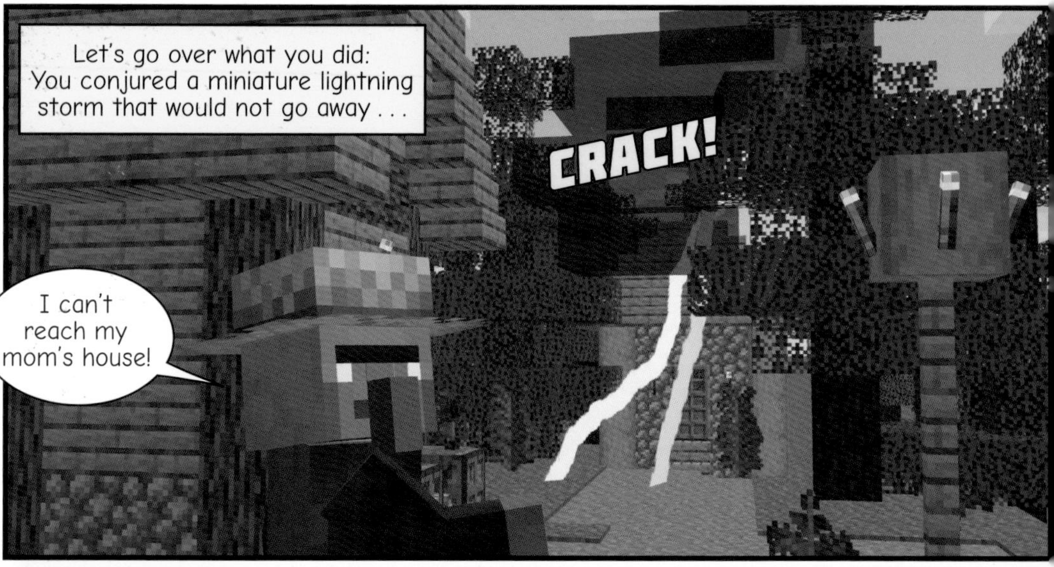
Let's go over what you did: You conjured a miniature lightning storm that would not go away . . .
CRACK!
I can't reach my mom's house!

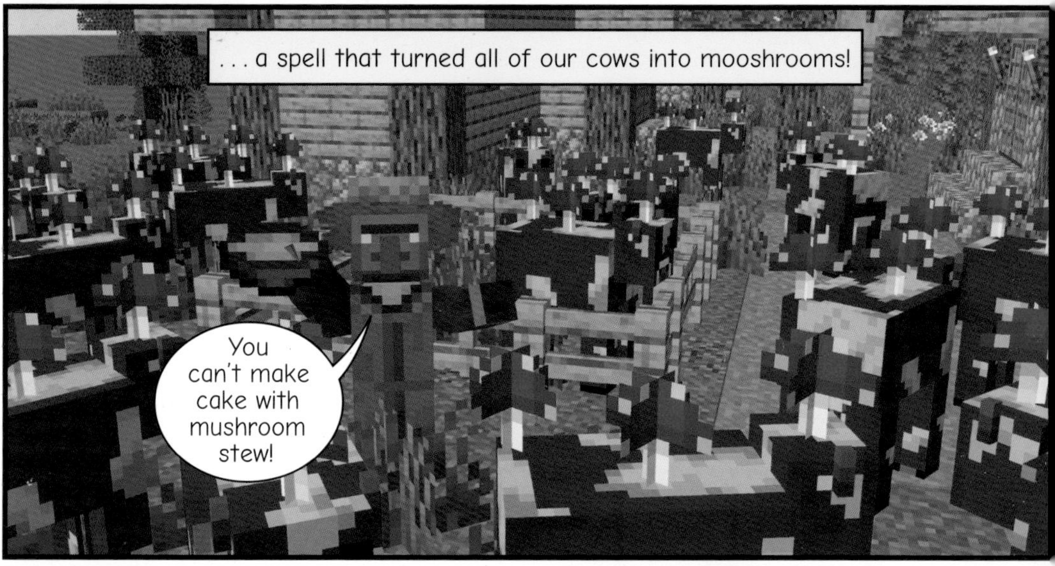
. . . a spell that turned all of our cows into mooshrooms!
You can't make cake with mushroom stew!

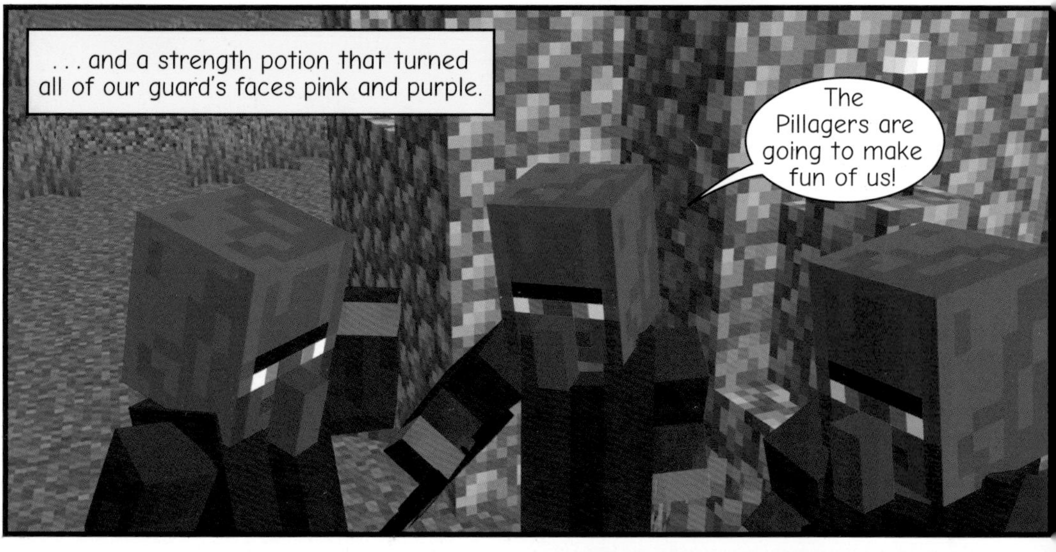
. . . and a strength potion that turned all of our guard's faces pink and purple.
The Pillagers are going to make fun of us!

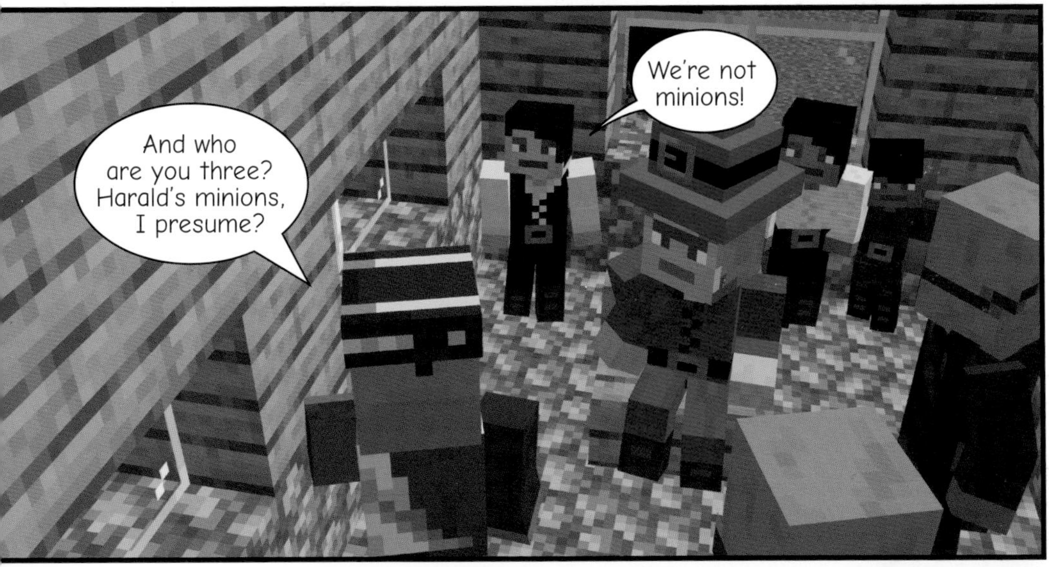
And who are you three? Harald's minions, I presume?
We're not minions!
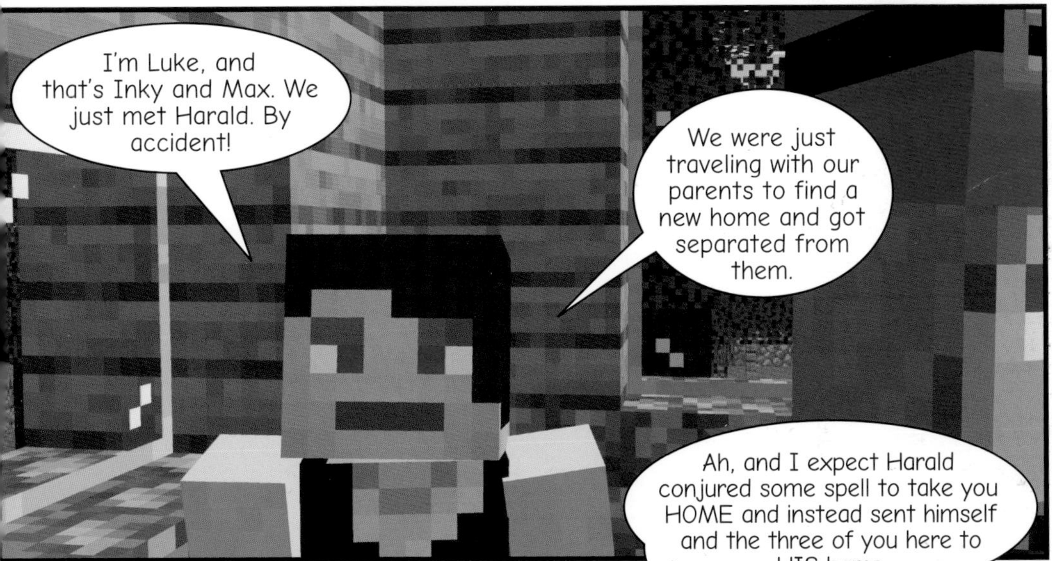
I'm Luke, and that's Inky and Max. We just met Harald. By accident!
We were just traveling with our parents to find a new home and got separated from them.
Ah, and I expect Harald conjured some spell to take you HOME and instead sent himself and the three of you here to HIS home.
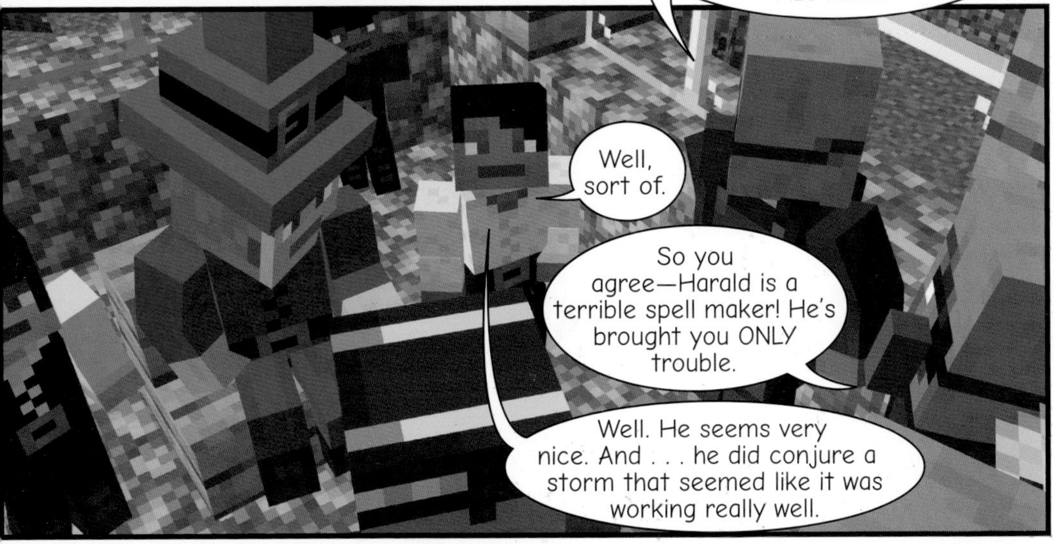
Well, sort of.
So you agree—Harald is a terrible spell maker! He's brought you ONLY trouble.
Well. He seems very nice. And . . . he did conjure a storm that seemed like it was working really well.

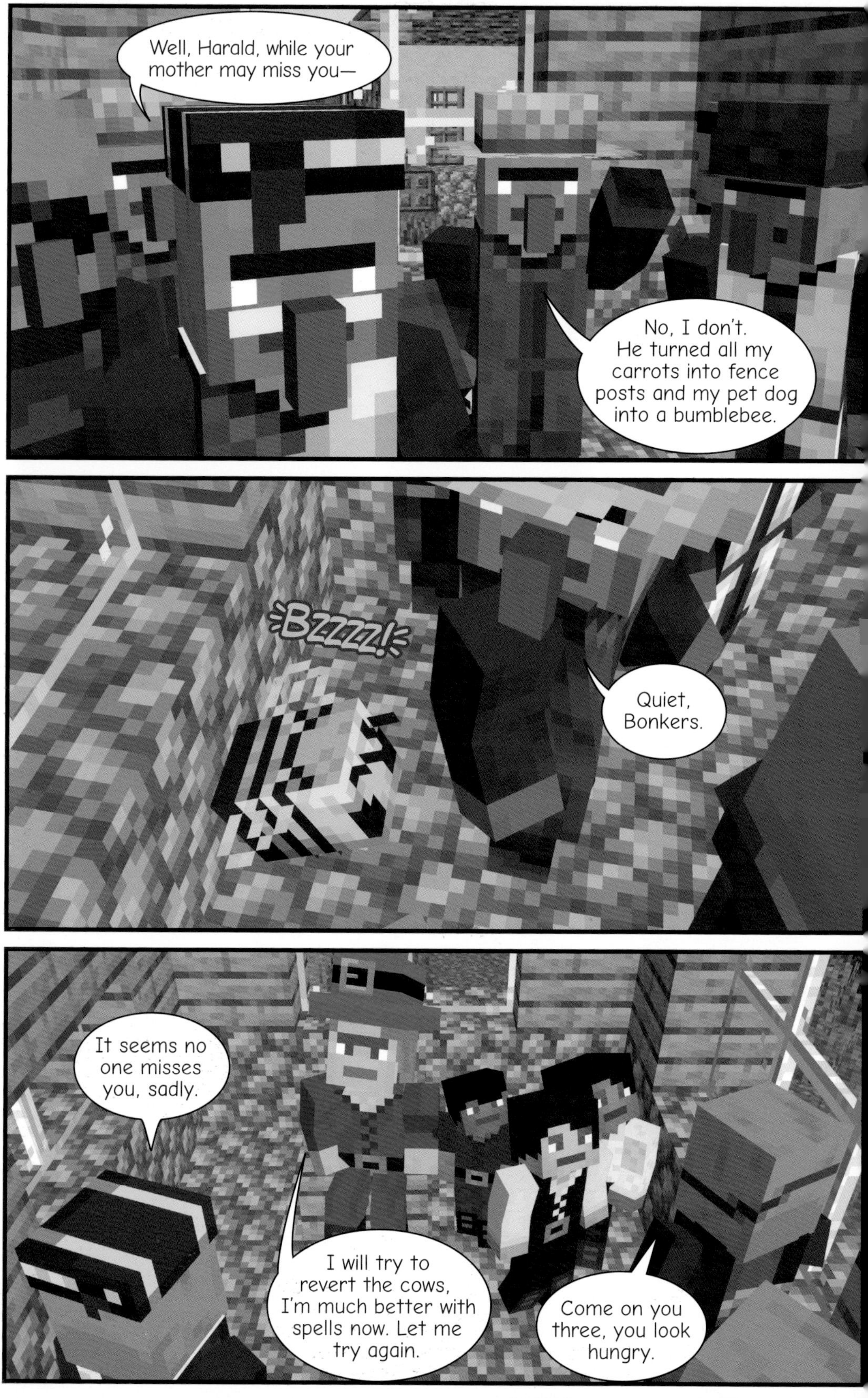
Well, Harald, while your mother may miss you—
No, I don't. He turned all my carrots into fence posts and my pet dog into a bumblebee.
BZZZZ!
Quiet, Bonkers.
It seems no one misses you, sadly.
I will try to revert the cows, I'm much better with spells now. Let me try again.
Come on you three, you look hungry.

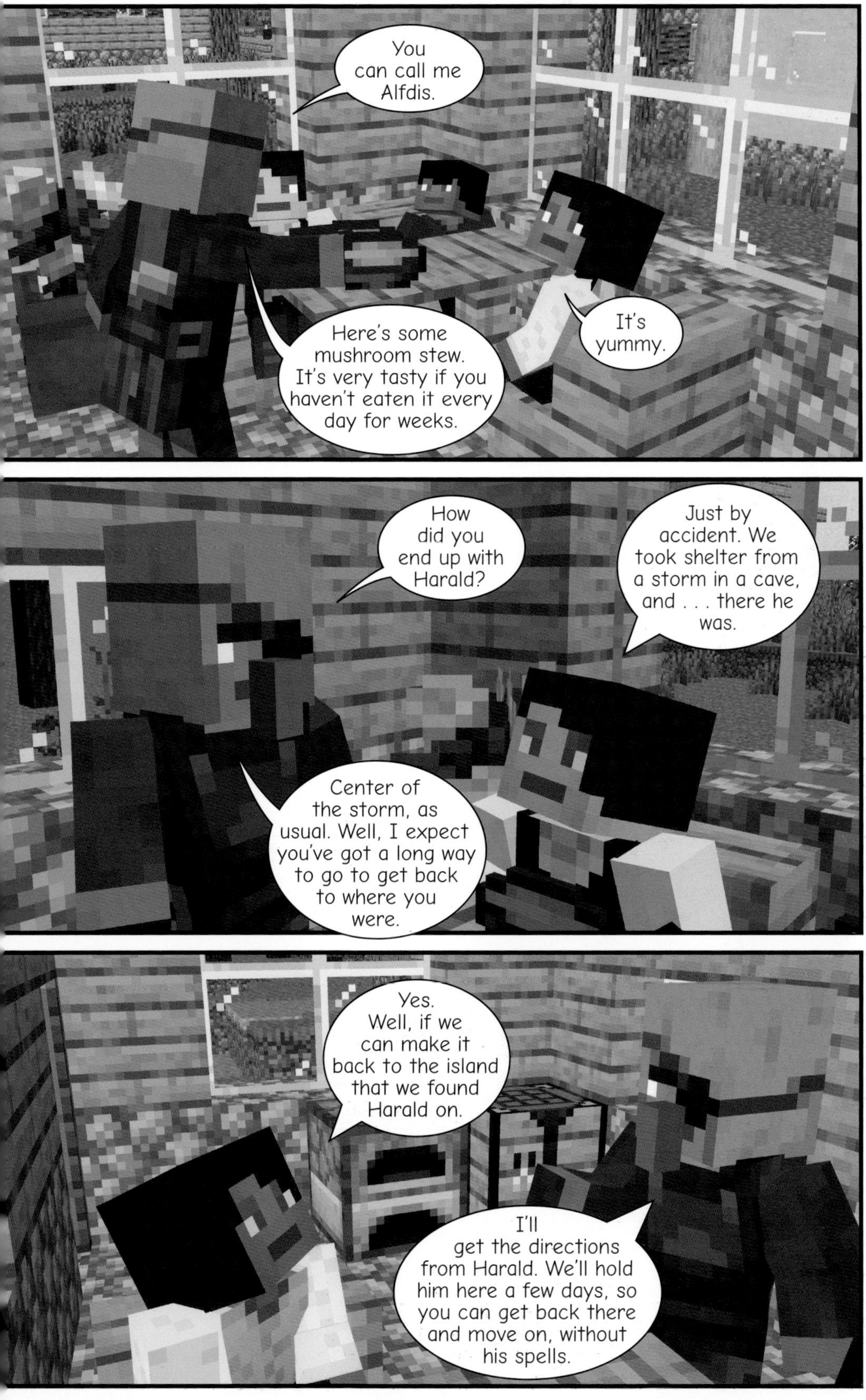
You can call me Alfdis.
Here's some mushroom stew. It's very tasty if you haven't eaten it every day for weeks.
It's yummy.
How did you end up with Harald?
Just by accident. We took shelter from a storm in a cave, and . . . there he was.
Center of the storm, as usual. Well, I expect you've got a long way to go to get back to where you were.
Yes. Well, if we can make it back to the island that we found Harald on.
I'll get the directions from Harald. We'll hold him here a few days, so you can get back there and move on, without his spells.

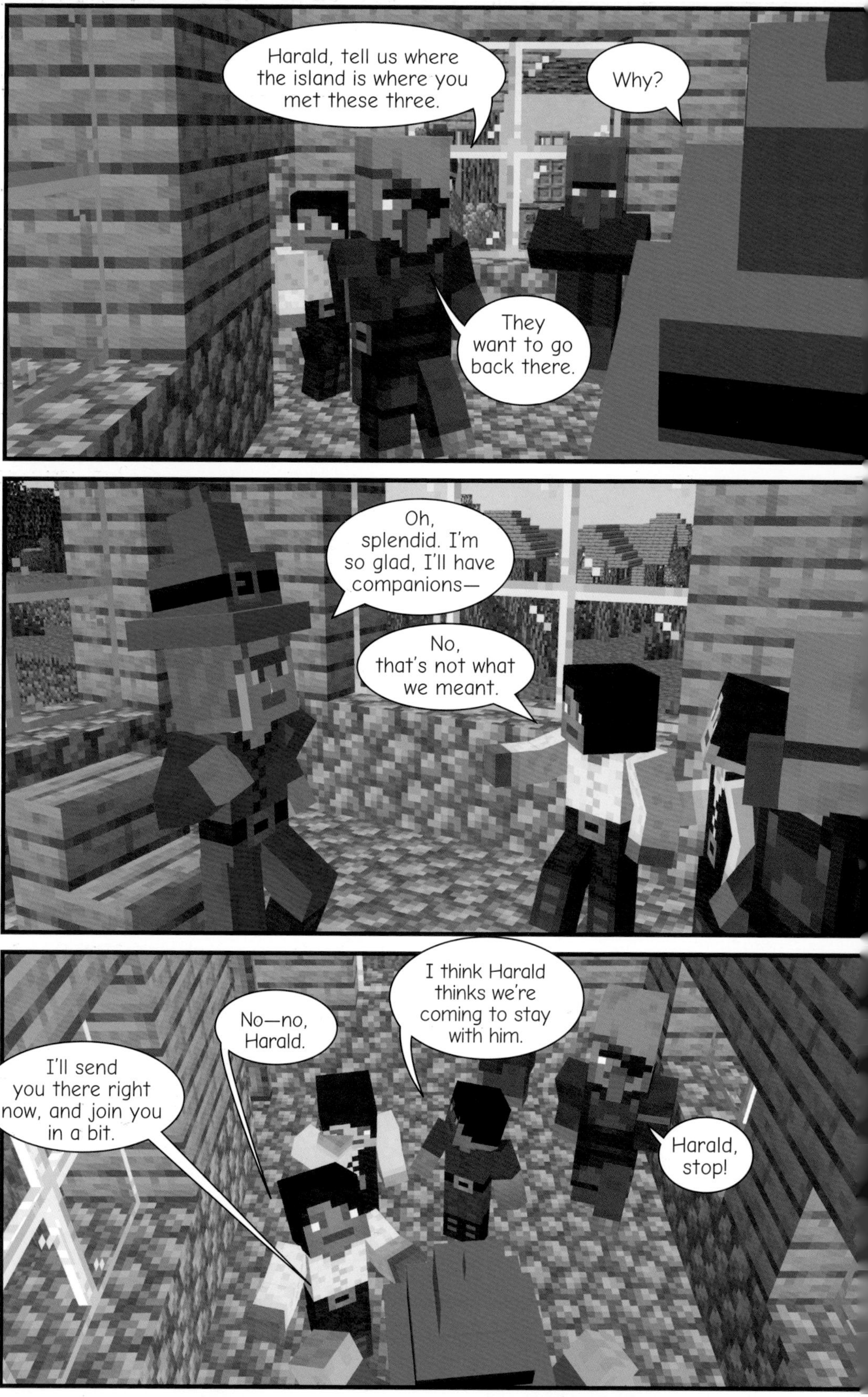
Harald, tell us where the island is where you met these three.
Why?
They want to go back there.
Oh, splendid. I'm so glad, I'll have companions—
No, that's not what we meant.
No—no, Harald.
I think Harald thinks we're coming to stay with him.
I'll send you there right now, and join you in a bit.
Harald, stop!

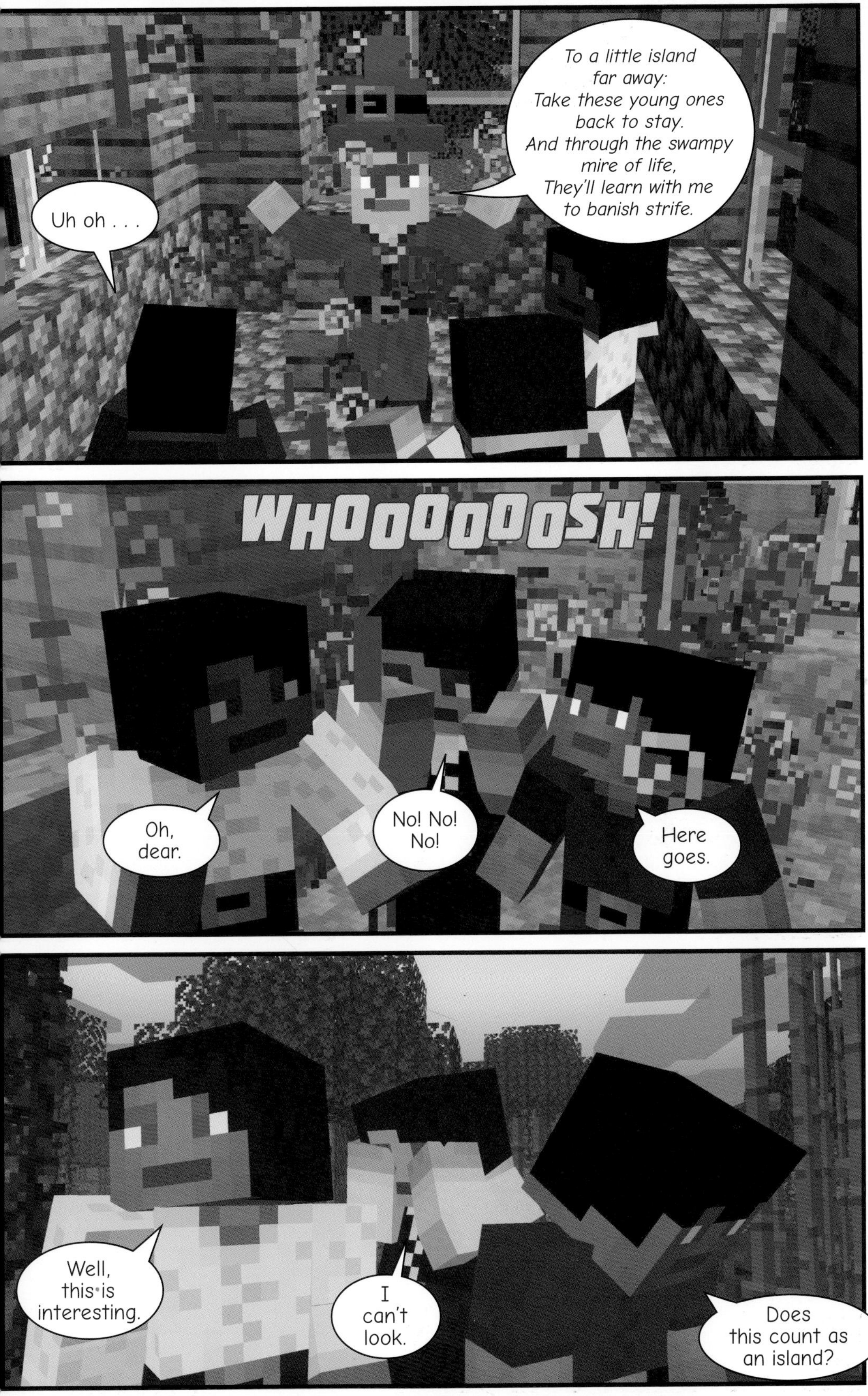
To a little island far away: Take these young ones back to stay. And through the swampy mire of life, They'll learn with me to banish strife.
Uh oh . . .
WHOOOOOOSH!
Oh, dear.
No! No! No!
Here goes.
Well, this is interesting.
I can't look.
Does this count as an island?

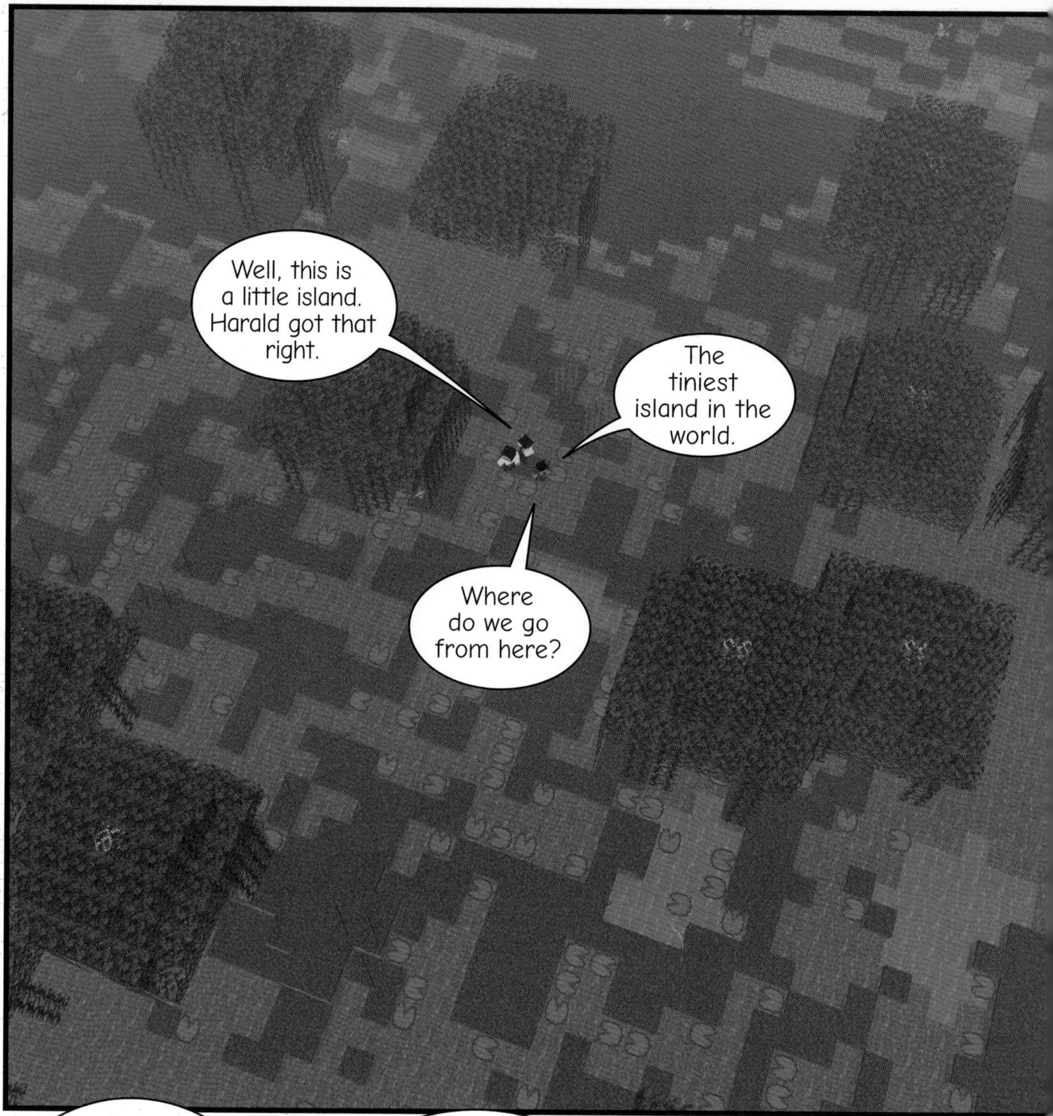

Well, this is a little island. Harald got that right.
The tiniest island in the world.
Where do we go from here?

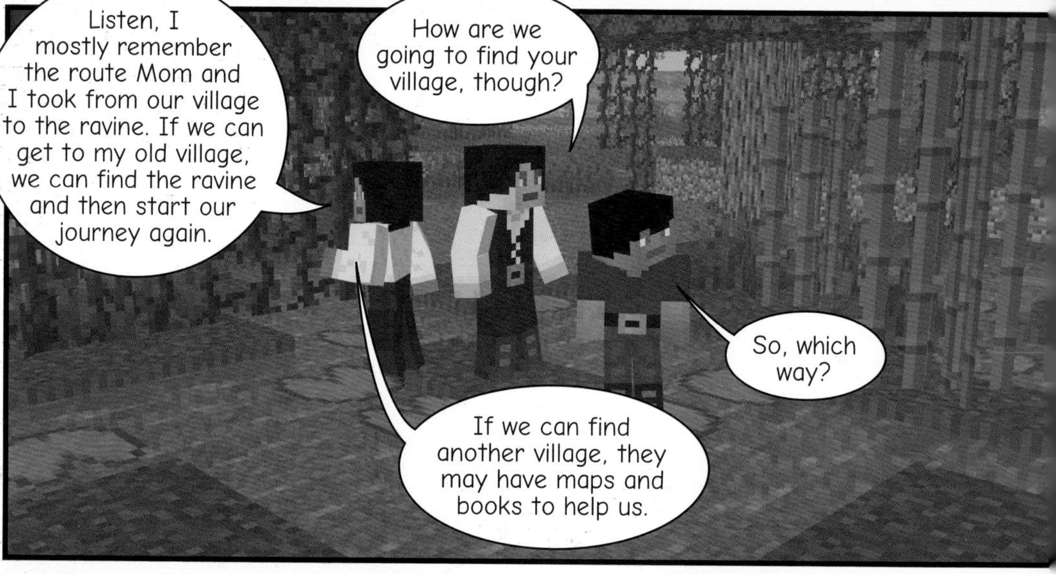

Listen, I mostly remember the route Mom and I took from our village to the ravine. If we can get to my old village, we can find the ravine and then start our journey again.
How are we going to find your village, though?
So, which way?
If we can find another village, they may have maps and books to help us.

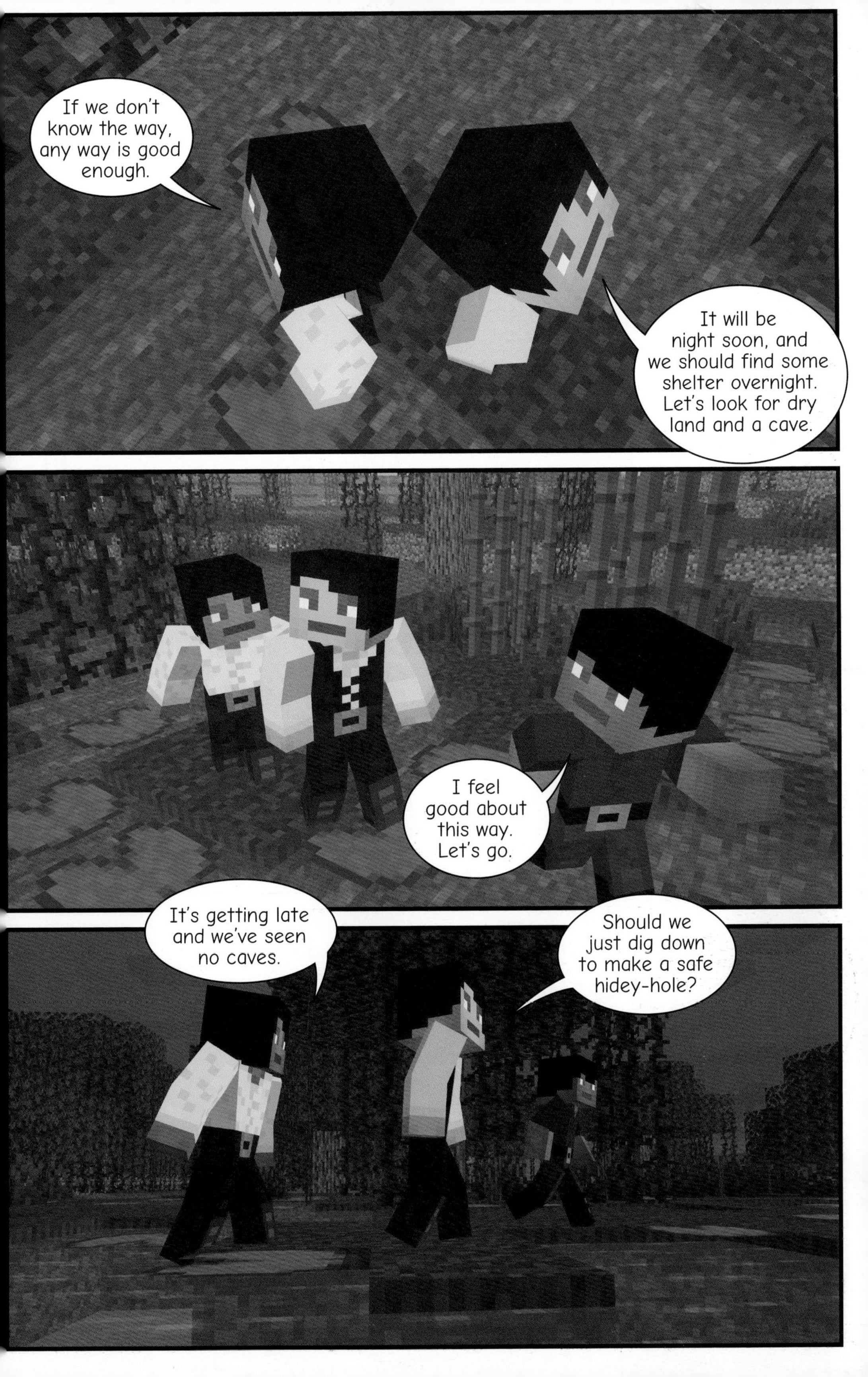
If we don't know the way, any way is good enough.
It will be night soon, and we should find some shelter overnight. Let's look for dry land and a cave.
I feel good about this way. Let's go.
It's getting late and we've seen no caves.
Should we just dig down to make a safe hidey-hole?

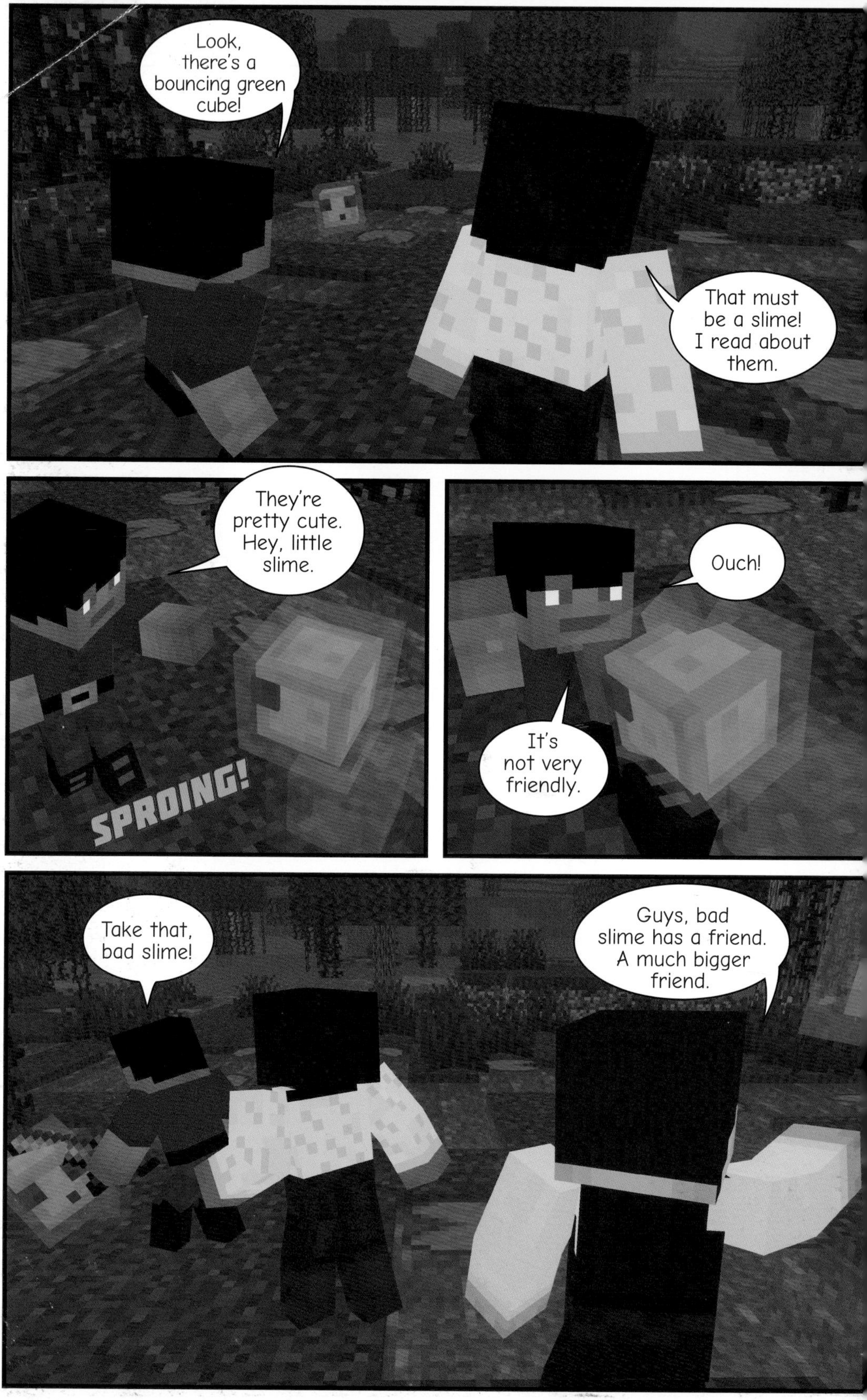
Look, there's a bouncing green cube!
That must be a slime! I read about them.
They're pretty cute. Hey, little slime.
SPROING!
Ouch!
It's not very friendly.
Take that, bad slime!
Guys, bad slime has a friend. A much bigger friend.

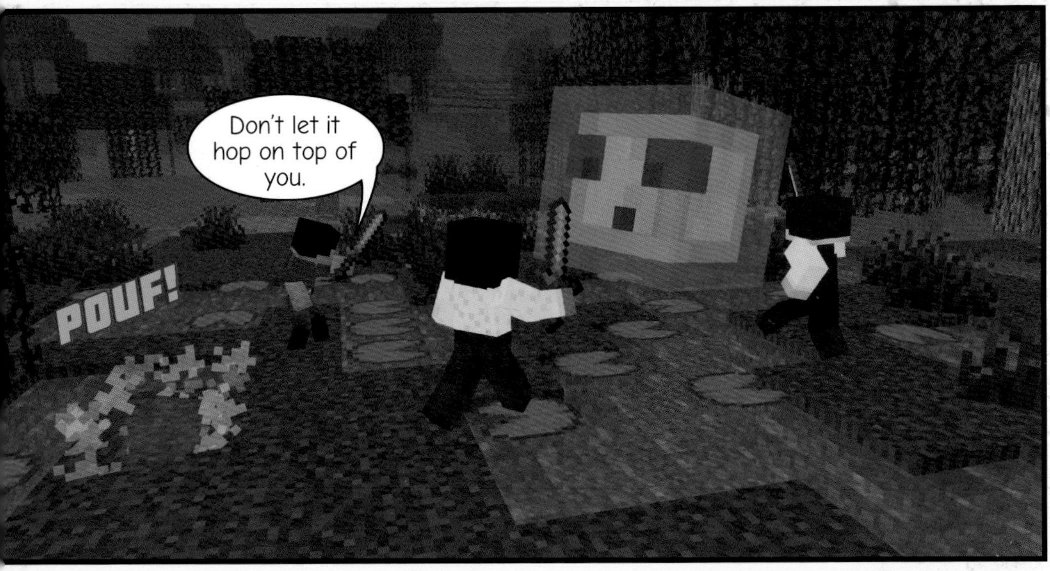
Don't let it hop on top of you.
POUF!

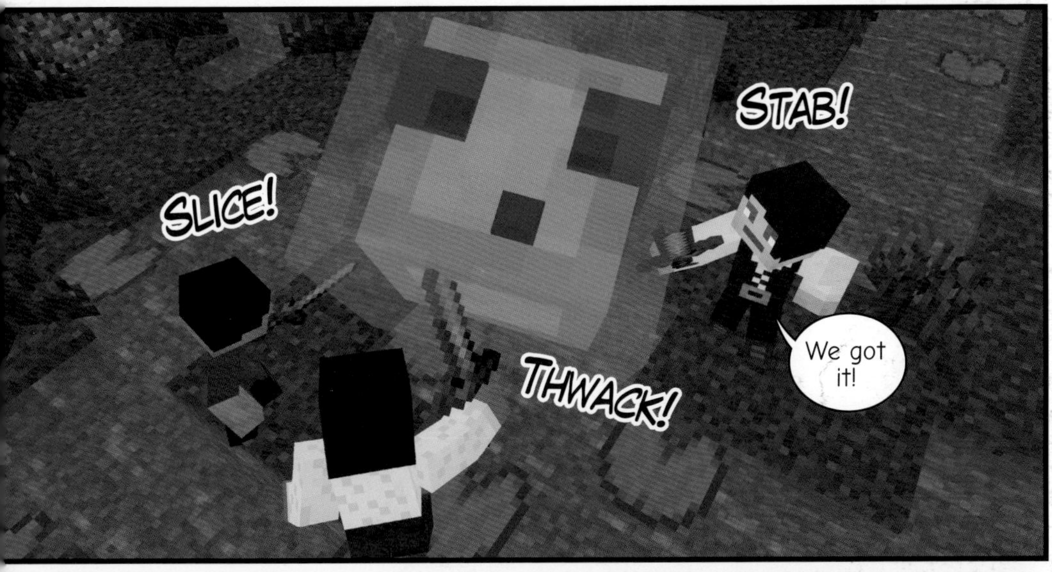
STAB!
SLICE!
THWACK!
We got it!

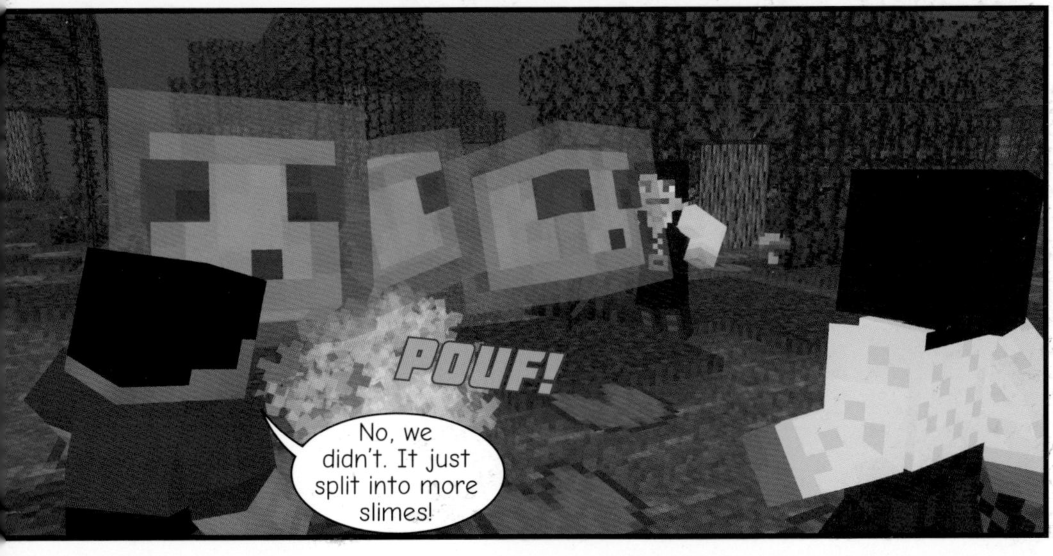
POUF!
No, we didn't. It just split into more slimes!

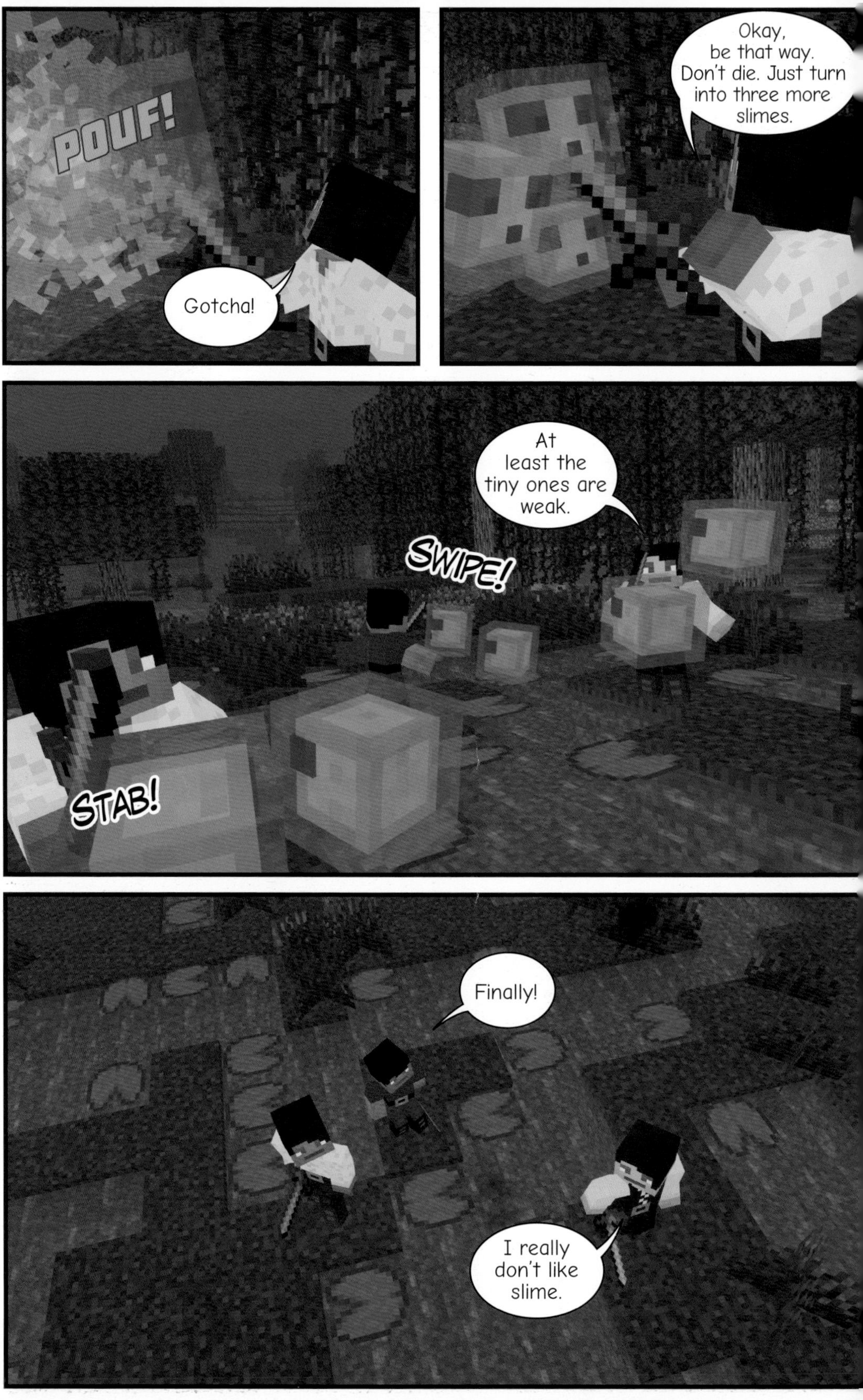
POUF!
Gotcha!
Okay, be that way. Don't die. Just turn into three more slimes.
At least the tiny ones are weak.
SWIPE!
STAB!
Finally!
I really don't like slime.

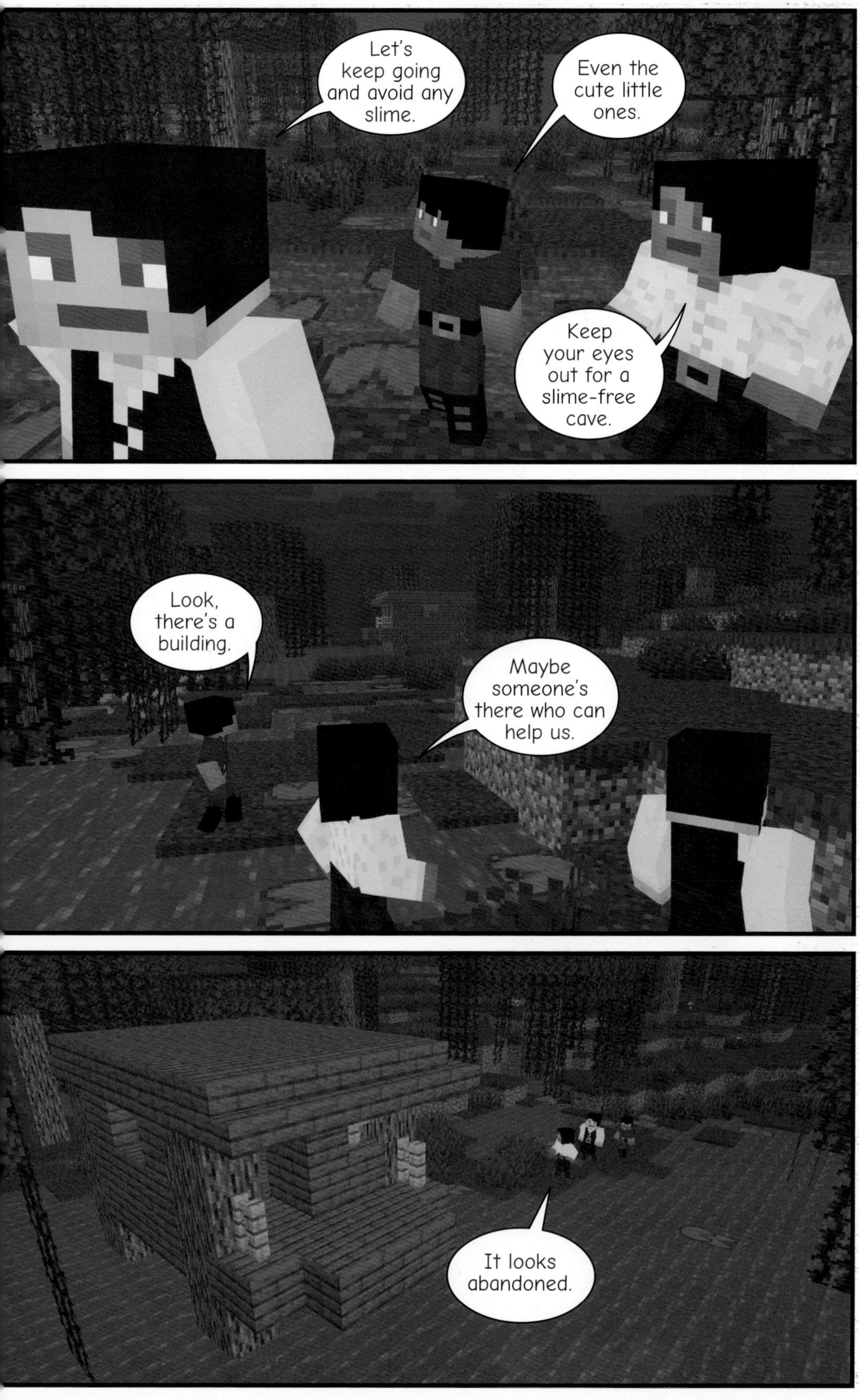
Let's keep going and avoid any slime.
Even the cute little ones.
Keep your eyes out for a slime-free cave.
Look, there's a building.
Maybe someone's there who can help us.
It looks abandoned.

I see cobwebs.
Okay, let's rest here.
WHO IS IN MY HUT?
What . . . ?

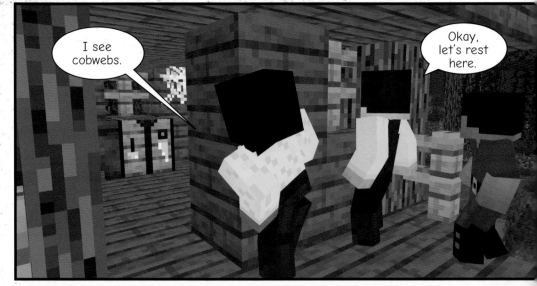

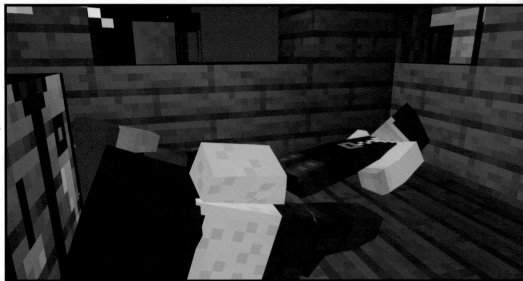

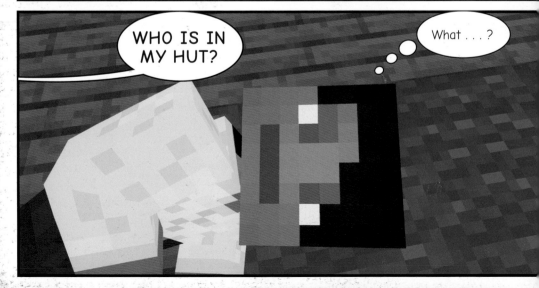

Chapter 7
The Really
Bad Witch

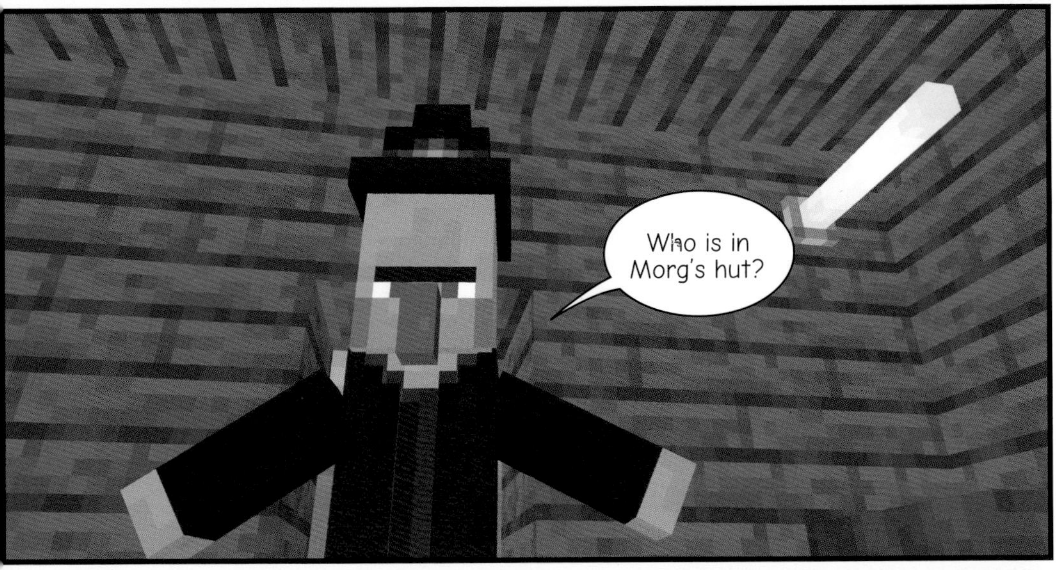
Who is in
Morg's hut?

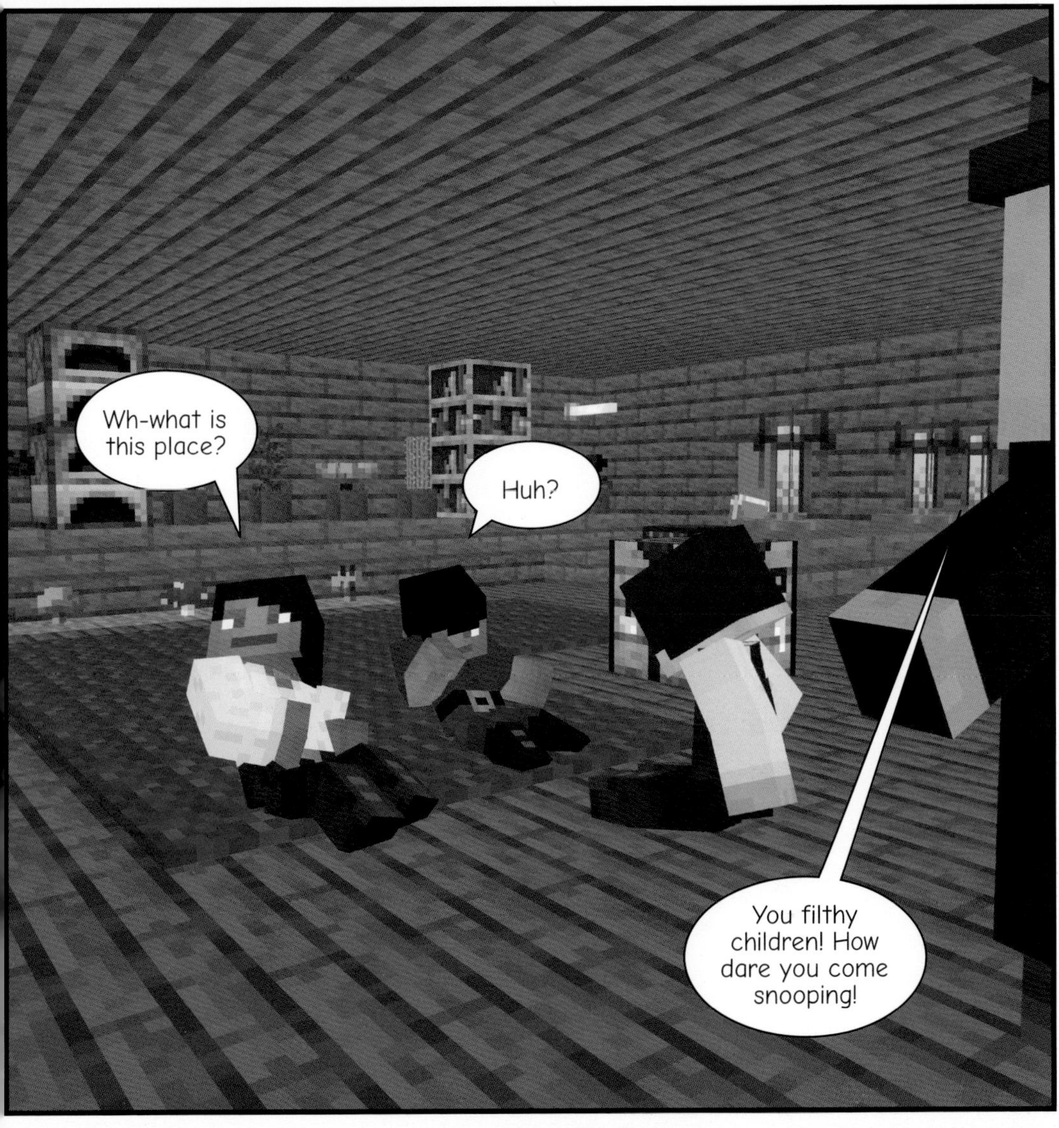
Wh-what is
this place?
Huh?
You filthy
children! How
dare you come
snooping!

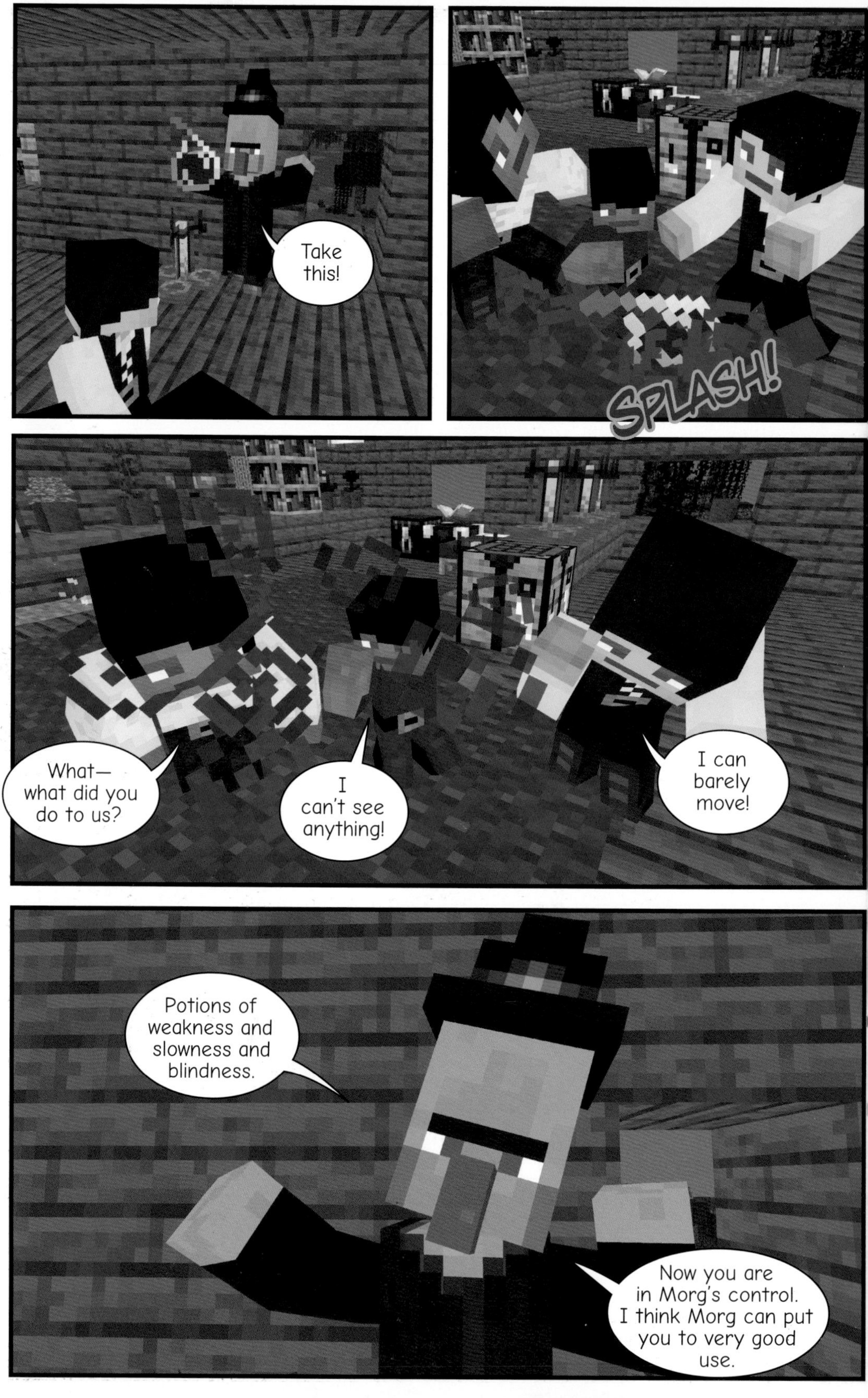
Take this!
SPLASH!
What—what did you do to us?
I can't see anything!
I can barely move!
Potions of weakness and slowness and blindness.
Now you are in Morg's control. I think Morg can put you to very good use.

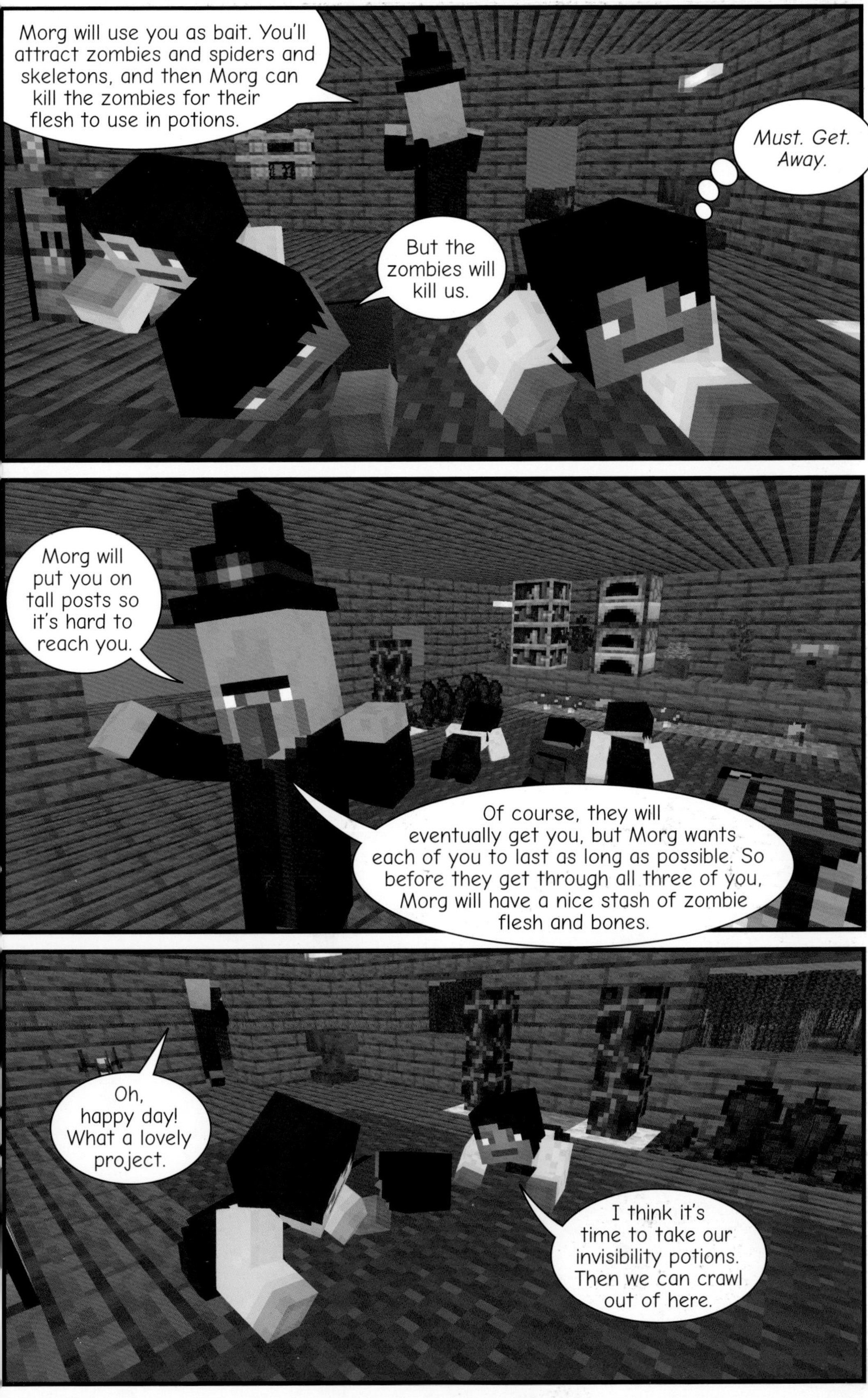
Morg will use you as bait. You'll attract zombies and spiders and skeletons, and then Morg can kill the zombies for their flesh to use in potions.
Must. Get. Away.
But the zombies will kill us.
Morg will put you on tall posts so it's hard to reach you.
Of course, they will eventually get you, but Morg wants each of you to last as long as possible. So before they get through all three of you, Morg will have a nice stash of zombie flesh and bones.
Oh, happy day! What a lovely project.
I think it's time to take our invisibility potions. Then we can crawl out of here.

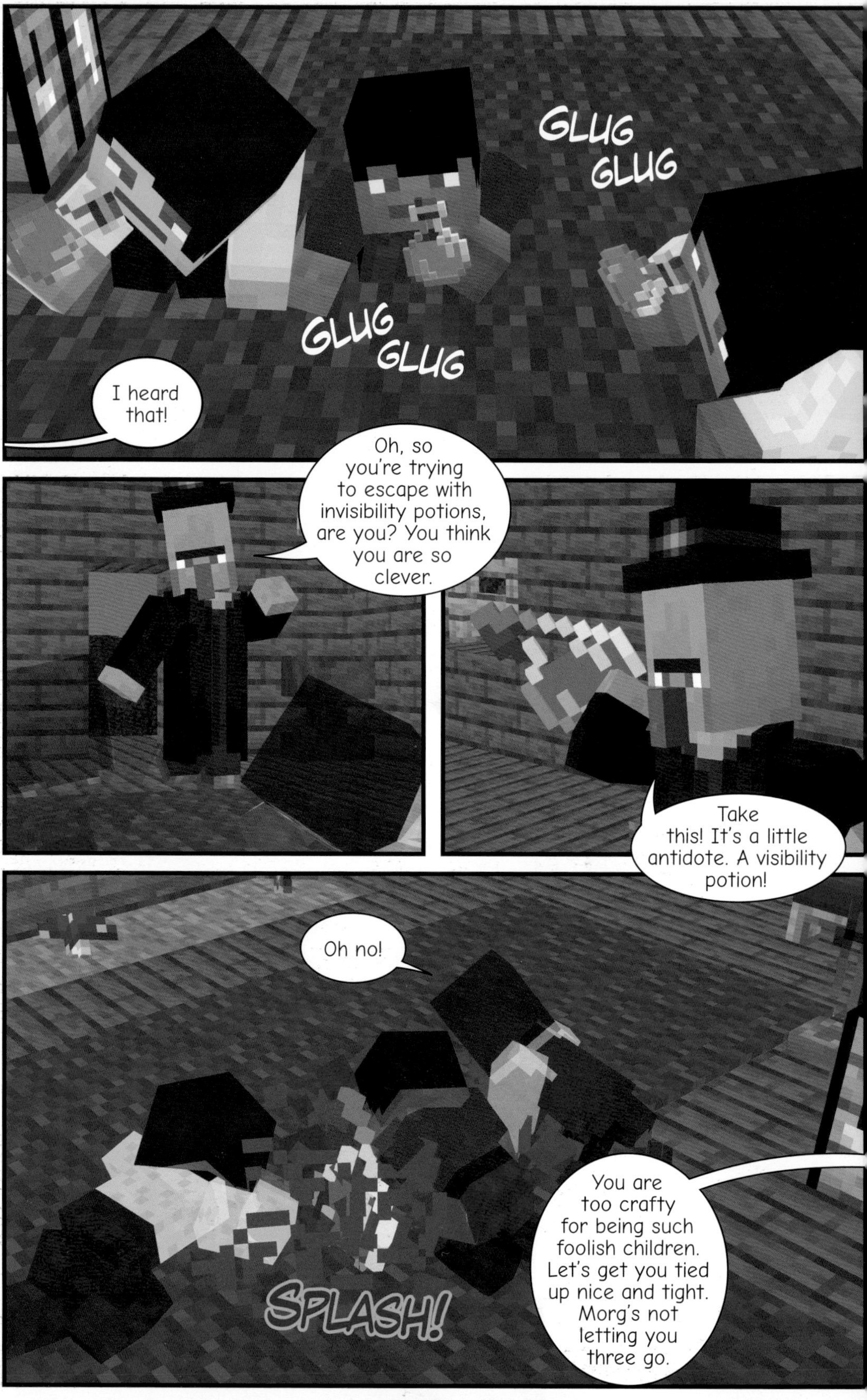
GLUG GLUG
GLUG GLUG
I heard that!
Oh, so you're trying to escape with invisibility potions, are you? You think you are so clever.
Take this! It's a little antidote. A visibility potion!
Oh no!
SPLASH!
You are too crafty for being such foolish children. Let's get you tied up nice and tight. Morg's not letting you three go.

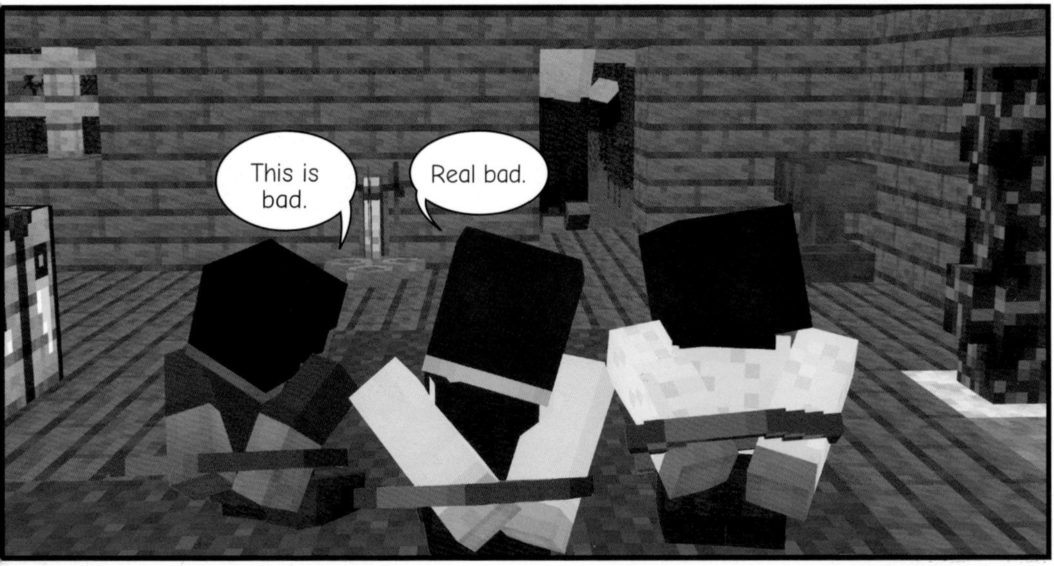
This is bad.
Real bad.

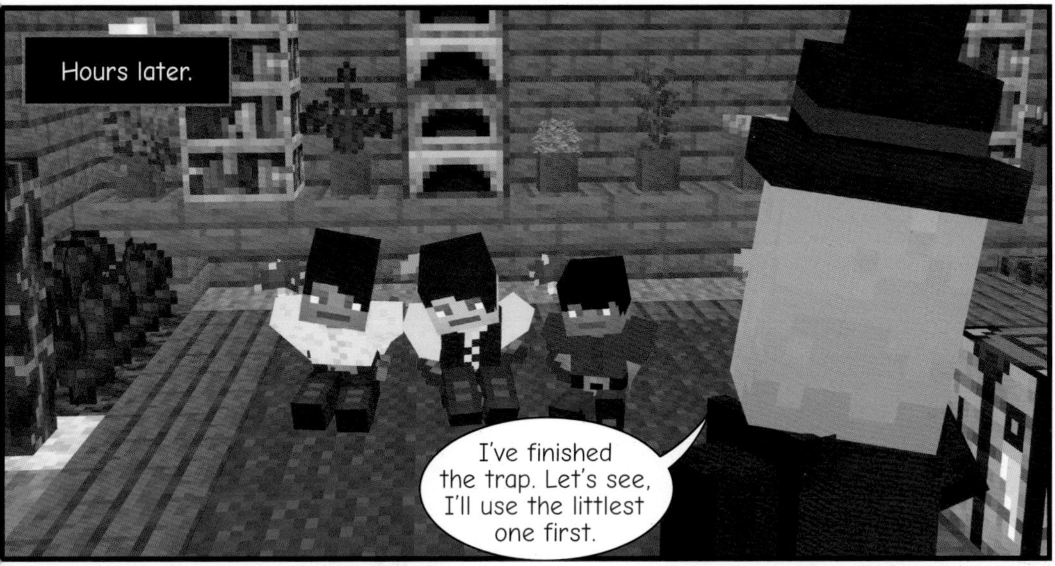
Hours later.
I've finished the trap. Let's see, I'll use the littlest one first.

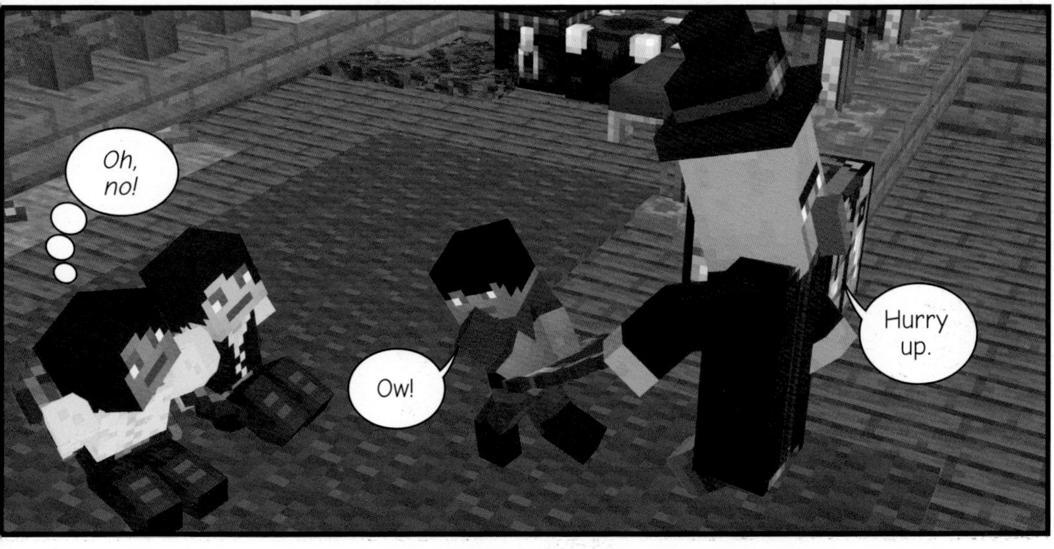
Oh, no!
Ow!
Hurry up.

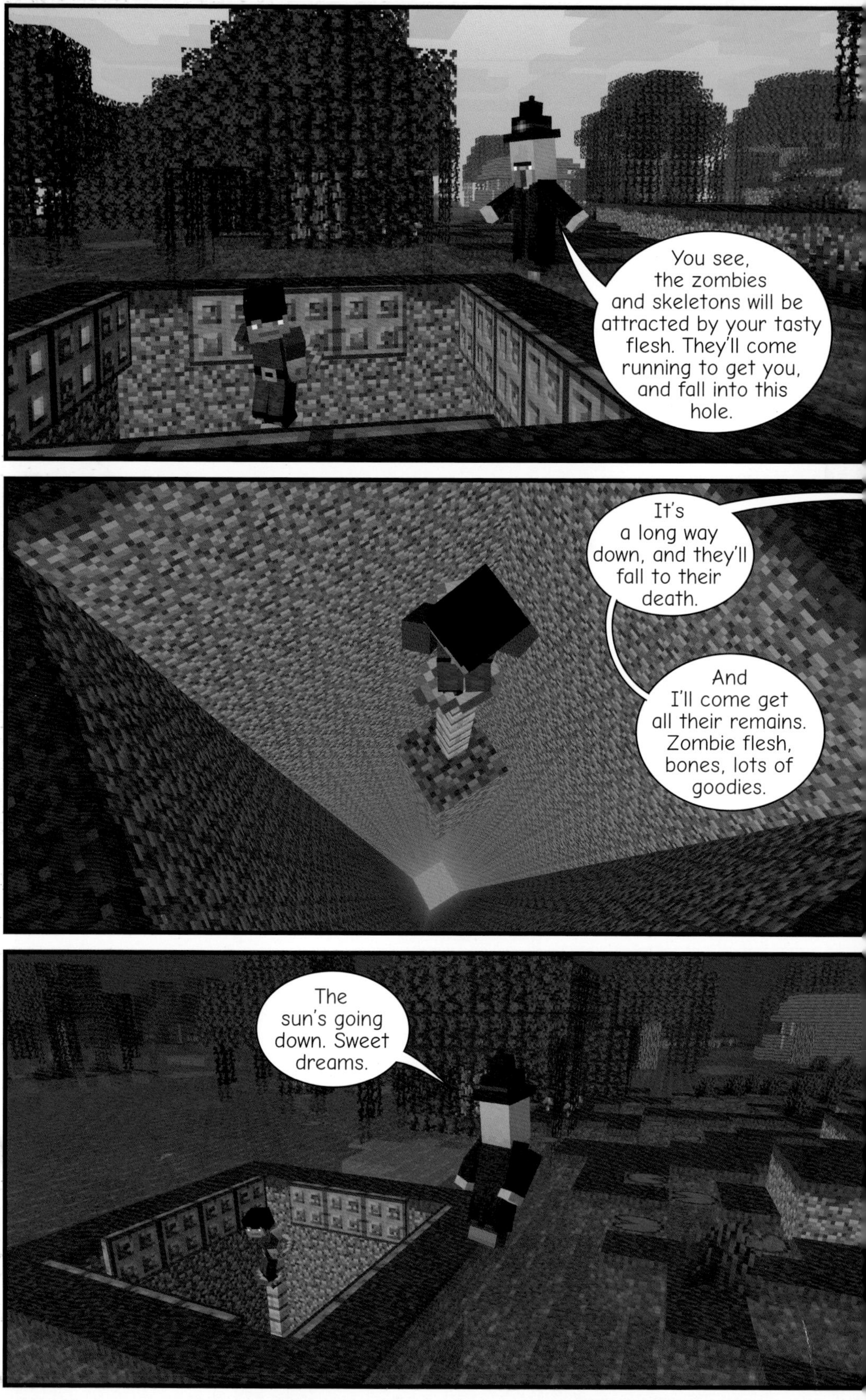
You see, the zombies and skeletons will be attracted by your tasty flesh. They'll come running to get you, and fall into this hole.
It's a long way down, and they'll fall to their death.
And I'll come get all their remains. Zombie flesh, bones, lots of goodies.
The sun's going down. Sweet dreams.

URRRRGH!

AARRGH!

RRRRRRR!

That sounds like a zombie!

And it sees me!

It's here!

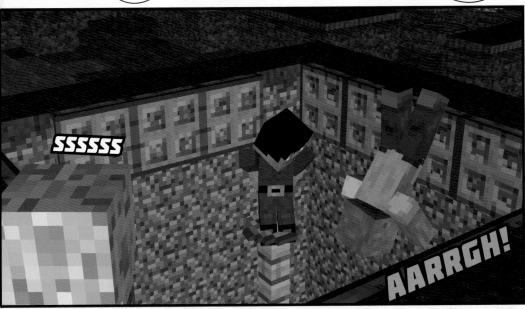

SSSSSS

AARRGH!

Please don't blow up!

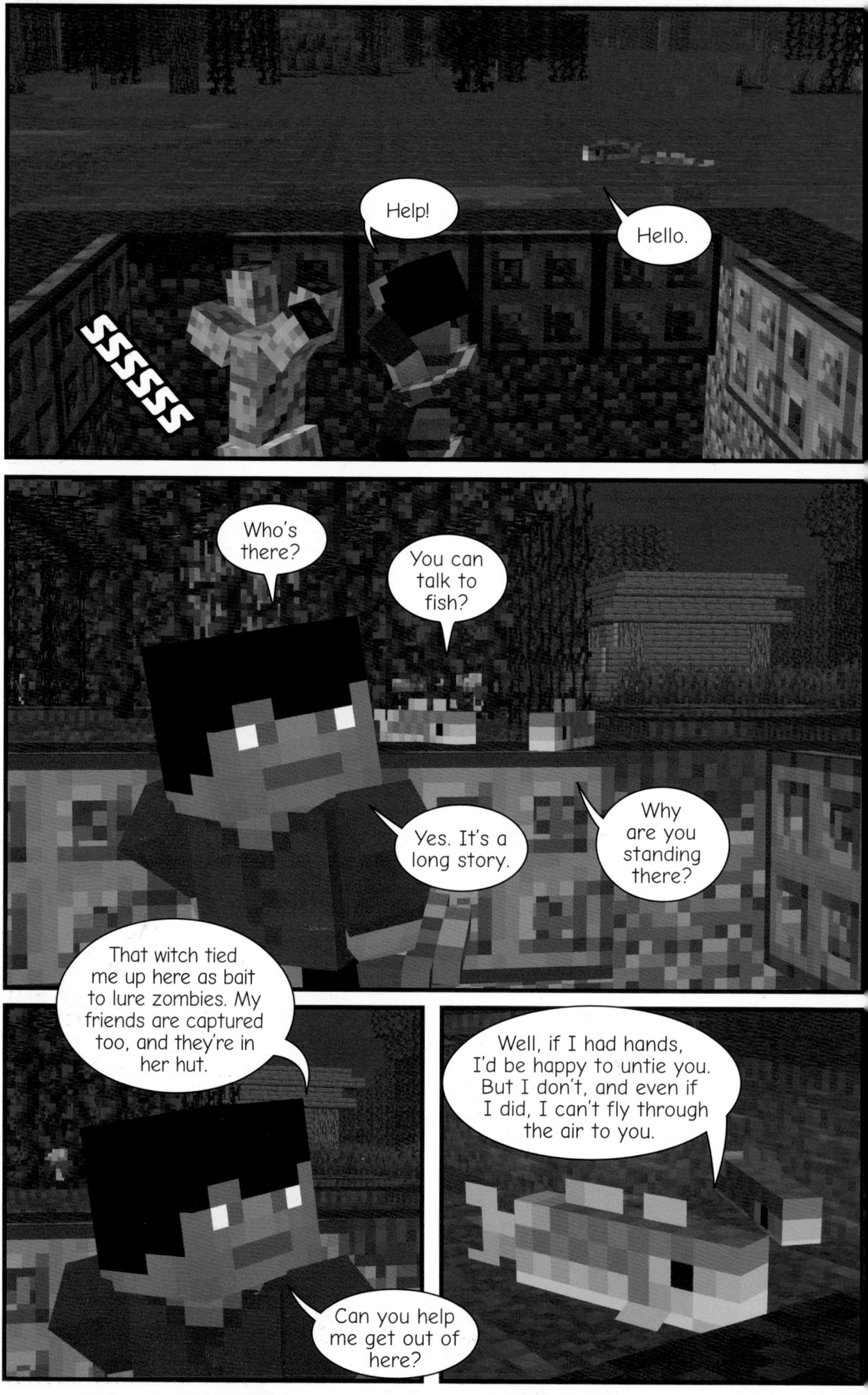
SSSSSS
Help!
Hello.
Who's there?
You can talk to fish?
Yes. It's a long story.
Why are you standing there?
That witch tied me up here as bait to lure zombies. My friends are captured too, and they're in her hut.
Can you help me get out of here?
Well, if I had hands, I'd be happy to untie you. But I don't, and even if I did, I can't fly through the air to you.

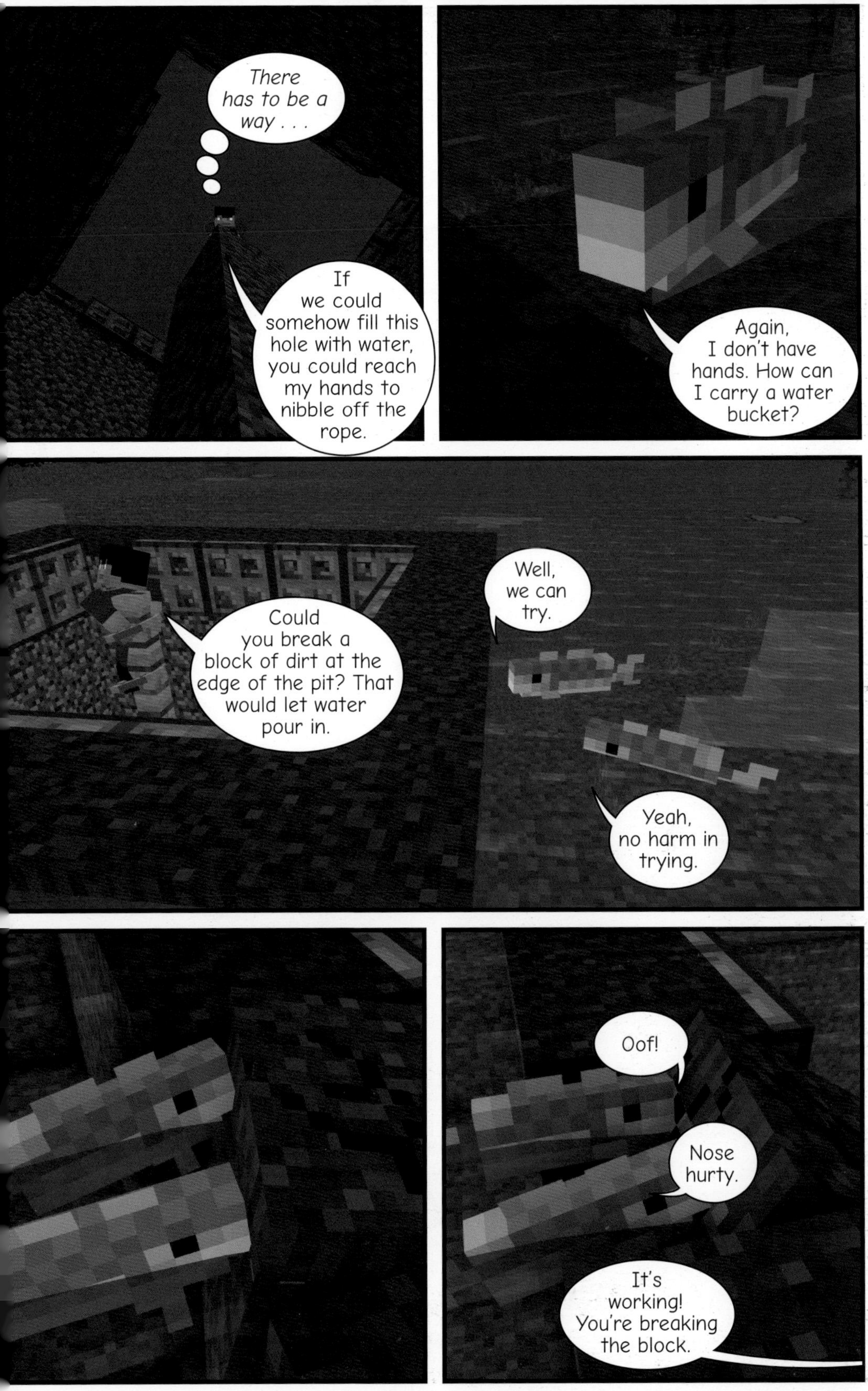
There has to be a way . . .
If we could somehow fill this hole with water, you could reach my hands to nibble off the rope.
Again, I don't have hands. How can I carry a water bucket?
Could you break a block of dirt at the edge of the pit? That would let water pour in.
Well, we can try.
Yeah, no harm in trying.
Oof!
Nose hurty.
It's working! You're breaking the block.

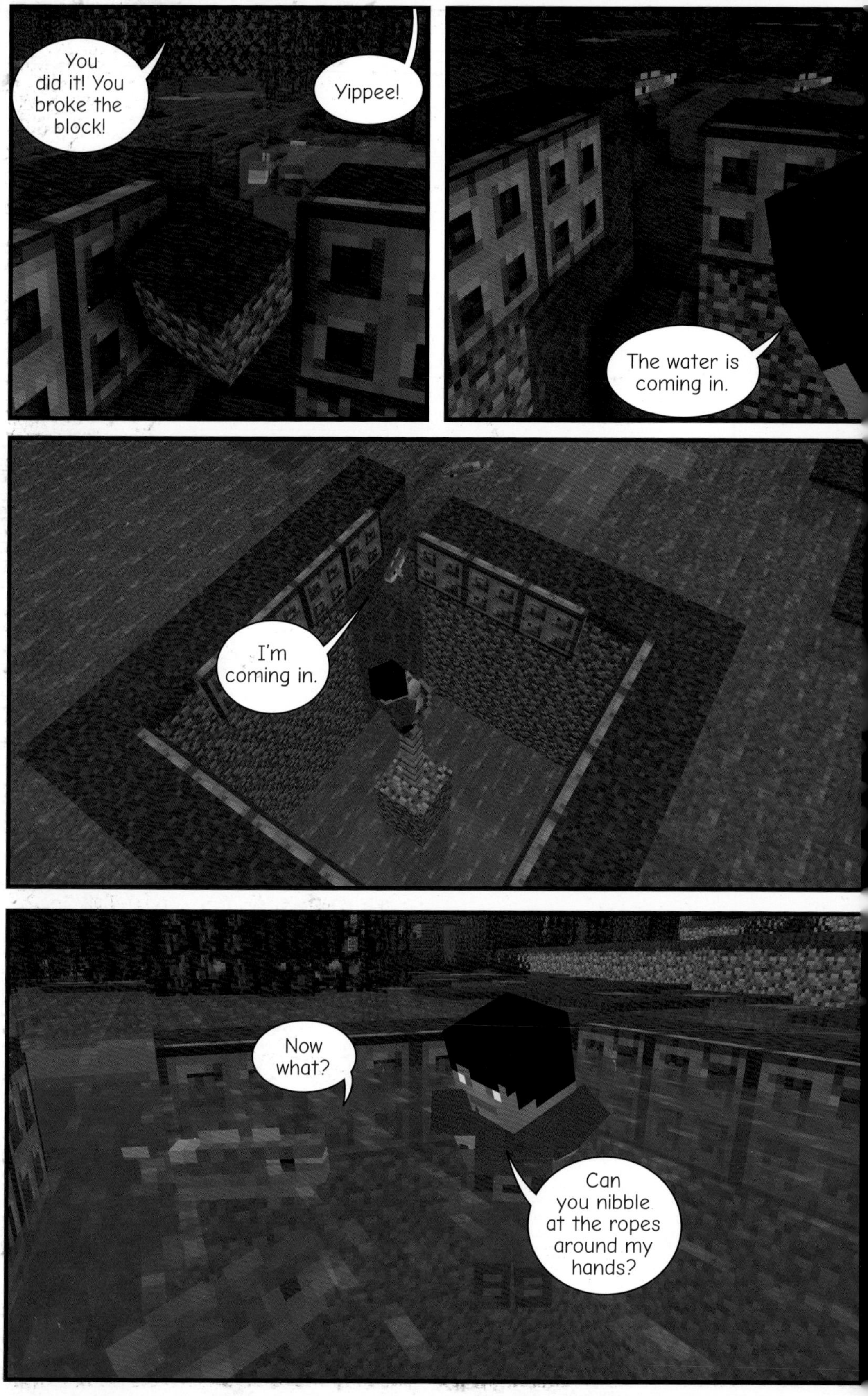
You did it! You broke the block!
Yippee!
The water is coming in.
I'm coming in.
Now what?
Can you nibble at the ropes around my hands?

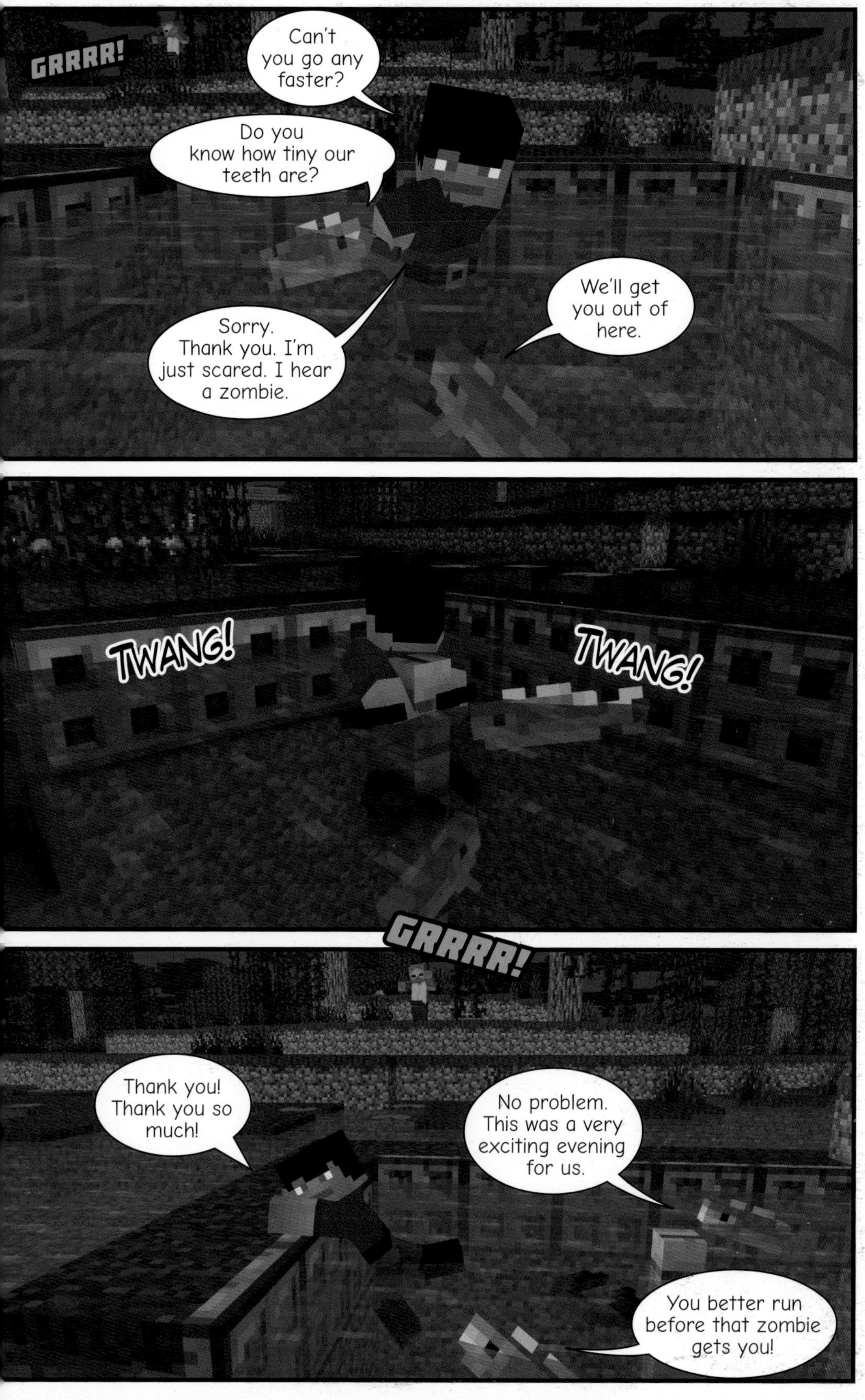
GRRRR!
Can't you go any faster?
Do you know how tiny our teeth are?
Sorry. Thank you. I'm just scared. I hear a zombie.
We'll get you out of here.
TWANG!
TWANG!
GRRRR!
Thank you! Thank you so much!
No problem. This was a very exciting evening for us.
You better run before that zombie gets you!

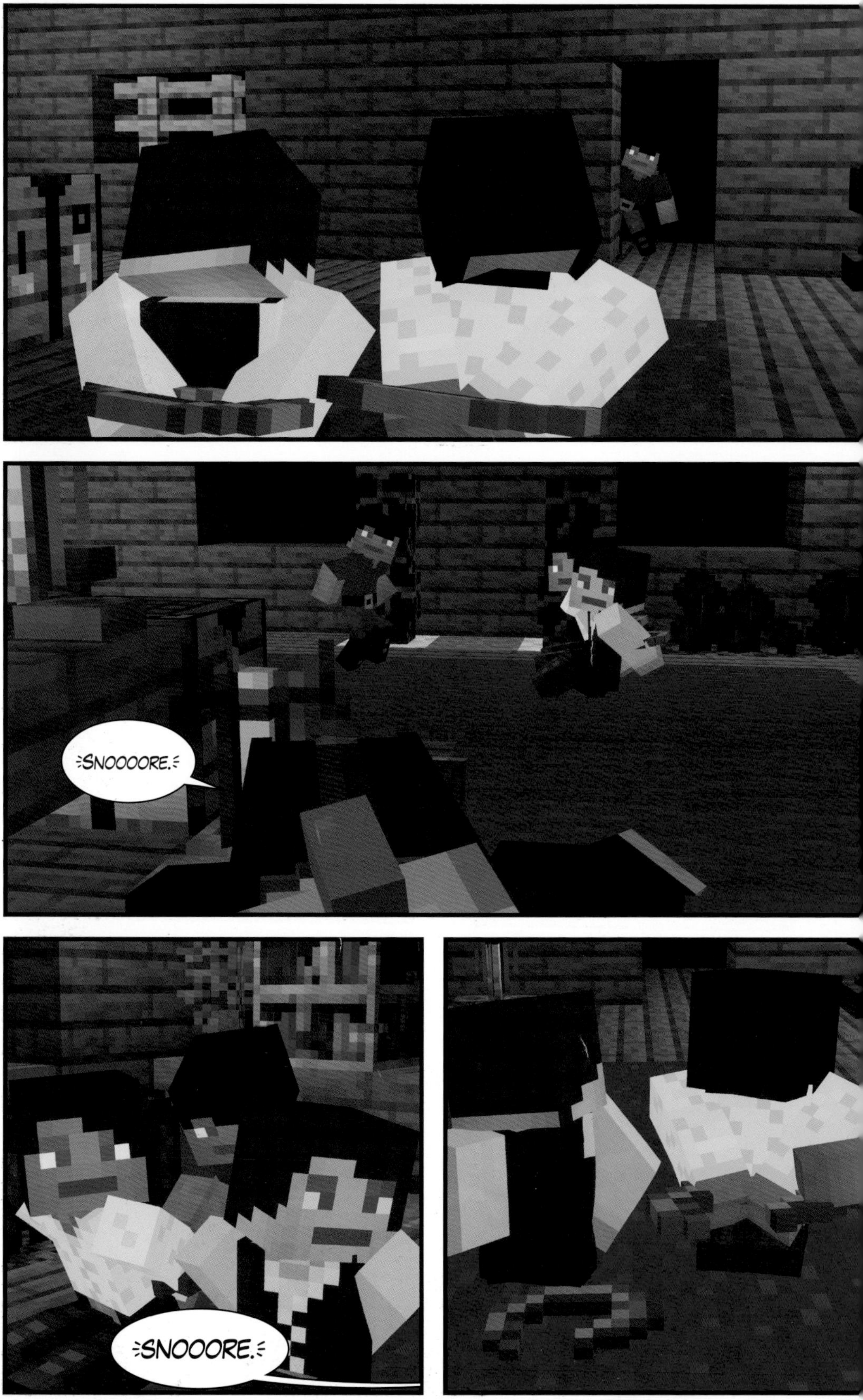
SNOOOORE.
SNOOORE.

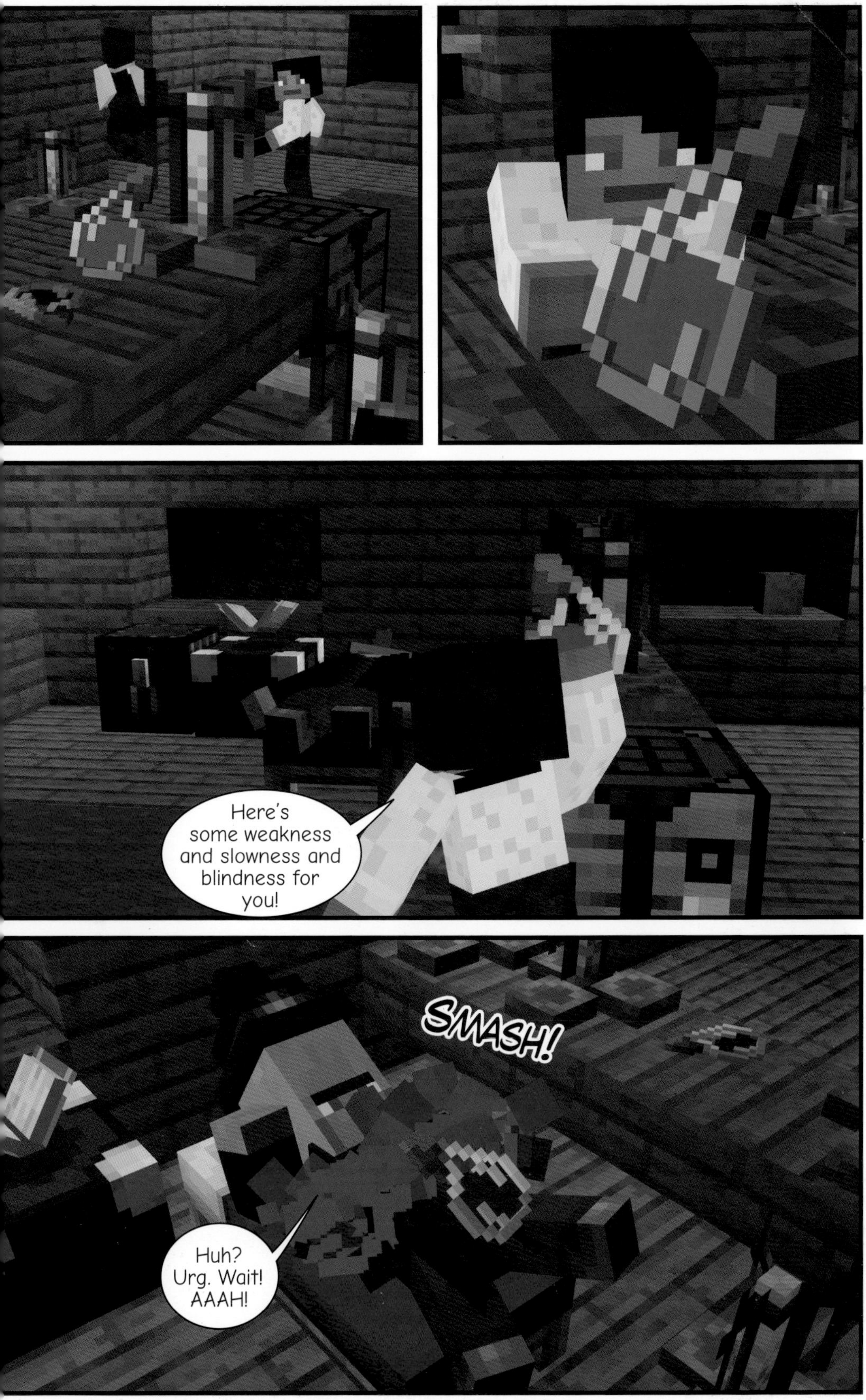
Here's some weakness and slowness and blindness for you!
SMASH!
Huh? Urg. Wait! AAAH!

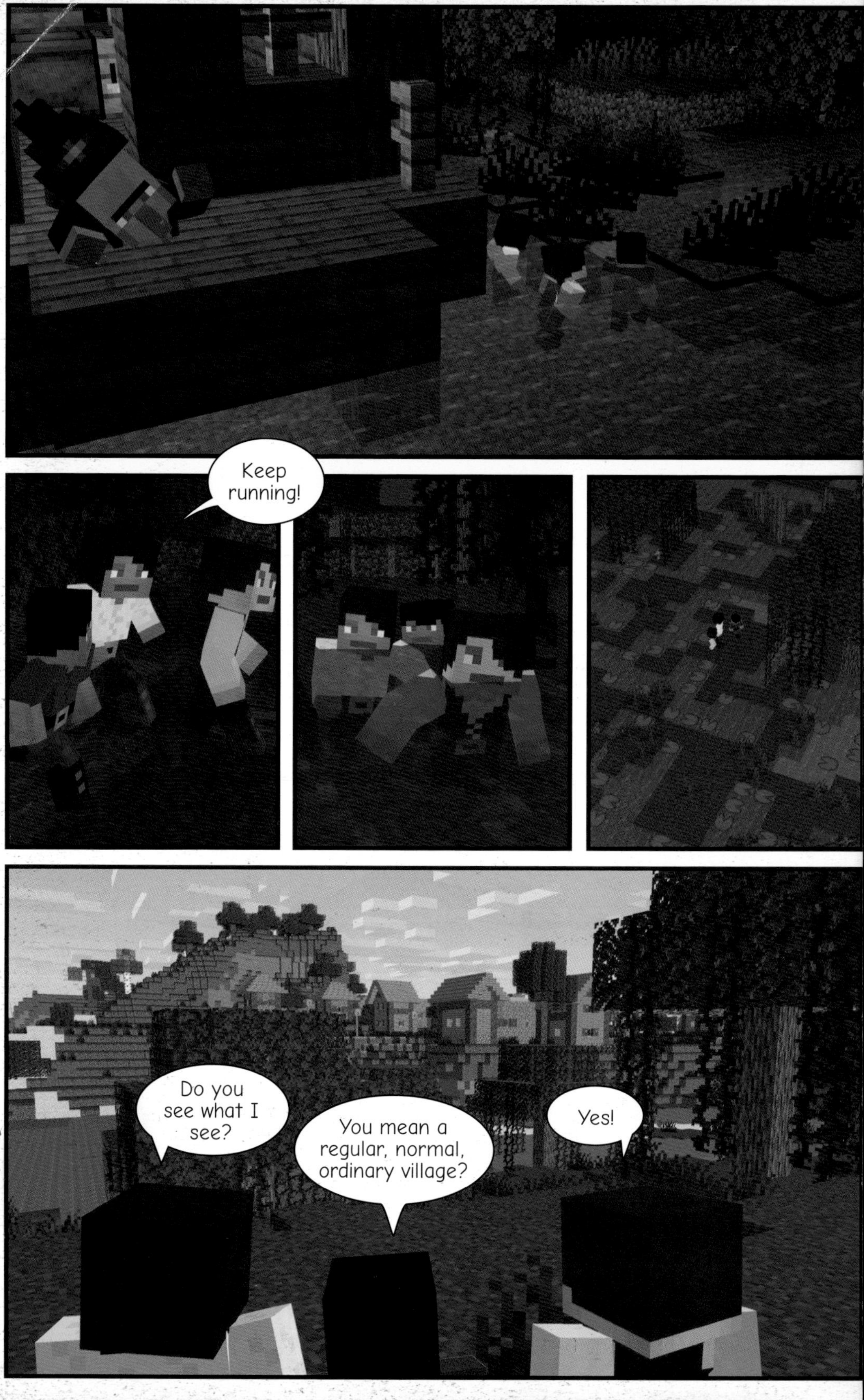
Keep running!
Do you see what I see?
You mean a regular, normal, ordinary village?
Yes!

Chapter 8
Swamp's Edge

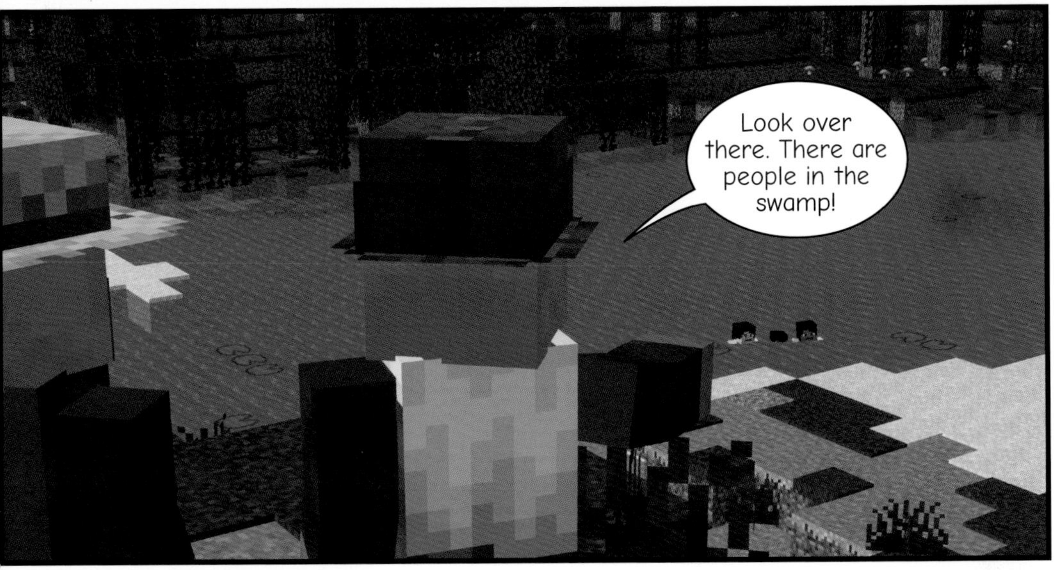
Look over there. There are people in the swamp!

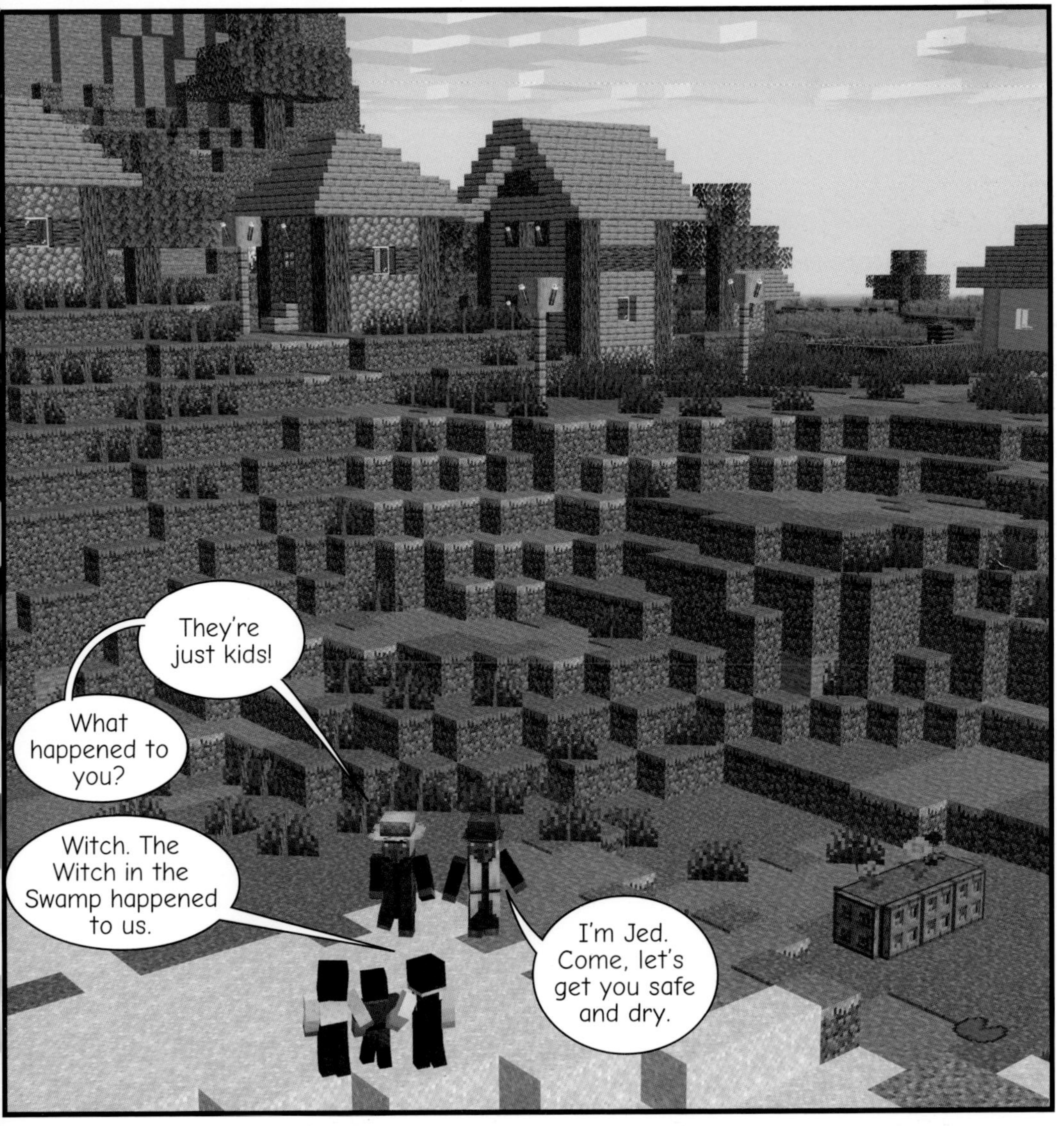
They're just kids!
What happened to you?
Witch. The Witch in the Swamp happened to us.
I'm Jed. Come, let's get you safe and dry.

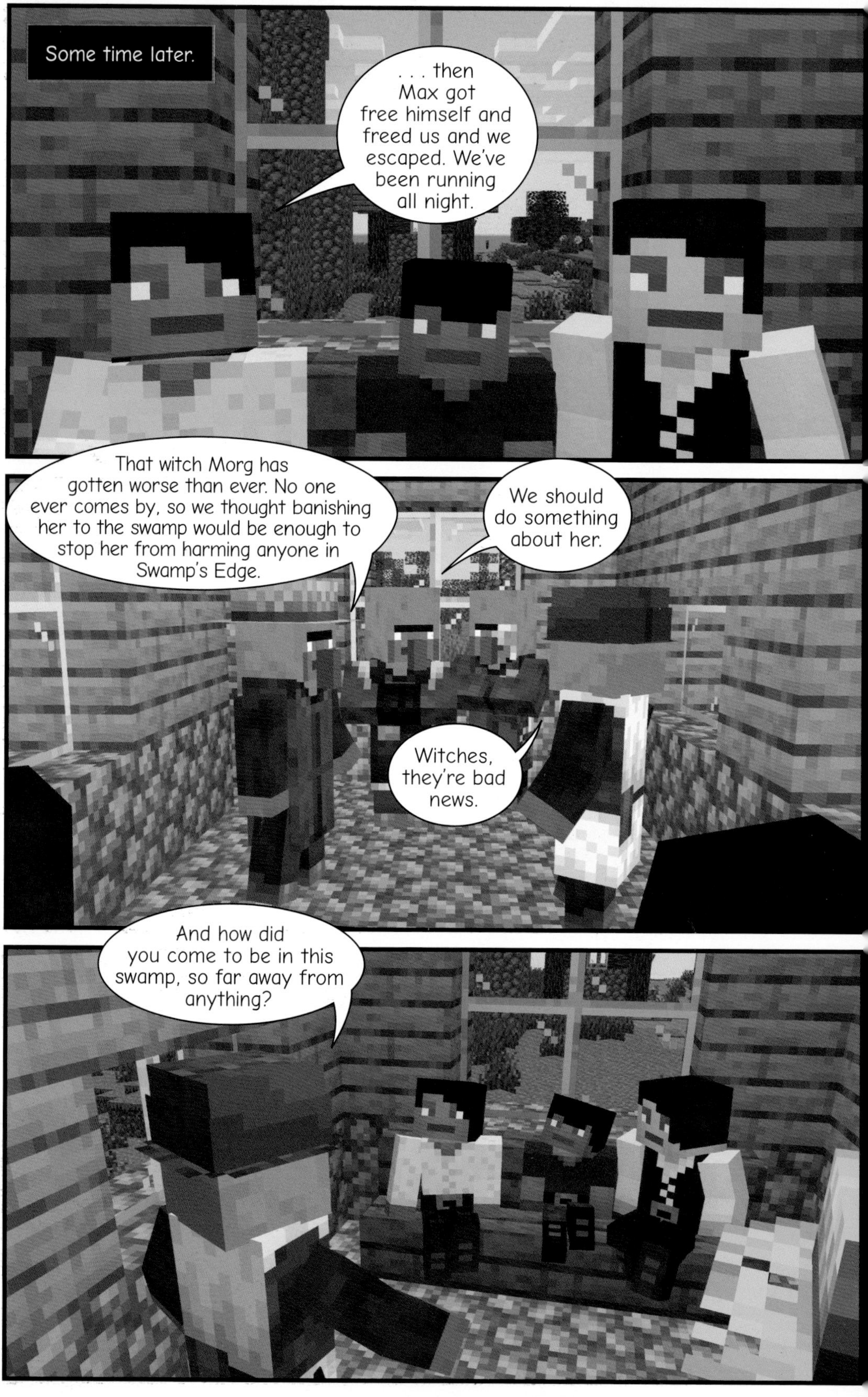
Some time later.
. . . then Max got free himself and freed us and we escaped. We've been running all night.
That witch Morg has gotten worse than ever. No one ever comes by, so we thought banishing her to the swamp would be enough to stop her from harming anyone in Swamp's Edge.
We should do something about her.
Witches, they're bad news.
And how did you come to be in this swamp, so far away from anything?

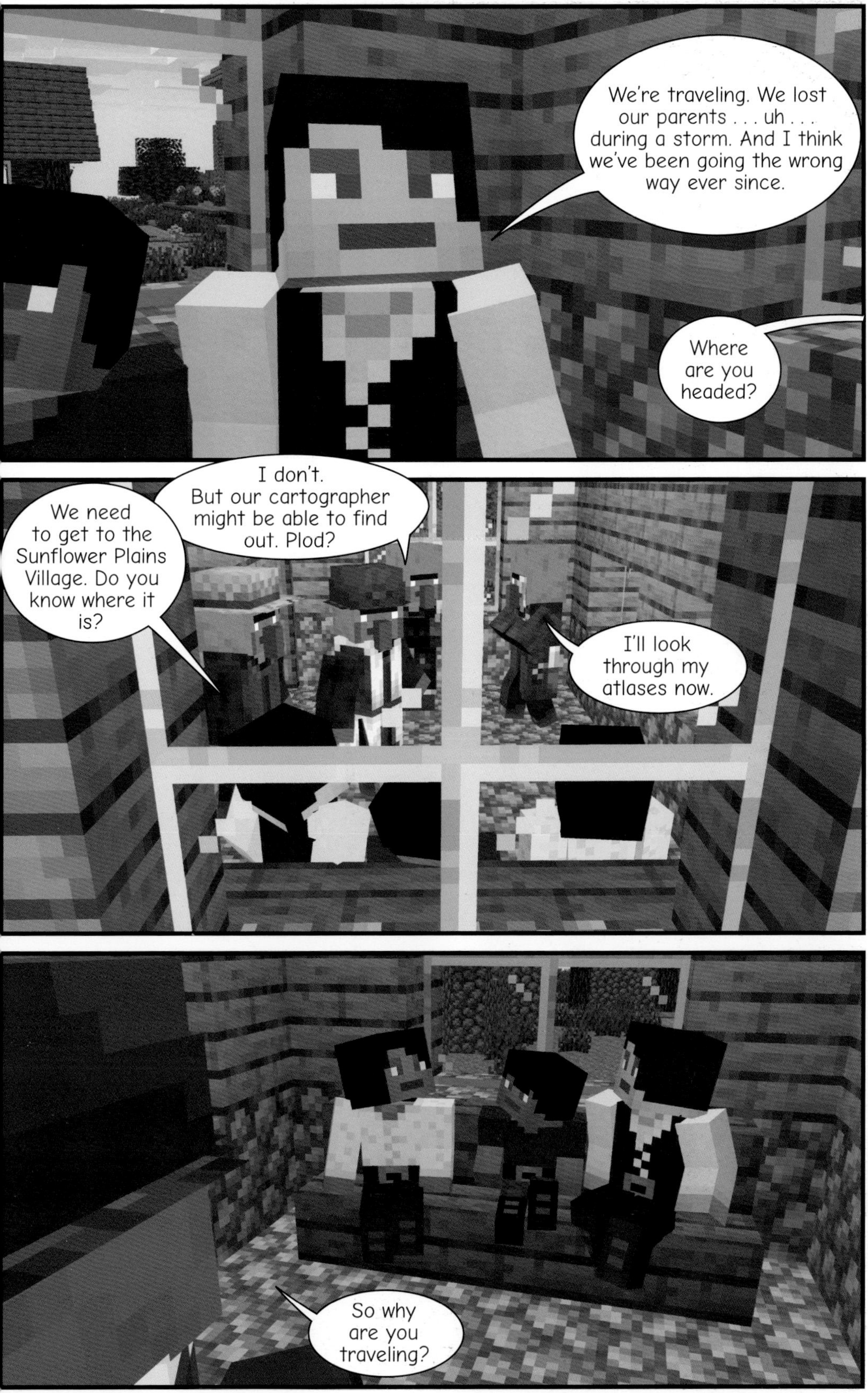
We're traveling. We lost our parents . . . uh . . . during a storm. And I think we've been going the wrong way ever since.
Where are you headed?
We need to get to the Sunflower Plains Village. Do you know where it is?
I don't. But our cartographer might be able to find out. Plod?
I'll look through my atlases now.
So why are you traveling?

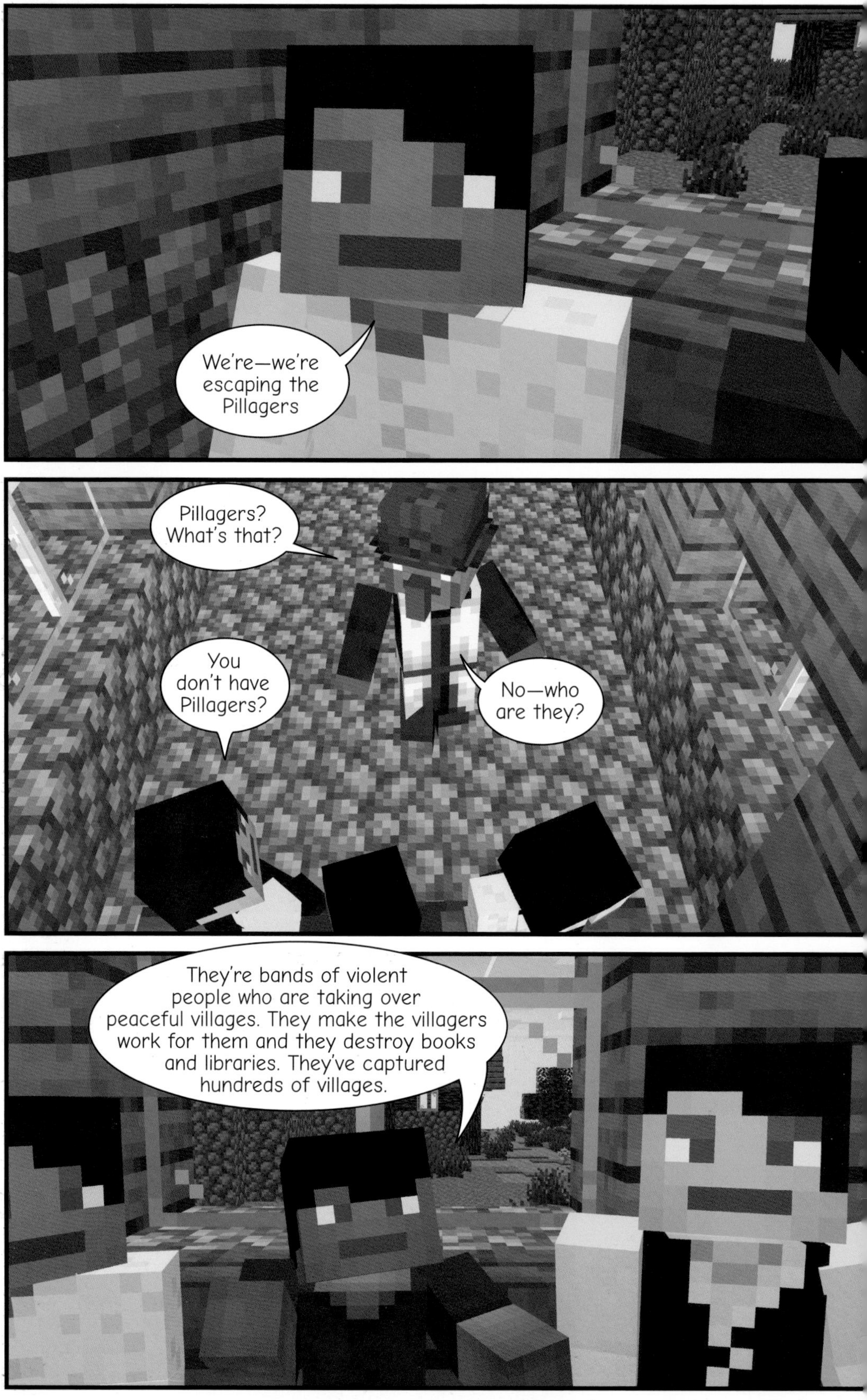
We're—we're escaping the Pillagers
Pillagers? What's that?
You don't have Pillagers?
No—who are they?
They're bands of violent people who are taking over peaceful villages. They make the villagers work for them and they destroy books and libraries. They've captured hundreds of villages.

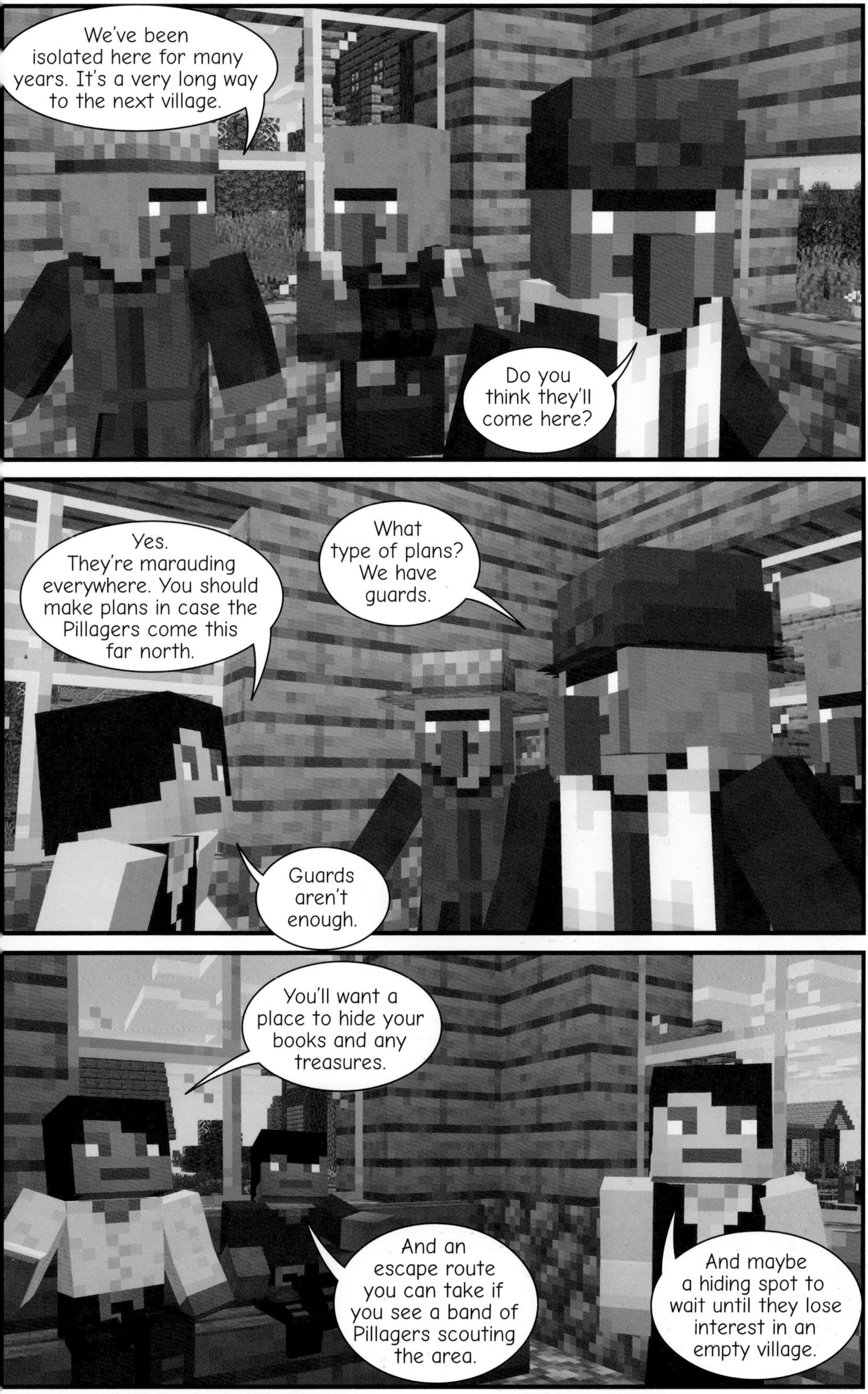
We've been isolated here for many years. It's a very long way to the next village.
Do you think they'll come here?
Yes. They're marauding everywhere. You should make plans in case the Pillagers come this far north.
What type of plans? We have guards.
Guards aren't enough.
You'll want a place to hide your books and any treasures.
And an escape route you can take if you see a band of Pillagers scouting the area.
And maybe a hiding spot to wait until they lose interest in an empty village.

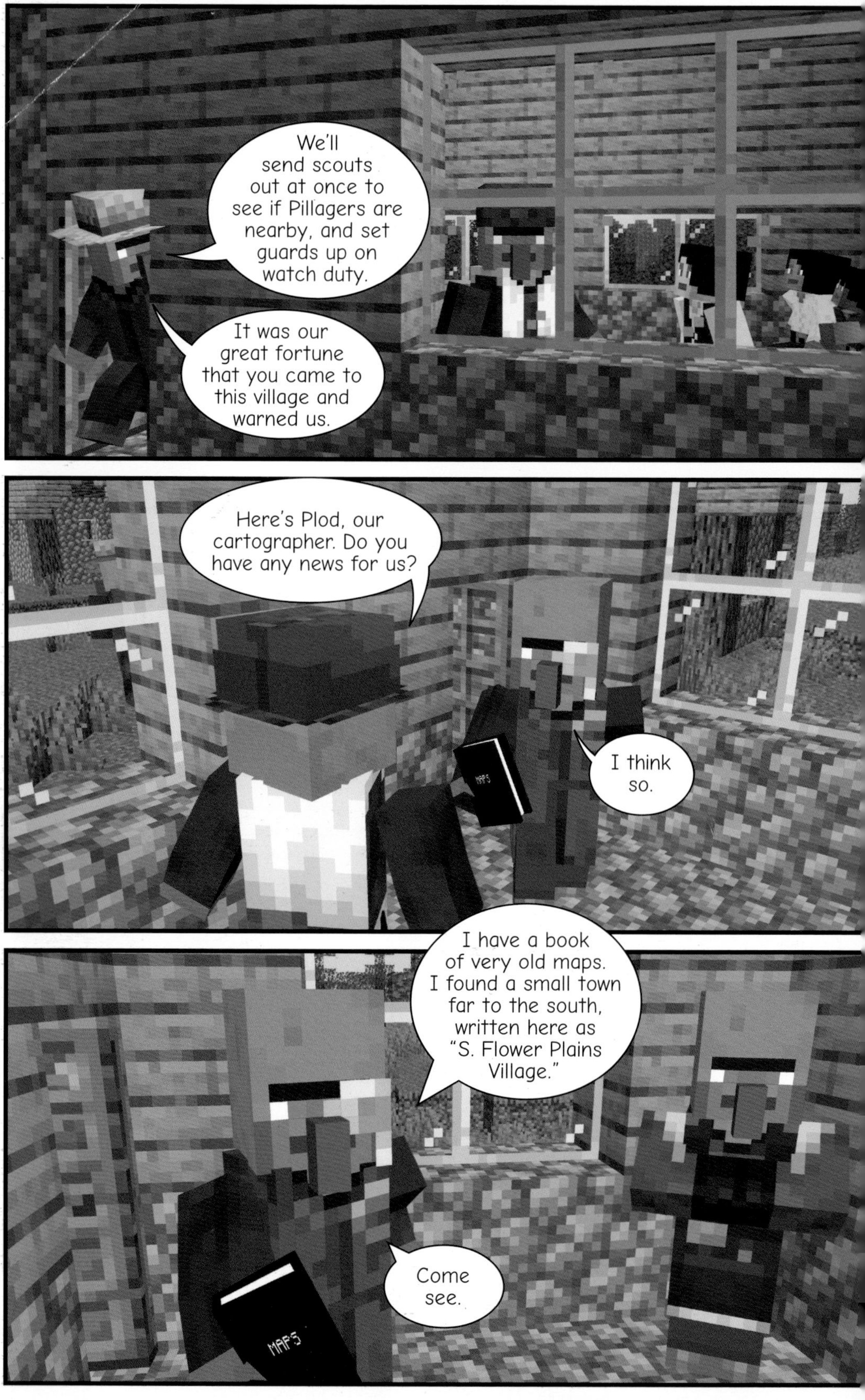
We'll send scouts out at once to see if Pillagers are nearby, and set guards up on watch duty.
It was our great fortune that you came to this village and warned us.
Here's Plod, our cartographer. Do you have any news for us?
MAPS
I think so.
I have a book of very old maps. I found a small town far to the south, written here as "S. Flower Plains Village."
Come see.
MAPS

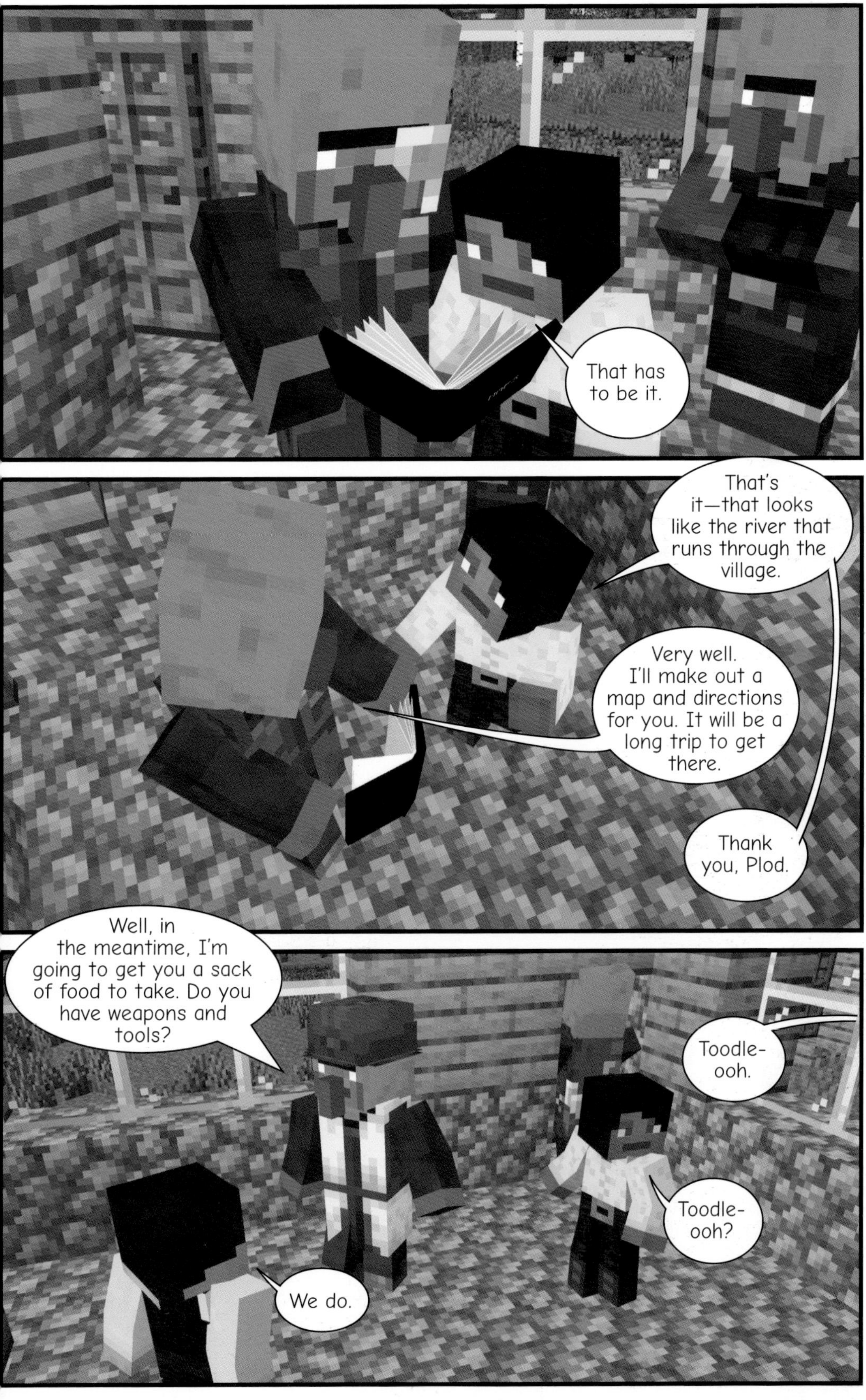
That has to be it.
That's it—that looks like the river that runs through the village.
Very well. I'll make out a map and directions for you. It will be a long trip to get there.
Thank you, Plod.
Well, in the meantime, I'm going to get you a sack of food to take. Do you have weapons and tools?
Toodle-ooh.
Toodle-ooh?
We do.

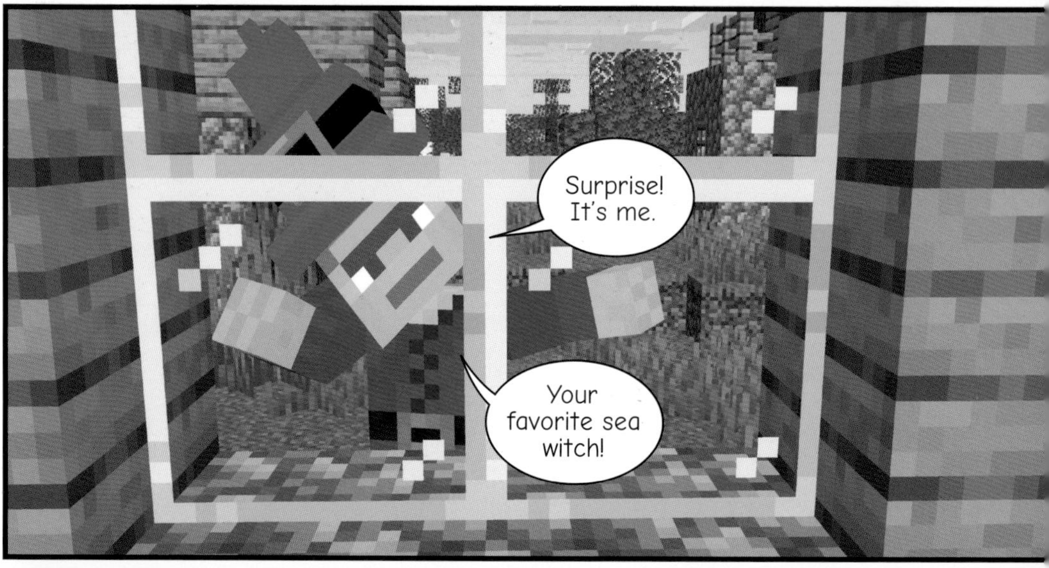
Surprise! It's me.
Your favorite sea witch!

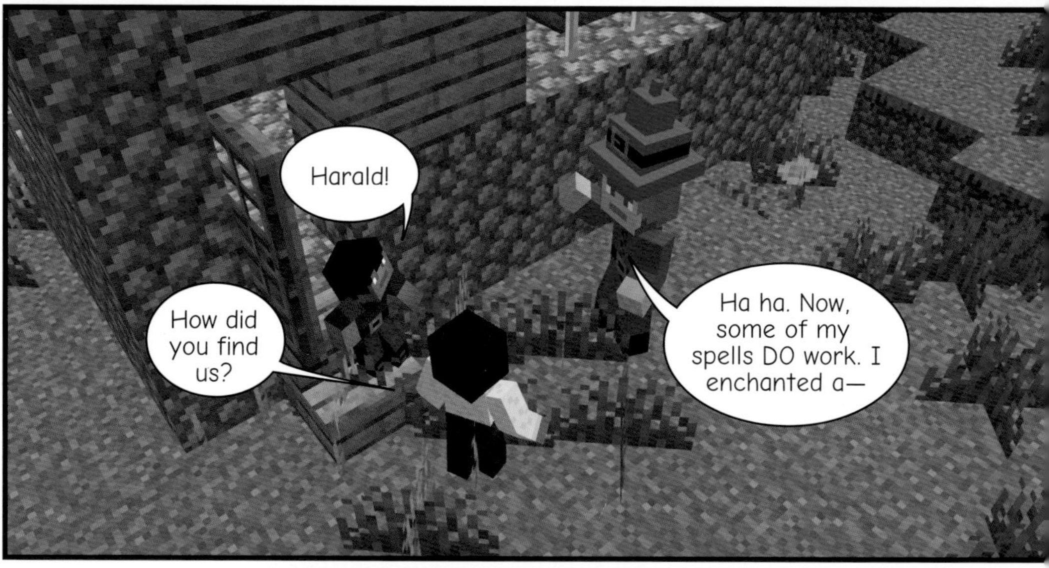
Harald!
How did you find us?
Ha ha. Now, some of my spells DO work. I enchanted a—

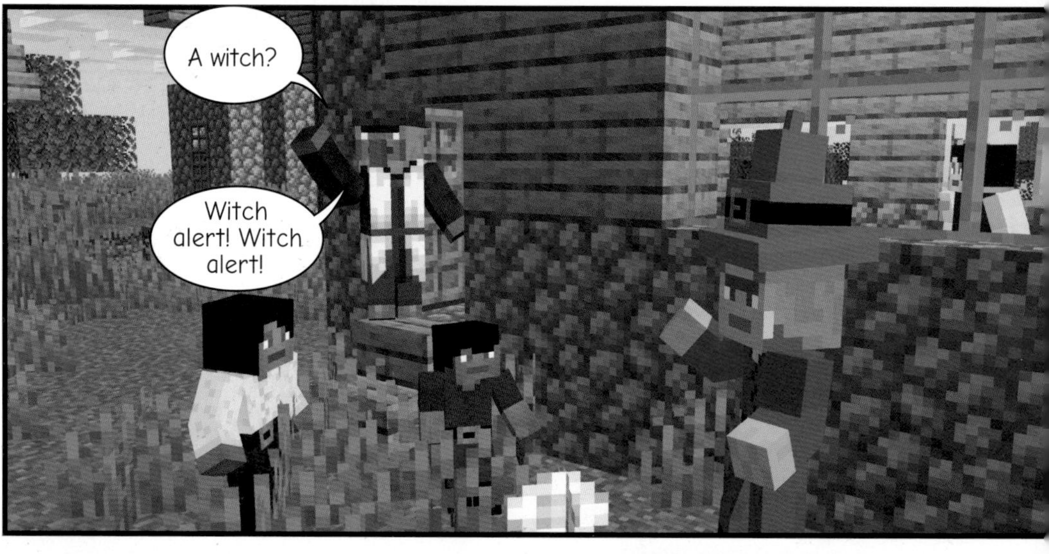
A witch?
Witch alert! Witch alert!

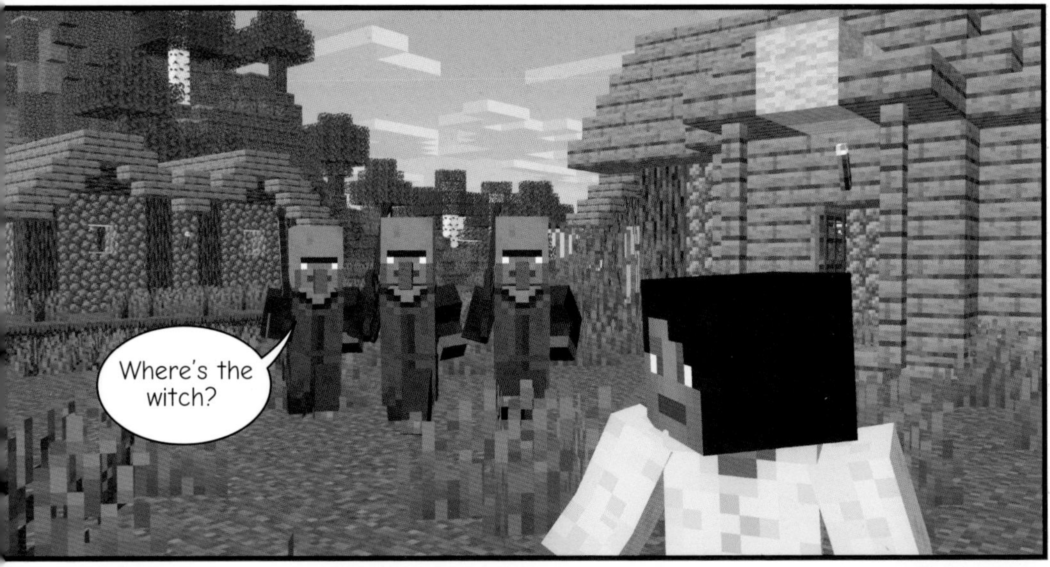
Where's the witch?

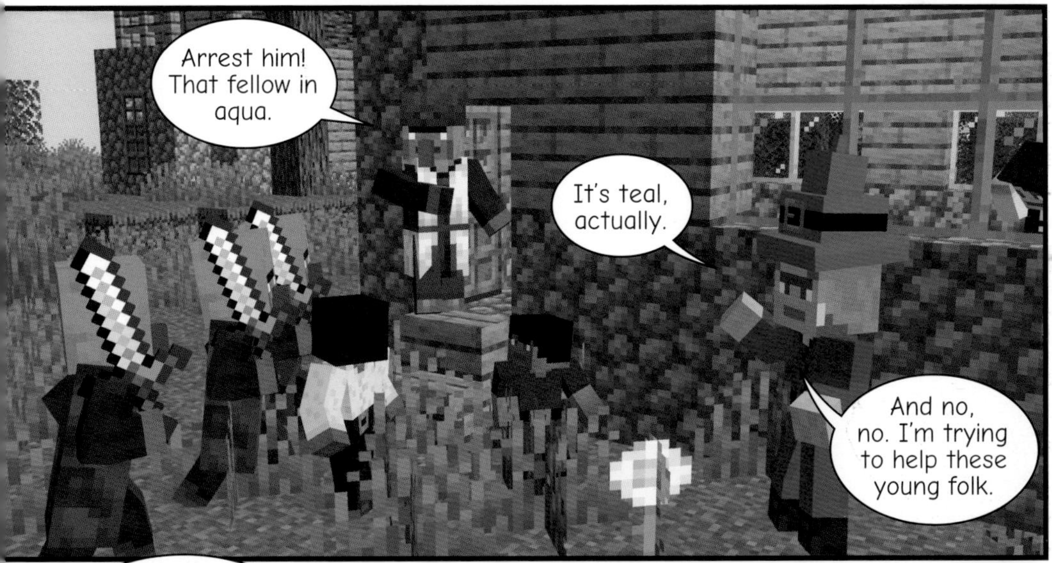
Arrest him! That fellow in aqua.
It's teal, actually.
And no, no. I'm trying to help these young folk.

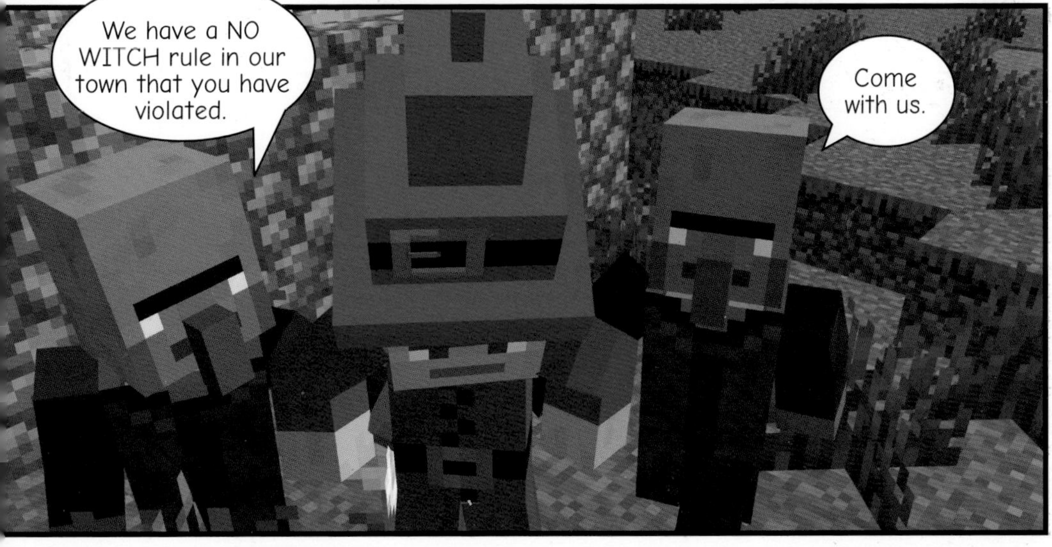
We have a NO WITCH rule in our town that you have violated.
Come with us.

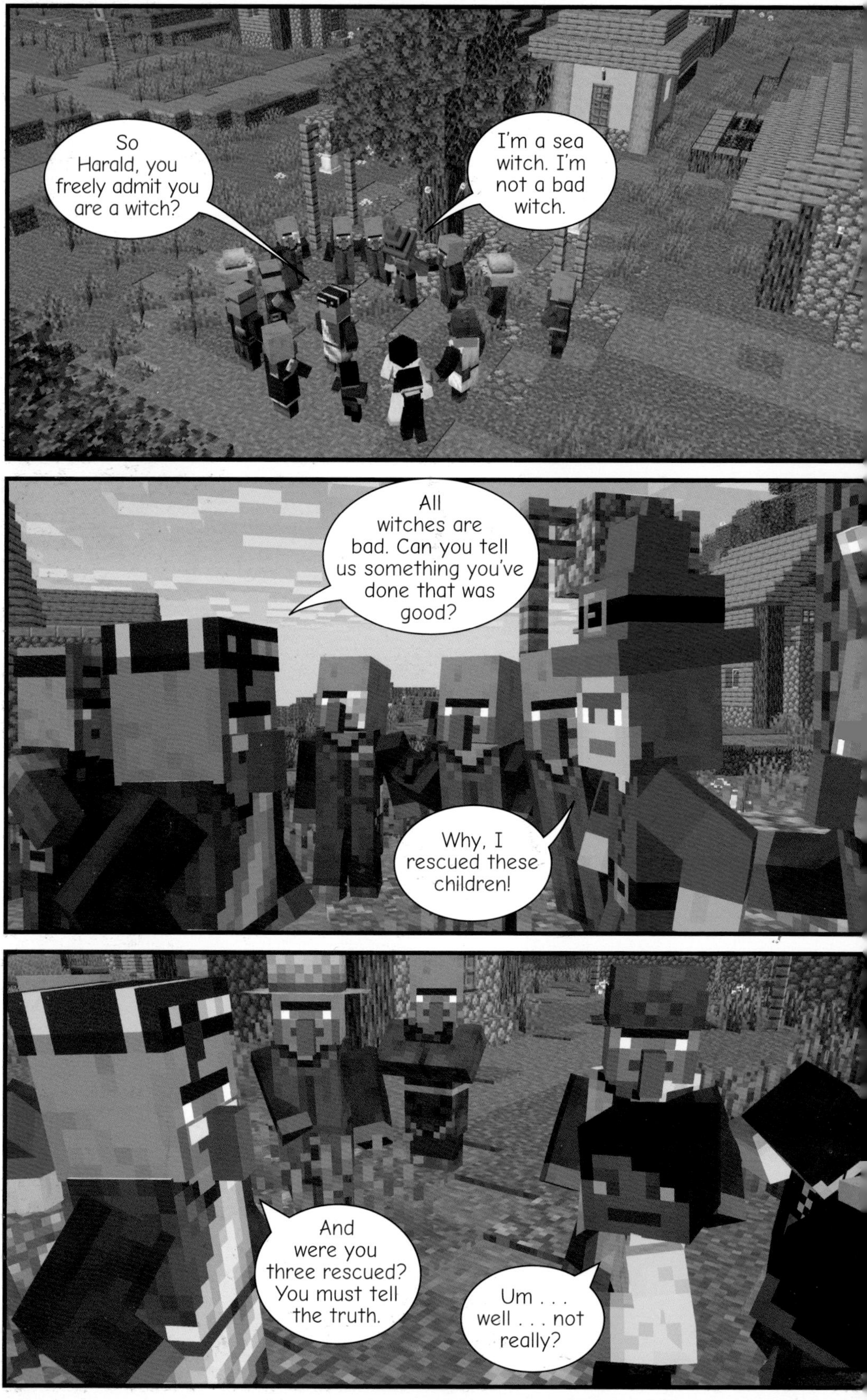
So Harald, you freely admit you are a witch?
I'm a sea witch. I'm not a bad witch.
All witches are bad. Can you tell us something you've done that was good?
Why, I rescued these children!
And were you three rescued? You must tell the truth.
Um . . . well . . . not really?

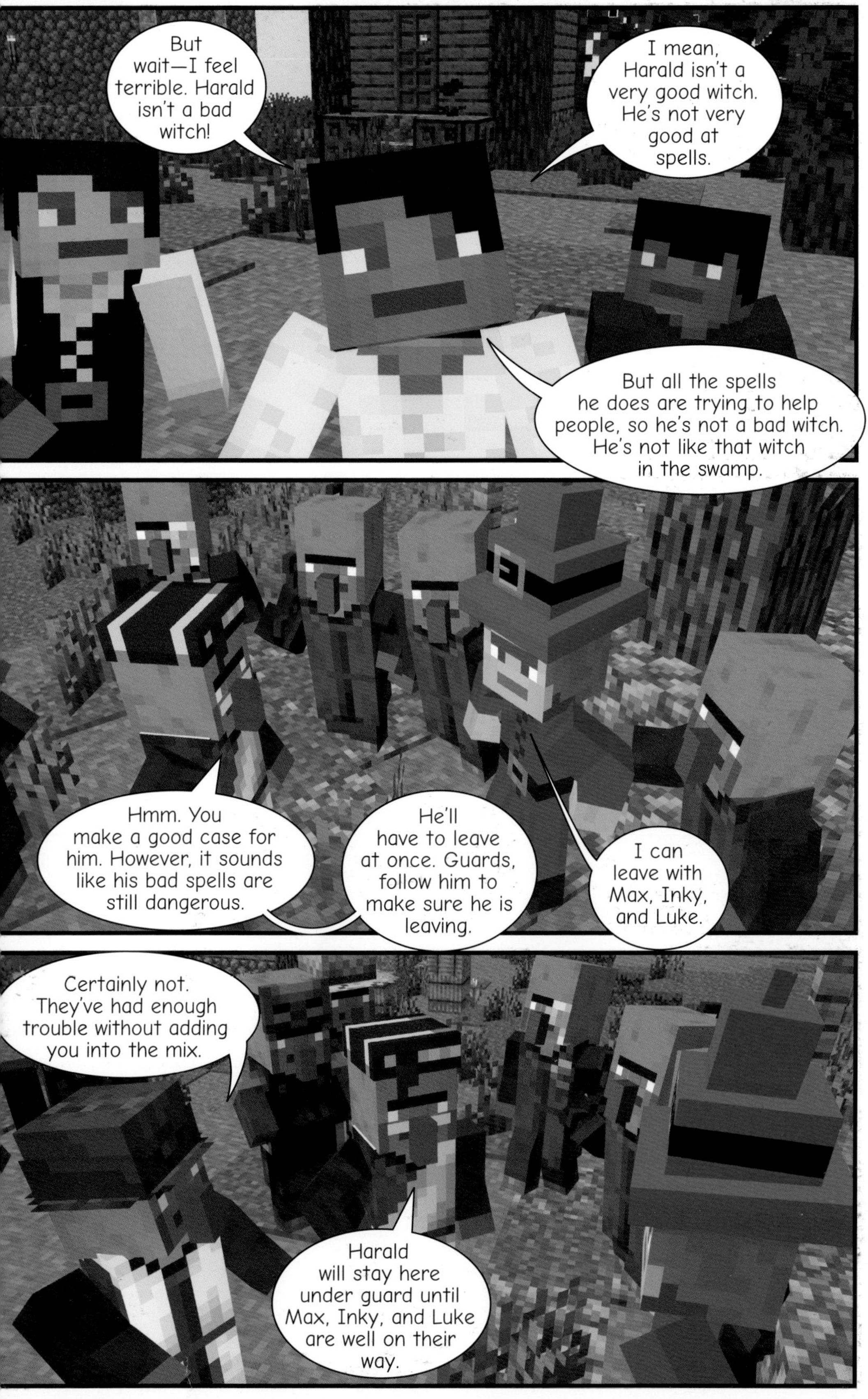
But wait—I feel terrible. Harald isn't a bad witch!
I mean, Harald isn't a very good witch. He's not very good at spells.
But all the spells he does are trying to help people, so he's not a bad witch. He's not like that witch in the swamp.
Hmm. You make a good case for him. However, it sounds like his bad spells are still dangerous.
He'll have to leave at once. Guards, follow him to make sure he is leaving.
I can leave with Max, Inky, and Luke.
Certainly not. They've had enough trouble without adding you into the mix.
Harald will stay here under guard until Max, Inky, and Luke are well on their way.

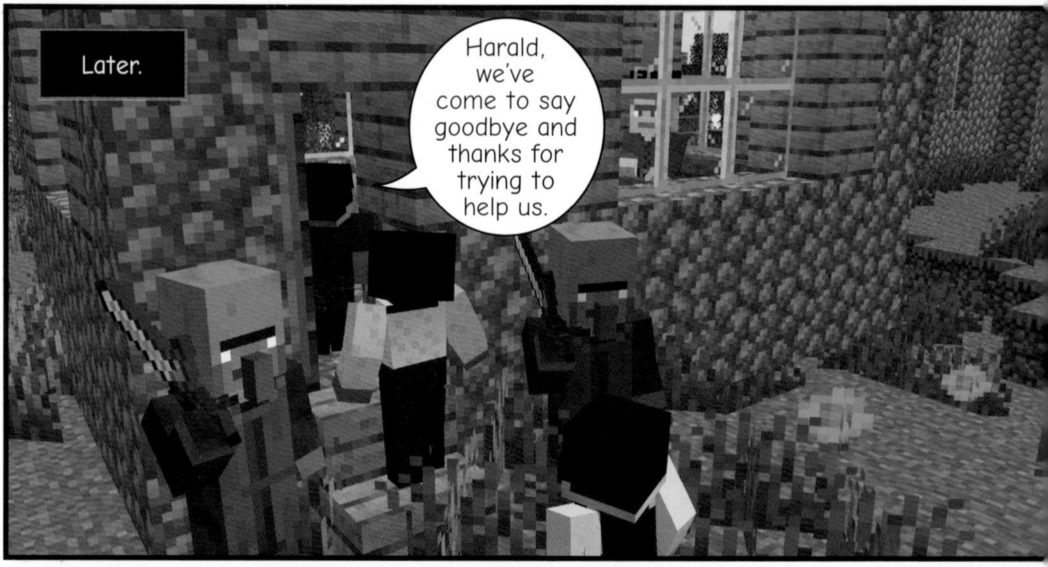
Later.
Harald, we've come to say goodbye and thanks for trying to help us.

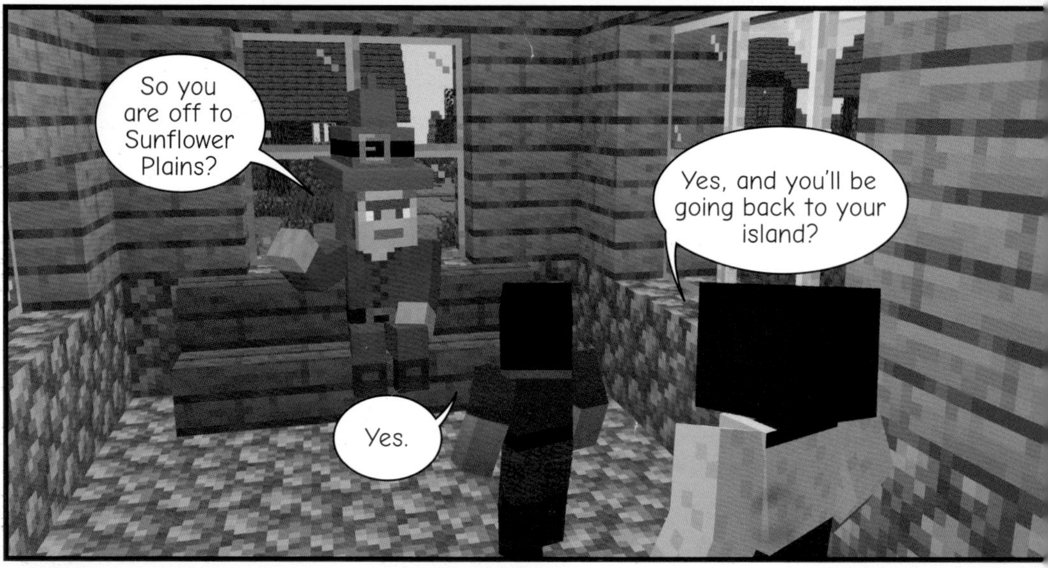
So you are off to Sunflower Plains?
Yes, and you'll be going back to your island?
Yes.

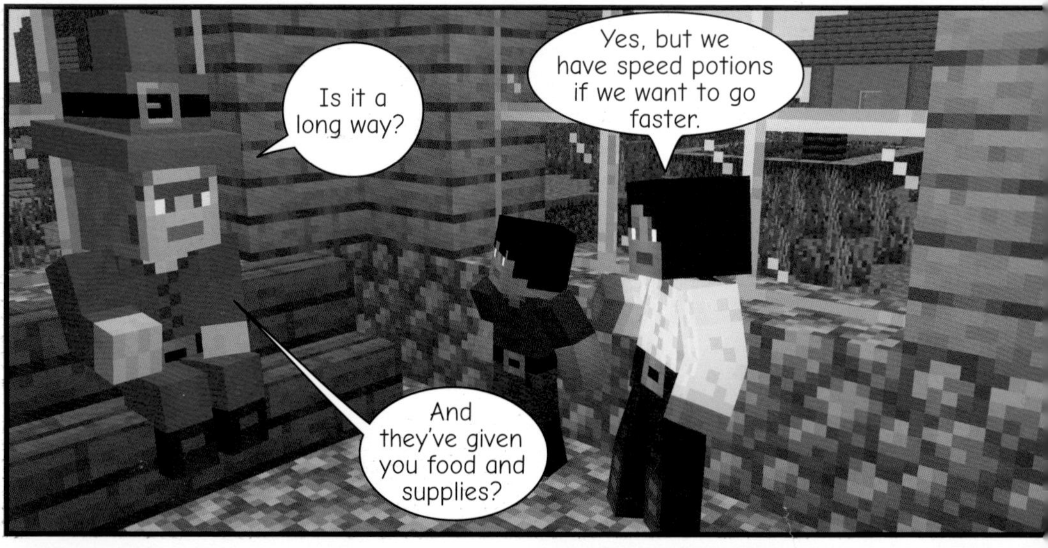
Is it a long way?
Yes, but we have speed potions if we want to go faster.
And they've given you food and supplies?

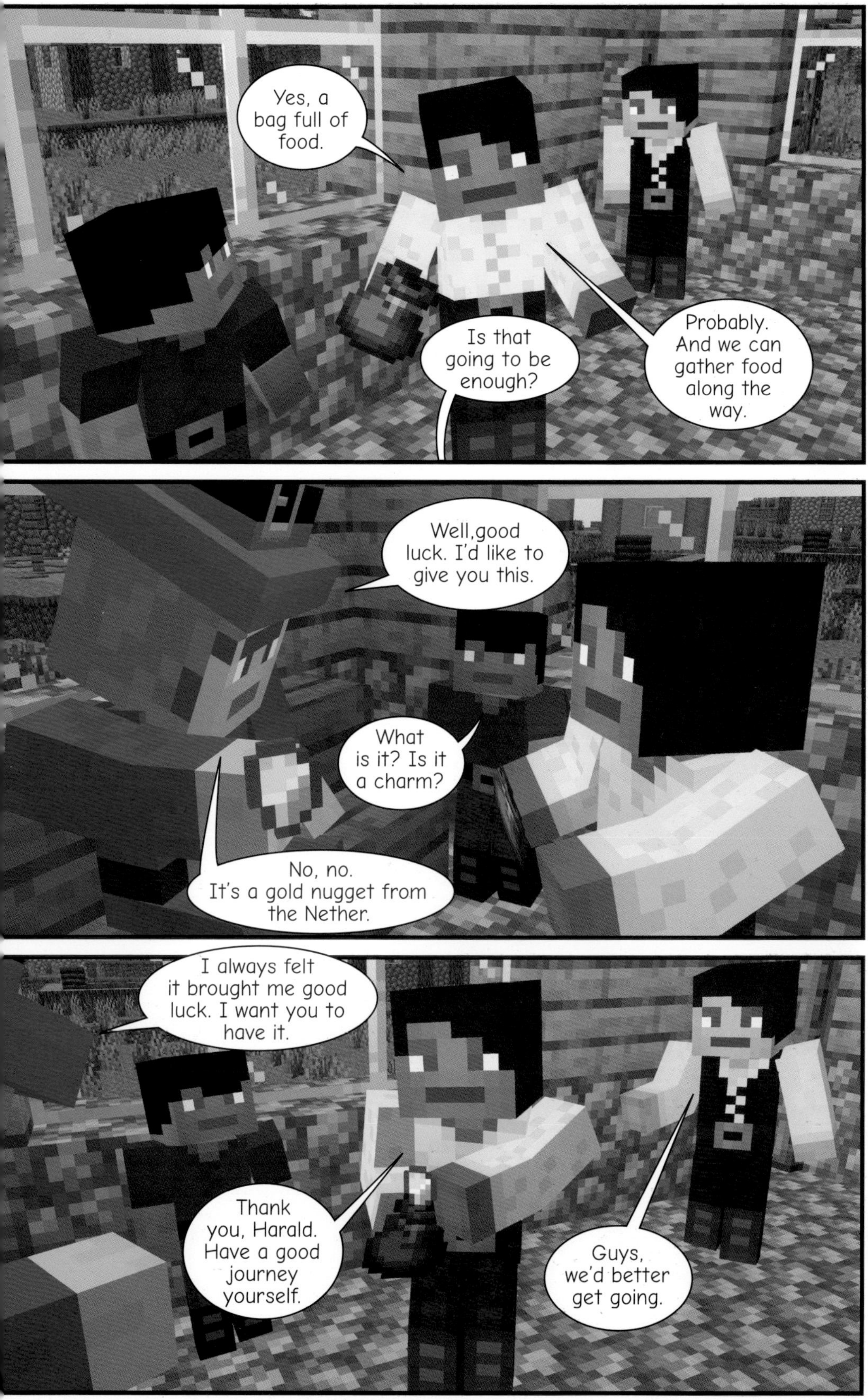

Yes, a bag full of food.
Is that going to be enough?
Probably. And we can gather food along the way.
Well,good luck. I'd like to give you this.
What is it? Is it a charm?
No, no. It's a gold nugget from the Nether.
I always felt it brought me good luck. I want you to have it.
Thank you, Harald. Have a good journey yourself.
Guys, we'd better get going.

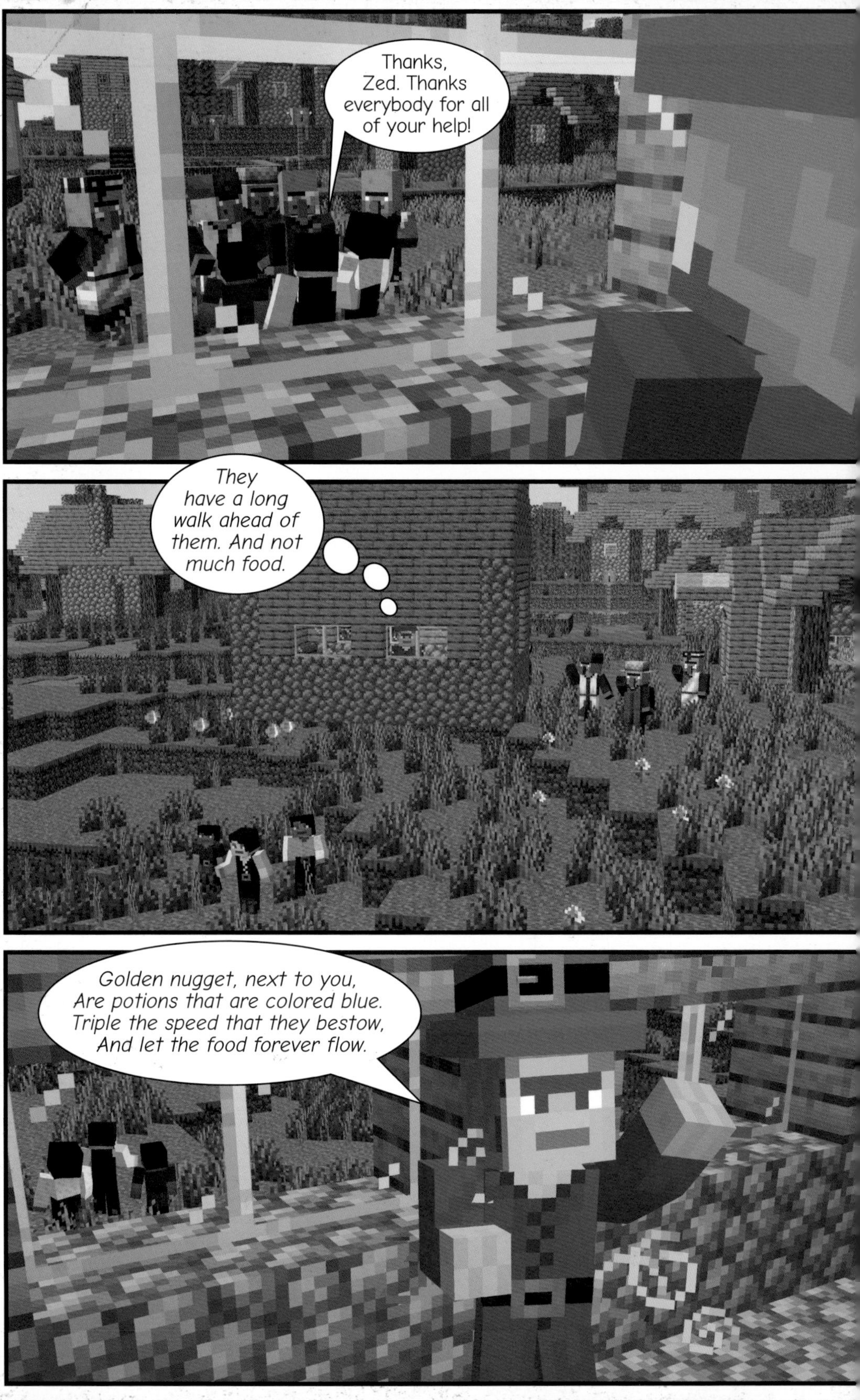
Thanks, Zed. Thanks everybody for all of your help!
They have a long walk ahead of them. And not much food.
Golden nugget, next to you, Are potions that are colored blue. Triple the speed that they bestow, And let the food forever flow.

Chapter 9
To Sunflower
Plains

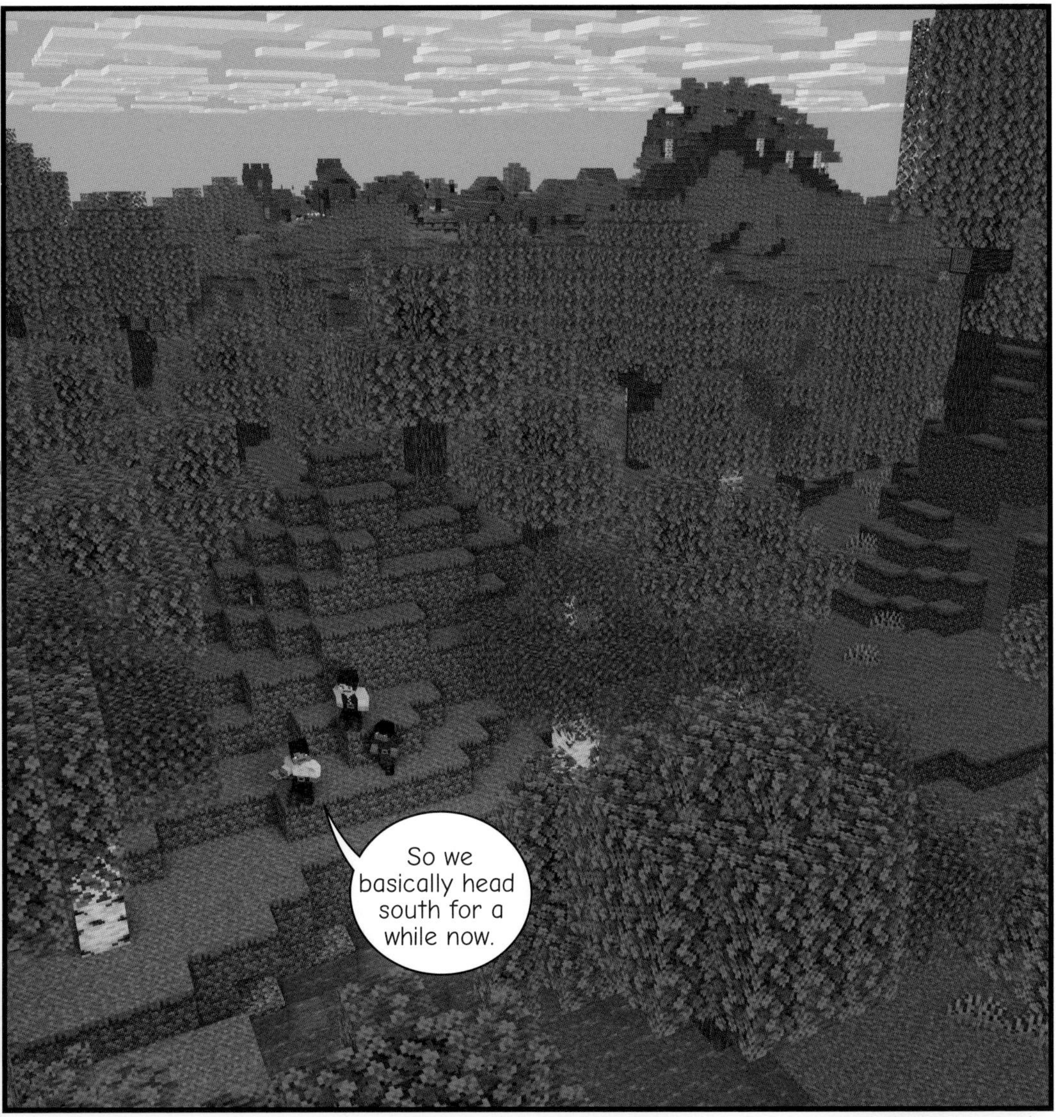
So we basically head south for a while now.

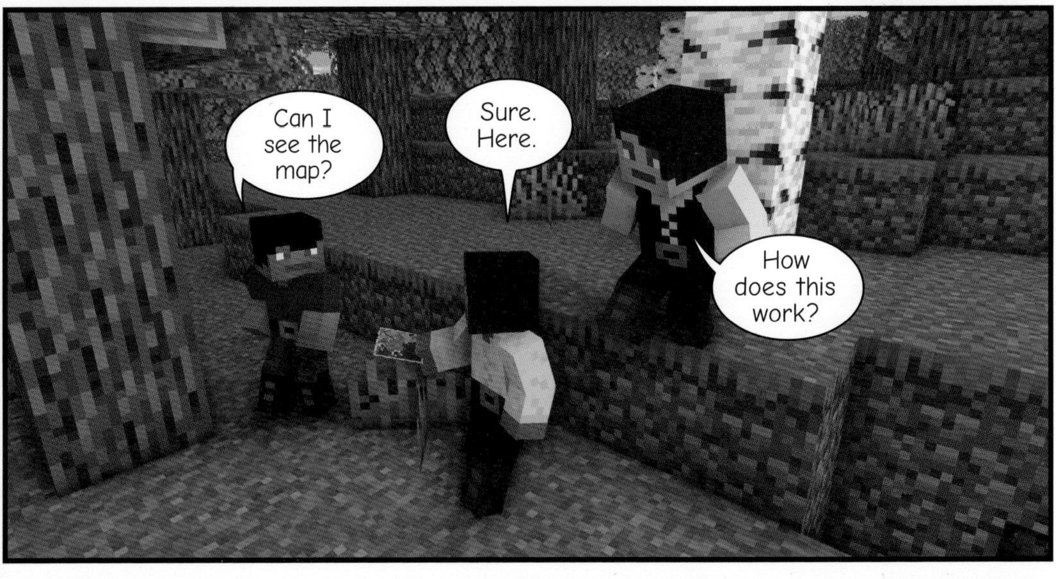
Can I see the map?
Sure. Here.
How does this work?

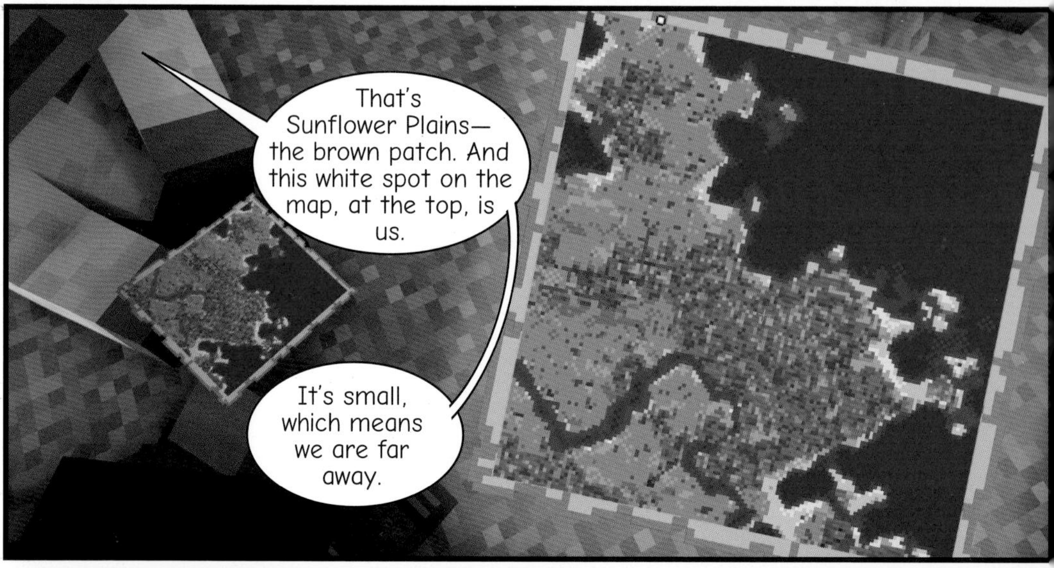
That's Sunflower Plains—the brown patch. And this white spot on the map, at the top, is us.
It's small, which means we are far away.

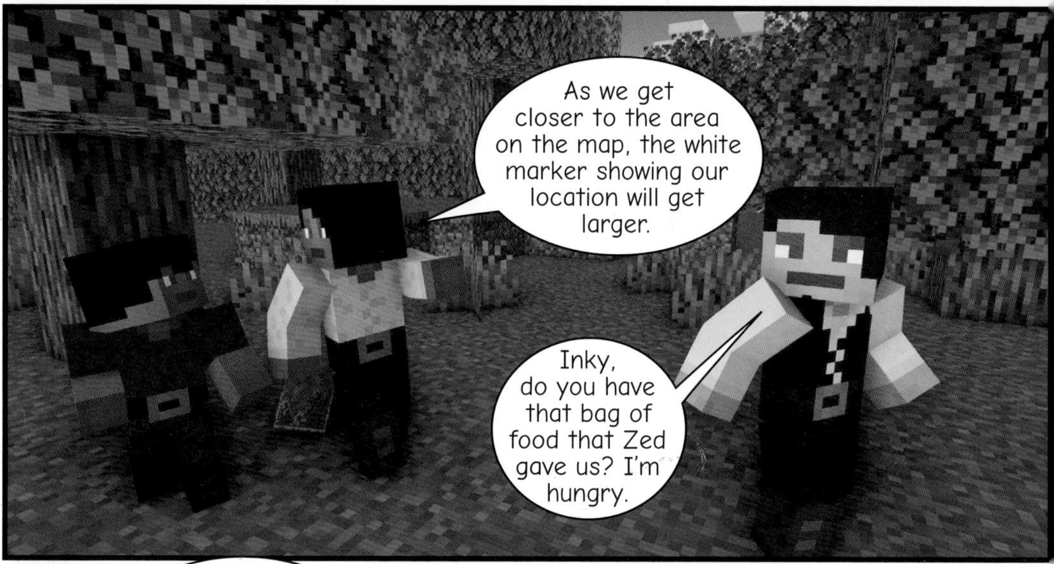
As we get closer to the area on the map, the white marker showing our location will get larger.
Inky, do you have that bag of food that Zed gave us? I'm hungry.

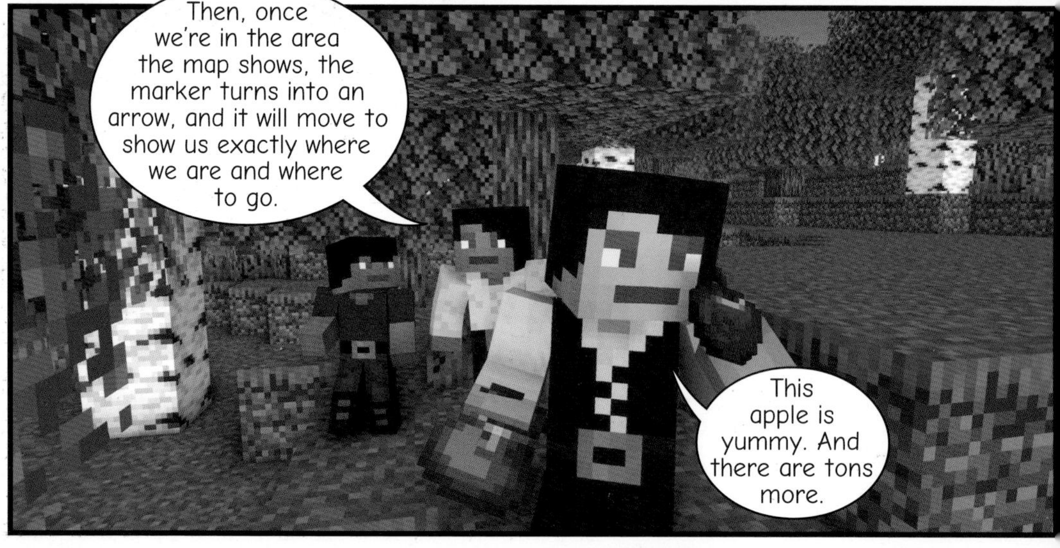
Then, once we're in the area the map shows, the marker turns into an arrow, and it will move to show us exactly where we are and where to go.
This apple is yummy. And there are tons more.

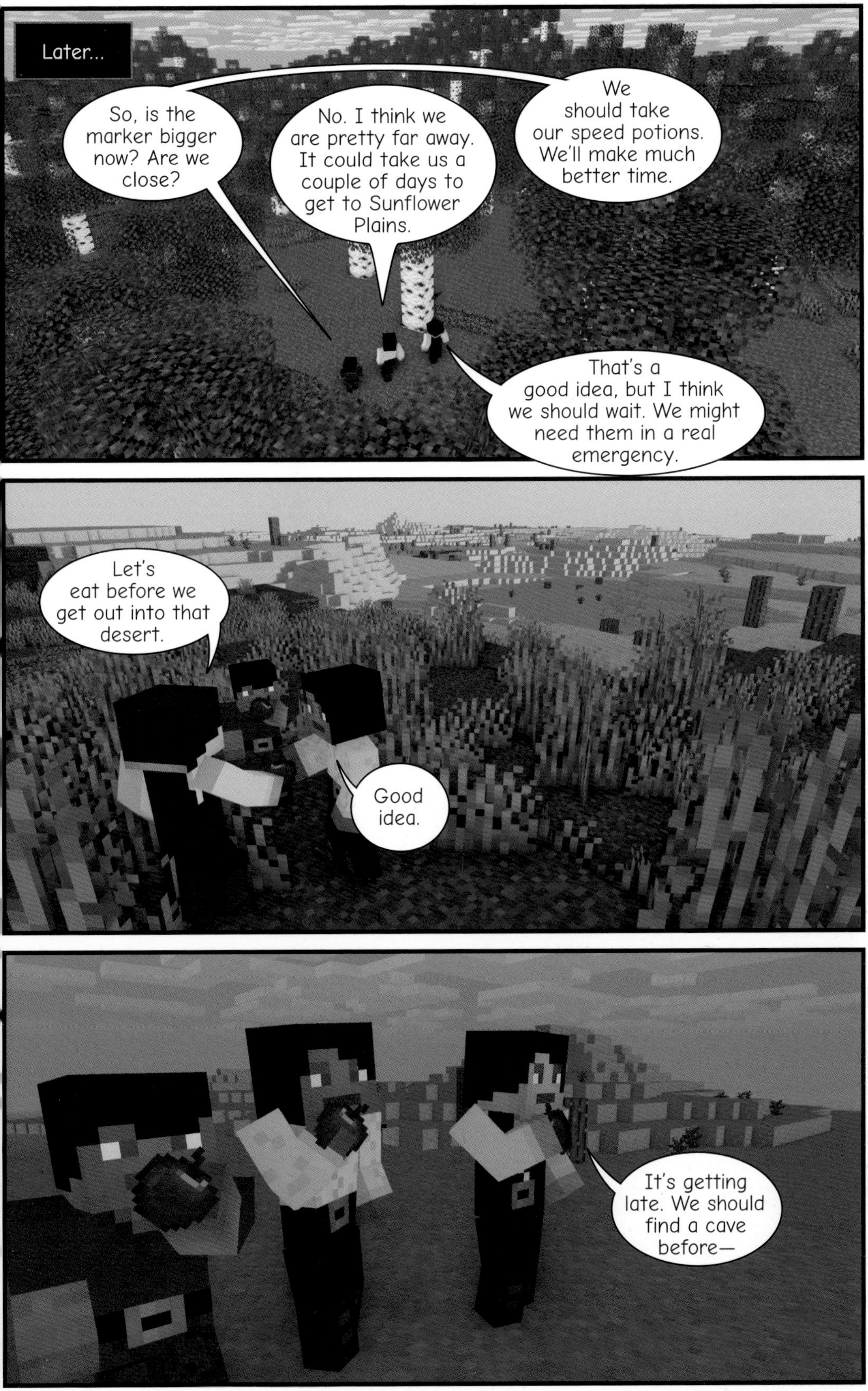
Later...
So, is the marker bigger now? Are we close?
No. I think we are pretty far away. It could take us a couple of days to get to Sunflower Plains.
We should take our speed potions. We'll make much better time.
That's a good idea, but I think we should wait. We might need them in a real emergency.
Let's eat before we get out into that desert.
Good idea.
It's getting late. We should find a cave before—

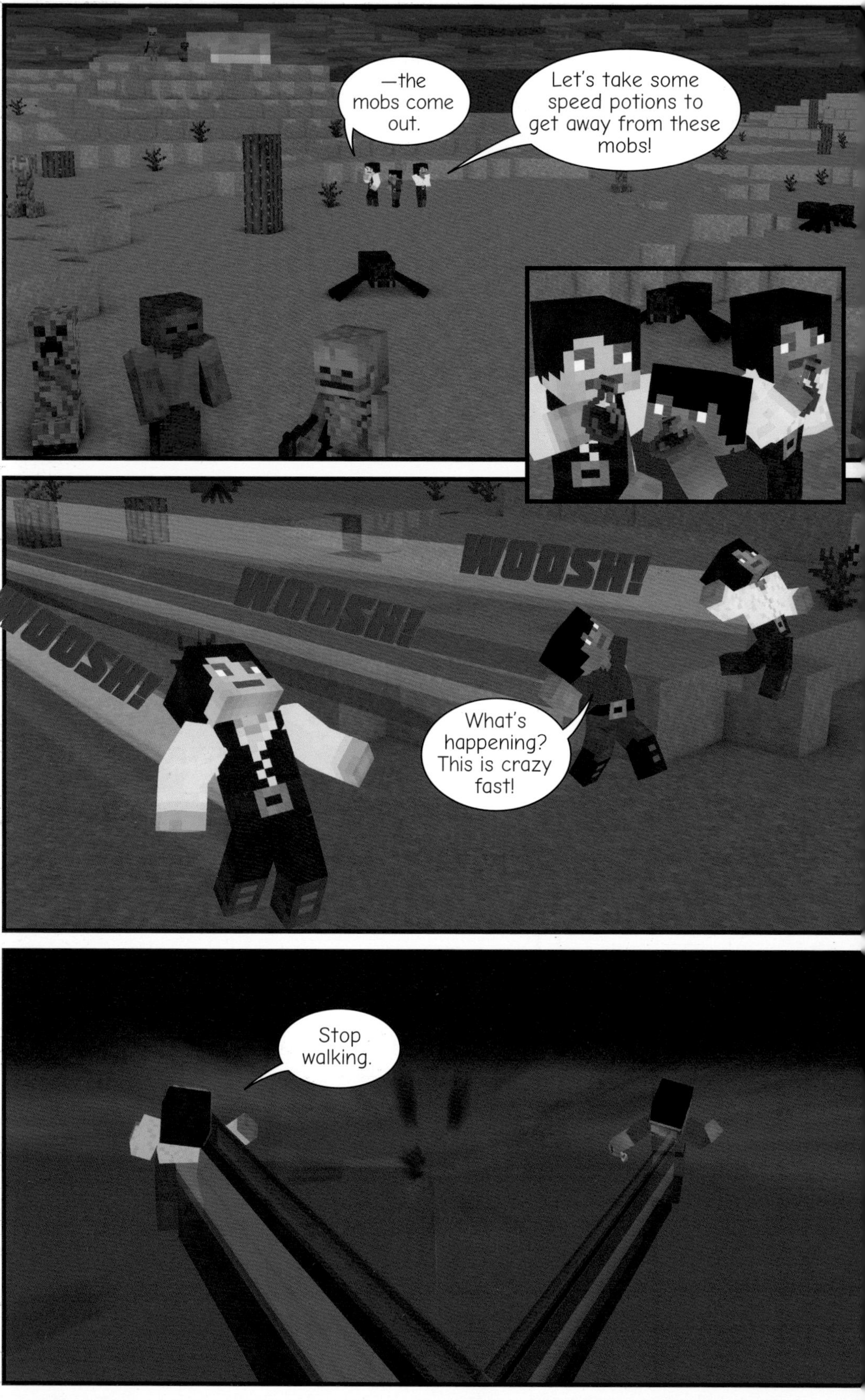
—the mobs come out.
Let's take some speed potions to get away from these mobs!
WOOSH!
WOOSH!
WOOSH!
What's happening? This is crazy fast!
Stop walking.

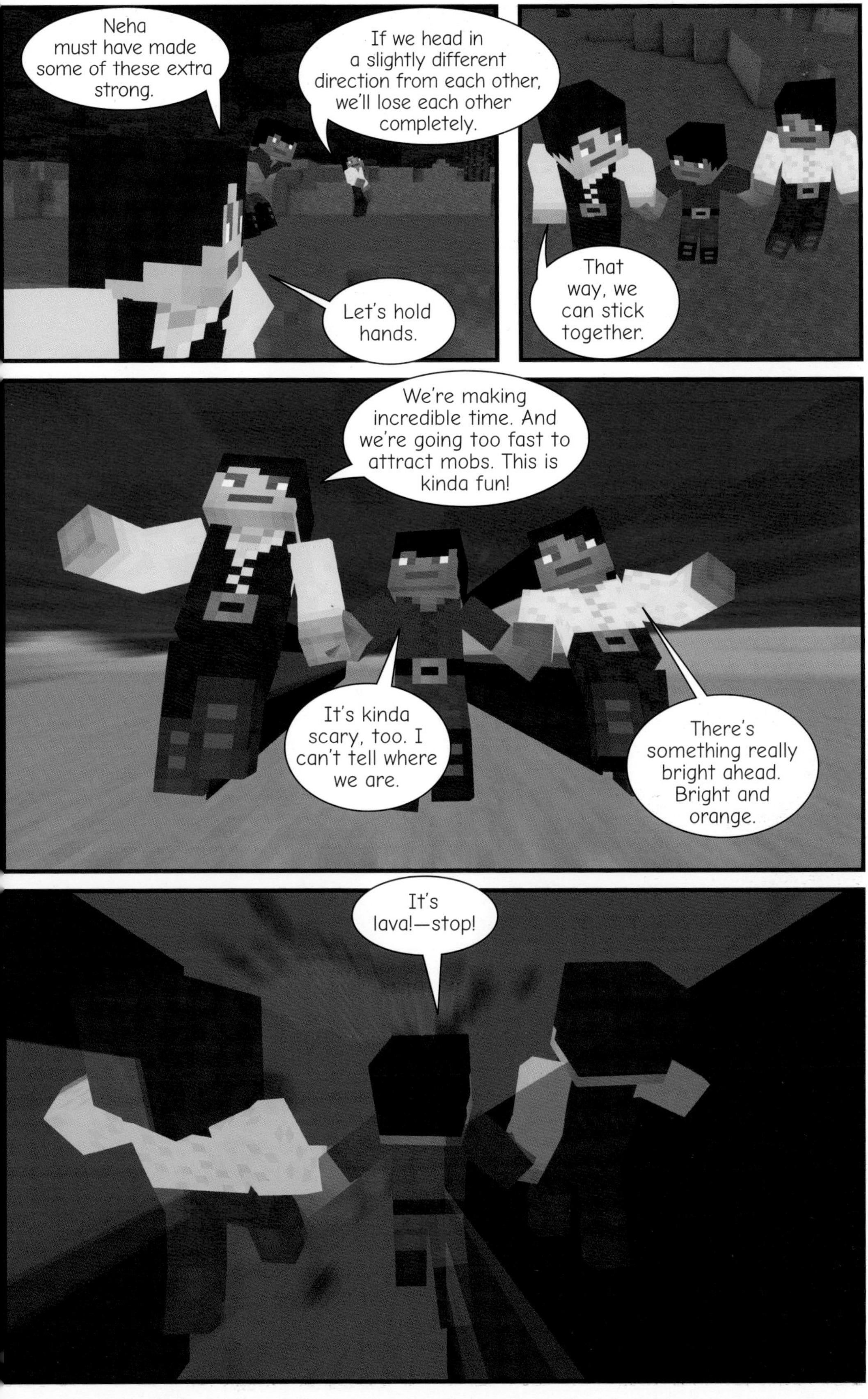
Neha must have made some of these extra strong.
If we head in a slightly different direction from each other, we'll lose each other completely.
Let's hold hands.
That way, we can stick together.
We're making incredible time. And we're going too fast to attract mobs. This is kinda fun!
It's kinda scary, too. I can't tell where we are.
There's something really bright ahead. Bright and orange.
It's lava!—stop!

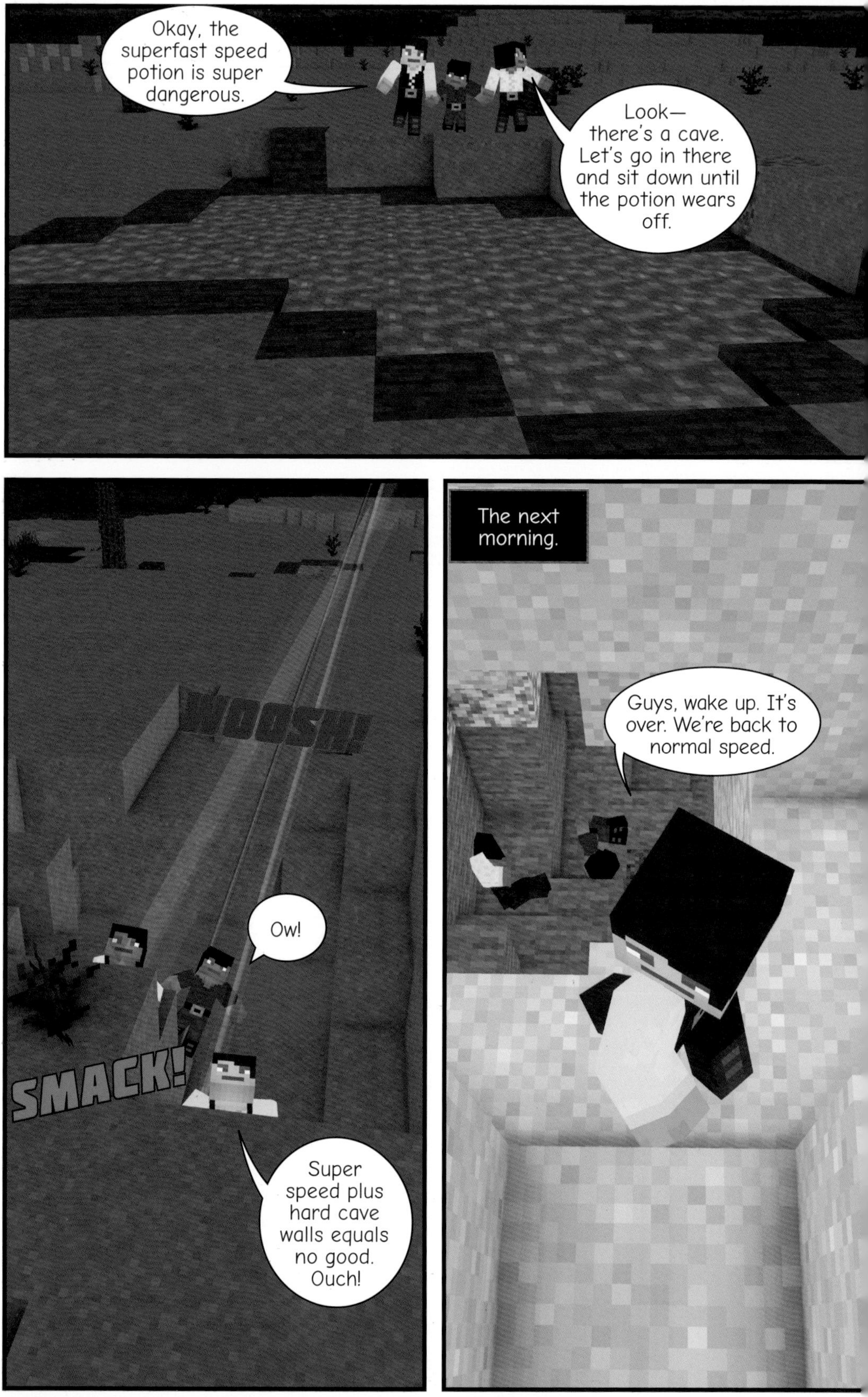
Okay, the superfast speed potion is super dangerous.
Look—there's a cave. Let's go in there and sit down until the potion wears off.
WOOSH!
Ow!
SMACK!
Super speed plus hard cave walls equals no good. Ouch!
The next morning.
Guys, wake up. It's over. We're back to normal speed.

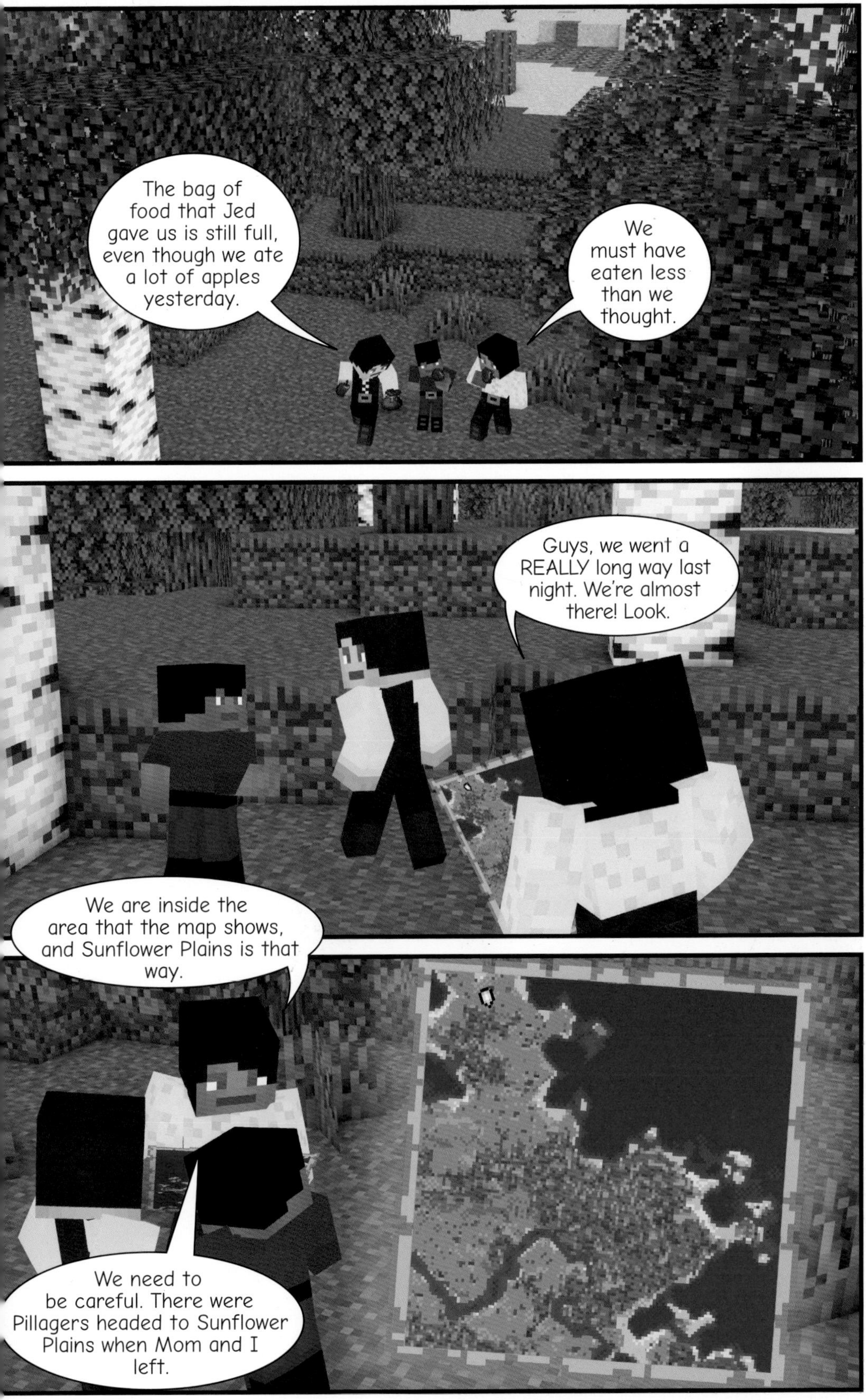

The bag of food that Jed gave us is still full, even though we ate a lot of apples yesterday.
We must have eaten less than we thought.
Guys, we went a REALLY long way last night. We're almost there! Look.
We are inside the area that the map shows, and Sunflower Plains is that way.
We need to be careful. There were Pillagers headed to Sunflower Plains when Mom and I left.

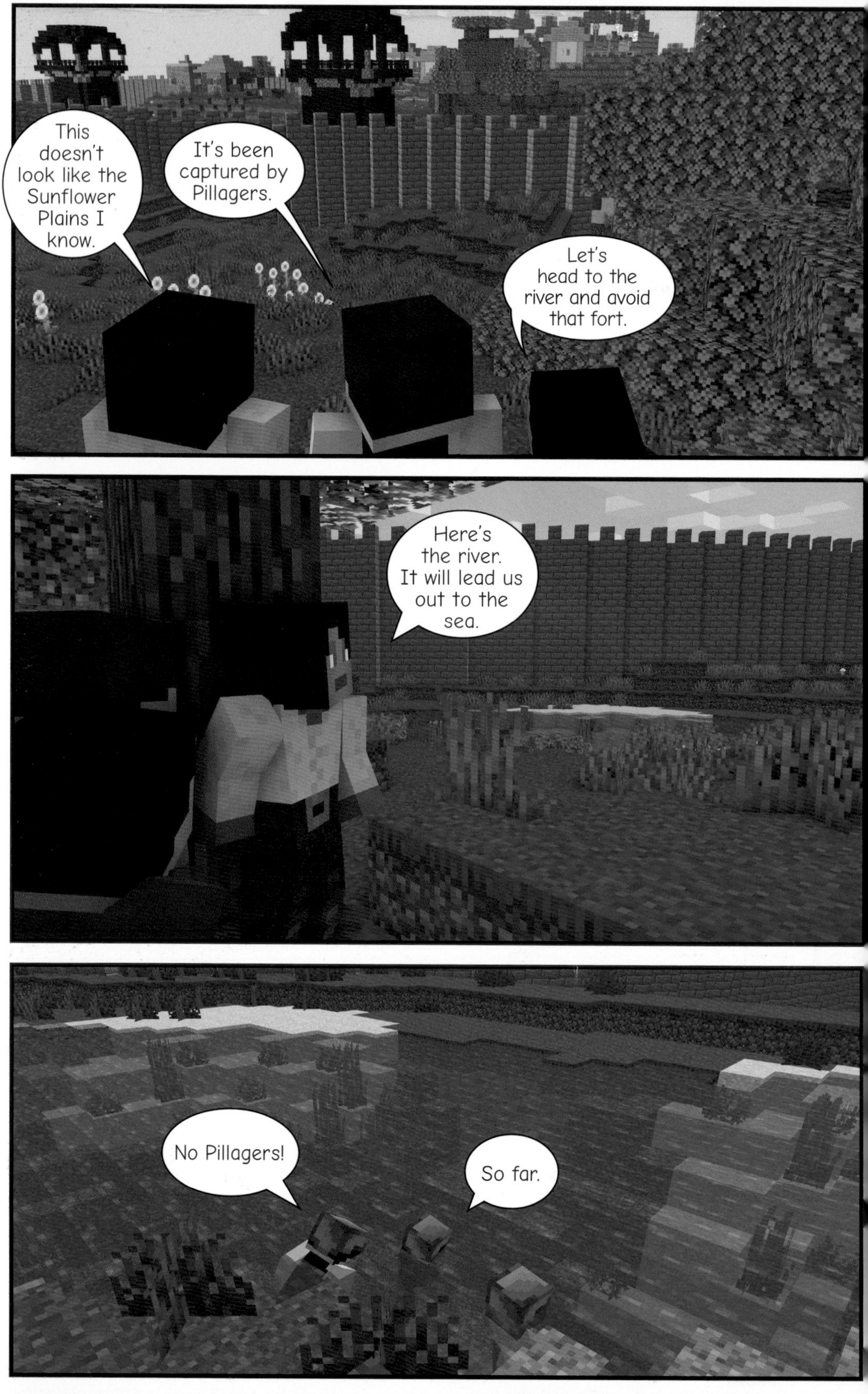

This doesn't look like the Sunflower Plains I know.
It's been captured by Pillagers.
Let's head to the river and avoid that fort.
Here's the river. It will lead us out to the sea.
No Pillagers!
So far.

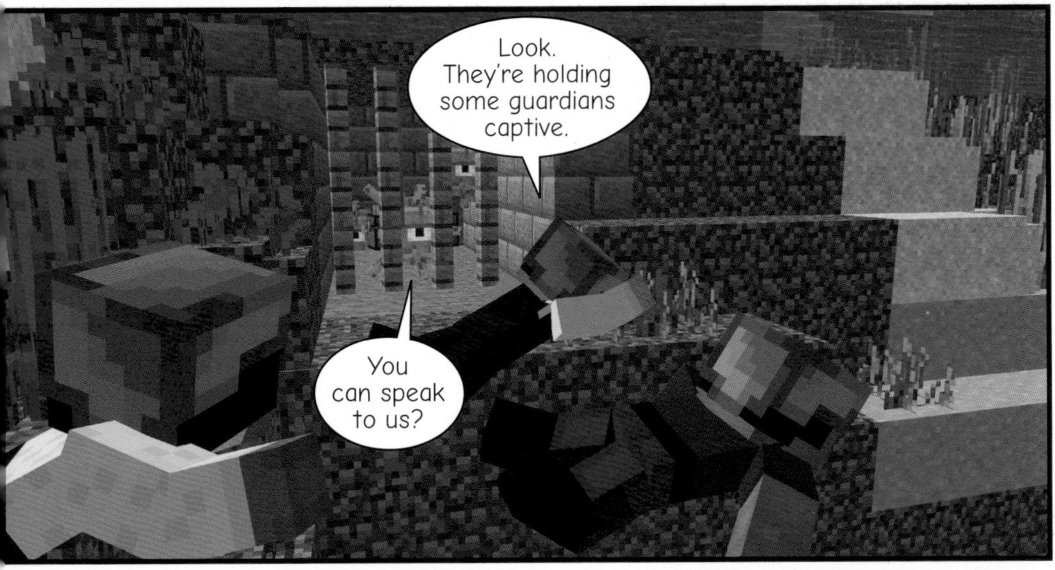
Look. They're holding some guardians captive.
You can speak to us?
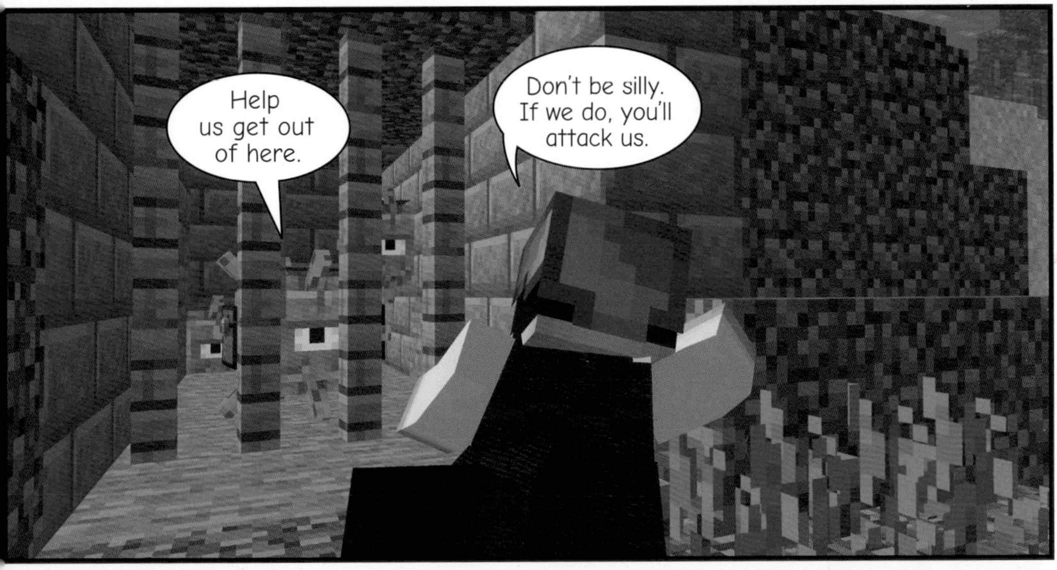
Help us get out of here.
Don't be silly. If we do, you'll attack us.
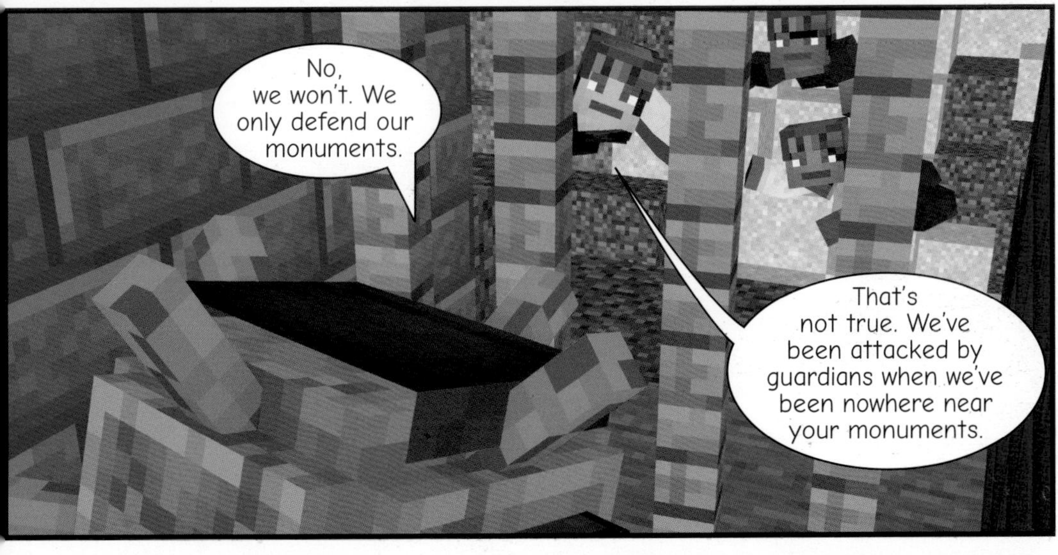
No, we won't. We only defend our monuments.
That's not true. We've been attacked by guardians when we've been nowhere near your monuments.

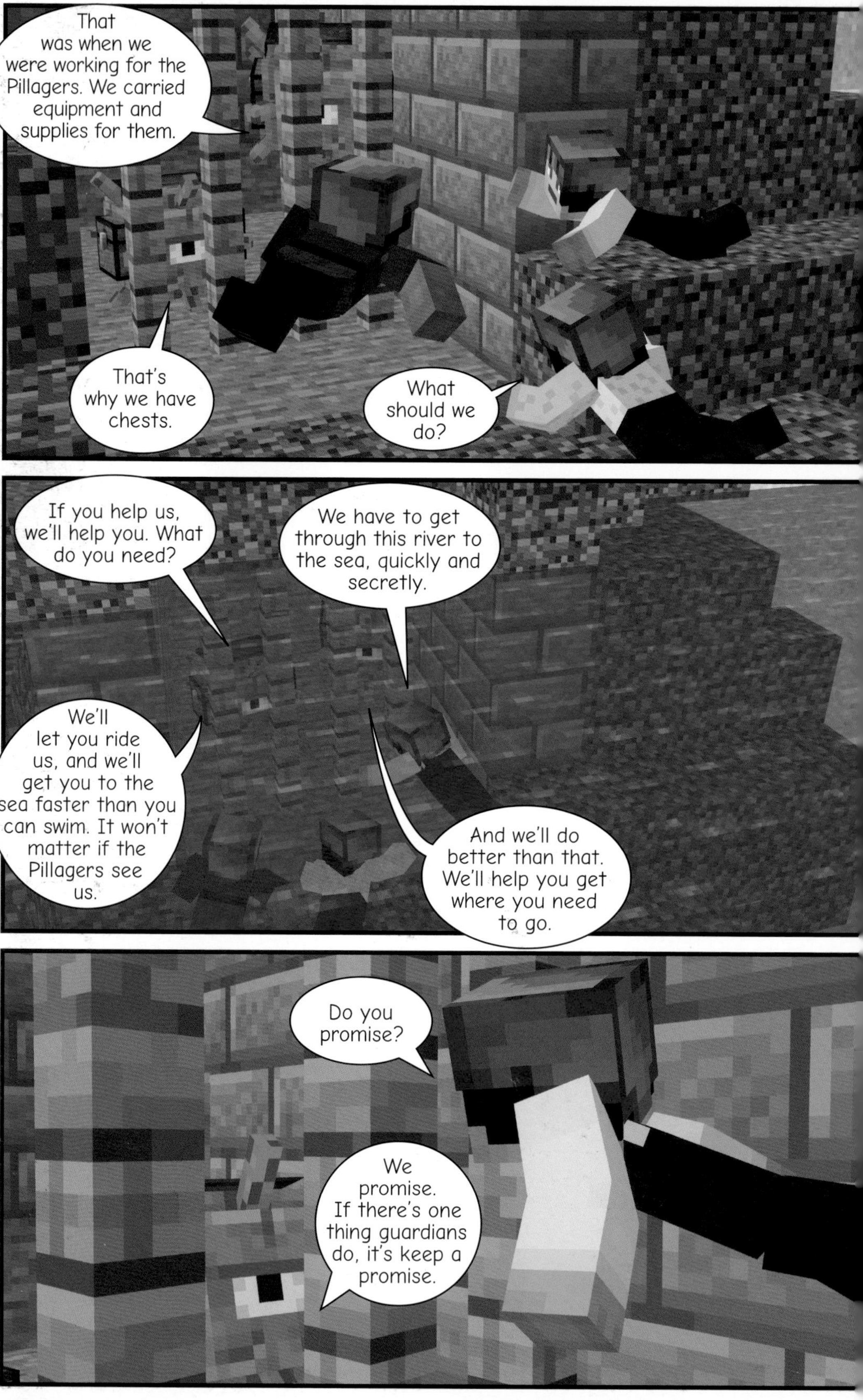
That was when we were working for the Pillagers. We carried equipment and supplies for them.
That's why we have chests.
What should we do?
If you help us, we'll help you. What do you need?
We have to get through this river to the sea, quickly and secretly.
We'll let you ride us, and we'll get you to the sea faster than you can swim. It won't matter if the Pillagers see us.
And we'll do better than that. We'll help you get where you need to go.
Do you promise?
We promise. If there's one thing guardians do, it's keep a promise.

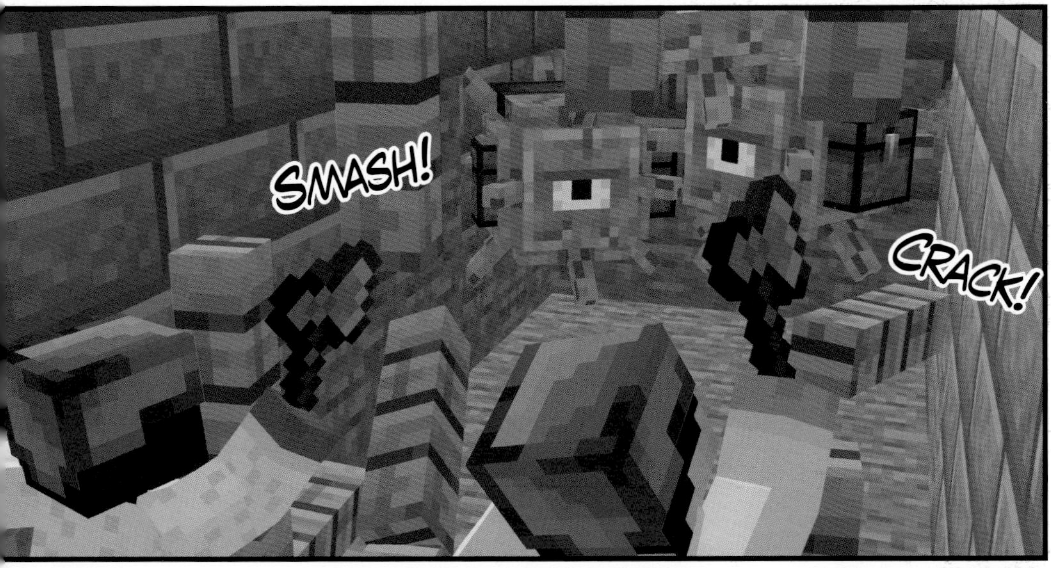
SMASH!
CRACK!
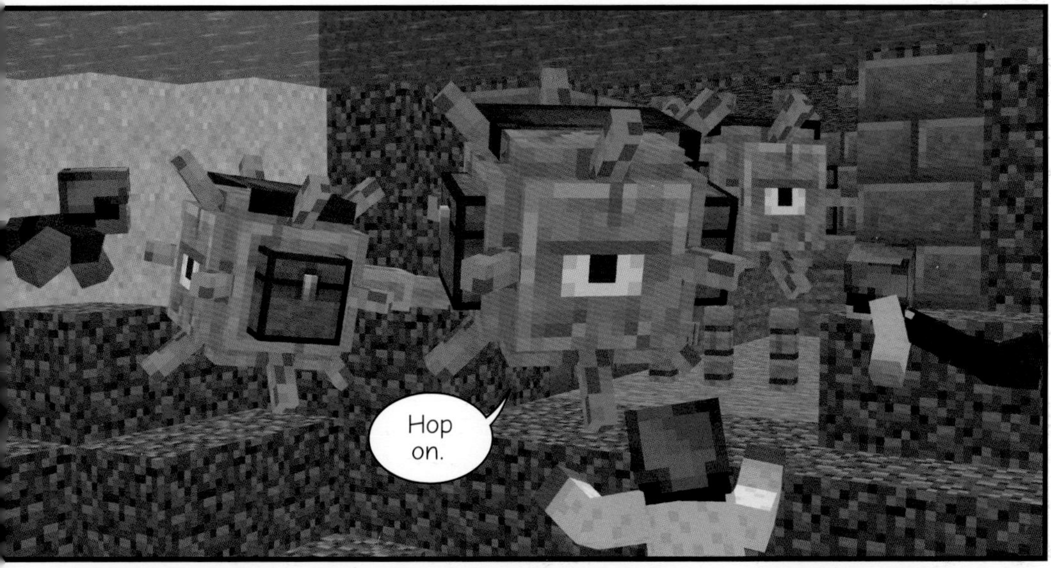
Hop on.
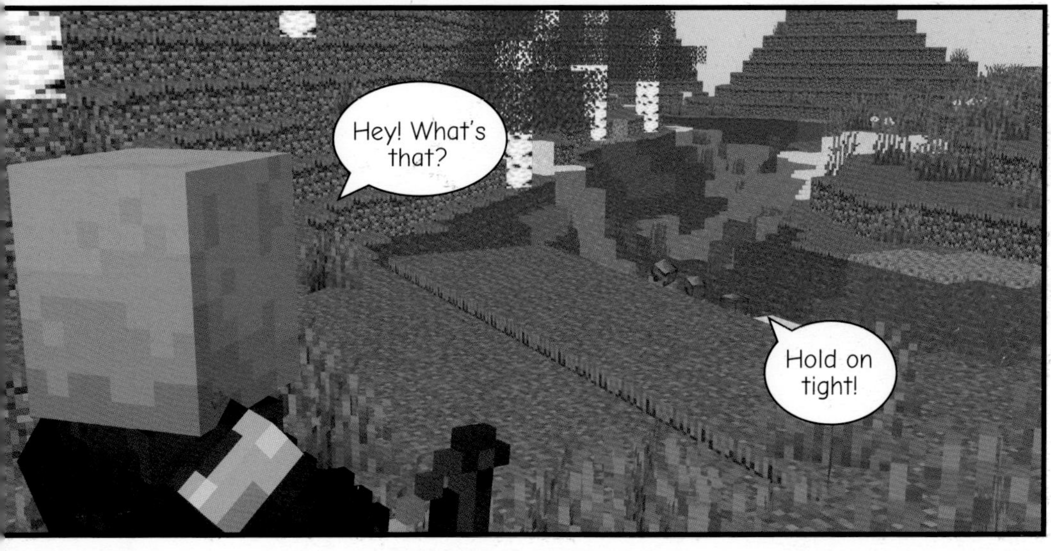
Hey! What's that?
Hold on tight!

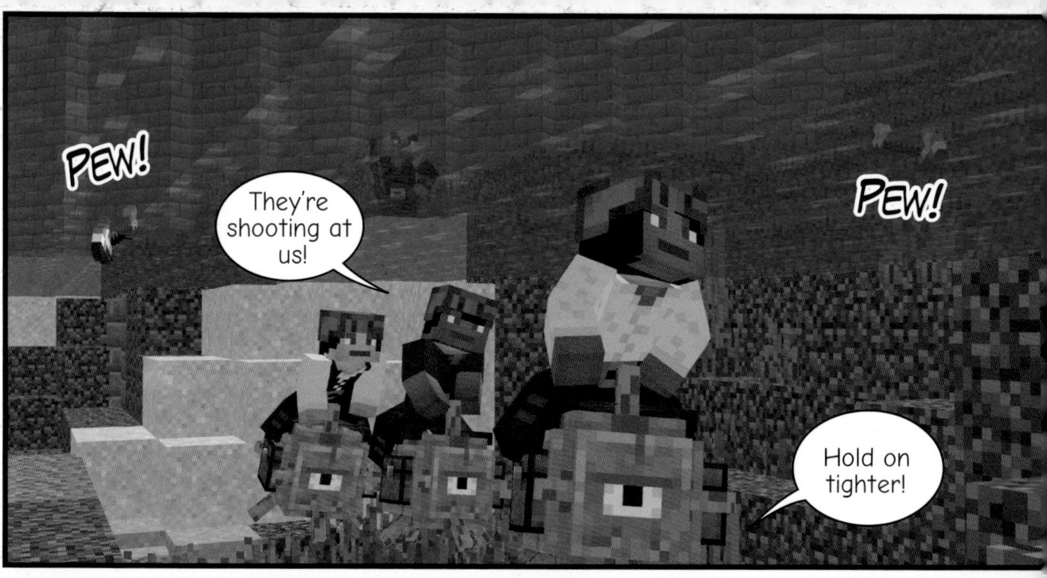
PEW!
They're shooting at us!
PEW!
Hold on tighter!

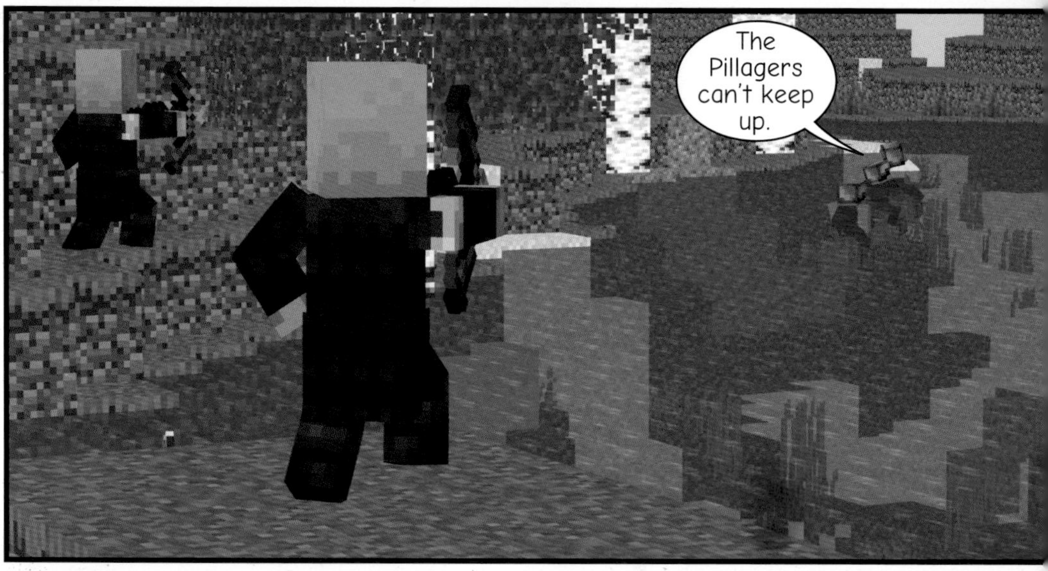
The Pillagers can't keep up.

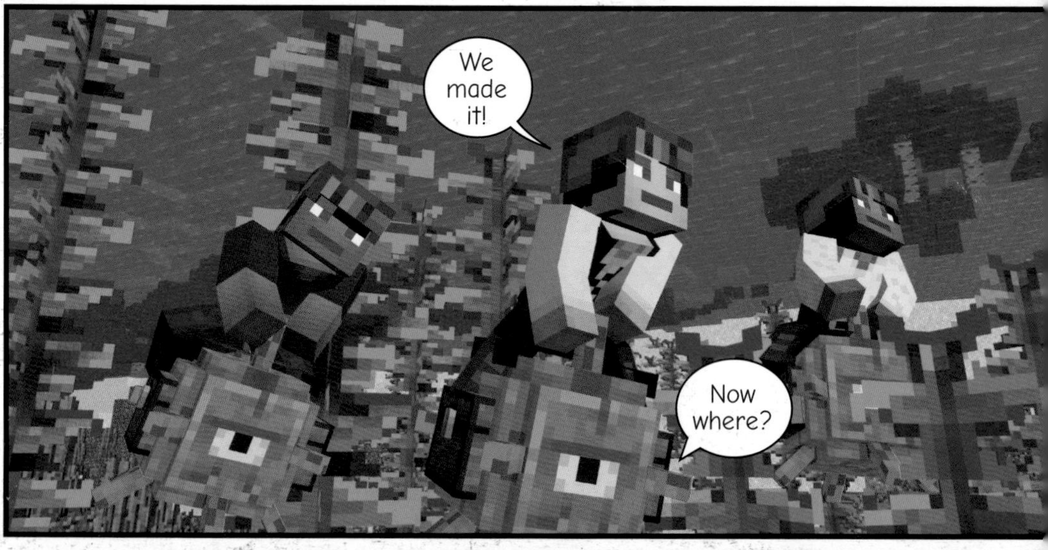
We made it!
Now where?

Chapter 10
Danger Nearby

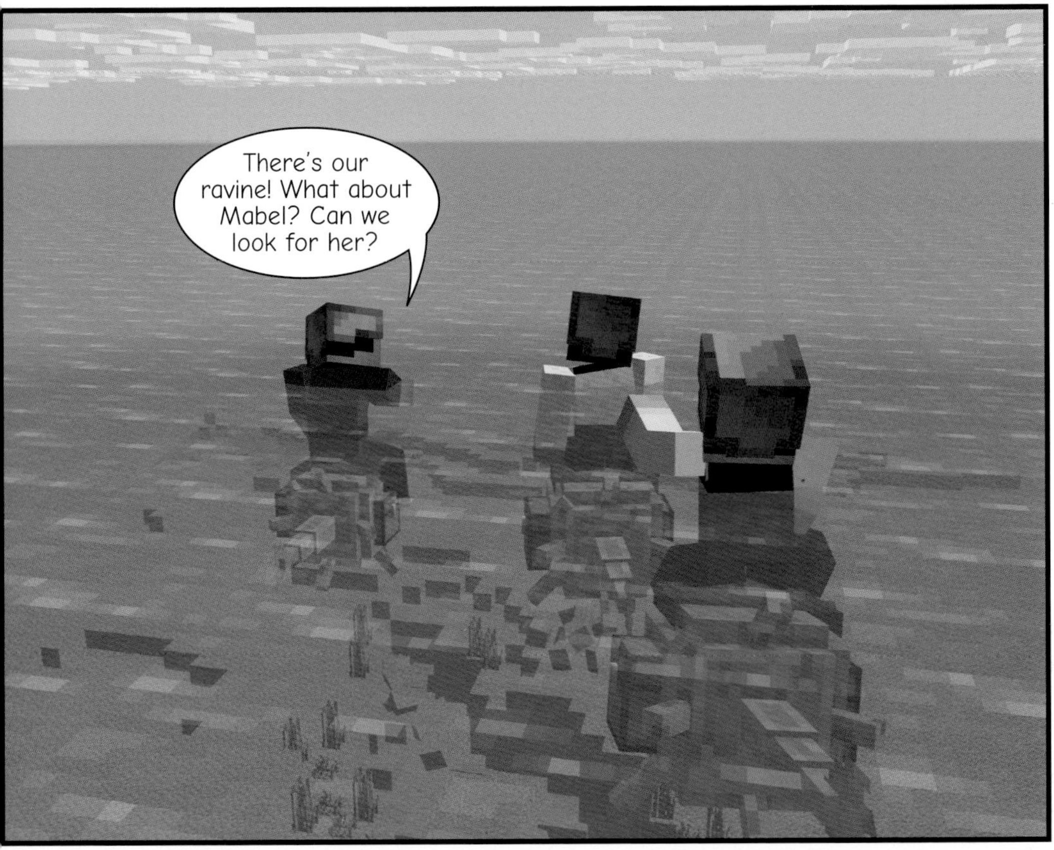
There's our ravine! What about Mabel? Can we look for her?

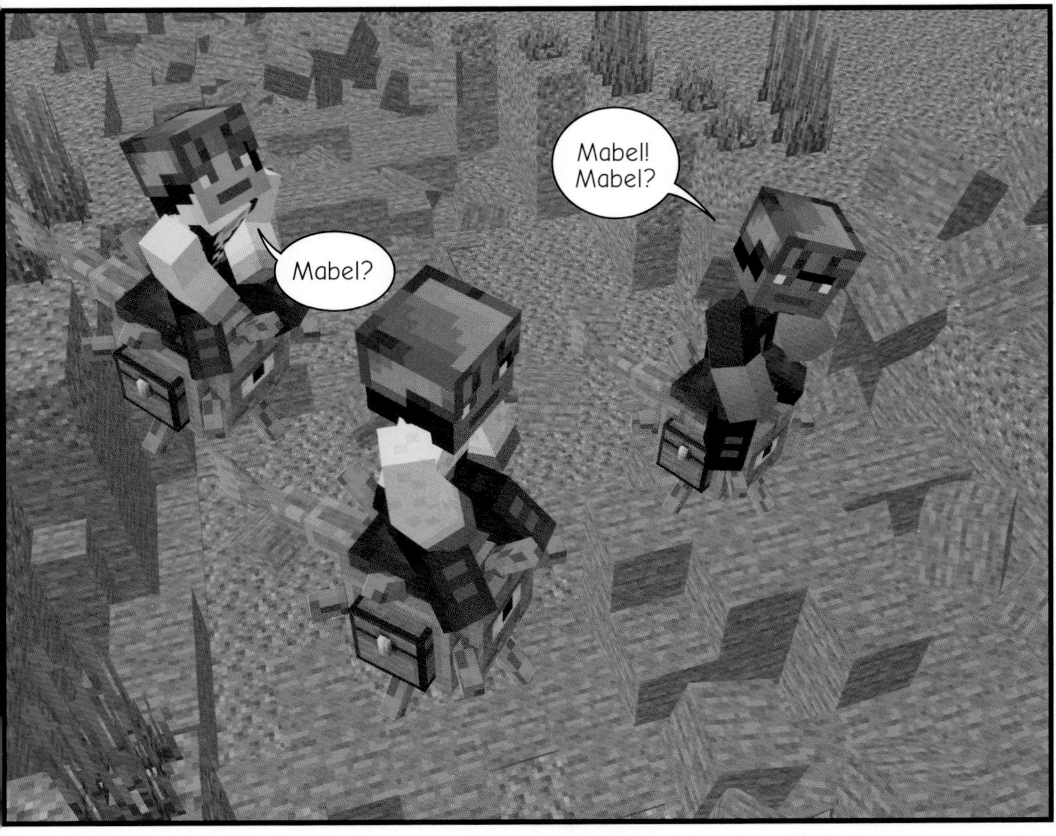
Mabel?
Mabel! Mabel?

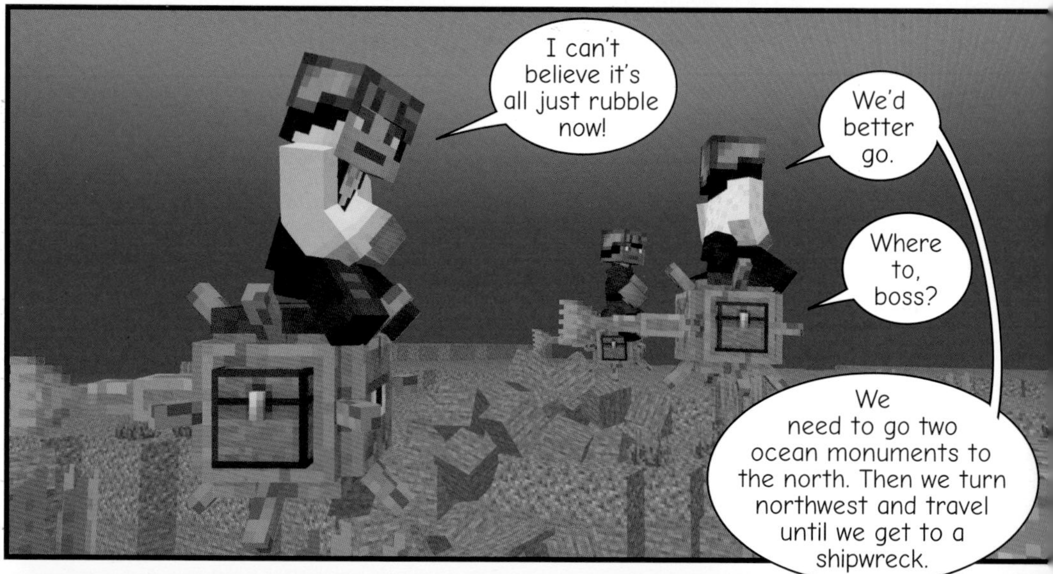
I can't believe it's all just rubble now!
We'd better go.
Where to, boss?
We need to go two ocean monuments to the north. Then we turn northwest and travel until we get to a shipwreck.

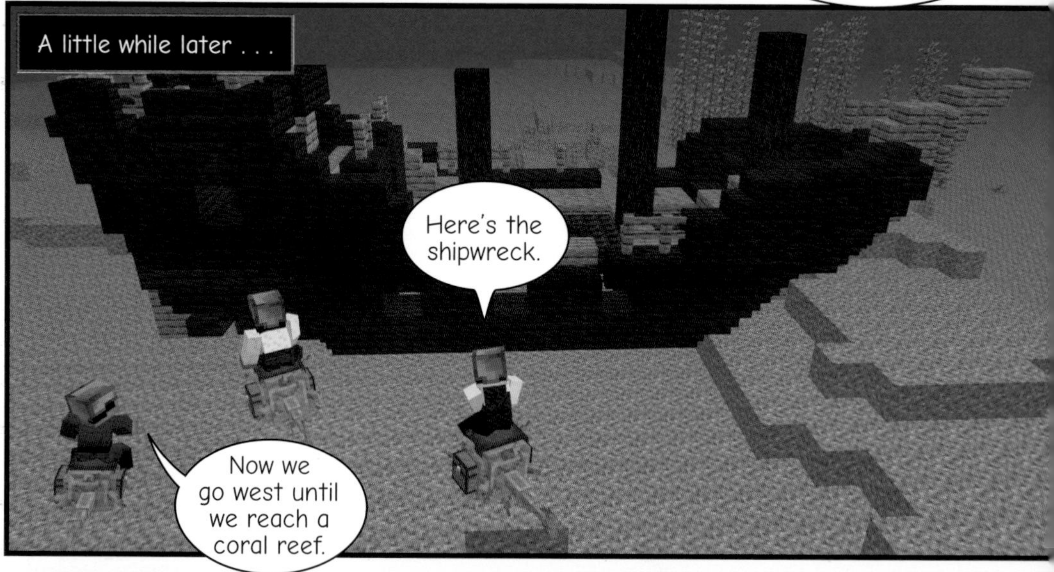
A little while later . . .
Here's the shipwreck.
Now we go west until we reach a coral reef.

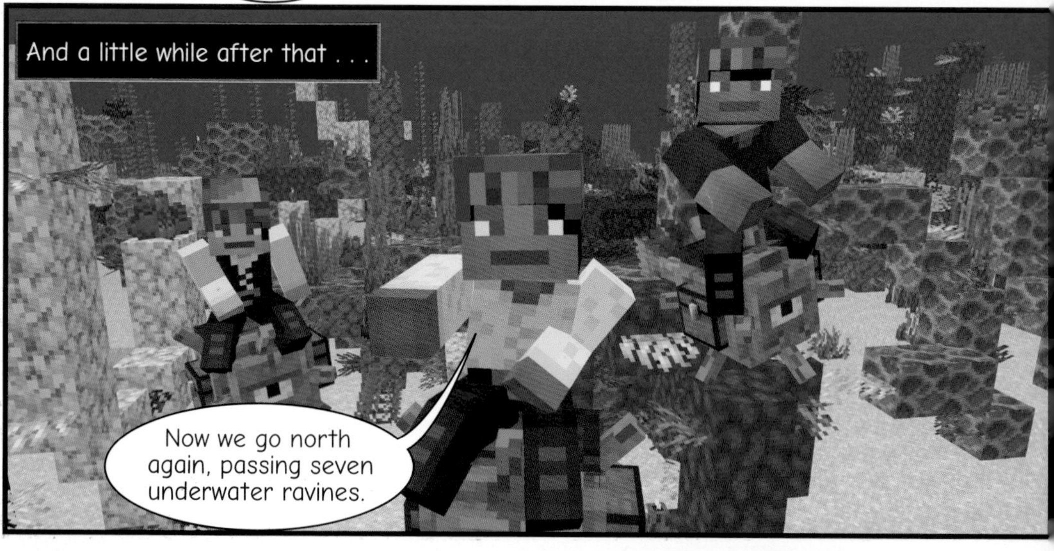
And a little while after that . . .
Now we go north again, passing seven underwater ravines.

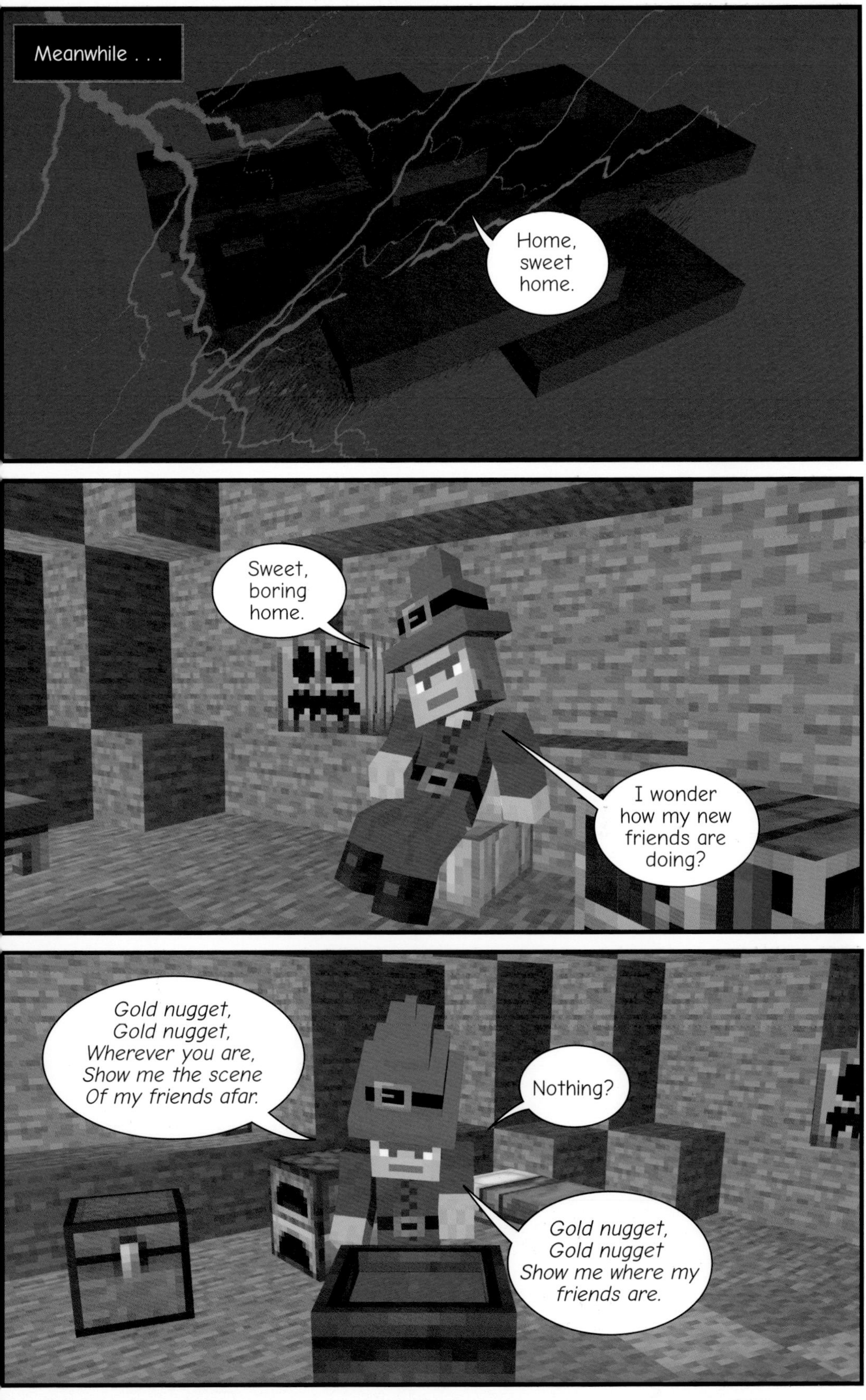
Meanwhile . . .
Home, sweet home.
Sweet, boring home.
I wonder how my new friends are doing?
Gold nugget, Gold nugget, Wherever you are, Show me the scene Of my friends afar.
Nothing?
Gold nugget, Gold nugget Show me where my friends are.

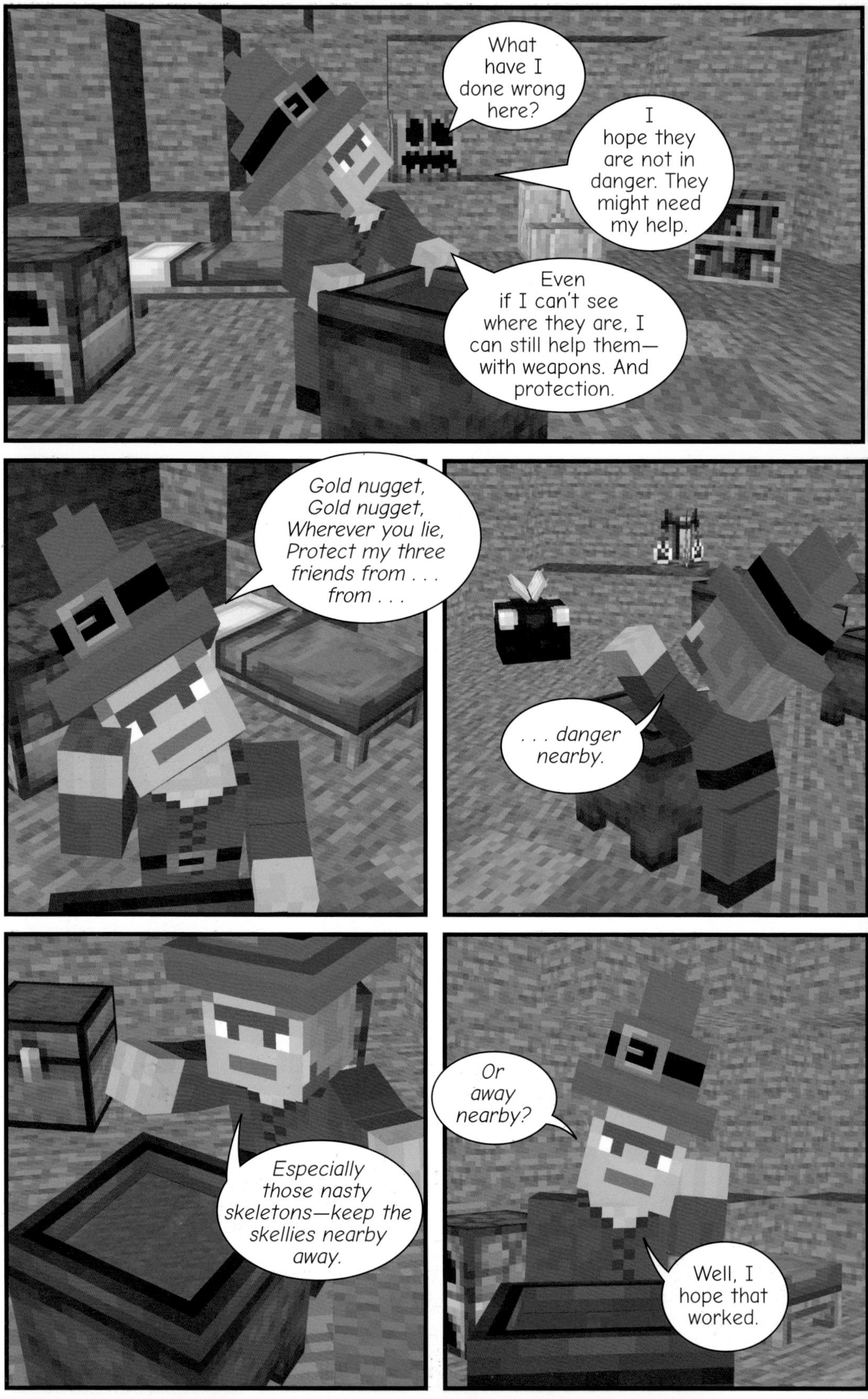

What have I done wrong here?
I hope they are not in danger. They might need my help.
Even if I can't see where they are, I can still help them—with weapons. And protection.
Gold nugget, Gold nugget, Wherever you lie, Protect my three friends from . . . from . . .
. . . danger nearby.
Especially those nasty skeletons—keep the skellies nearby away.
Or away nearby?
Well, I hope that worked.

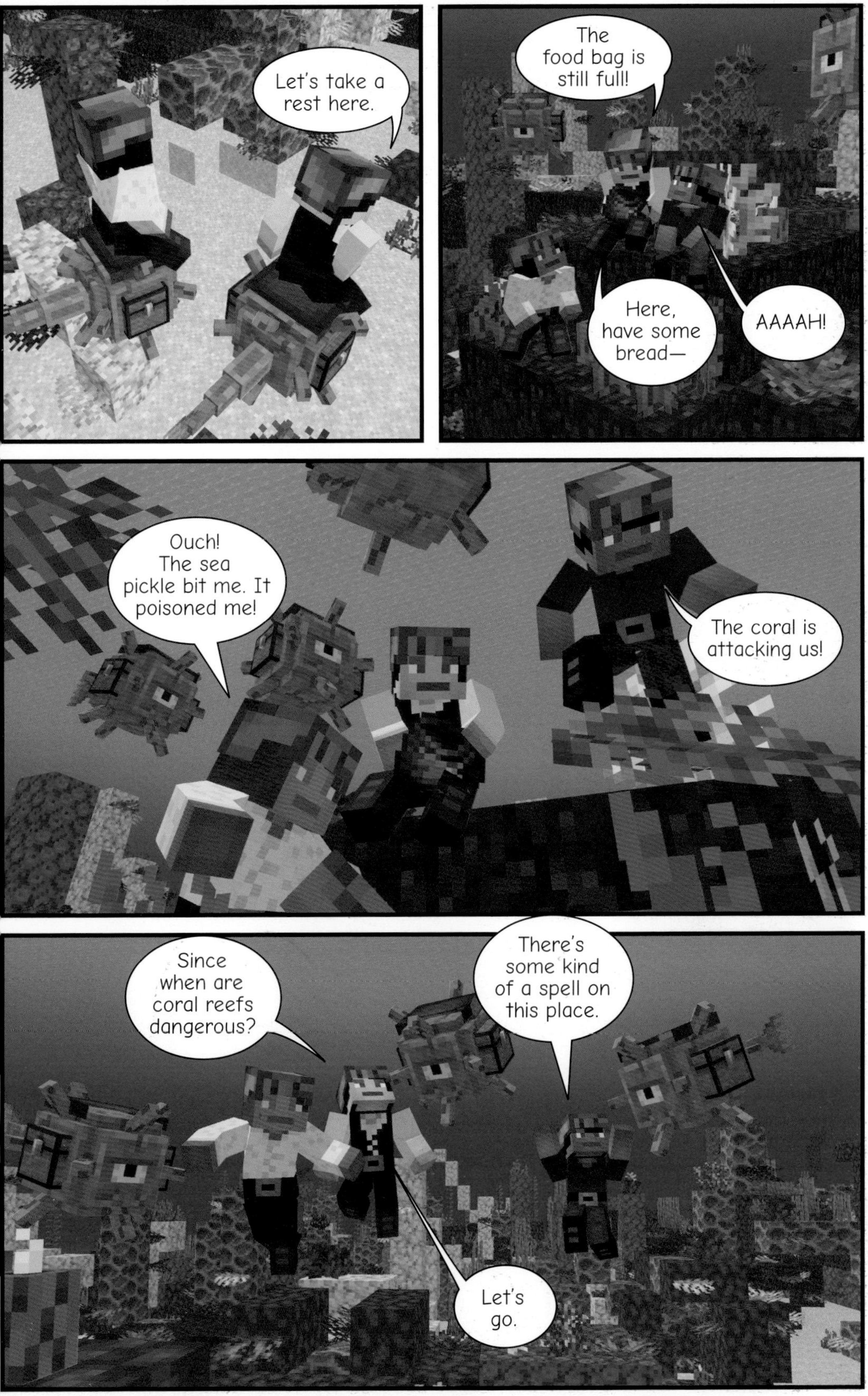
Let's take a rest here.
The food bag is still full!
Here, have some bread—
AAAAH!
Ouch! The sea pickle bit me. It poisoned me!
The coral is attacking us!
Since when are coral reefs dangerous?
There's some kind of a spell on this place.
Let's go.

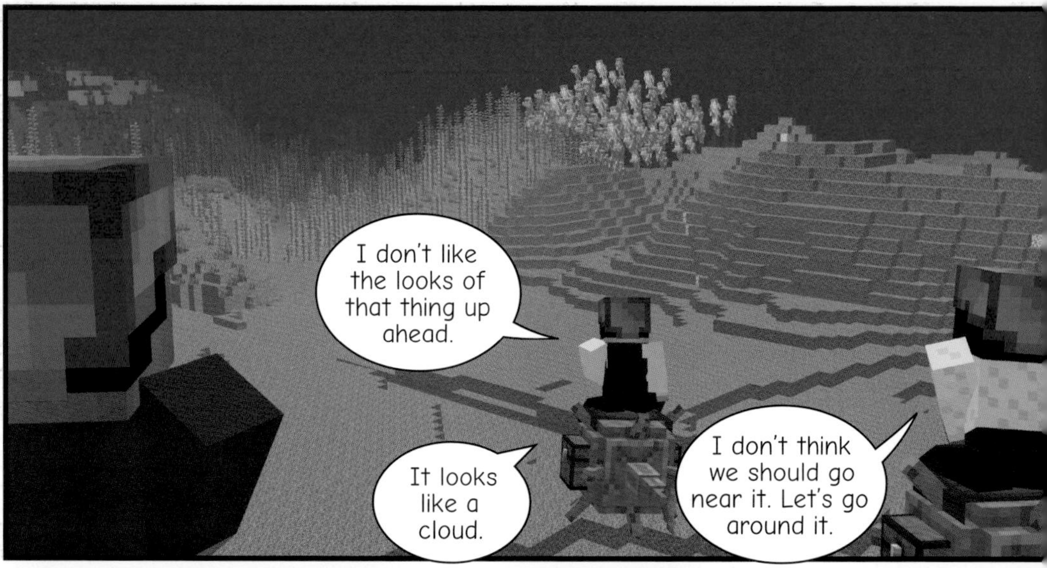
I don't like the looks of that thing up ahead.
It looks like a cloud.
I don't think we should go near it. Let's go around it.

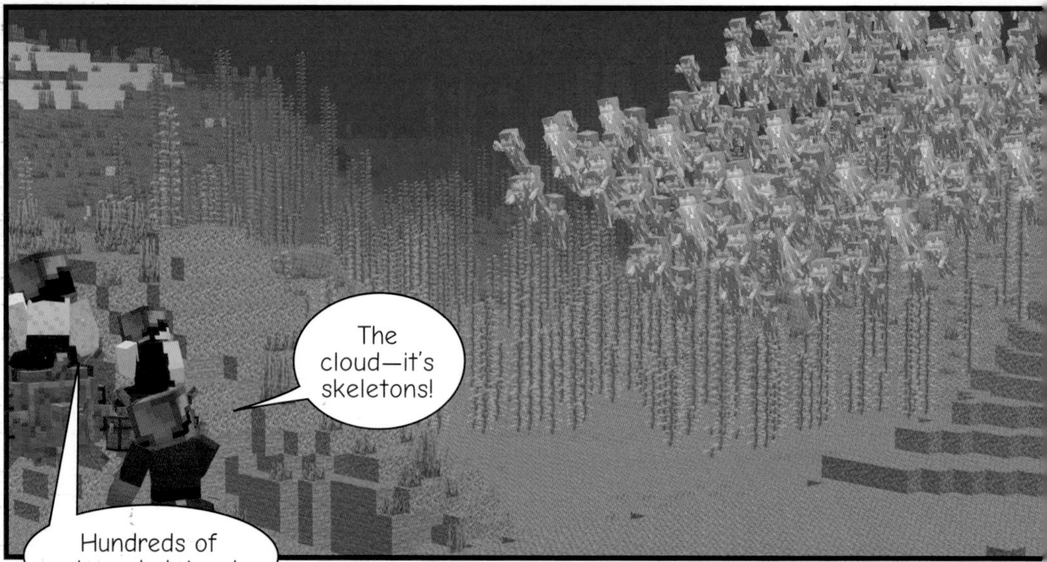
The cloud—it's skeletons!
Hundreds of stray skeletons!

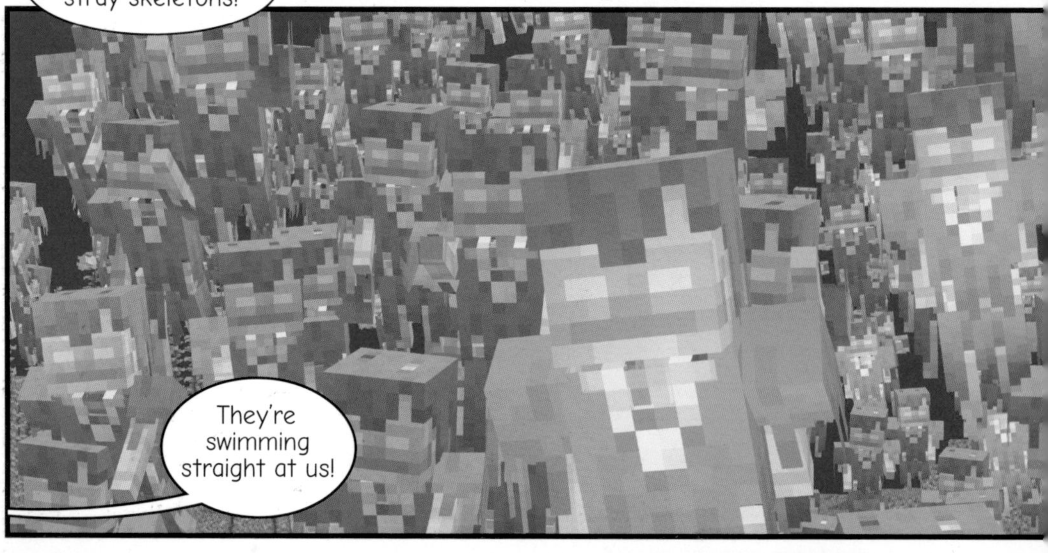
They're swimming straight at us!

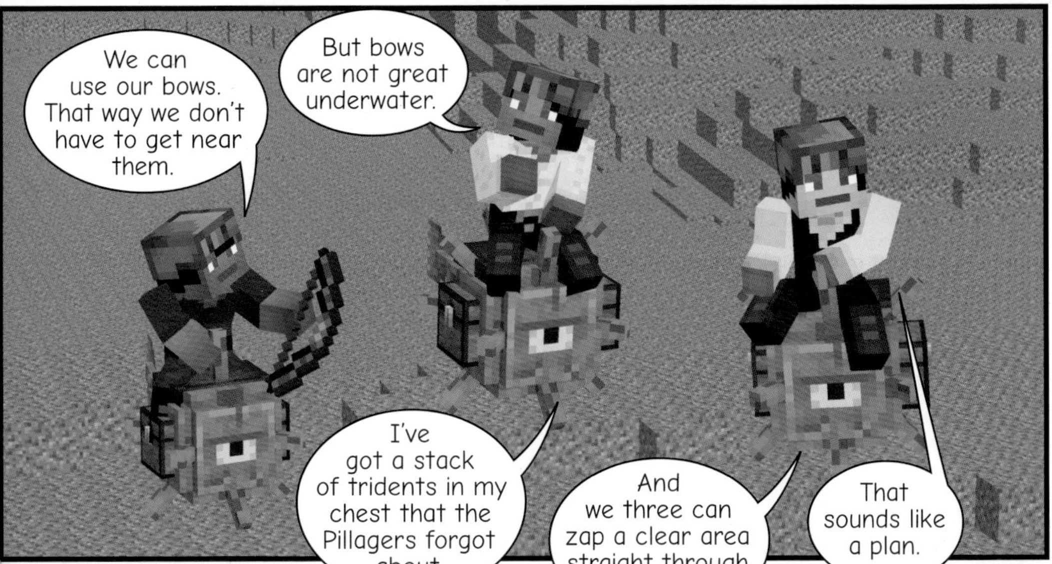
We can use our bows. That way we don't have to get near them.
But bows are not great underwater.
I've got a stack of tridents in my chest that the Pillagers forgot about.
And we three can zap a clear area straight through them.
That sounds like a plan.

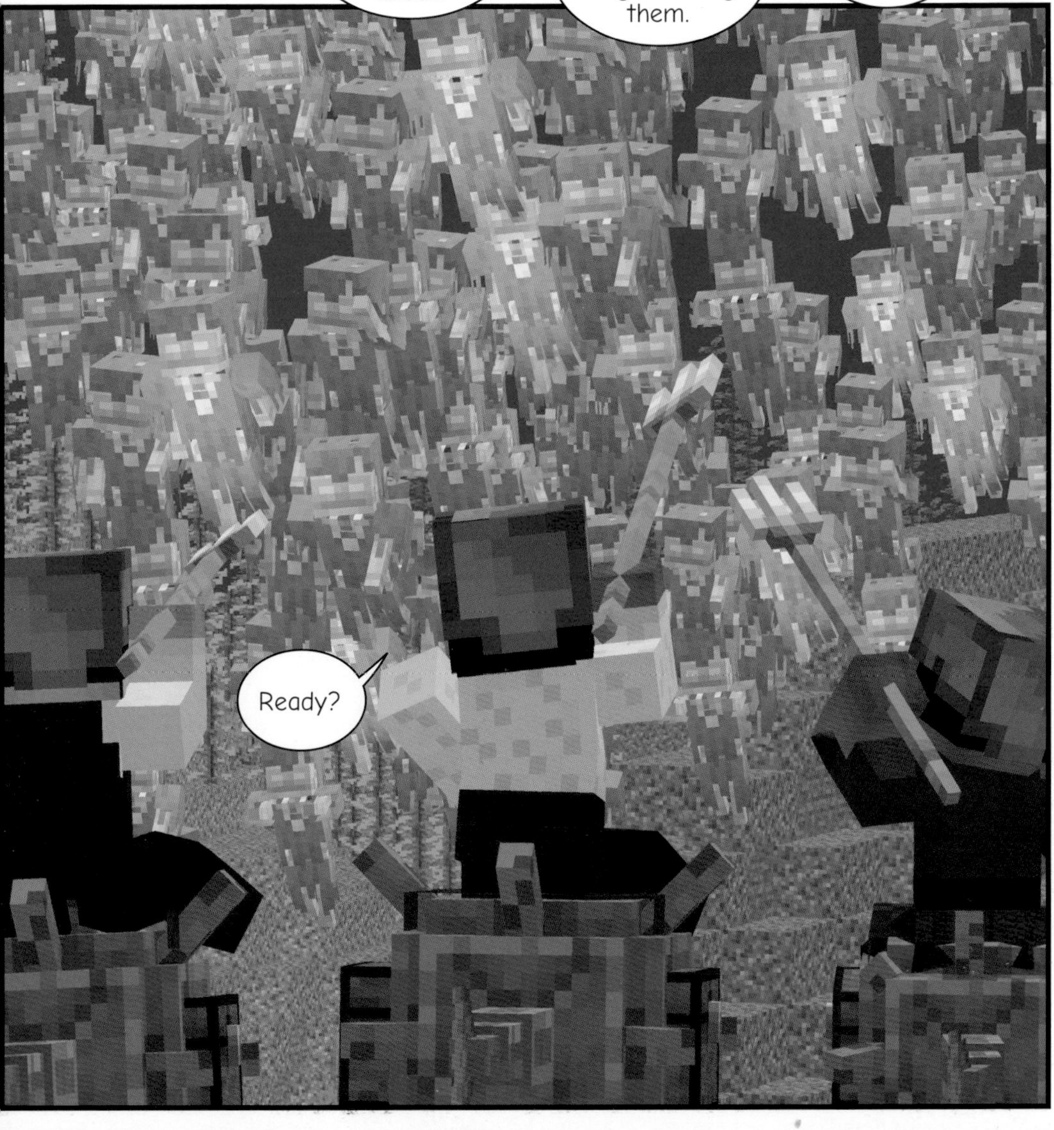
Ready?

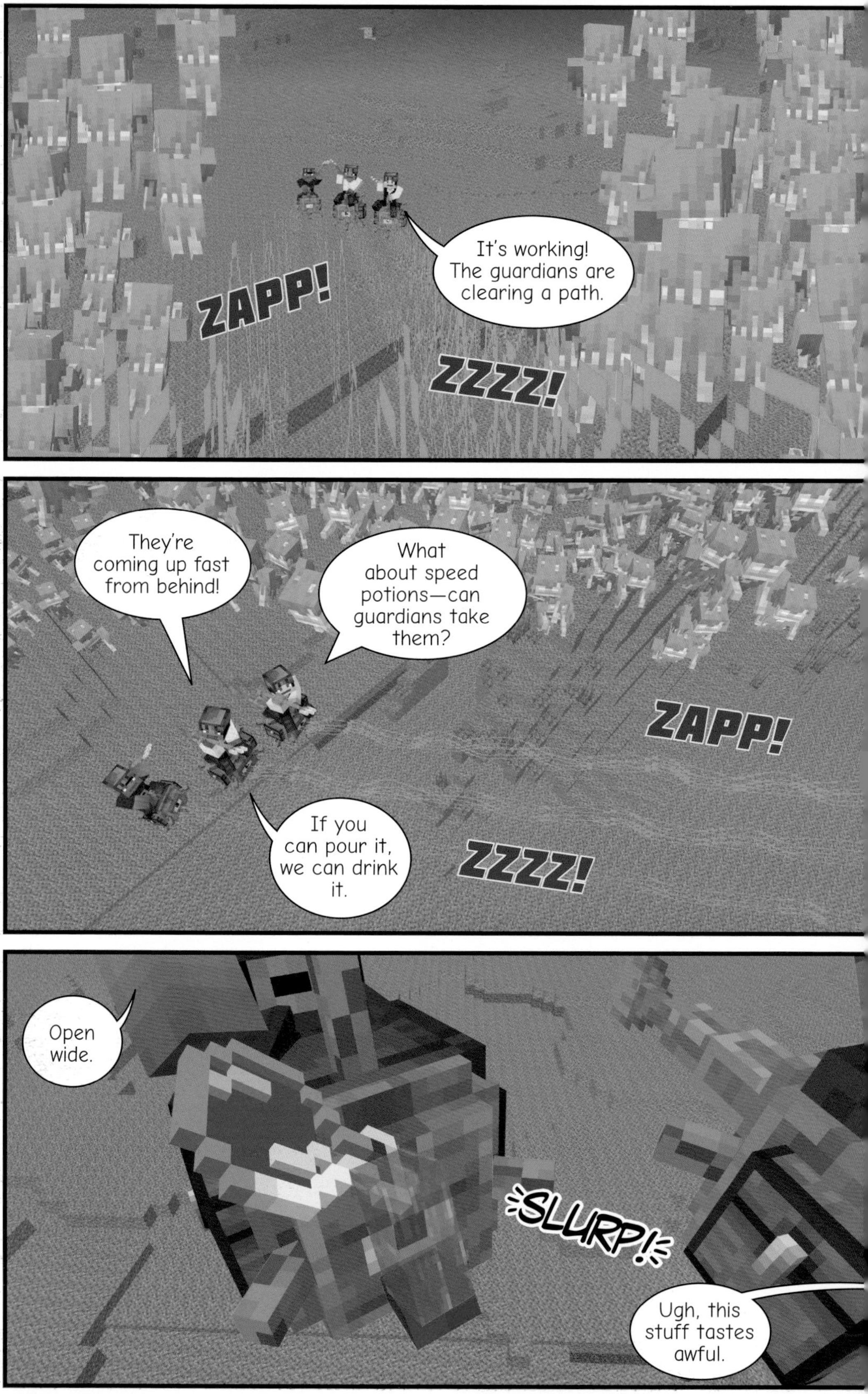
It's working! The guardians are clearing a path.
ZAPP!
ZZZZ!
They're coming up fast from behind!
What about speed potions—can guardians take them?
ZAPP!
If you can pour it, we can drink it.
ZZZZ!
Open wide.
SLURP!
Ugh, this stuff tastes awful.

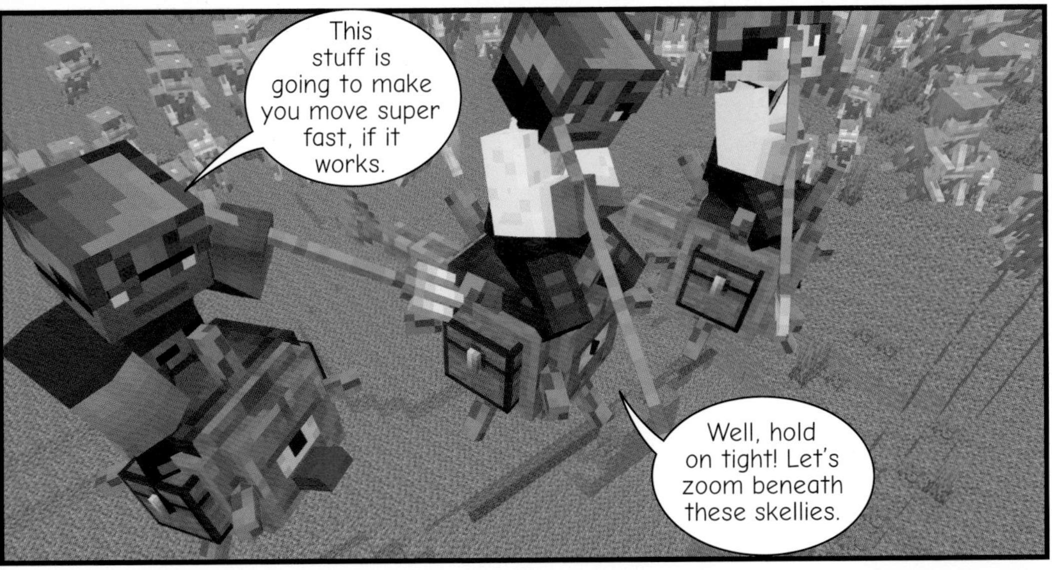
This stuff is going to make you move super fast, if it works.
Well, hold on tight! Let's zoom beneath these skellies.

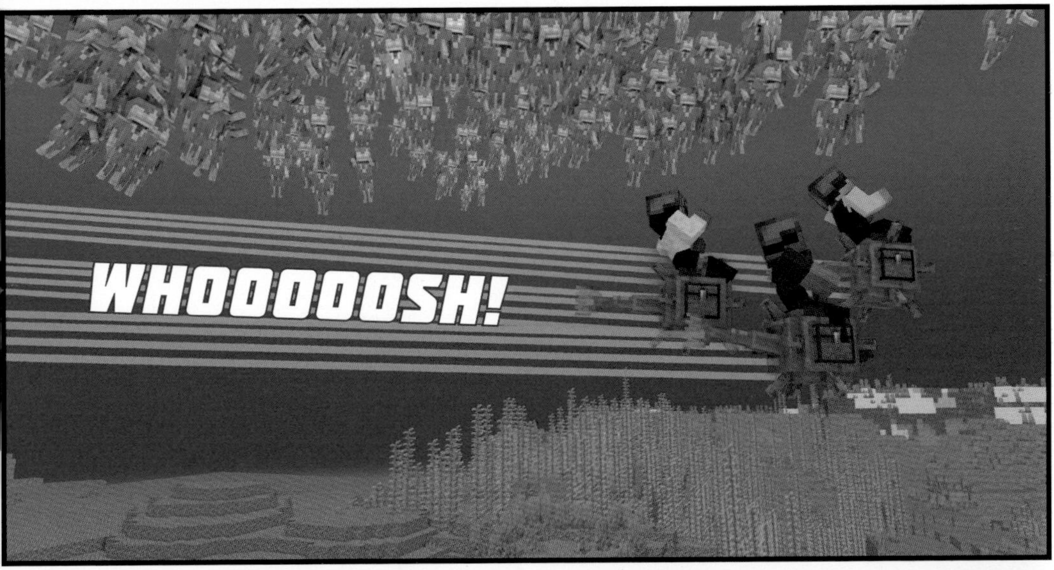
WHOOOOOSH!

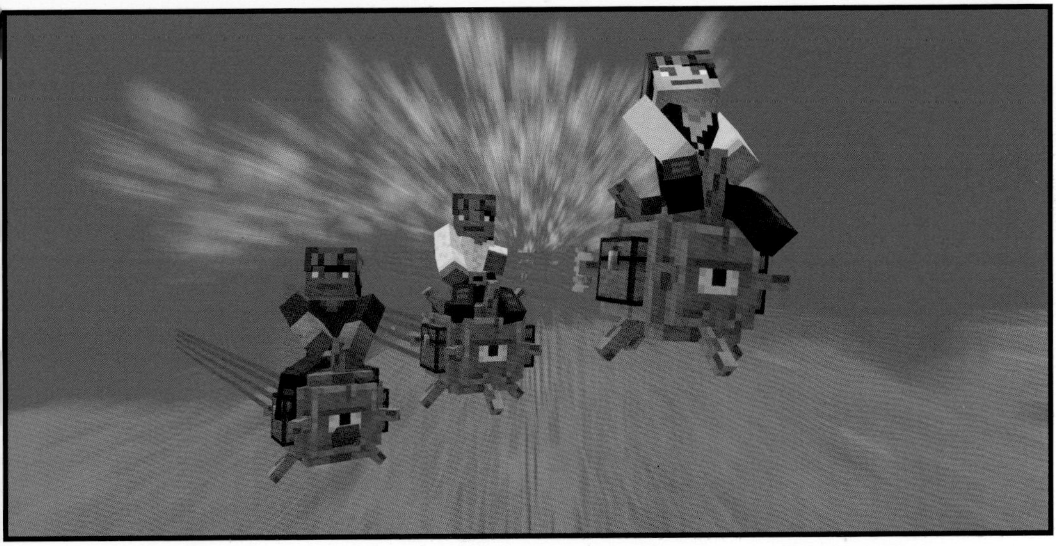

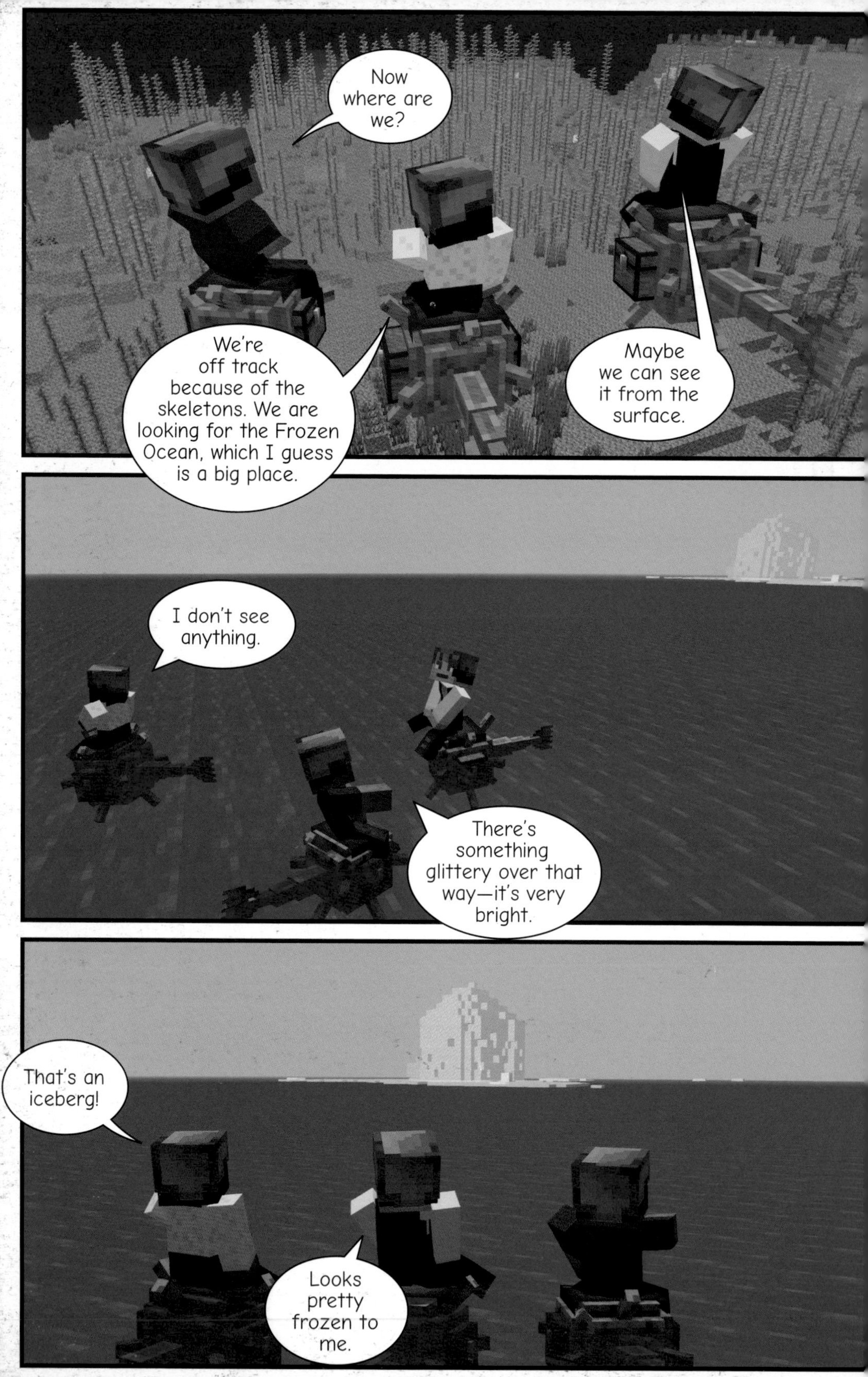
Now where are we?
We're off track because of the skeletons. We are looking for the Frozen Ocean, which I guess is a big place.
Maybe we can see it from the surface.
I don't see anything.
There's something glittery over that way—it's very bright.
That's an iceberg!
Looks pretty frozen to me.

Chapter 11
The Frozen
Ocean

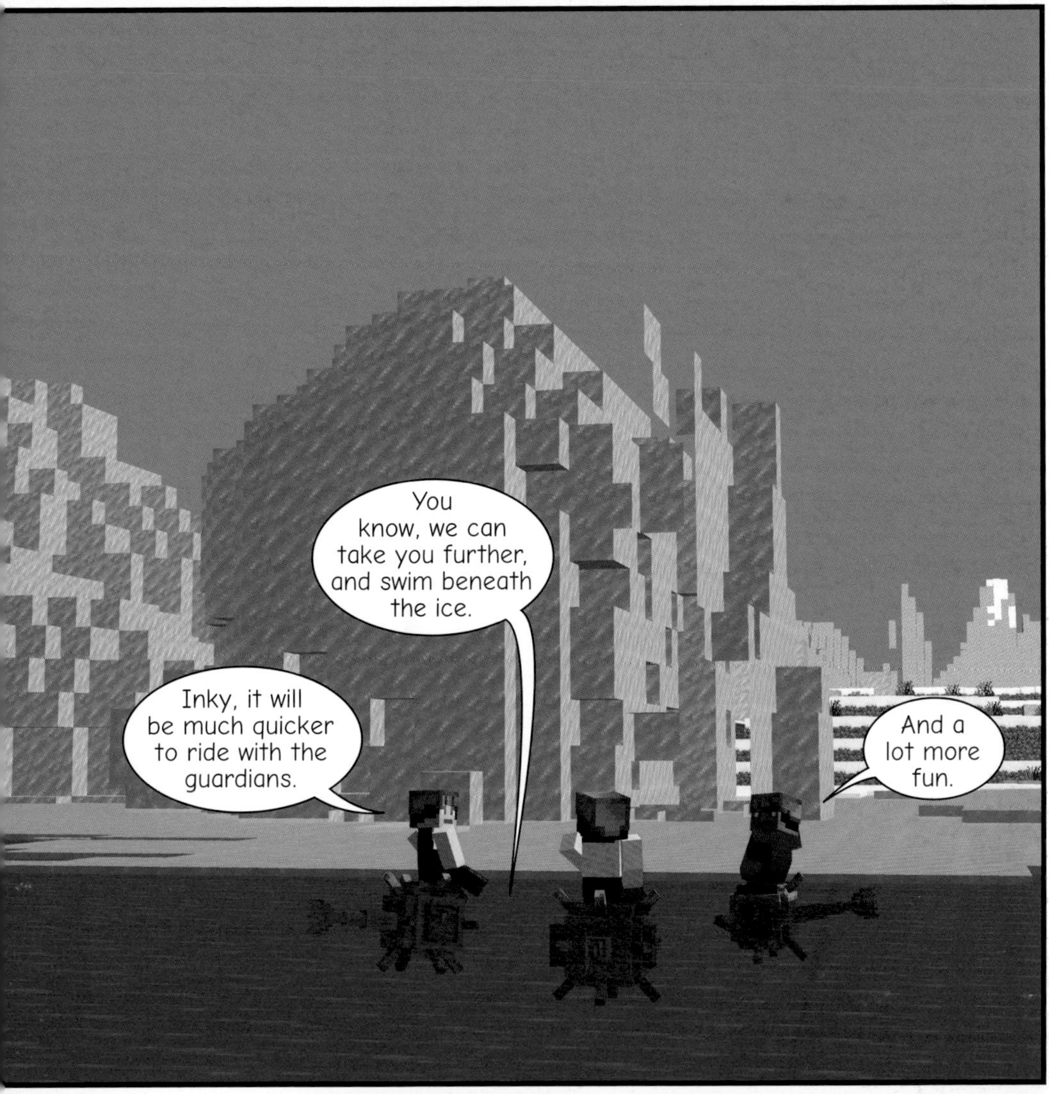
Inky, it will be much quicker to ride with the guardians.
You know, we can take you further, and swim beneath the ice.
And a lot more fun.

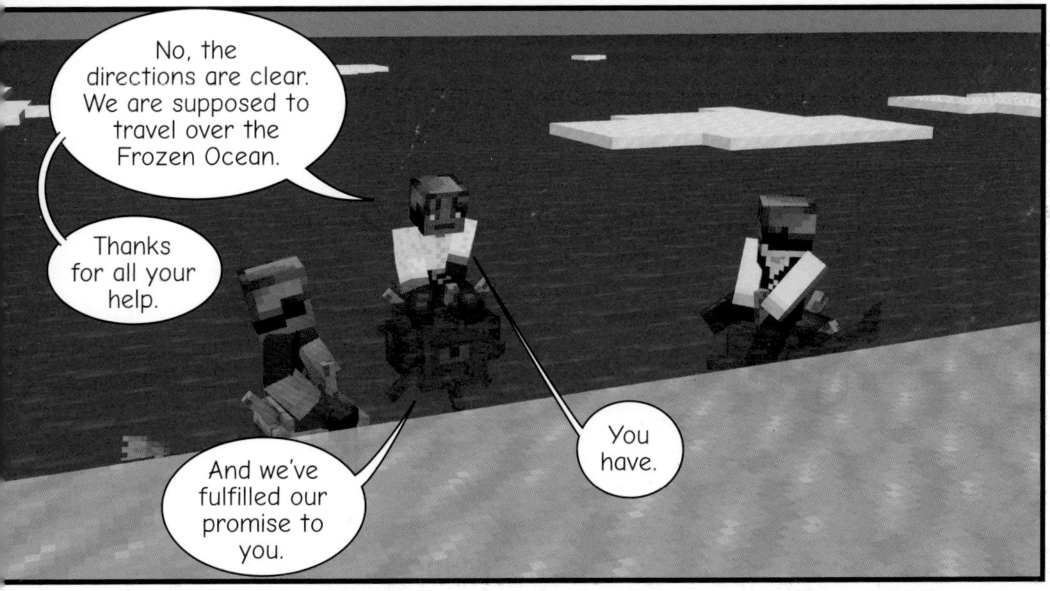
No, the directions are clear. We are supposed to travel over the Frozen Ocean.
Thanks for all your help.
You have.
And we've fulfilled our promise to you.

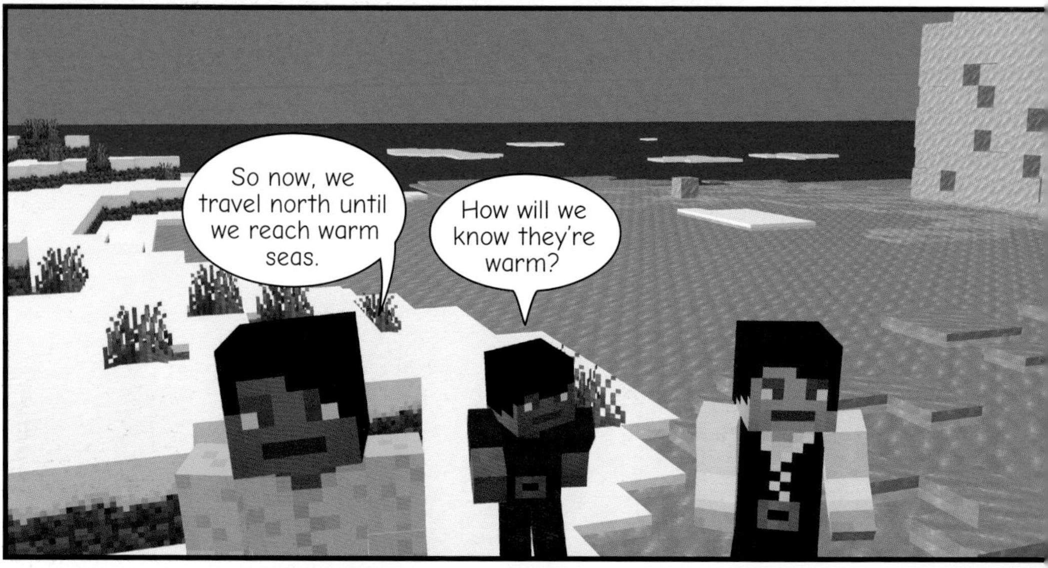
So now, we travel north until we reach warm seas.
How will we know they're warm?

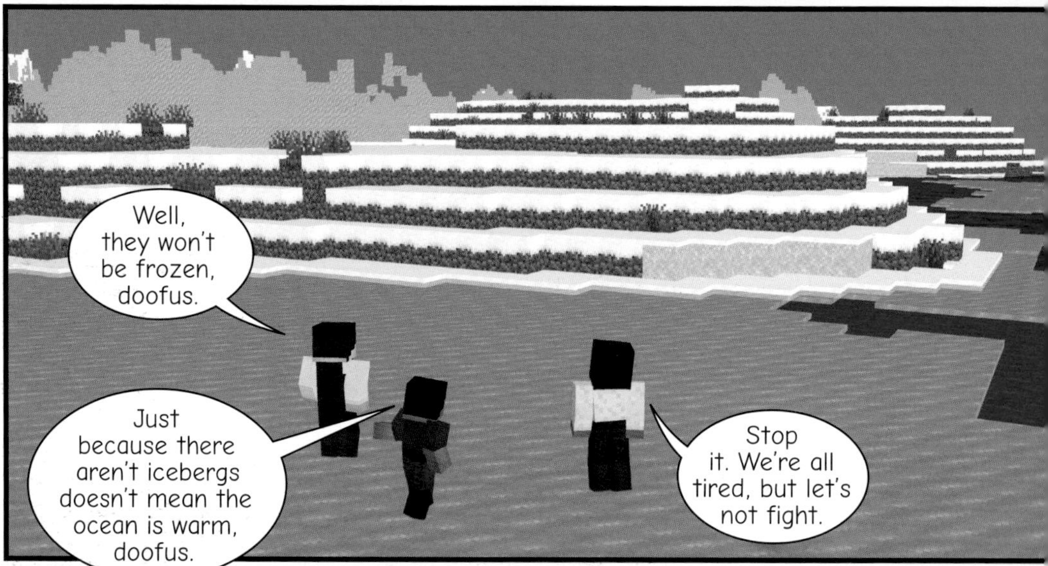
Well, they won't be frozen, doofus.
Just because there aren't icebergs doesn't mean the ocean is warm, doofus.
Stop it. We're all tired, but let's not fight.

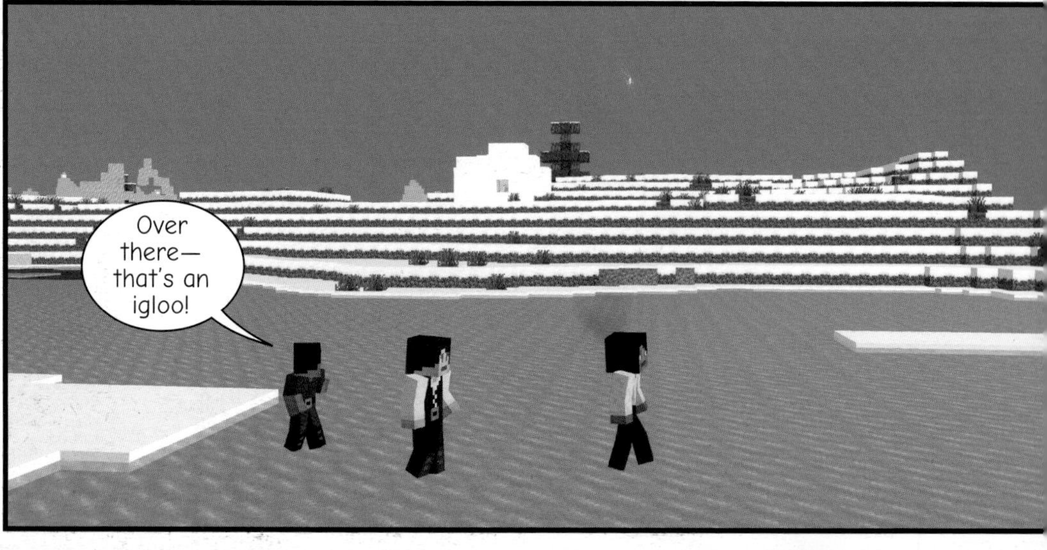
Over there—that's an igloo!

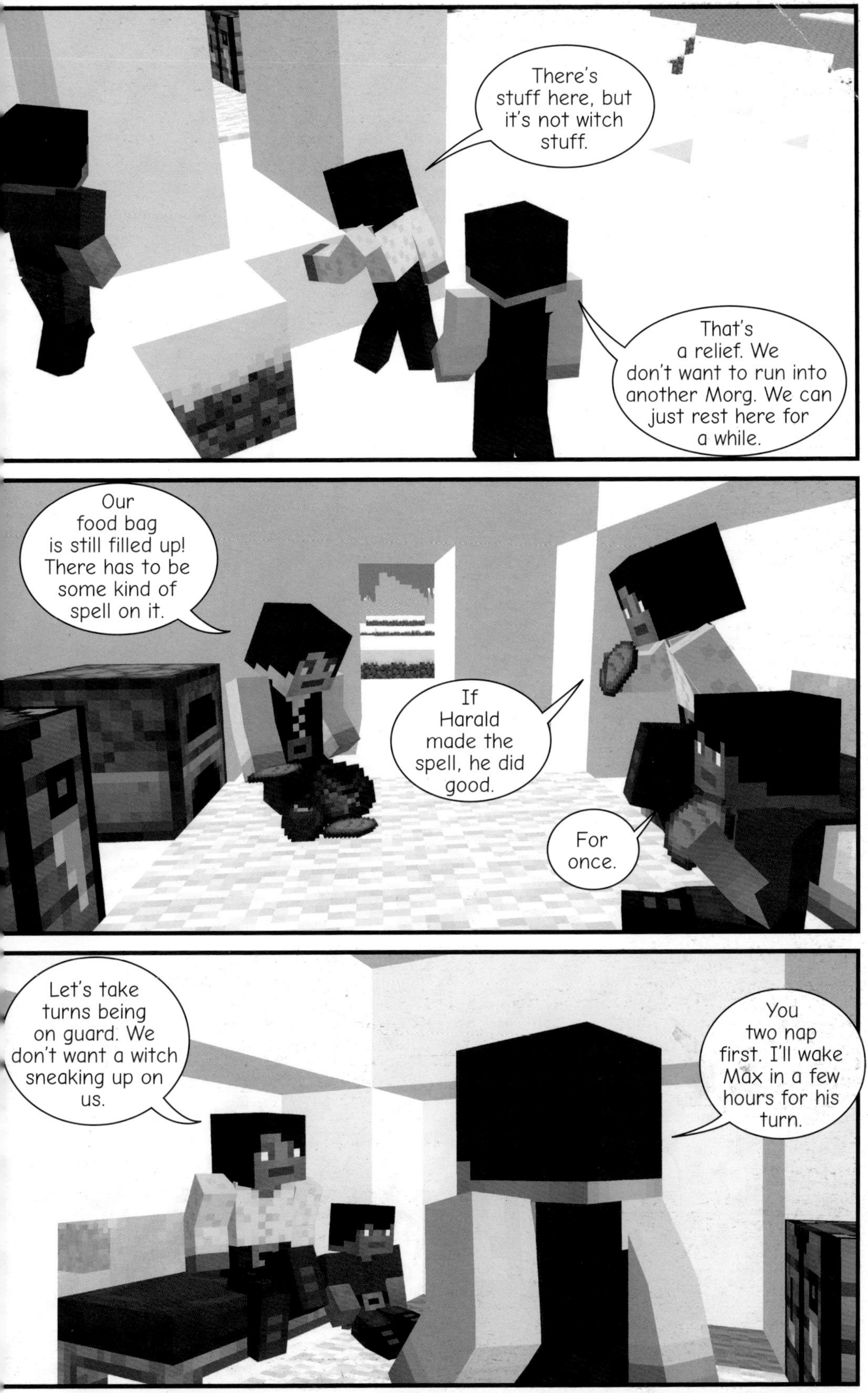
There's stuff here, but it's not witch stuff.
That's a relief. We don't want to run into another Morg. We can just rest here for a while.
Our food bag is still filled up! There has to be some kind of spell on it.
If Harald made the spell, he did good.
For once.
Let's take turns being on guard. We don't want a witch sneaking up on us.
You two nap first. I'll wake Max in a few hours for his turn.

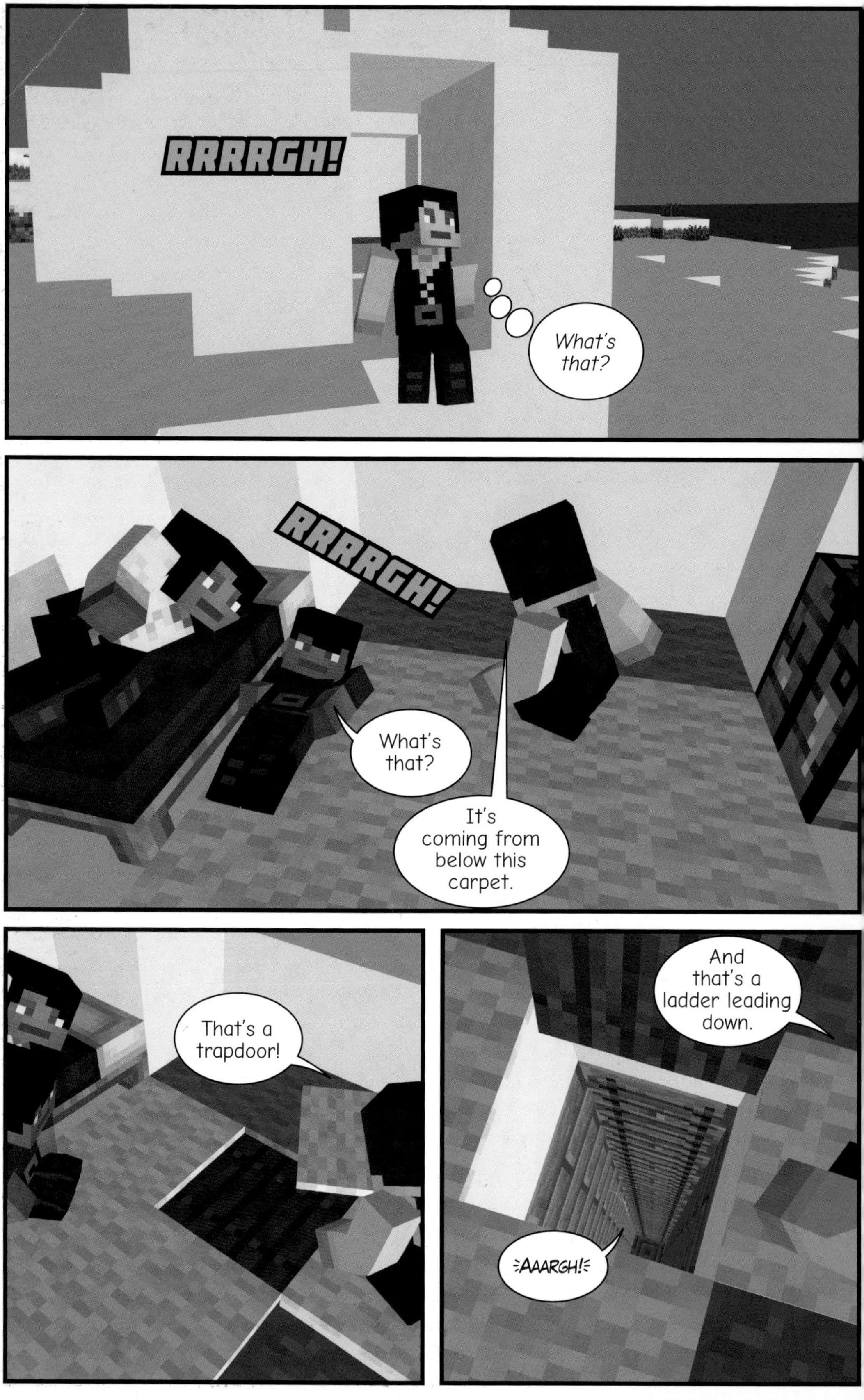
RRRRGH!
What's that?
RRRRGH!
What's that?
It's coming from below this carpet.
That's a trapdoor!
And that's a ladder leading down.
AAARGH!

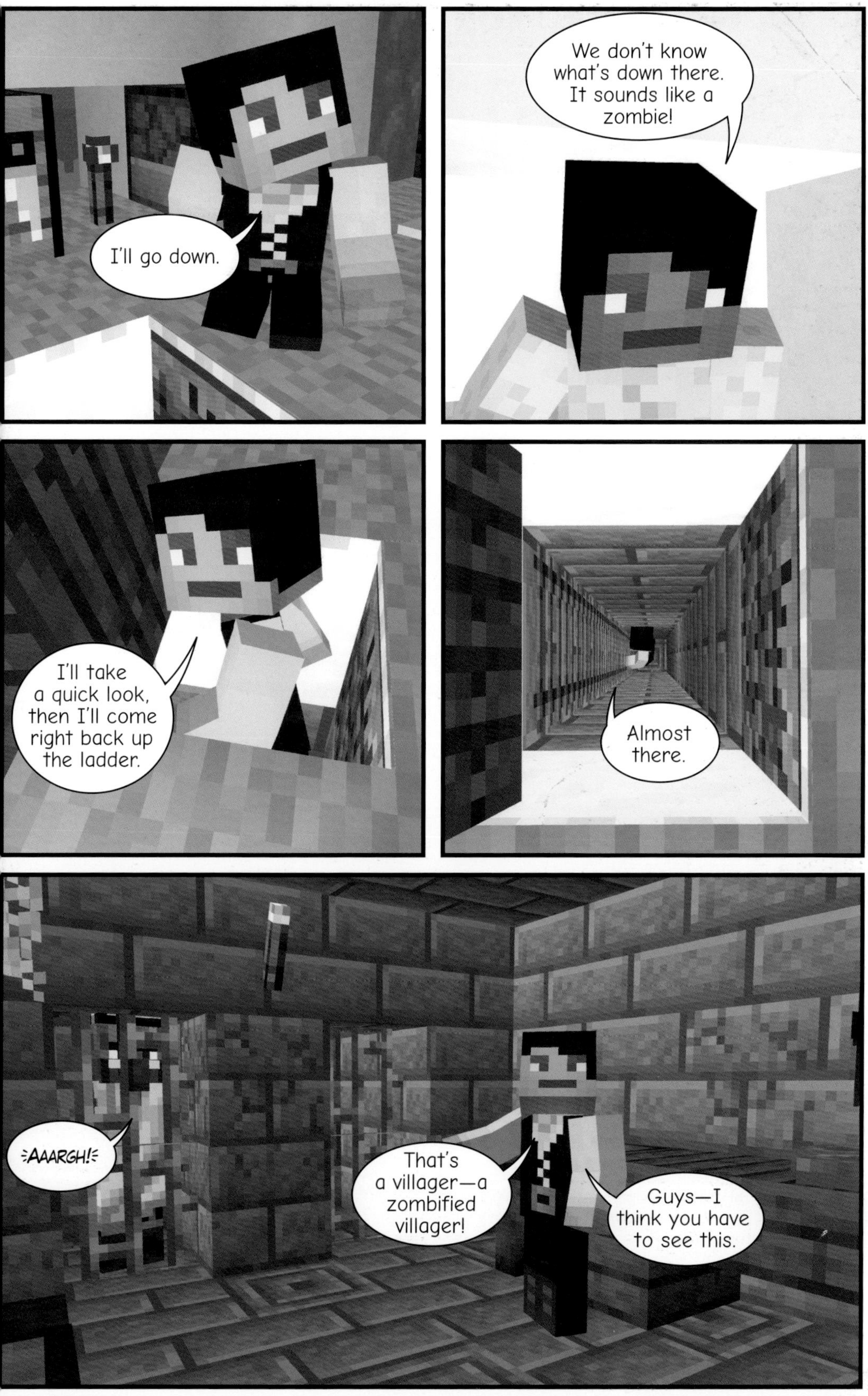
I'll go down.
We don't know what's down there. It sounds like a zombie!
I'll take a quick look, then I'll come right back up the ladder.
Almost there.
AAARGH!
That's a villager—a zombified villager!
Guys—I think you have to see this.

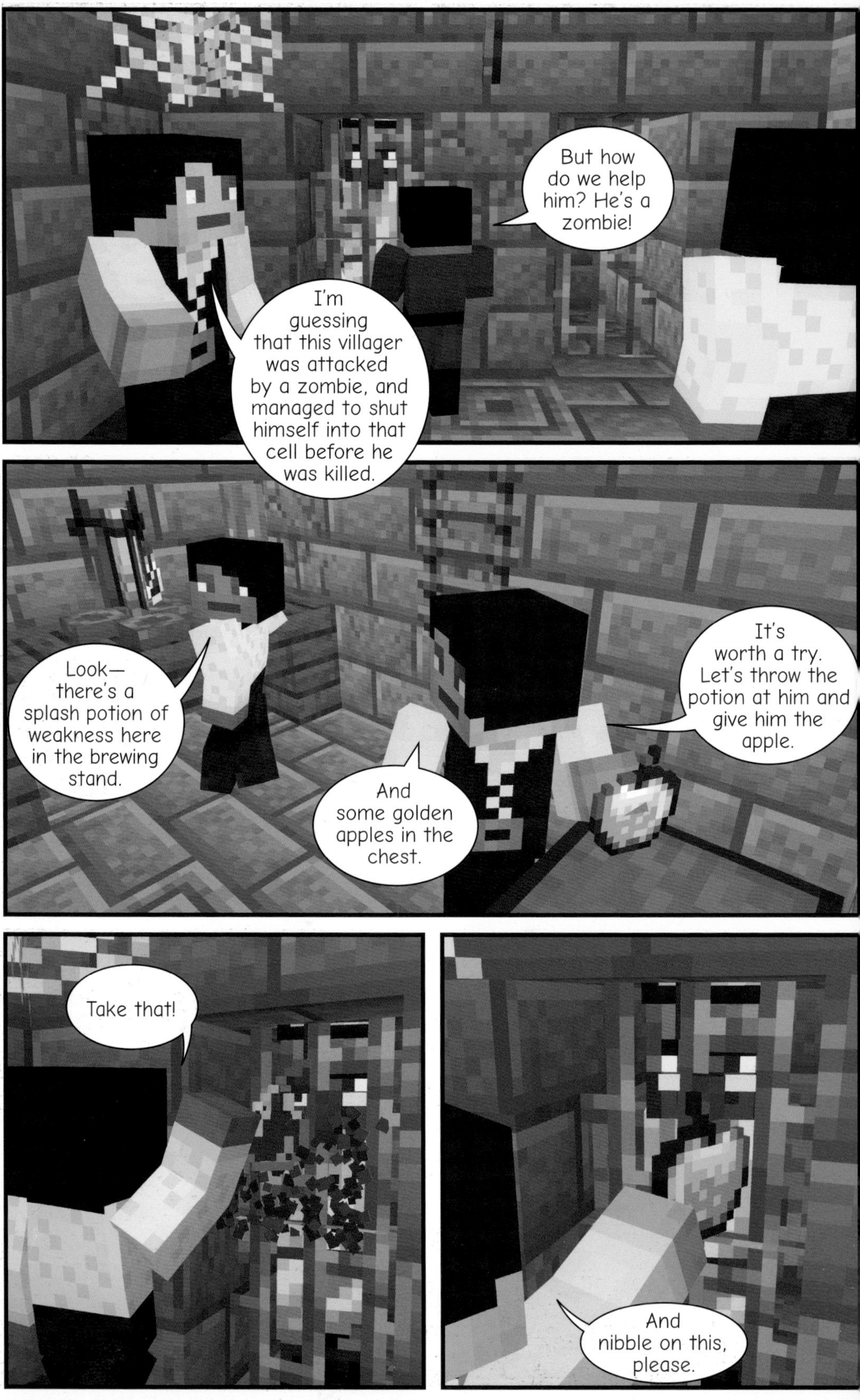
But how do we help him? He's a zombie!
I'm guessing that this villager was attacked by a zombie, and managed to shut himself into that cell before he was killed.
Look— there's a splash potion of weakness here in the brewing stand.
And some golden apples in the chest.
It's worth a try. Let's throw the potion at him and give him the apple.
Take that!
And nibble on this, please.

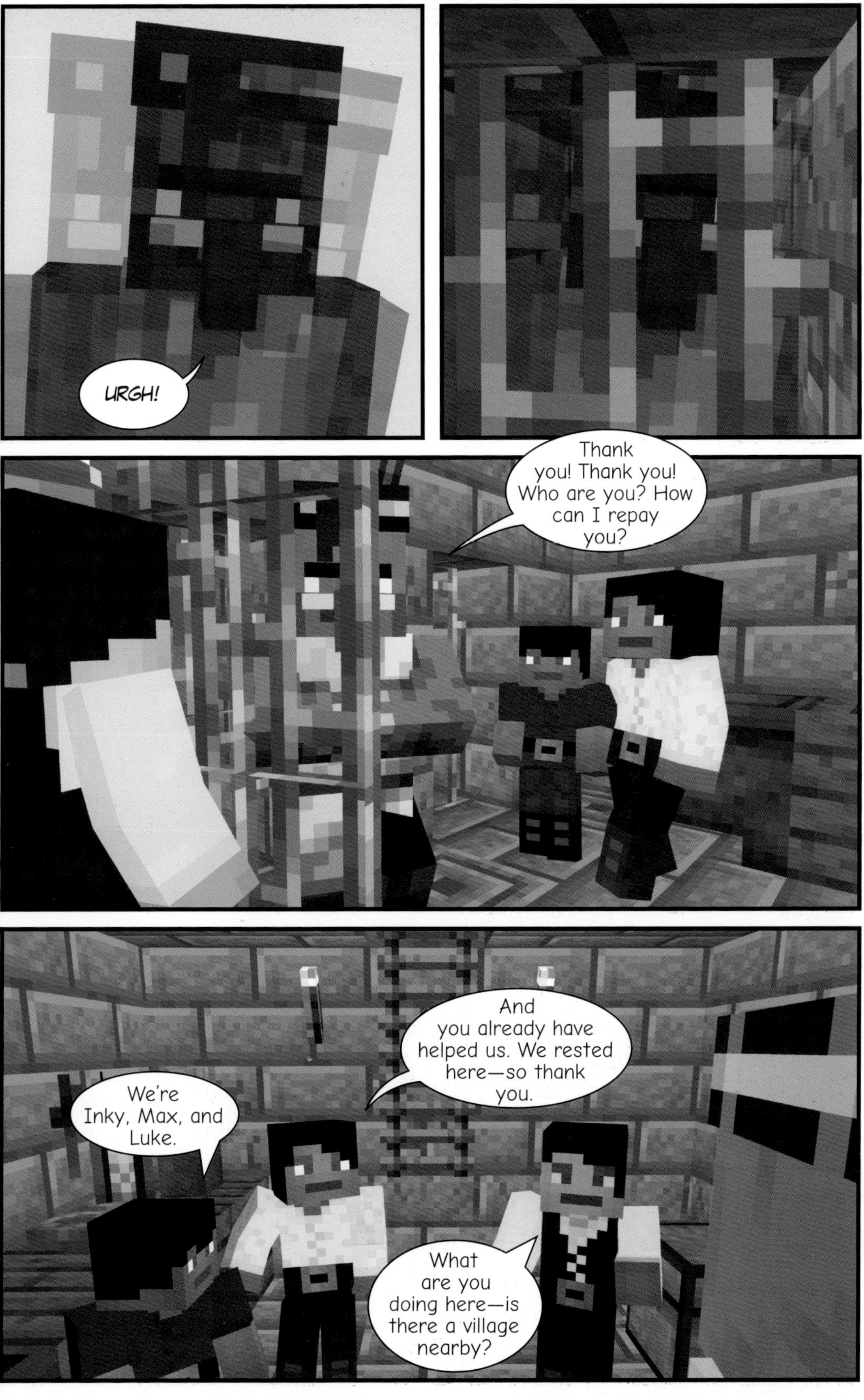
URGH!
Thank you! Thank you! Who are you? How can I repay you?
We're Inky, Max, and Luke.
And you already have helped us. We rested here—so thank you.
What are you doing here—is there a village nearby?

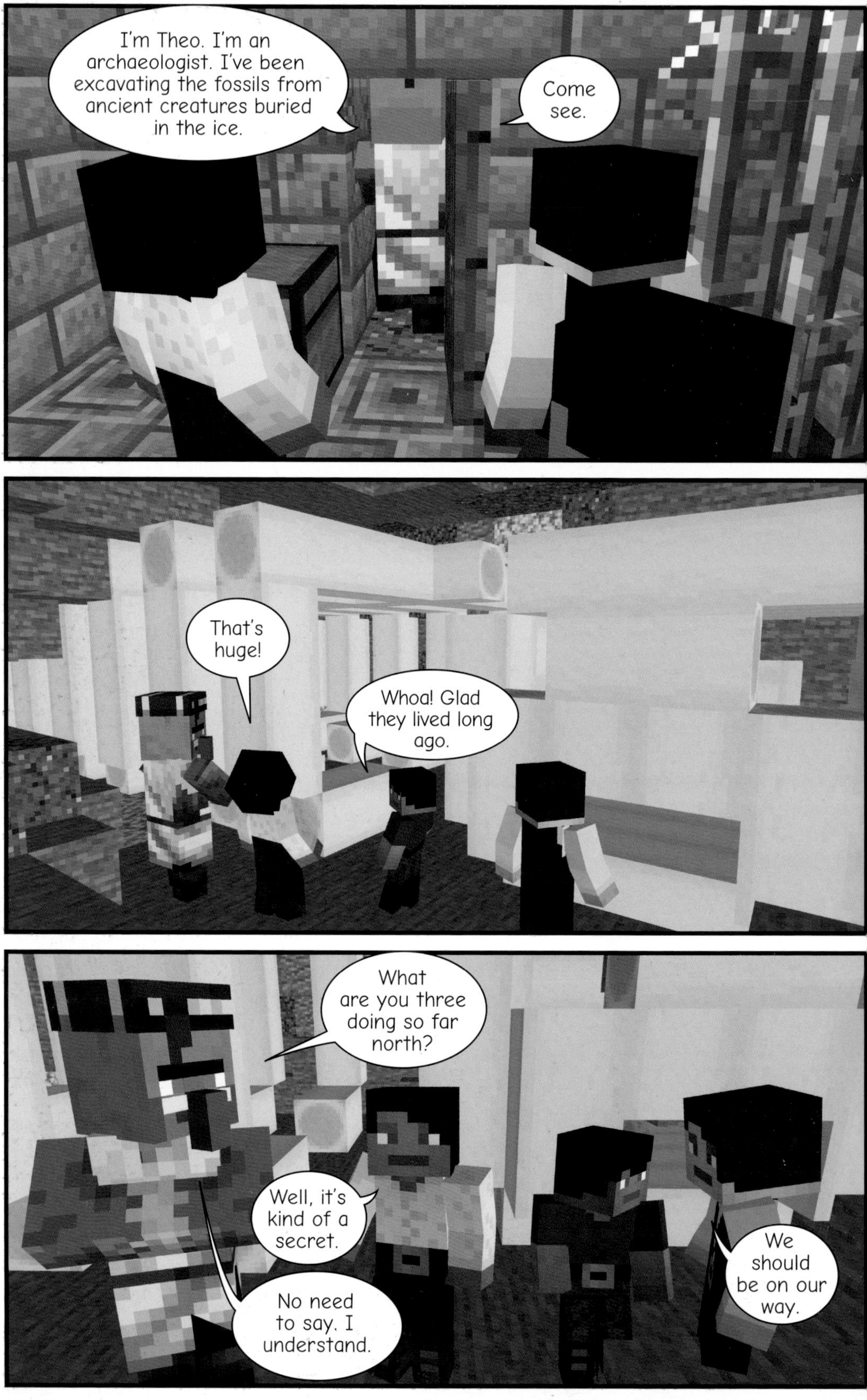
I'm Theo. I'm an archaeologist. I've been excavating the fossils from ancient creatures buried in the ice.
Come see.
That's huge!
Whoa! Glad they lived long ago.
What are you three doing so far north?
Well, it's kind of a secret.
No need to say. I understand.
We should be on our way.

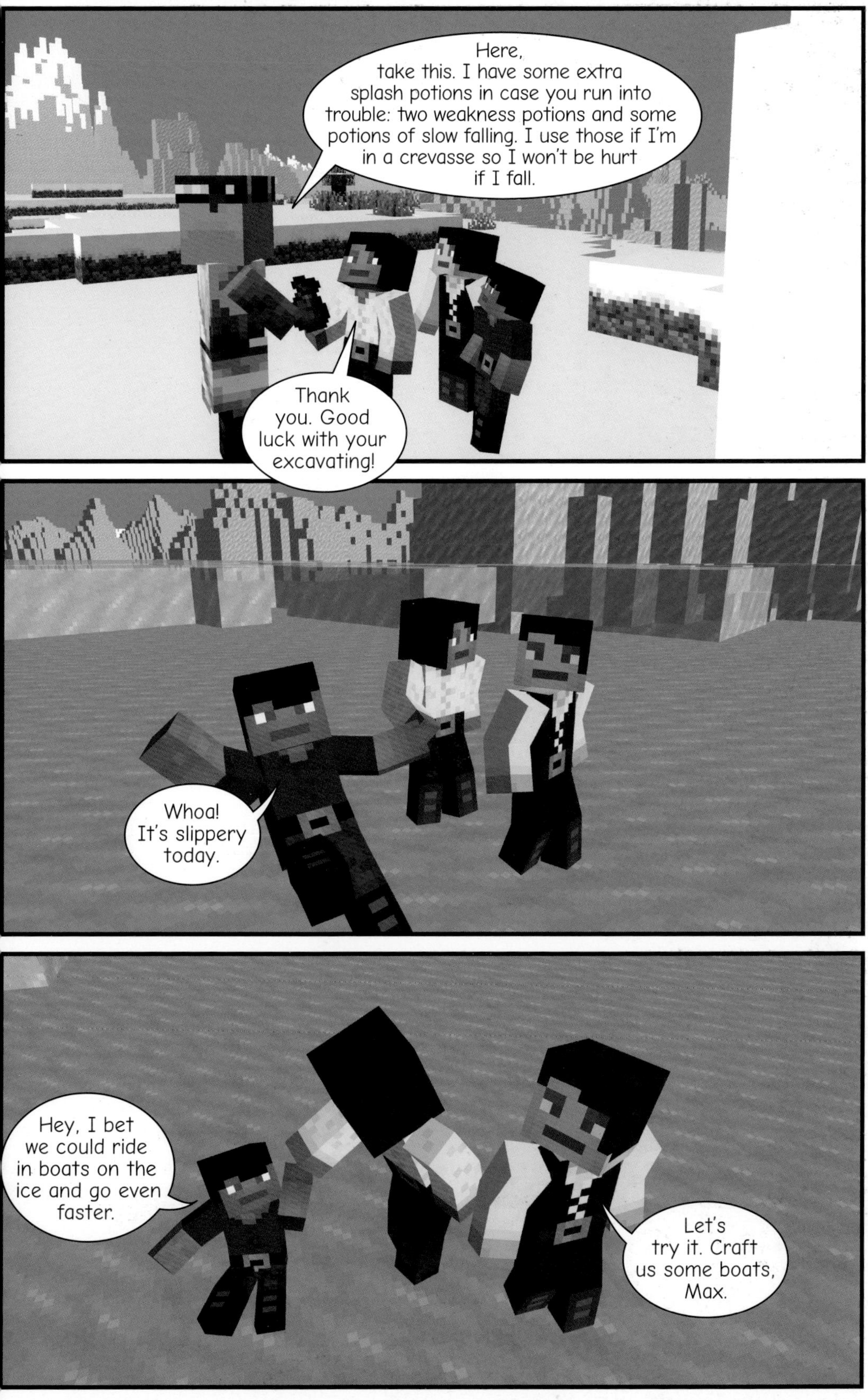

Here, take this. I have some extra splash potions in case you run into trouble: two weakness potions and some potions of slow falling. I use those if I'm in a crevasse so I won't be hurt if I fall.
Thank you. Good luck with your excavating!
Whoa! It's slippery today.
Hey, I bet we could ride in boats on the ice and go even faster.
Let's try it. Craft us some boats, Max.

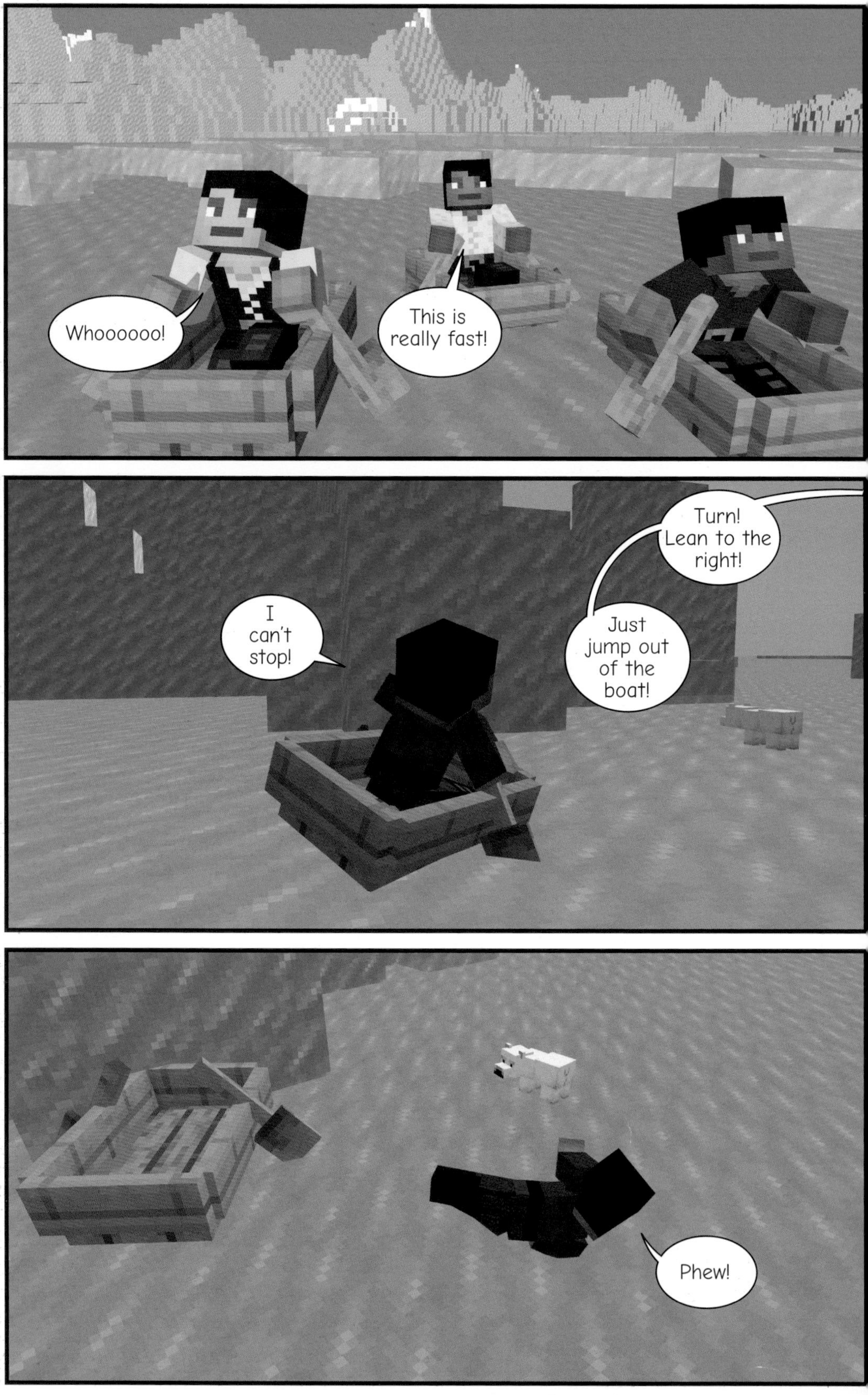
Whooooooo!
This is really fast!
I can't stop!
Turn! Lean to the right!
Just jump out of the boat!
Phew!

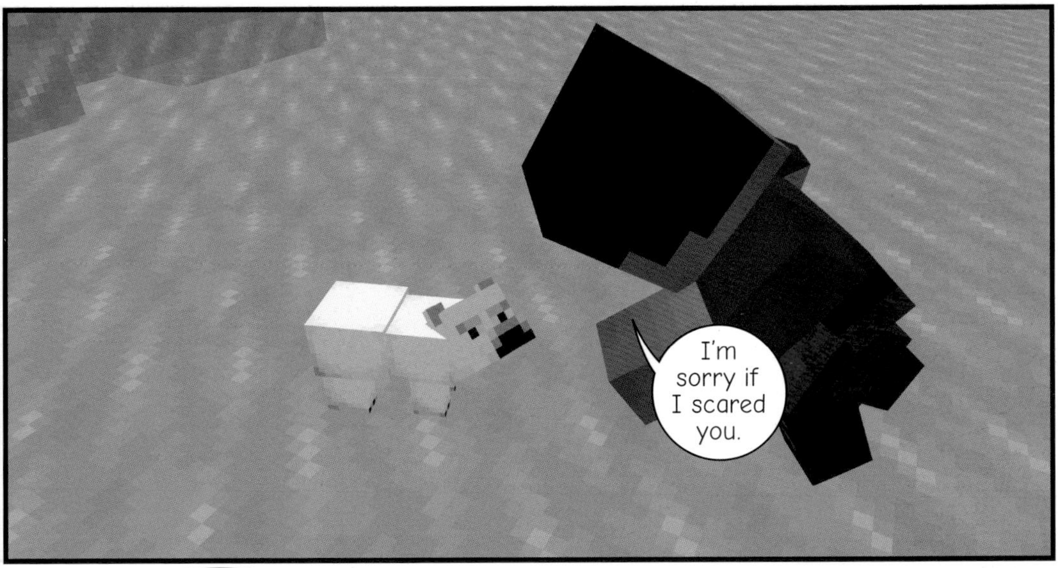
I'm sorry if I scared you.

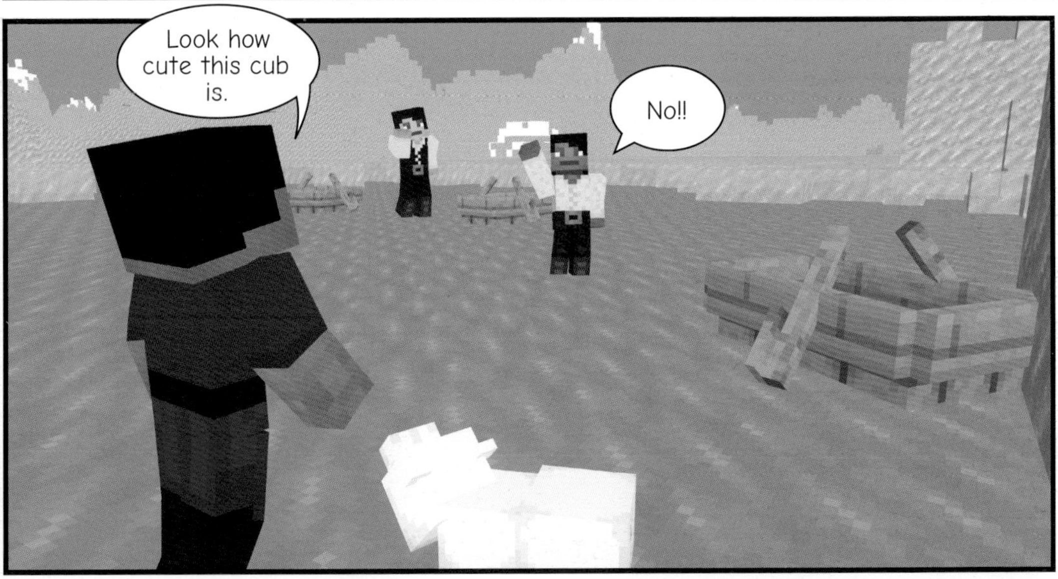
Look how cute this cub is.
No!!

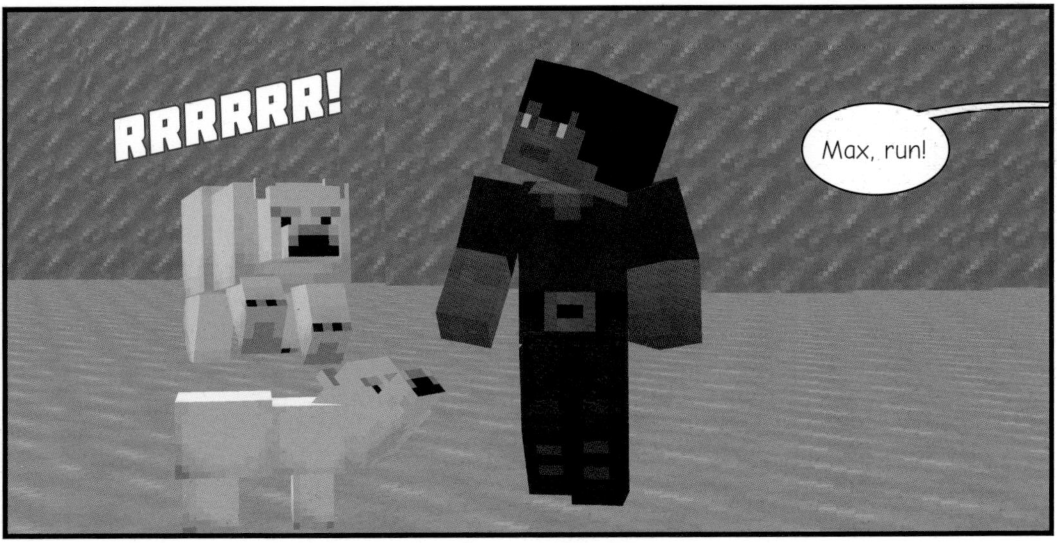
RRRRRR!
Max, run!

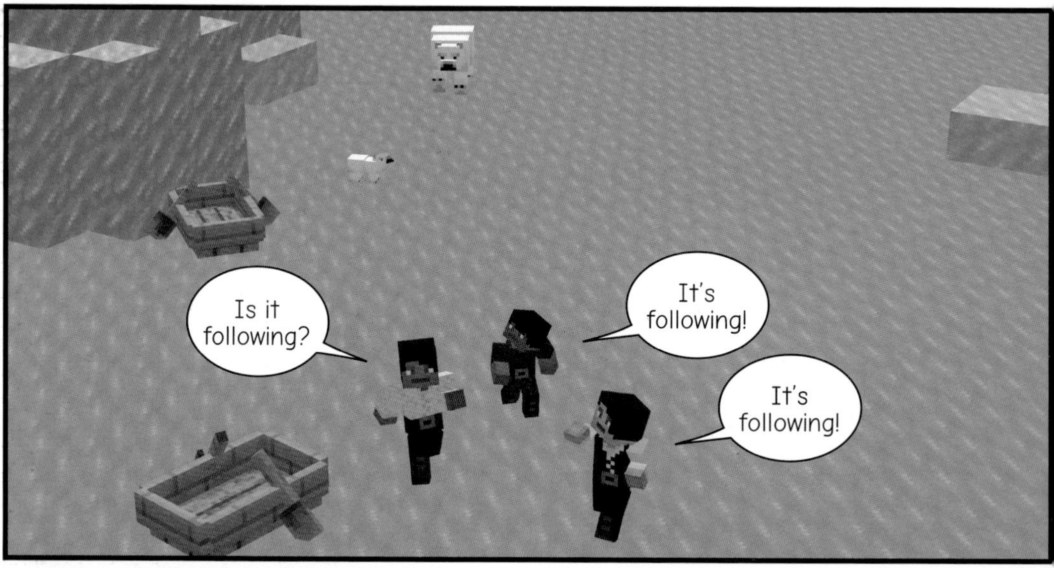
Is it following?
It's following!
It's following!

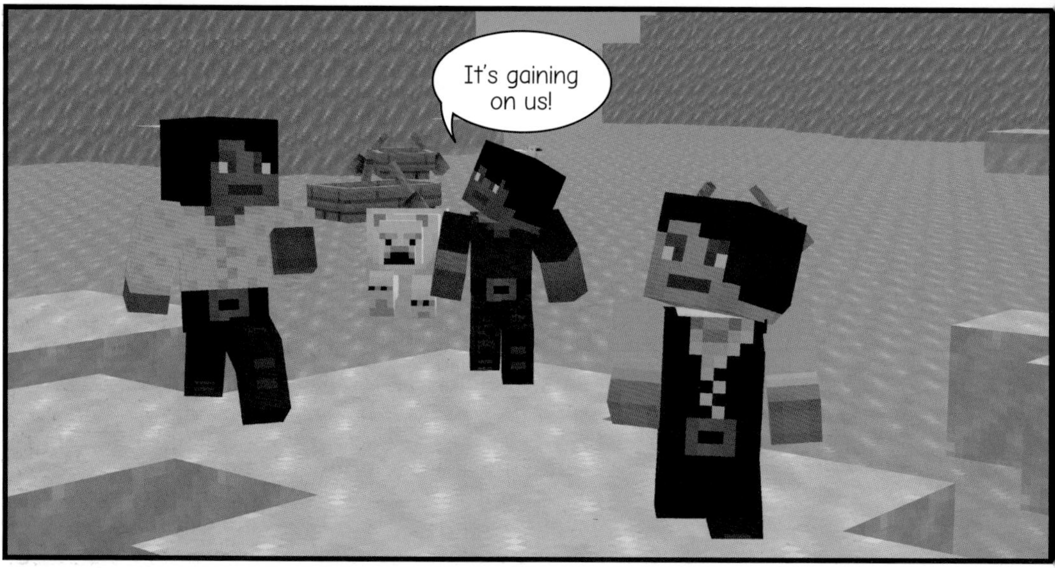
It's gaining on us!

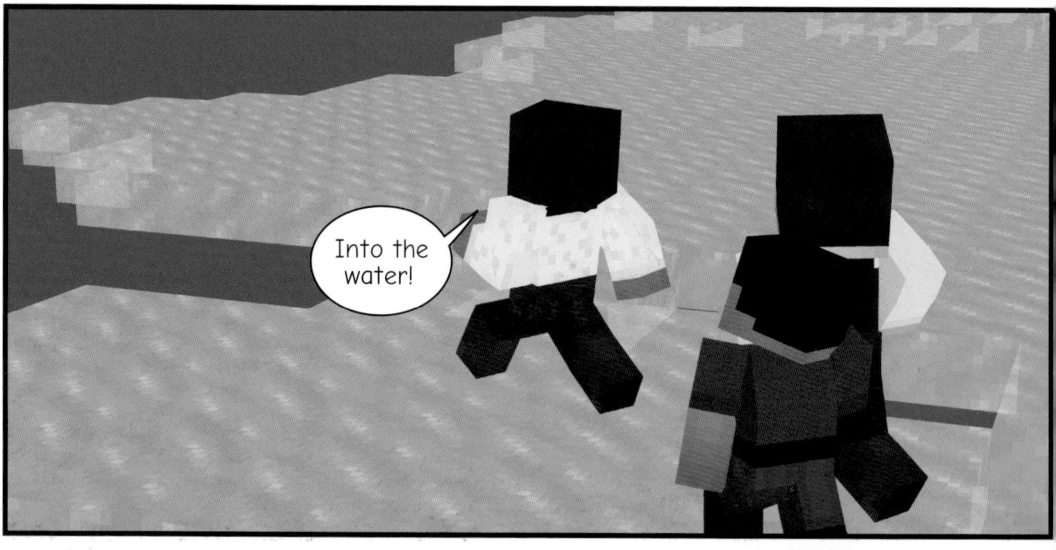
Into the water!

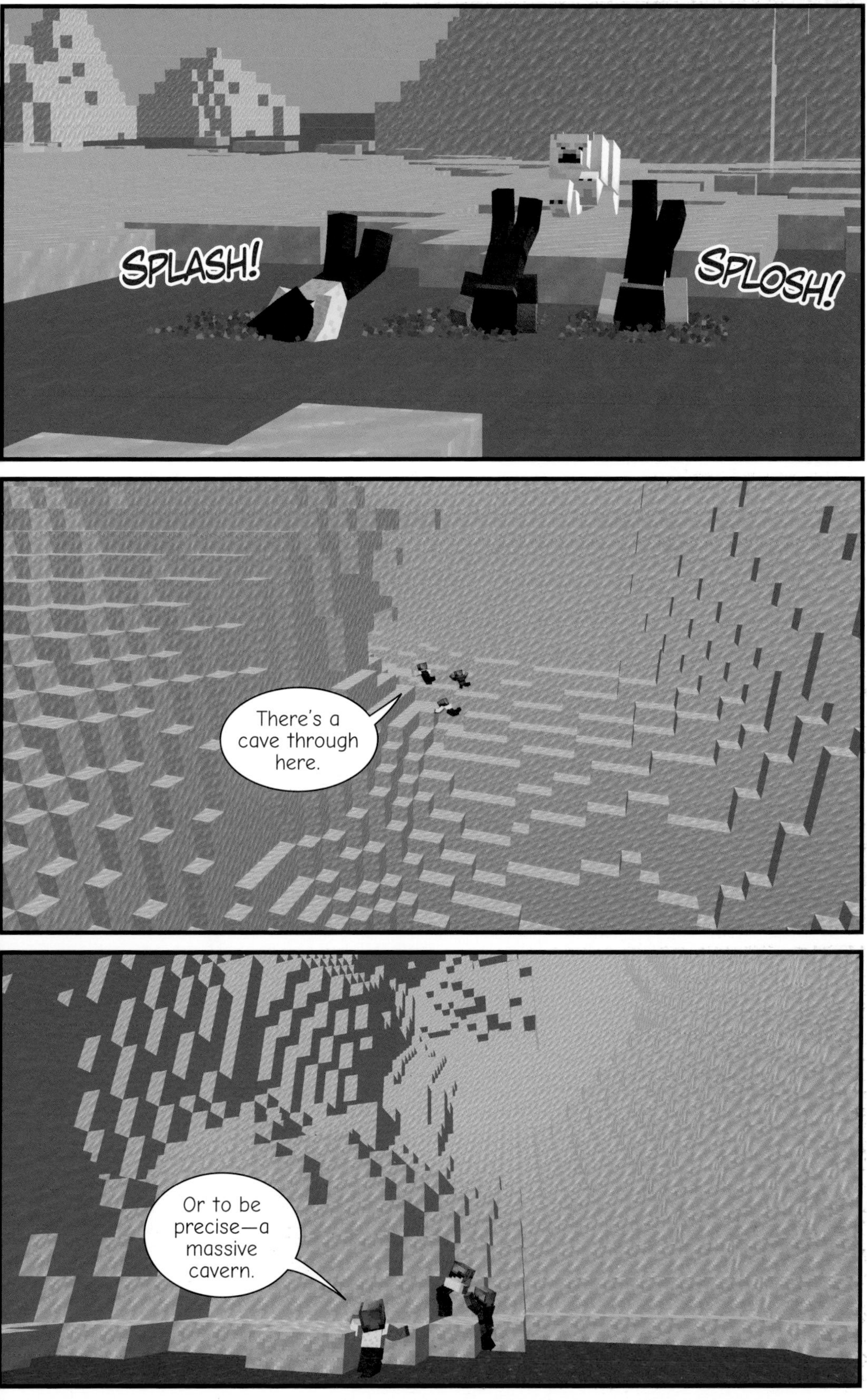
SPLASH!
SPLOSH!
There's a cave through here.
Or to be precise—a massive cavern.

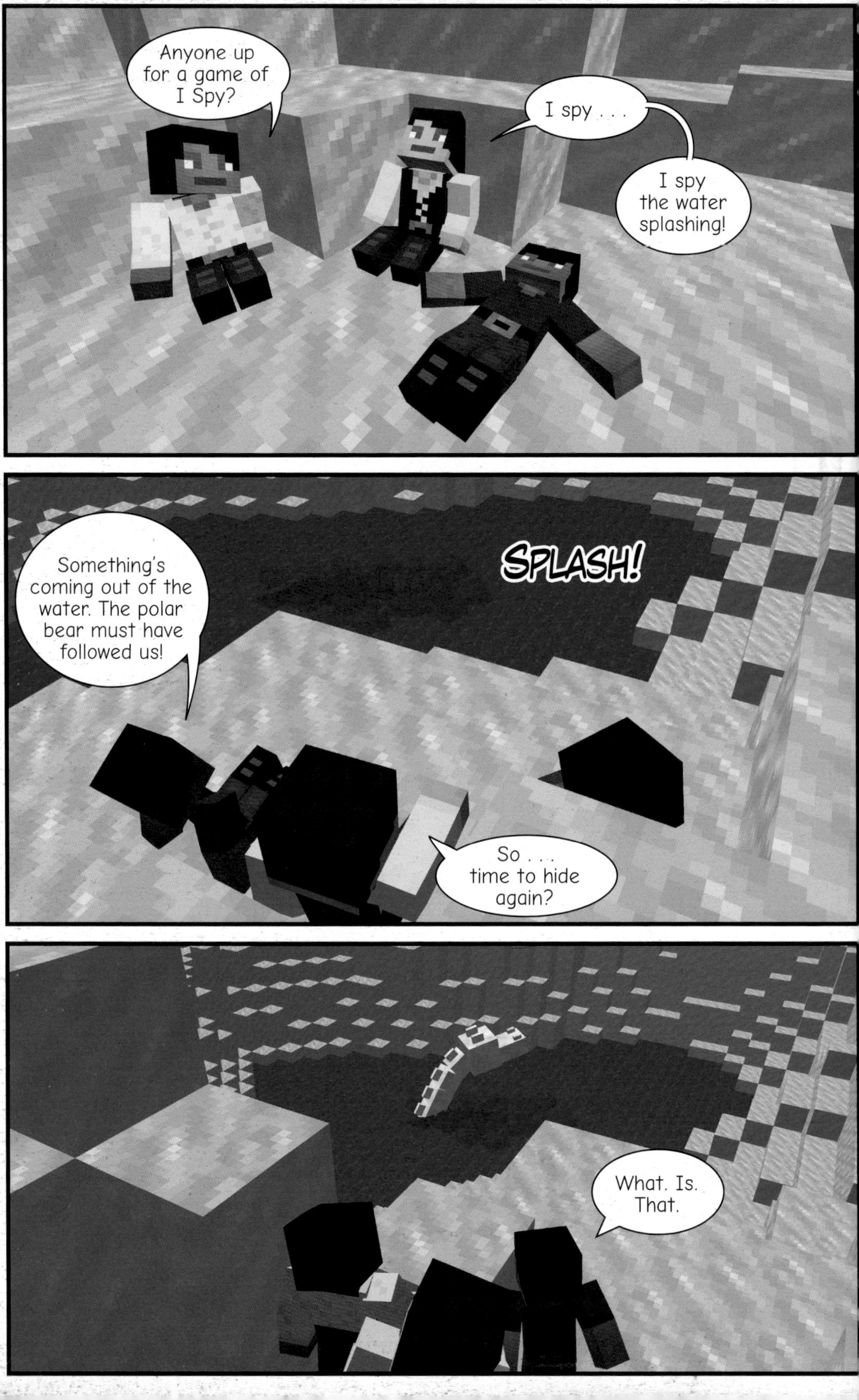
Anyone up for a game of I Spy?
I spy . . .
I spy the water splashing!
SPLASH!
Something's coming out of the water. The polar bear must have followed us!
So . . . time to hide again?
What. Is. That.

Chapter 12
Ice Dragon

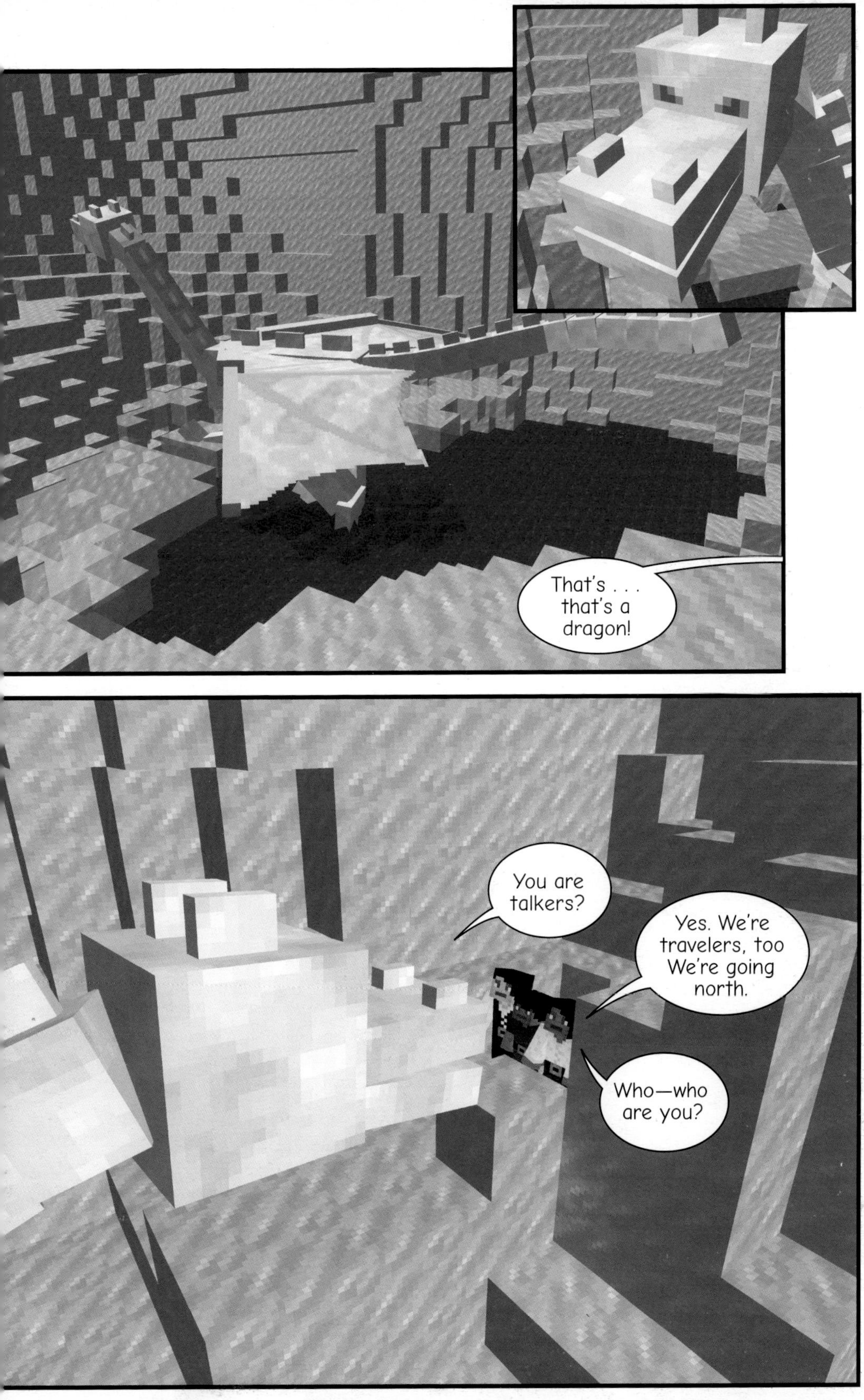
That's . . . that's a dragon!
You are talkers?
Yes. We're travelers, too We're going north.
Who—who are you?

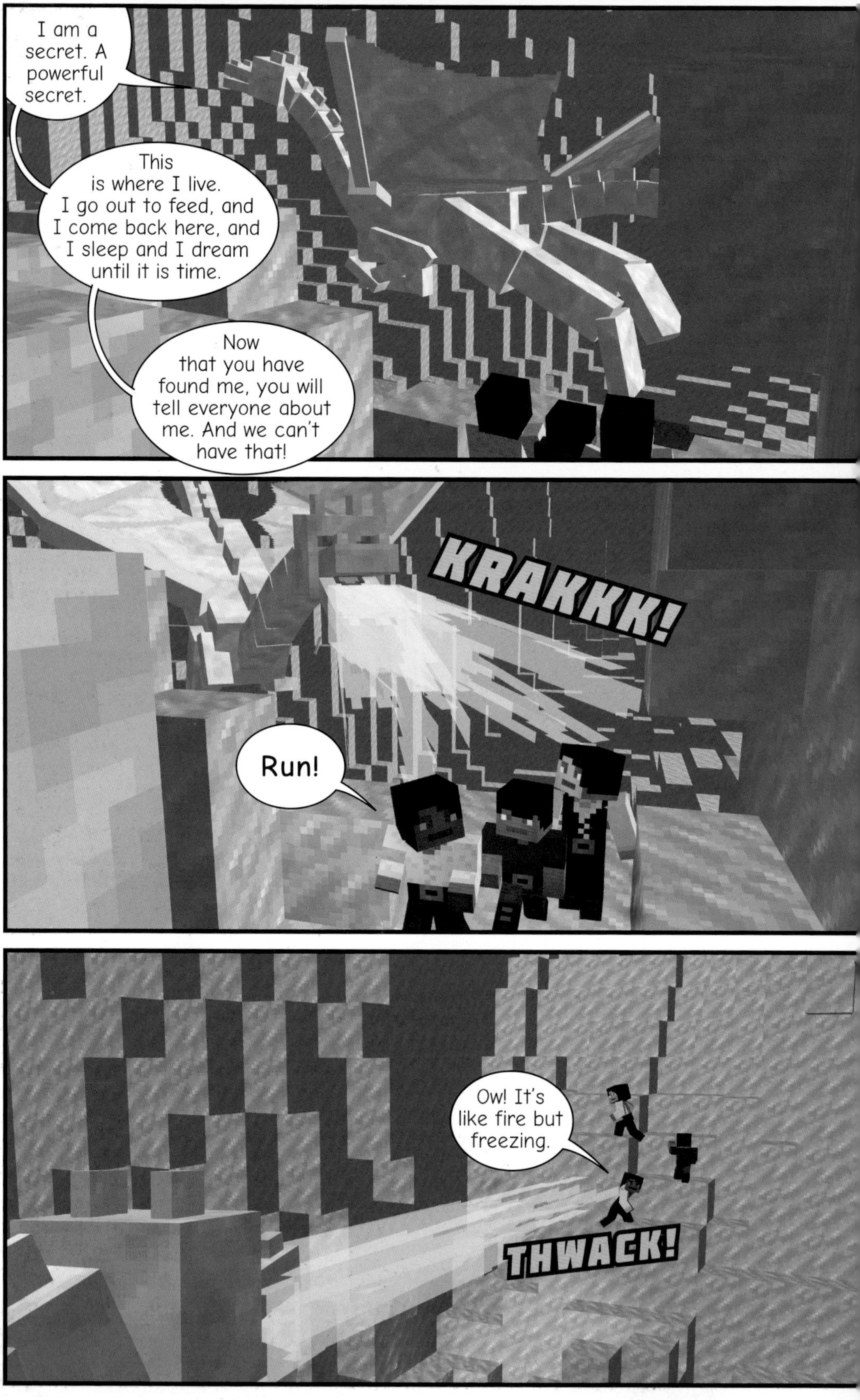
I am a secret. A powerful secret.
This is where I live. I go out to feed, and I come back here, and I sleep and I dream until it is time.
Now that you have found me, you will tell everyone about me. And we can't have that!
KRAKKKK!
Run!
Ow! It's like fire but freezing.
THWACK!

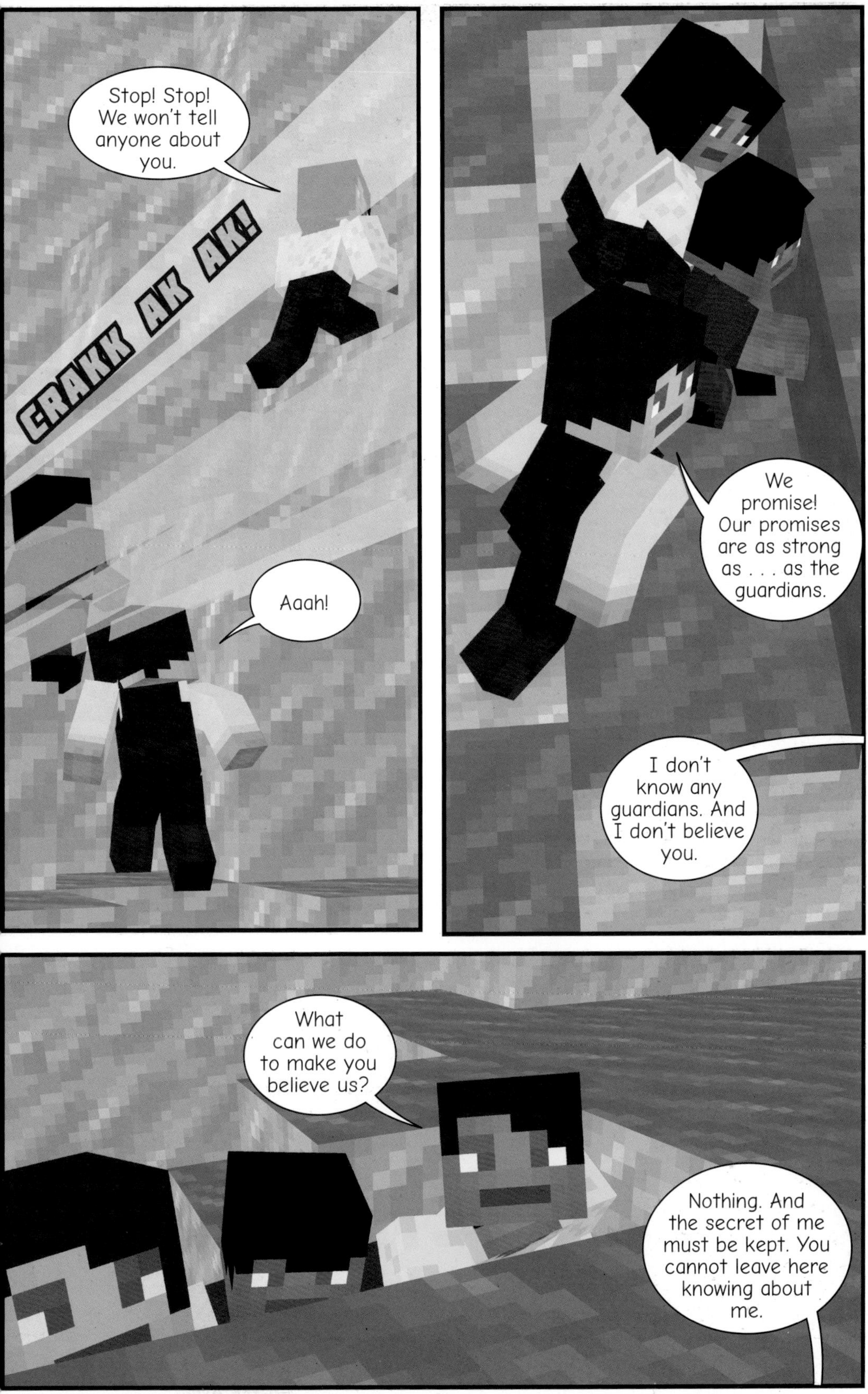
Stop! Stop! We won't tell anyone about you.
CRAKK AK AK!
Aaah!
We promise! Our promises are as strong as . . . as the guardians.
I don't know any guardians. And I don't believe you.
What can we do to make you believe us?
Nothing. And the secret of me must be kept. You cannot leave here knowing about me.

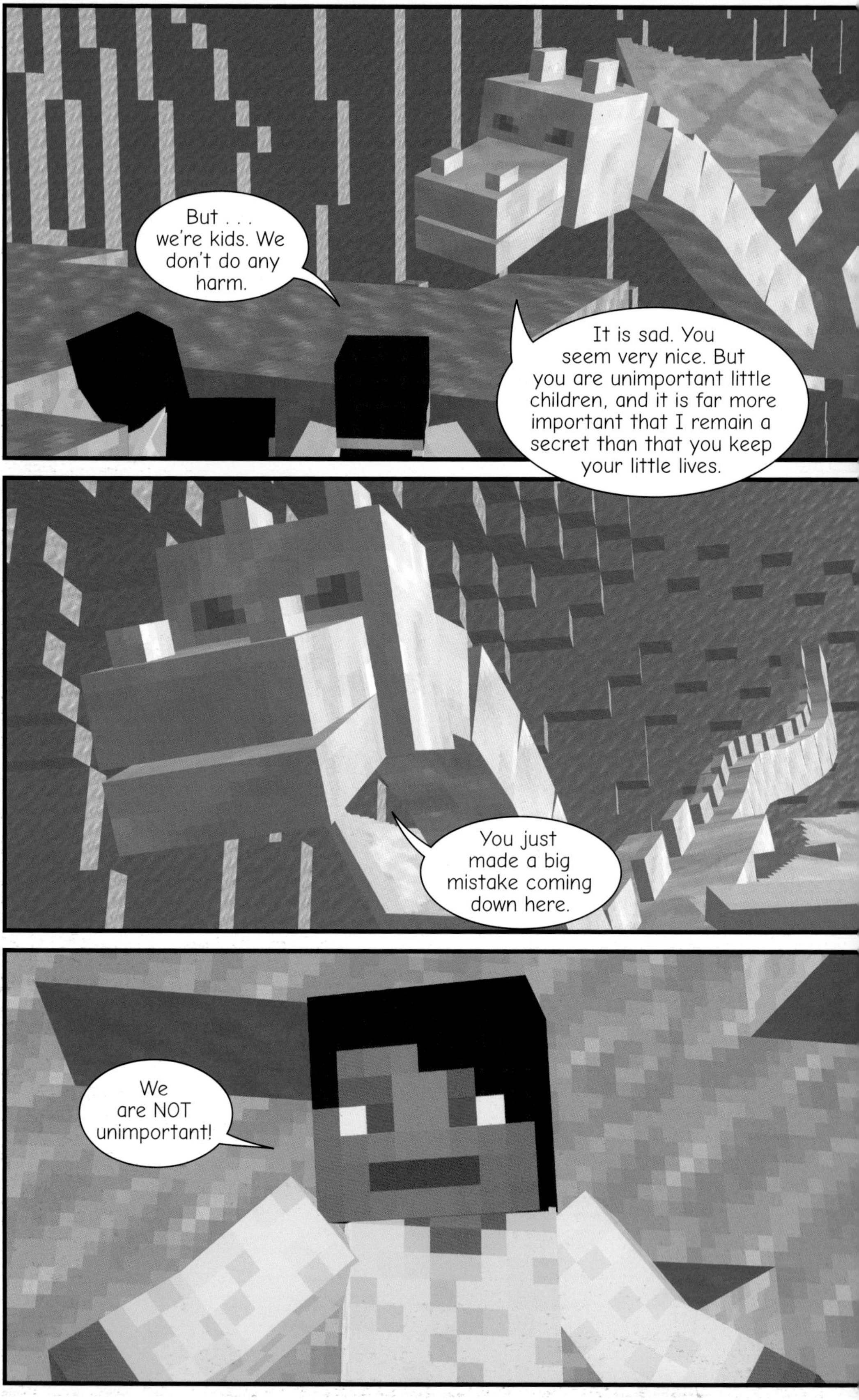
But . . . we're kids. We don't do any harm.
It is sad. You seem very nice. But you are unimportant little children, and it is far more important that I remain a secret than that you keep your little lives.
You just made a big mistake coming down here.
We are NOT unimportant!

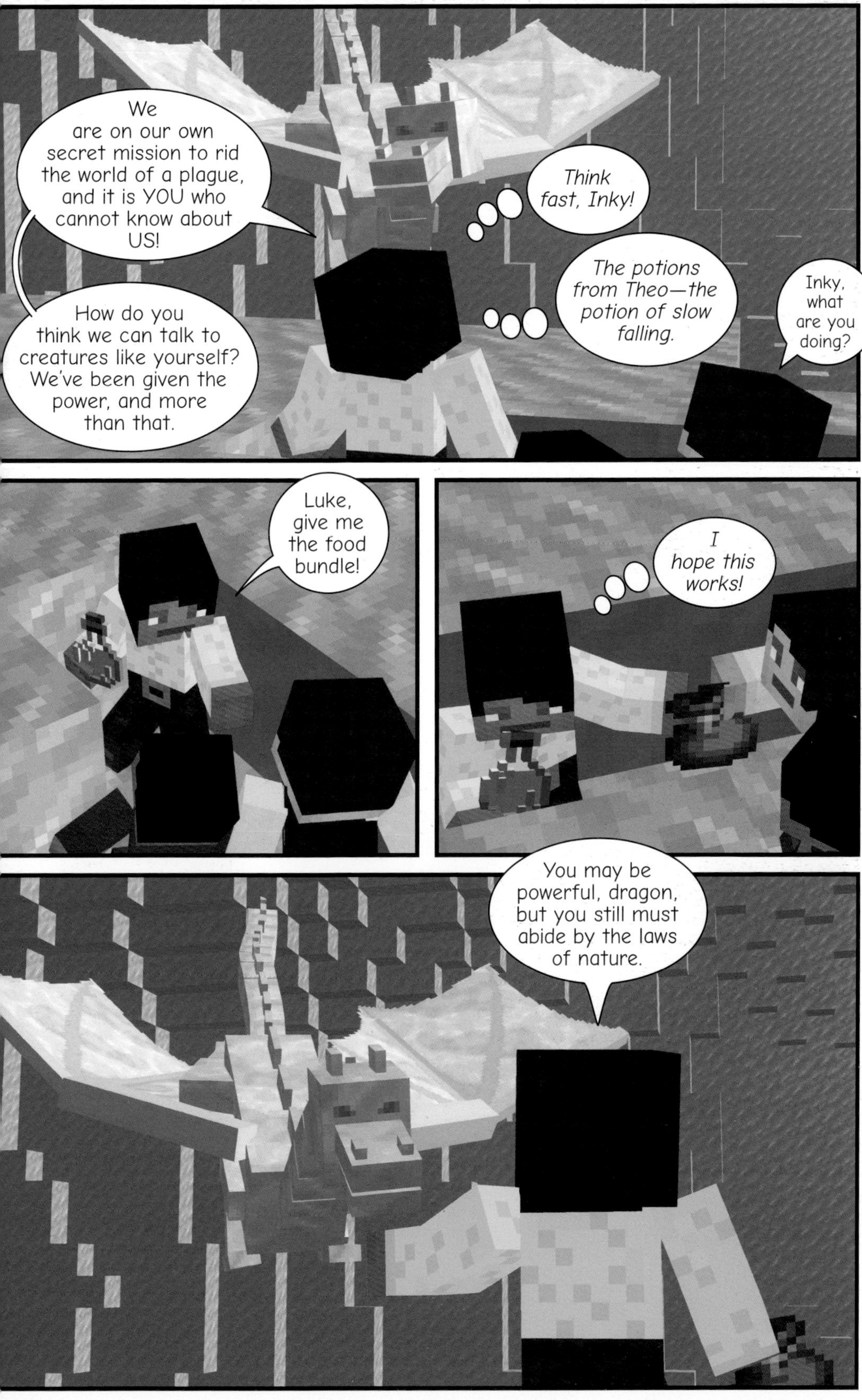
We are on our own secret mission to rid the world of a plague, and it is YOU who cannot know about US!
How do you think we can talk to creatures like yourself? We've been given the power, and more than that.
Think fast, Inky!
The potions from Theo—the potion of slow falling.
Inky, what are you doing?
Luke, give me the food bundle!
I hope this works!
You may be powerful, dragon, but you still must abide by the laws of nature.

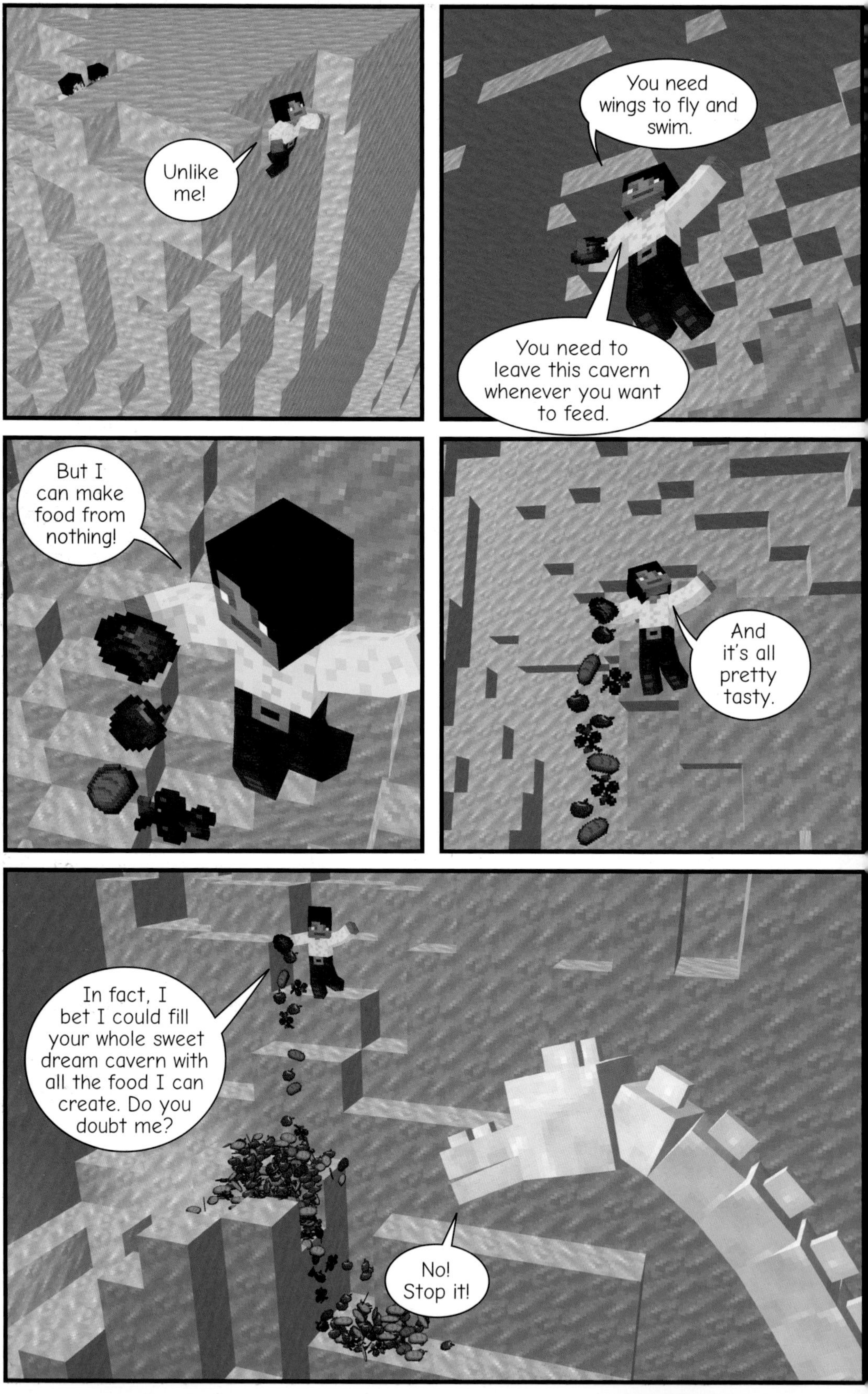
Unlike me!
You need wings to fly and swim.
You need to leave this cavern whenever you want to feed.
But I can make food from nothing!
And it's all pretty tasty.
In fact, I bet I could fill your whole sweet dream cavern with all the food I can create. Do you doubt me?
No! Stop it!

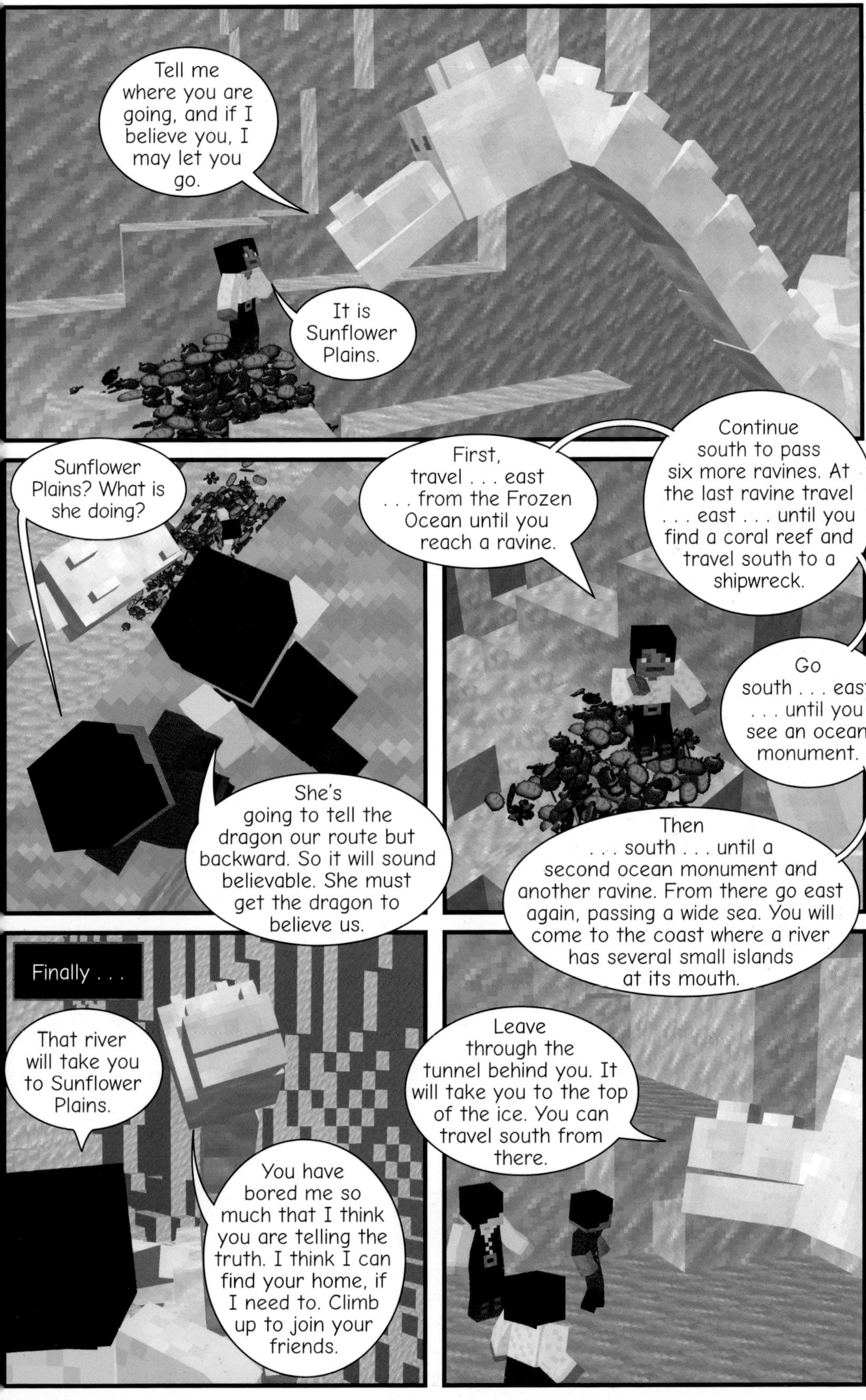
Tell me where you are going, and if I believe you, I may let you go.
It is Sunflower Plains.
Sunflower Plains? What is she doing?
First, travel . . . east . . . from the Frozen Ocean until you reach a ravine.
Continue south to pass six more ravines. At the last ravine travel . . . east . . . until you find a coral reef and travel south to a shipwreck.
Go south . . . east . . . until you see an ocean monument.
She's going to tell the dragon our route but backward. So it will sound believable. She must get the dragon to believe us.
Then . . . south . . . until a second ocean monument and another ravine. From there go east again, passing a wide sea. You will come to the coast where a river has several small islands at its mouth.
Finally . . .
That river will take you to Sunflower Plains.
You have bored me so much that I think you are telling the truth. I think I can find your home, if I need to. Climb up to join your friends.
Leave through the tunnel behind you. It will take you to the top of the ice. You can travel south from there.

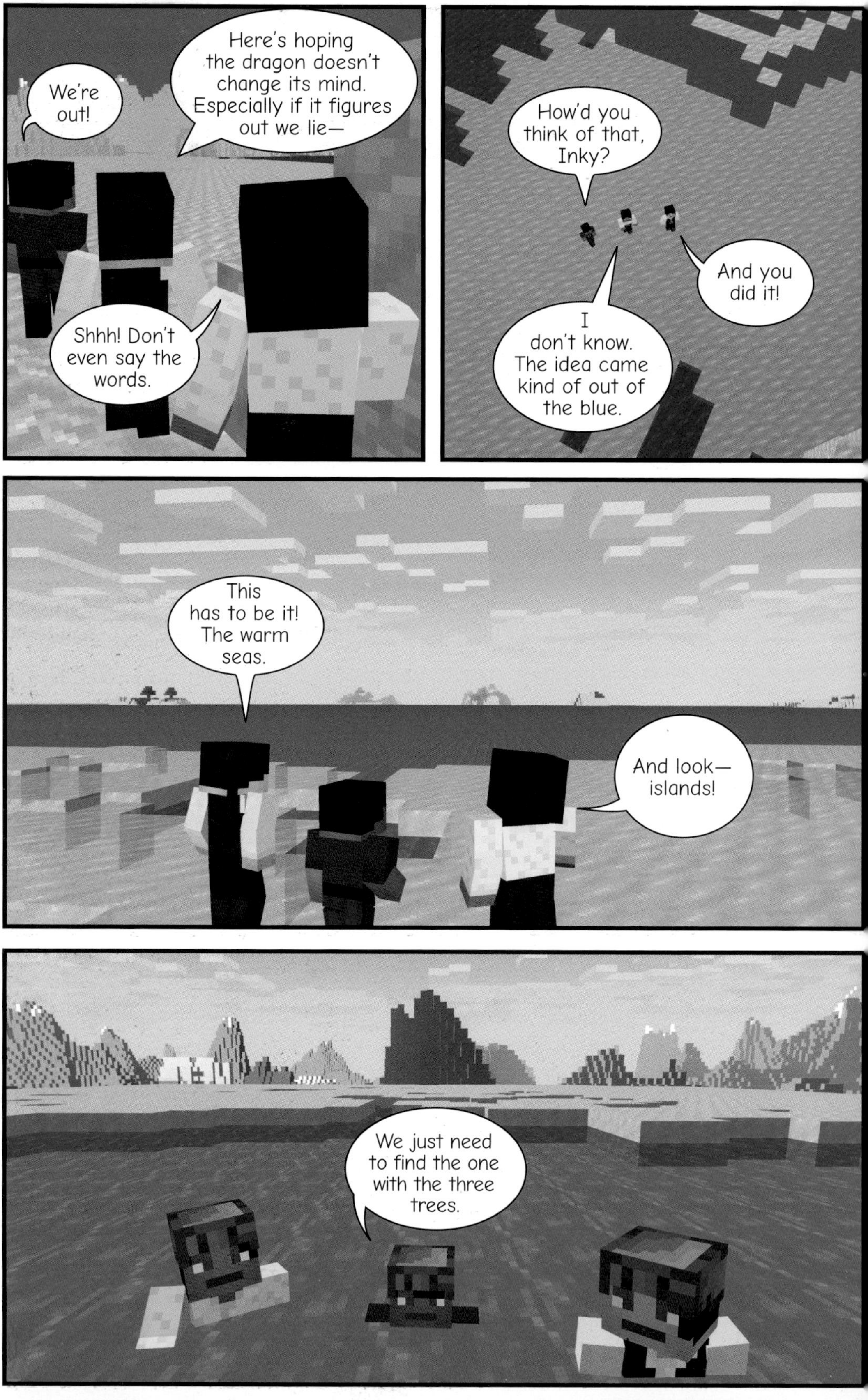
We're out!
Here's hoping the dragon doesn't change its mind. Especially if it figures out we lie—
Shhh! Don't even say the words.
How'd you think of that, Inky?
I don't know. The idea came kind of out of the blue.
And you did it!
This has to be it! The warm seas.
And look—islands!
We just need to find the one with the three trees.

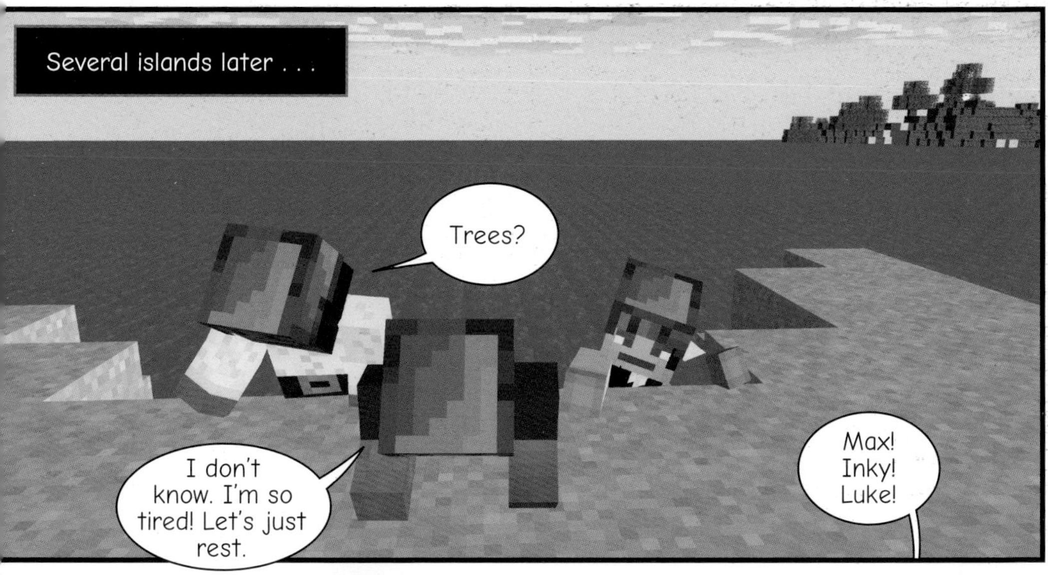
Several islands later . . .
Trees?
I don't know. I'm so tired! Let's just rest.
Max! Inky! Luke!

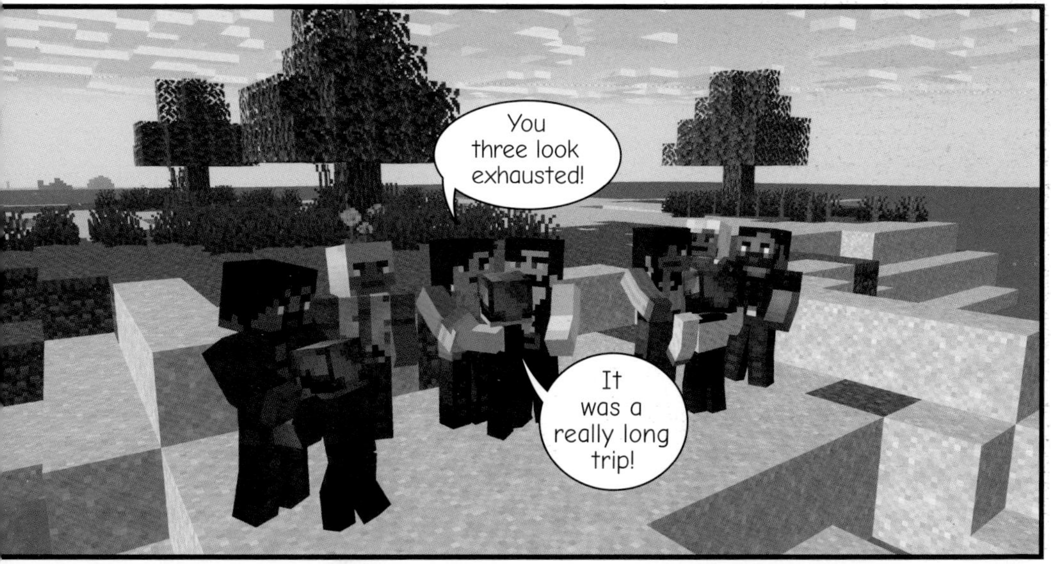
You three look exhausted!
It was a really long trip!

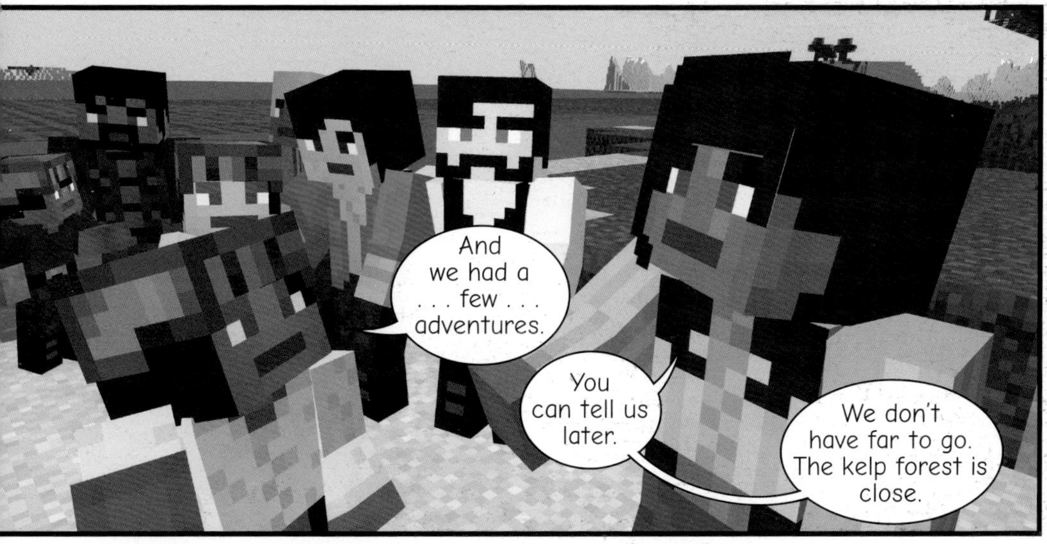
And we had a . . . few . . . adventures.
You can tell us later.
We don't have far to go. The kelp forest is close.

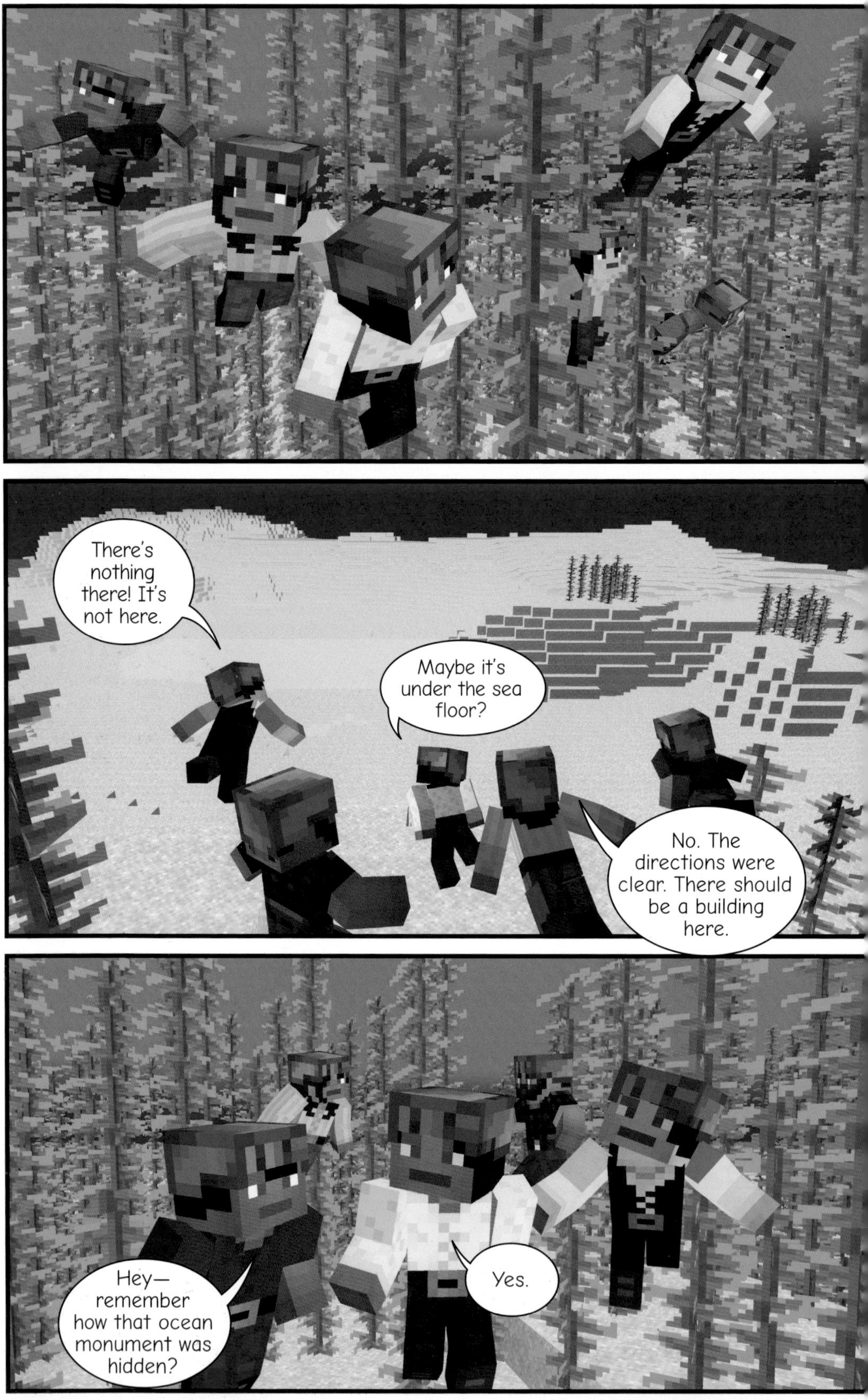
There's nothing there! It's not here.
Maybe it's under the sea floor?
No. The directions were clear. There should be a building here.
Hey—remember how that ocean monument was hidden?
Yes.

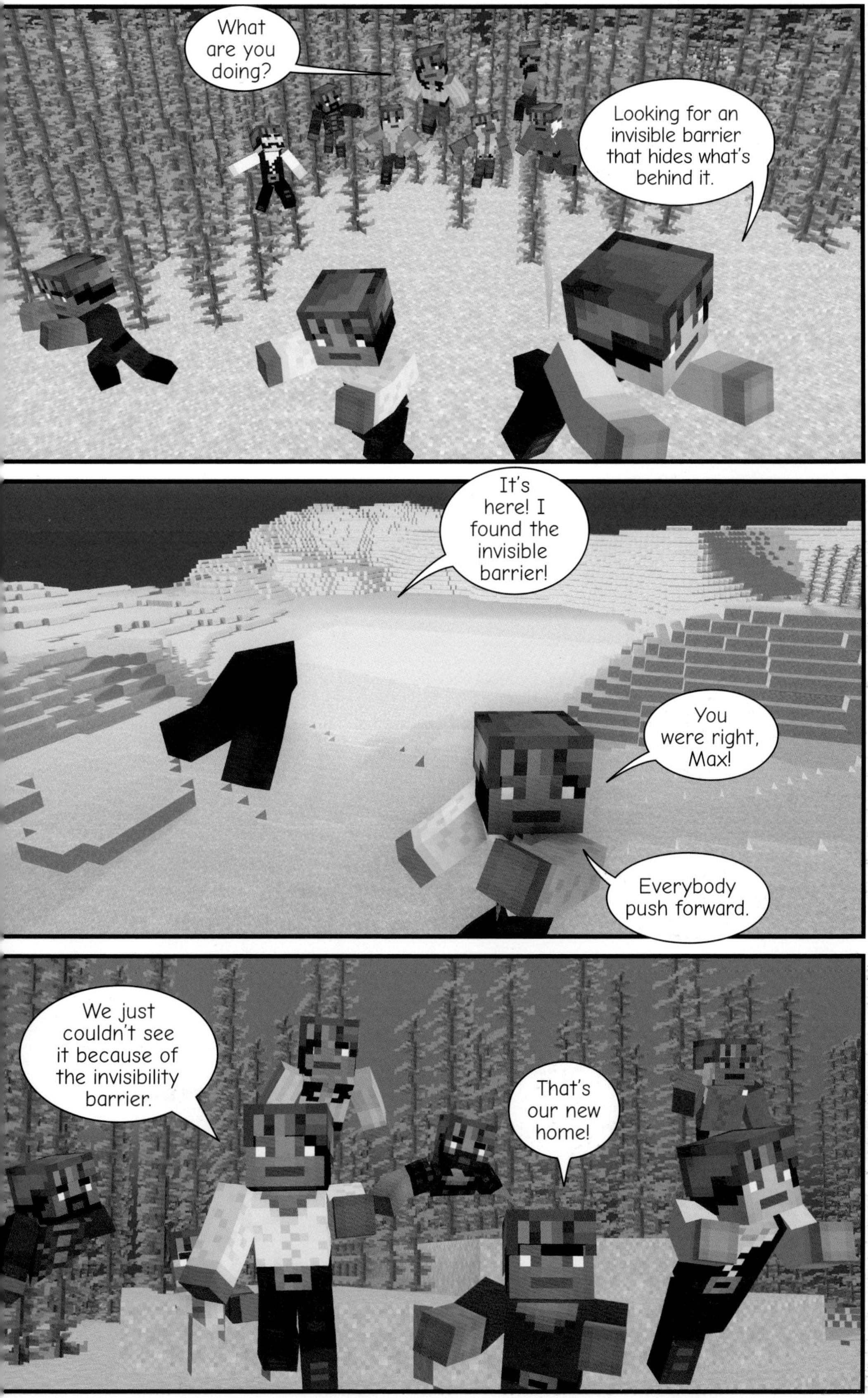
What are you doing?
Looking for an invisible barrier that hides what's behind it.
It's here! I found the invisible barrier!
You were right, Max!
Everybody push forward.
We just couldn't see it because of the invisibility barrier.
That's our new home!

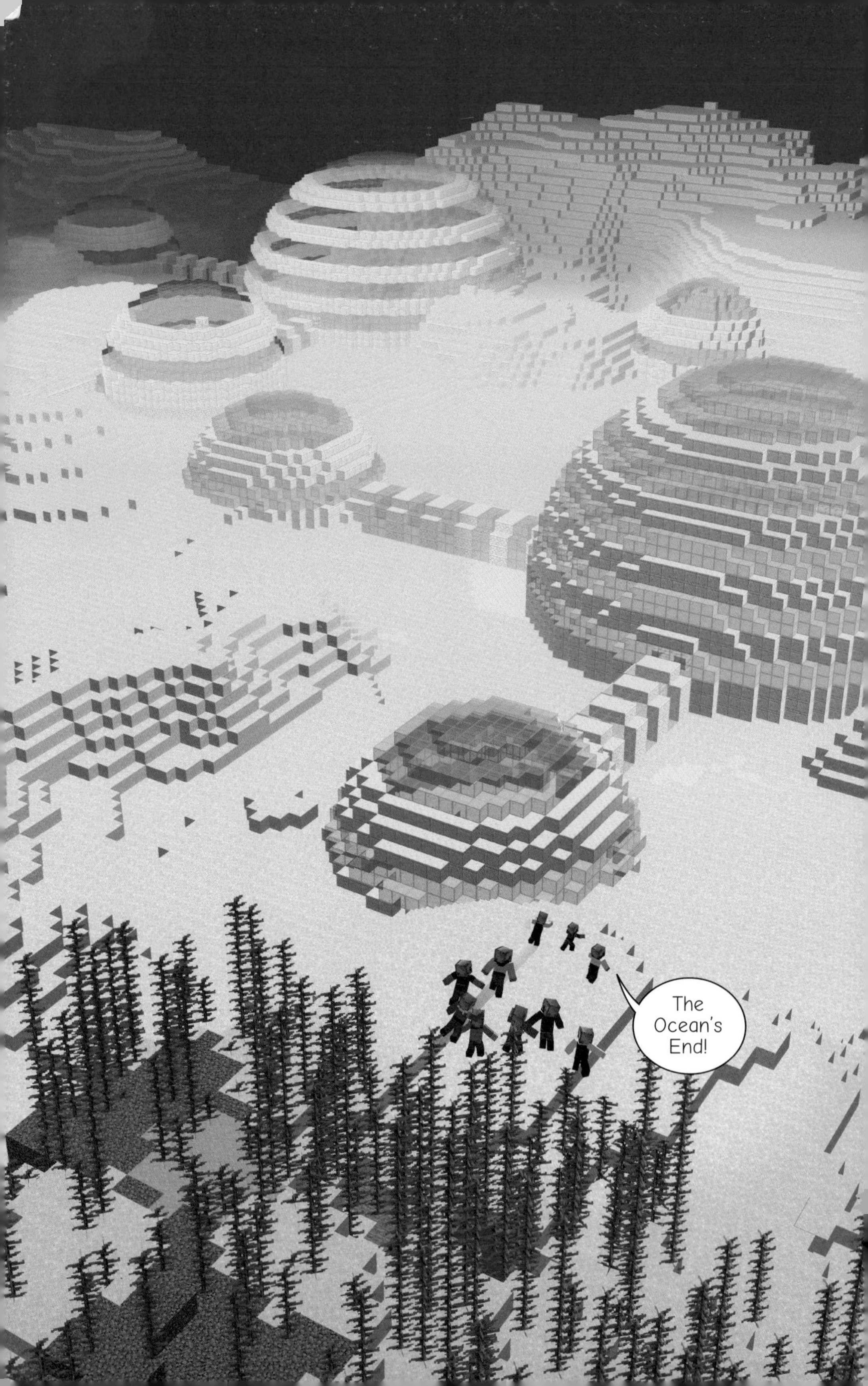
The Ocean's End!